POISONED

JENNIFER DONNELLY

HOT
KEY
BOOKS

First published in Great Britain in 2020 by
HOT KEY BOOKS
80–81 Wimpole St, London W1G 9RE
Owned by Bonnier Books
Sveavägen 56, Stockholm, Sweden
www.hotkeybooks.com

A CIP catalogue record for this book is available from the British Library.

ISBN: 9781471408144
also available as an ebook

1

This book is typeset using Atomik ePublisher
Printed and bound in Great Britain by Clays Ltd, Elcograf S.p.A.

Hot Key Books is an imprint of Bonnier Books UK
www.bonnierbooks.co.uk

POISONED

ALSO BY JENNIFER DONNELLY

Stepsister
These Shallow Graves
A Gathering Light

For Mallory Kass, my wonderful editor,
with gratitude and admiration

PROLOGUE

Once upon long ago, always and evermore, a girl rode into the Darkwood.

Her lips were the color of ripe cherries, her skin as soft as new-fallen snow, her hair as dark as midnight.

The tall pines whispered and sighed as she passed under them, the queen's huntsman at her side. Crows, perched high in the branches, blinked their bright black eyes.

As the sky lightened, the huntsman pointed to a pond ahead and told the girl that they must dismount to let the horses drink. She did so, walking side by side with him. Lost in her thoughts, she did not hear the soft hiss of a dagger leaving its sheath. She did not see the huntsman lift his face to the dawn, or glimpse the anguish in his eyes.

A gasp of shock escaped the girl as the huntsman pulled her close, his broad hand spanning her narrow back. Her eyes, wide and questioning, sought his. She was not afraid—not yet. She felt almost nothing as he slid the blade between her ribs, just a slight, soft push and then a bloom of warmth, as if she'd spilled tea down her dress.

But then the pain came, red clawed and snarling.

The girl threw her head back and screamed. A stag bolted from the brush at the sound. The crows burst from their roosts, their wings beating madly.

The huntsman was skilled. He was quick. He had gutted a thousand deer. A few expert cuts with a knife so sharp it could slice blue from the sky and the delicate ribs were cleaved, the flesh and veins severed.

The girl's head lolled back. Her legs gave out. Gently, the huntsman lowered her to the ground, then knelt beside her.

"Forgive me, dear princess. Forgive me," he begged. "This foul deed was not my wish, but the queen's command."

"Why?" the girl cried, with her dying breath.

But the huntsman, tears in his eyes, could not speak. He finished his grim task and got to his feet. As he did, the girl got her answer. For the last thing she saw before her eyes closed was her heart, small and perfect, in the huntsman's trembling hands.

In the forest, the birds have gone silent. The creatures are still. Gloom lingers under the trees. And on the cold ground, a girl lies dying, a ragged red hole where her heart used to be.

"Hang the huntsman!" you shout. "Burn the evil queen!" And who would fault you?

But you've missed the real villain.

It's easily done. He's stealthy and sly and comes when you're alone. He stands in the shadows and whispers his poison. His words drip, drip, drip into the small, secret chambers of your heart.

You think you know this tale, but you only know what

2

you've been told. "Who are you? How do you know these things?" you ask.

Fair questions, both.

I am the huntsman. Dead now, but that's no matter. The dead speak. With tongues blackened by time and regret. You can hear us if you listen.

You will say that I'm telling you tales. Fairy stories. That it's all make-believe. But there are more things afoot in the Darkwood than you can imagine, and only a fool would call them make-believe.

Keep to the path, the old wives say. Stay out of the forest.

But one day, you will have to walk deep into those dark woods and find what's waiting there.

For if you do not, it will surely find you.

ONE

The day before . . .

"Tally ho!" shouted the queen, spurring her fierce courser on.

The hounds had flushed their quarry. A gray wolf broke from the cover of a blackbriar patch and ran for the deep woods. The pack swept after it, baying for blood.

The bravest members of the hunting party followed the queen, galloping hard to keep up with her, but the princess, riding a swift, nimble palfrey, boldly streaked past her. She chased the wolf at breakneck speed, weaving in and out of trees, her skirts billowing behind her. She jumped a stone wall, a stream, a tangle of brush so high, there was no telling what lay beyond it. Her hat came off; her black hair unfurled like ribbons of night.

The queen couldn't catch her. Nor could the princes, Haakon and Rodrigo. I saw them flashing through the woods, the queen in white, her nobles in rich hues of russet, moss, and ochre. I saw a baron crouched low over his horse's neck, his hands high up in the animal's mane. He narrowed the distance between himself and the queen, but just as he was about to pass her, his horse stumbled. The baron lost his balance. There was a cry, then a sickening crack as he hit the ground.

"Leave him, huntsman!" the queen shouted. "Leave anyone who falls!"

The man lay crumpled under a tree, his eyes closed, his head bloodied. I thundered past him; the rest of the riders did, too. Only the princess cast a look back.

We trailed the hounds, navigating by their cries, swerving through the woods as they changed direction. I lost sight of the queen as she rode through a pocket of mist, then found her again, some moments later, with the pack. And the princess.

The hounds had surrounded the wolf. The creature was huge and fearsome. It had killed two dogs already. Their broken bodies lay nearby.

And him? Oh, yes. He was there, too.

He was always close by. Watching. Waiting.

I heard him in the wolf's low growl. Felt him in the nervous stamping of the horses. I saw him rise from the depths of the princess's eyes, like a corpse bobbing up in a river.

And then, without warning, the wolf charged the horses, snarling. The palfrey whinnied and reared, but the princess kept her seat. The courser's nostrils flared, he flattened his ears, but he stood his ground as the queen jumped down from her saddle.

Circling the fray, she shouted at the hounds, exhorting them to attack. They did, barking and slavering, snapping at their prey's haunches. The wolf rounded on them, but it was one against many. The hounds knew it and grew bolder, but one, small and slight, hung back from the pack.

The queen saw it; her eyes darkened. "Fight, you coward!" she shouted.

5

The hound tucked its tail and retreated. Furious, the queen snatched a whip out of a groom's hands and started after the dog.

"Your Grace! The wolf is escaping!"

It was Prince Haakon. He'd just caught up to the pack. The queen threw the whip down and ran to her horse, but by the time she'd swung back into her saddle, the pack—and the princess—was already gone, in hot pursuit once more.

For a long and treacherous mile, the princess pursued the wolf, until a ravine brought them up short. She stopped her horse a few yards from the edge, but the wolf ran right to it. When it saw the sheer drop, it tried to backtrack, but the hounds closed in from the left. A tangle of blackbriar, a good ten feet high, ran from the woods to the edge of the ravine creating a wall on the right. The frantic animal paced back and forth, tensed itself to jump across the chasm, but saw that it was hopeless. Shoulders high, head low, it turned and readied itself for its last fight.

The princess had moved closer. She could see the scruff of white at the animal's throat now, the ragged edge of one ear. The wolf looked up at her, and she saw the fear in its silvery eyes. In a heartbeat, she was out of her saddle. Striding among the frenzied hounds, she drove them back, yelling at them, stamping them away, until she'd created an opening for the wolf.

"Go! Get out of here!" she shouted at the creature.

The wolf spied a small opening at the bottom of the blackbriar. The thorns were curved and cruel; they carved stripes in the desperate creature's snout and tore at its ears, but it pushed under the dense vines and disappeared. The hounds rushed after it, but their snouts were tender, their hides thin; they could not break through.

The princess thought she was alone; she thought that no one saw this, but I did. I'd caught up to her but stayed hidden. I hunted many things for the queen, not all of them wolves.

I saw the princess lean her head into her horse's lathered neck. I saw a deep weariness settle on her shoulders like a shroud. I saw her press a hand to her chest, as if to soothe a fierce ache under her ribs.

How it cost her, this charade. How it would cost us all.

Hoofbeats sounded in the distance. Shouts echoed. By the time the queen drew up, with Haakon and a few other riders, the princess's back was straight again, her weariness buried.

"I'm afraid our sport is over, Stepmother," she said with feigned regret, nodding at the ravine. "The wolf chose a quicker death."

The queen rode to the edge and looked over it, frowning. "What a pity," she said, "that we are robbed of our kill."

Her eyes traveled to the hounds, then to the blackbriar. Her gaze sharpened. The princess did not see what had caught the queen's attention, for she was climbing back into her saddle, but I did. Snagged in the thorns was a tuft of fur. Gray fur. Wolf's fur.

The queen's frown hardened. "Blow for home, huntsman!" she commanded.

I sounded my trumpet, and the hounds set off, noses skimming the ground. The small, frightened one, her tail still between her legs, skittered along at the edge of the pack. The riders followed, chatting and laughing.

As the hoofbeats faded from the clearing, there was a dry, rustling sound, like the whispering of silk skirts. I looked up and saw a crow, blueblack and shrewd, drop down from the high branch where he'd perched.

He let out a shrill caw, then flew off into the Darkwood. I hear his call still, echoing down the centuries.

It sounded like a warning.

It sounded like a death knell.

It sounded, most of all, like laughter.

TWO

There was blood on the reins.

Sophie saw it as she handed them to a groom.

She turned her palms up. Four thin crimson crescents lay across each one, gouged by her own fingernails. Terror had flooded through her as she'd galloped through the woods. The horse she'd ridden was so fast, so high-strung, it had taken all her strength to control her. With every hoofbeat, Sophie had been certain she would fall and break her neck. She'd been frightened as she'd faced the wolf, too. The creature was huge; it could've torn her to shreds.

But her horse, the wolf—neither was the reason for the cuts in her palms, and she knew it. Her legs were still trembling even though the hunt was long over.

"Stupid, stupid, girl," she hissed at herself.

What if the queen had seen her let the wolf go? What if someone else had? Her stepmother had eyes and ears everywhere.

Quickly, she pulled her gloves from her jacket pocket and slipped them on. The bold, fearless girl who could outride the princes, the huntsman, even the queen herself; the heartless girl who was keen to chase down an animal just to watch a pack of hounds kill it, that girl was a lie. The cuts were the truth, written in blood, and no one must ever read it. Rulers were ruthless. They did not show weakness or fear. They did not cry. They made others cry. Hadn't her stepmother told her that a thousand times?

Sophie was standing in a large cobbled courtyard shared by the stables and kennels. She glanced around it now for the queen and her retinue, but they had not returned yet. *Good*, she thought. The hunt itself, the small talk made during the ride back, the constant pressure to be captivating and witty—it had all exhausted her. She wanted nothing more than to slip away to her chambers, get out of her sweaty clothing, and sink into a hot bath.

Servants had set out a long, linen-draped table in the courtyard. It was laden with meat pies, roasted game birds, smoked hams, cheeses, nuts, and fruit. Sophie made her way past it, head down, hoping to go unnoticed.

"Hail, bold Artemis, goddess of the hunt!" a voice bellowed from across the yard.

Sophie's heart sank. *So much for my escape*, she thought.

She looked up and saw Haakon making his way toward her. Handsome Haakon, golden-haired and bronzed, his face as perfect as a marble god's. Rodrigo was right behind him, his full lips curved into a seductive smile, his dark eyes full of promises. Sophie smiled brightly at them; she had no choice. One of these men might well become her husband.

The morning's hunt was the first in a series of events over the next few days to celebrate her birthday. There would be a ball tonight as well, here in Konigsburg, at the palace. It would be a glittering affair with members of her stepmother's court and rulers from all the foreign realms in attendance. She would turn seventeen tomorrow and inherit her father's crown. Once she was queen, Sophie could marry, and her stepmother was determined to make Sophie an advantageous match with a powerful, titled man.

"The young prince of Skandinay, perhaps," the queen had said when she'd first raised the topic. "The emperor's nephew. Or the sultan's son."

"But, Stepmother, I don't even know these men. What if I don't fall in love with any of them?" Sophie had asked.

"Love?" the queen had said, contempt dripping from her voice. "Love is nothing but a fable, and a dangerous one at that. Your suitors should recite the size of their armies to you and the strength of their fortresses, not silly poems about flowers and doves."

There was a reason why her stepmother wanted a powerful husband for her, a shameful reason, and Sophie knew it—the queen thought her weak. The entire court did.

Sophie had grown up hearing the whispers, mocking her for being a shy, softhearted child. They'd begun as soon as the queen had married Sophie's father and had only grown louder over the years. The poisonous words had lodged in her heart like blackbriar thorns. They echoed there still . . . *The princess will never make a good queen . . . She's not smart enough . . . not tough enough . . .*

Haakon swaggered over to Sophie now. He was the eldest son of the king of Skandinay, and her stepmother's first choice

11

for her. He lifted the tankard of ale he was holding to her. "Fair Artemis has won my heart, but, oh, cruel, selfish deity! She will not give me hers!"

Rodrigo snorted. "Can you blame her?"

"I pine. I languish. I *starve* for love," Haakon said, pressing a hand to his heart. Then he leaned over the breakfast table and tore a leg off a chicken. "I endure unending torment. Give me your heart, cold goddess, and end my torment!"

"That is impossible, sir," Sophie said, her eyes teasing, her voice so breezy and bemused that no one would have guessed how desperately she longed for the quiet of her chambers.

"Why the devil not?" Haakon asked, gnawing the chicken leg. "Good-looking lad like me . . . Why, I'm probably a god myself. I must be." He frowned, then nodded. "In fact, I'm sure of it. I'm the god . . . mmm, *Apollo*! Yes, that's the fellow!" He pointed at Sophie with the chicken leg. "What a pair we would make, the two of us."

"If you recall your classics, and I'm certain that you do—" Sophie began.

"Scholar that you are," Rodrigo cut in.

"—then you know that Artemis swore she would never marry. And were she to break that vow, I doubt it would be for Apollo. Since he is her brother."

Haakon wrinkled his nose. "Ew."

"Very," said Rodrigo.

Sophie laughed despite herself. It was impossible not to. Haakon was a bright, golden sun who pulled everyone into his orbit. He was arrogant and annoying but astonishingly beautiful, and beautiful people are so easily forgiven. Every woman in the palace was in love with him. Sophie was a little, too, though she hated to admit it.

More members of the hunting party trotted into the courtyard now. Grooms and hounds followed them. Sophie thought she heard the queen's lord commander among them, barking orders. Haakon and Rodrigo turned to the party and waved some of the riders over. As they did, Sophie heard a smaller, softer sound than clopping hooves or Haakon's booming voice. She heard footsteps. They were quick but shambling.

"Tom?" she said, turning around.

A young boy was running toward her. He was undersized for his age, awkward, and shy.

"Be careful, Tom. Slow down before—" Sophie started to say. But it was too late. Tom caught the toe of his boot on a cobblestone, stumbled, and fell. Sophie bent down to help him up.

"Clumsy ox," a voice said.

"Should've drowned him at birth. Isn't that what one does with runts?" Tom winced at their cruel words. Sophie could see that they hurt him more than the fall. The women who'd made them, two of the queen's ladies-in-waiting, laughed as they hurried by.

"Don't listen to them," Sophie said, trying to make the boy feel better. "If you want to see clumsy, you should see Baroness von Arnim"—she nodded at the shorter of the two women—"dance a sarabande. She looks like a donkey on ice!"

Tom laughed and Sophie smiled, but her smile faded as she saw the boy's skinned knees. "You mustn't run," she scolded. "Haven't I told you so?" He was like the puppies he cared for, all loose limbs and big feet.

13

Tom brushed his bangs out of his eyes. "But I couldn't help it, Your Grace! I had to tell you!"

"Tell me what?" Sophie asked.

"Duchess had her puppies!" Duchess was Sophie's favorite spaniel. "She didn't!" Sophie said, her eyes widening with excitement.

"She did! Seven healthy pups! All as fat as sausages, with snub noses and pink feet! Come see them!"

Tom grew so excited that he forgot himself and reached for Sophie's hand. Sophie forgot herself and took it.

"What are you doing? Have you gone mad, boy?" a voice thundered. "How dare you put your hands on the princess!"

It was the lord commander, the man in charge of the queen's military. He strode up to Tom, grabbed his shoulder, and gave him a tooth-rattling shake. As he did, Sophie brusquely pulled her hand away. As if it were all Tom's doing.

It was a cowardly move, and shame curdled Sophie's insides. She knew that she should come to Tom's defense. She should explain to the lord commander that they'd both been carried away. But she did not. Holding hands with kennel boys, playing with puppies—this was not how a ruler behaved. Strong rulers were distant and aloof. If the queen heard of her lapse, she would be angry. This was not the wolf hunt, where there was no one at the ravine to see her weakness. Here, at the palace, the wolves were the ones who hunted.

"It won't happen again, Your Grace," the lord commander said to Sophie. Then he turned back to Tom. "Remember your place," he growled, giving the boy another shake before he walked away.

14

Tom raised his eyes to Sophie's. The hurt and confusion she saw in them twisted her heart. "I-I'm sorry, Your Grace. I didn't . . . I didn't mean to—"

Tom's words were abruptly cut off by a blood-chilling sound. It was a high, keening wail.

And it was rising over the courtyard.

THREE

The wretched creature had been backed into a corner.

It was a hound, and it was crying and cowering, trying to make itself as small as possible. Sophie recognized it. It was the small, skittish dog that had refused to attack the wolf.

The queen had hit the creature with her riding crop and was now pointing at it. "That animal's worthless," she spat. "I want it killed."

Sophie stood frozen to the spot, horrified. It was Tom who tried to stop the queen.

"No!" he cried, lurching toward the hound. "Please don't, Your Grace! She's a good dog!"

The queen whirled around, incensed. Her eyes sought the one who'd dared to censure her. "Am I to be shouted at by a kennel boy?" she asked, her hand tightening on the crop.

Alistair, the kennel master and Tom's father, had come running from the dog pens, alarmed by the cries. He saw what was about to happen, and his eyes widened in terror. He grabbed Tom by the back of his shirt and pulled the boy to him just as the crop came whistling through the air. The blow missed the child but caught Alistair and split his cheek open.

Heedless of his pain and of the blood dripping from his jaw, Alistair begged for his son. "He's very sorry, Your Grace. He'll never do it again. Please forgive him. Apologize, Tom—"

"But, Papa—"

"Apologize!" Alistair shouted. *"Now!"*

It wasn't anger that made him shout at his boy. Sophie knew that. It was fear. The queen had carved a gully in Alistair's face, and he was a grown man. What would a blow like that have done to Tom's small body?

"I-I'm sorry, Your Grace," Tom stammered, looking at the ground.

"Attend to the rest of the hounds, both of you," the queen ordered.

Alistair let go of Tom. He drew a cloth from his pocket, pressed it to his cheek, and then called the pack to him. The small dog stayed in the corner, hopeless, helpless. As if it knew it had been condemned.

"Come and see my new brood mare!" the queen said to a group of nobles.

As they headed to the stables, Tom made his way back to Sophie. "Don't let her be killed. Please, my lady," he begged, his voice breaking. "Her name's Zara. She was the runt of her litter. How can you kill a wolf if you're so small?"

"You can't, Tom," Sophie said, watching the queen head into the stables.

Sophie remained rooted to the spot, astonished by her stepmother's cruelty. Sorrow corseted her chest so tightly she could barely breathe, but another emotion simmered underneath it now—*anger*. Anger at the injustice of her stepmother's actions. Anger that no one cared, that every single person in the courtyard went on eating and drinking, laughing and chattering, as if nothing had happened.

No, you can't kill the wolf, she thought as the queen disappeared through the stable doors. *But maybe you can outfox her.*

Tom had not moved. He was still standing by Sophie's side, his hands clenched.

"Go help your father," Sophie said to him.

Tom's shoulders slumped. Hope drained from his small face. "But, my lady—"

"*Go.*"

Fear made her voice harsh. Allowing a wolf to escape was foolish; what she was about to do now was insanity.

As Tom moved off, Sophie glanced around. No one was paying attention to her. The lord commander was cutting into a flaky venison pie. Haakon was picking up a slice of ham with his fingers. Rodrigo was biting into a peach. She walked to the far end of the courtyard, where the hound, her eyes closed, had slumped to the ground.

Sophie took a deep breath to shore up her nerve. She was quaking inside, but then she thought of Tom, shouting at the queen to spare the dog. He did not wear his courage as she did, as a mask to be slipped on and off. If a small boy could be brave, so could she.

"Zara, is it? You're a beauty," she said softly as she approached the dog.

At the sound of her name, the hound got to her feet. Her eyes were huge and pleading.

"Steady, girl," Sophie said. "I'm not going to hurt you. No

18

one is. Not if we're quick, you and I." She hooked two fingers under Zara's collar and coaxed her away from the wall. Her skirts shielded the dog from view. "Come on, girl, just a bit farther . . . Hurry now . . ."

A wooden gate stood only a few feet away. Sophie led Zara to it, then quickly unlatched it. "Go!" she whispered as she opened it. "Run from here and never come back!"

The dog was off in a flash. Sophie's heart swelled as she watched the cream-colored blur streak across the fields and disappear into the woods. She latched the gate, then turned and glanced around again. All the members of the hunting party were still occupied with breakfast; the servants were busy with their duties. No one had seen her. Sophie allowed herself to exhale. As she walked back across the courtyard, she passed Tom. He was standing in the center, turning around in a slow circle.

"My father says I'm to find Zara and bring her to him," he said dully. "Did you see where she went, Your Grace?"

Sophie affected a regretful expression. "The little hound?" she said. "I'm afraid she ran off, Tom. I opened the gate, and I shouldn't have. I wasn't paying attention."

Tom smiled. With his mouth, his face, his whole body. Sophie winked at him, then walked on, eager to finally get to her chambers.

It was then that she saw her stepmother.

The queen was standing in the open doorway of the stables, watching her. Dread's thin, icy fingers closed around Sophie. *How long has she been standing there?* she wondered frantically. *How much did she see?*

The queen's silence, cold and forbidding, quieted the chattering court.

After a moment, she spoke, her voice ringing across the yard. "Cowardice is like a plague; it spreads. One sick individual can infect an entire population. The hound—the one I ordered to be put down, the one who appears to have escaped—that hound should have attacked when it was ordered to. What will happen next time, should the other hounds decide to do as they wish, not as they're told? I shall tell you: The *wolf* will attack, and your queen will die."

Sophie's dread turned to fear. But not for herself. "It was my fault the dog got out, Your Grace. I opened the gate," she said, her words tumbling out in a rush.

"You are a princess of the realm, not a kennel hand," the queen retorted. "The boy was negligent. He should have leashed the dog immediately." She paused, allowing her gaze to settle on Tom. "I order every hound in the kennel to be slaughtered, lest any have caught the disease of cowardice. And I order that this boy here, who coddles cowards, who places more value on a dog's life than that of his queen . . . I order that he be taken to the guards' barracks, where he will receive ten lashes."

"No," Tom whispered, shaking his head. "*No.* Please. I'm sorry . . . I'm *sorry!*"

Sophie gasped. She wanted to shout at her stepmother, to beg her not to do this, but she knew she could do no such thing. So she watched, impotent and mute, as Tom backed away, stumbled, and fell once again. Two guards picked him up, then half marched, half dragged him out of the courtyard.

"Papa! *Papa!*" he cried, reaching back for his father.

Alistair took a step toward him, but the captain of the guards blocked his way. He turned toward the queen, to beg her to spare his child, but she was already gone.

Sophie knew what the queen was doing. She wished to teach lessons. Not to the boy. That was only a ruse. She wished to teach the powerful nobles who had accompanied her on the hunt that cowardice was dangerous and disobedience even more so.

And she wished to teach Sophie a lesson, too.

And that lesson was perfectly clear: There is nothing more dangerous than kindness.

FOUR

In her chambers, the queen stood gazing into a mirror.

The silver glass showed a tall, straight-backed woman with indigo eyes, blond hair, and high cheekbones. Her name was Adelaide.

She had once been more beautiful than the dawn, but the years had not been kind to her is how the storytellers start their tales about her. Or *Time had etched deep lines at the corners of her eyes and grooved furrows across her brow.*

Tell me, what stories of kings begin with their wrinkles?

Why did no one speak of her ferocious intelligence? Her bravery? Her strength?

The stone floor was ice-cold beneath the queen's bare feet, the air chilly on her skin. A shiver moved through her, for she had just bathed. Her skin was still damp, and the thin linen shift she wore provided little warmth, but she barely noticed. Her eyes, fever bright, were fixed on the silver glass as if searching its depths.

For what, no one could say. Though many did.

A lady-in-waiting appeared with a white satin gown and slipped it over the queen's head. Another laced her into a stiff bodice, then pulled the strings tight. Two more brought a golden surcoat embellished with scores of flawless diamonds.

"It's as heavy as a suit of armor," said Lady Beatrice, the eldest of the queen's attendants, as she settled the costly garment on her mistress's shoulders.

"It *is* armor," said the queen. "I will meet with the Hinterlands' ambassador in an hour to discuss disputed territories in the north. He's a treacherous old snake, just like his master."

As Beatrice left the room to fetch the queen's shoes, one of the younger ladies-in-waiting, Elizabetta, shyly stepped forward. "You look very beautiful, Your Grace," she said.

Her words were all wrong. The hapless woman saw that immediately. Anger blanched the queen's face. She knew what her enemies said about her. That she was jealous and vain. That she cared only for her own reflection. She motioned Elizabetta to her.

"Do you think I cover myself in shiny stones out of vanity?" she asked. "Do you think I care a fig about my appearance, when enemies of my realm prowl my borders?"

Elizabetta swallowed. She glanced left and right, hoping for a shred of support, but everyone in the room, from noble ladies to lowly maids, had averted her eyes.

"I—I think . . . Well, no," she stutteringly began. "Actually, I do *not* think—"

"That much is clear," said the queen.

She walked to a window and raised her arms. Rays of sun, streaming in through the panes, turned the jewels on her surcoat into prisms, encasing her in a brilliant light.

"I use these diamonds to head off war," she said. "When the

23

ambassador sees me, he will conclude that if I can afford to strew gemstones over myself like confetti, I can also afford to strew warships along my coast. The best way to win a war is by not starting one."

Elizabetta, her eyes downcast, nodded silently.

The queen lowered her arms. She glanced at a golden clock. "Where is she? Why is she not here?" she asked impatiently. "I summoned her half an hour ago."

"She *is* here, Your Grace," said Beatrice, returning with a pair of silk shoes. "She awaits you in your antechamber."

Beatrice placed the shoes on the floor, and the queen slipped her feet into them. Then she snatched a gray tuft off a table and marched out of her dressing room, heels clicking against the stone floor.

The princess stood silhouetted in a window in the queen's antechamber, twisting the ring on her left hand. It was the Ruler's Ring—a gold oval with a unicorn in its center, framed by diamonds—and had been handed down through the centuries from the Greenlands' monarchs to their heirs.

The queen could not think of anyone less suited to wear it. She walked up to the princess, took her hand, and smoothed it open, then dropped the fluff into it.

"Fur," she said. "Pulled from blackbriar thorns. The wolf *didn't* jump to its death, did it?"

Sophie stared down at the fluff. She made no reply.

The queen took hold of her chin and raised it. "You let it escape."

"Yes."

"Why?"

Sophie's eyes, bright with emotion, sought her stepmother's. "I—I felt sorry for it. It was so frightened."

With a snort of disgust, the queen released her. "The hunt was a chance for you to show strength, Sophia, not weakness."

Sophie lowered her eyes.

"You are soft when you should be shrewd, forgiving when you should be fierce," the queen continued. "You allow wolves to escape. You champion cowards and kennel boys."

"Ten lashes will kill him," Sophie said quietly.

"Ten lashes never killed anyone. And even if they did, what of it?" the queen snapped. "The boy, his father . . . They don't matter. Monarchs matter. Don't you see that?" She held her two hands out, palms up. "In my left hand, a boy. A weakling who likely won't live to see manhood," she said. "In my right hand, a queen . . . a ruler who must protect not one subject but an entire realm." Her left hand sank. Her right hand rose. "What is the life of one boy compared to a queen's?"

As the question hung in the air, the queen lowered her hands and asked another. "What kind of example does it set to allow disobedient creatures to go unpunished?"

It took all Sophie's courage to meet her stepmother's withering gaze again. "The dog was afraid. Is it so terrible to show a scared creature mercy?" she asked.

The queen laughed. It was a dry, dusty sound. "Mercy is just another word for weakness. Let a wolf live, and she'll repay your kindness by tearing out your throat. Fear is the only thing that keeps a queen safe. People obey me because they're frightened of me."

"People obeyed my father because they loved him."

The words popped out of Sophie's mouth before she could stop them. She regretted them immediately. Her stepmother hated any mention of her late husband, a man revered by his people.

"Your father had the luxury of love. He was a man," the queen spat. "No one, not even his enemies, questioned his right to sit on the throne. I do not have that luxury. You will not, either, you little fool. The people need a firm hand to keep them in place. I have been queen regent these past six years, ever since your father's death. Tomorrow is your coronation day. Tomorrow *you* become queen. How can you rule a country, Sophia, if you cannot rule yourself?"

Before Sophie could attempt to stammer out an answer, the sound of drums, beating like a dirge, was heard.

"Ah, I believe the captain of the guards is about to carry out my orders," said the queen. She opened the window and looked at the courtyard below. After a moment, she turned back to Sophie. "Would you like to watch?"

Sophie shook her head, her eyes shiny with tears.

"No? I didn't think so. It's too hard, too painful, isn't it? But that's what ruling is—hard and painful. It's making difficult decisions and handing down harsh sentences in order to keep your subjects in line and your enemies at bay." The queen pointed at her. "It's *your* fault the boy is being whipped, *your* fault the hounds will be slaughtered. Had you not set that cowardly dog free, none of this would be happening. Do you see now the havoc kindness wreaks?"

Sophie was unable to speak. Tears trickled down her cheeks. She pushed them away with the heel of her hand.

The queen clucked her tongue. "You are fortunate to have me here to help you rule until you marry." She jabbed a pointed nail into Sophie's ribs. "That thing in there . . . your soft, stupid heart? It will get you killed. Put it in a box and put that box on a high shelf. Never take it down."

"Am I dismissed?" Sophie asked in a small, broken voice, desperate to escape the terrible sound of the drums.

"Not yet. There is a ball tonight, as you are well aware. There are to be no red eyes, no blotchy cheeks. You have a stunning gown to wear, and a selection of jewels from the crown's vault will be brought to your chambers. You have your beauty and your youth. Use these things to secure a strong ruler for this realm. Today you have shown me, yet again, that it will need one."

Sophie, crumbling, gave a nod and hurried from the room. Adelaide watched her leave. Outside the window, the drumbeats stopped. The captain of the guards shouted his orders. The queen knew what was coming next. She could have closed her window, but she did not. Instead, she stood motionlessly, listening silently as the whip cracked. She did not blink. She did not flinch.

And if something flickered in her eyes, something like sorrow . . . well, what did it matter?

There was no one there to see it.

FIVE

There are bogs in the Darkwood, treacherous and deep. Take one wrong step, and they'll swallow you whole.

Most people stay well away from them, but in years past, when I'd stalked a stag too far into the forest and had to make my way home in the dark, I'd seen a lantern bobbing through the thick, clutching gloom that shrouds them. And then, days later, there came news of someone gone missing—a husband too ready with his fists, a mistress grown demanding, a miser with a sack of gold hidden under his floor.

The bodies were never found. The trials never held. The guilty went unpunished to comfortable graves in the churchyard. Time moved on. People forgot.

But the bogs never did.

Years, decades, sometimes centuries later, they gave up their restless dead, pushing the old bones out of their sodden black depths to the surface.

The truth is like that, too.

Bury it deep. Hope that it rots.

But one day, it will come back.

Tattered and shuffling and stinking of death, it comes home to knock on your door.

Adelaide committed many crimes. Rulers often do. A king beheads a wife for giving him daughters. A prince poisons a mutinous noble. A bishop burns a man at the stake because his God speaks English, not Latin. It is not murder, the history books say, but execution. Done to preserve the peace. Distasteful, yes, but necessary.

But in Adelaide's time, and perhaps still in yours, there was one crime that could not be countenanced. There was one abomination no king, no prince or pope could forgive . . .

A woman who wears a crown.

Mirror, mirror on the wall . . . who's the fairest of them all?

Do you know the villain yet? Do you see his face?

Ah, well, no matter. You will. He is coming ever closer.

SIX

"La volta! La volta!" a voice shouted as the last notes of the galliard faded.

Gasps rose from some of the older revelers. They were followed by laughter, whistles, even a few raucous catcalls from the younger ones.

If the galliard was a risqué dance, the volta was downright scandalous. It was a beautifully choreographed duel of desire. One partner advanced, the other retreated. One swayed close, the other turned away. Every glance was a provocation; every smile, a dare.

Music beckoned the dancers. Partners were sought. The flickering light of a thousand candles played over the faces of the guests and made their silk gowns and satin jackets shimmer. Jewels cascaded down powdered bosoms. Pearls as big as cherries dangled from earlobes. Gem-studded rings barnacled every hand.

The princess was standing off to one side of the Great Hall, trying not to gulp down a glass of punch. She was flushed and breathless, for she'd danced with passion and grace all night long, earning herself approving glances from her stepmother.

The gown she was wearing, of the deepest plum, set off her black hair and green eyes. The color was high in her cheeks.

She laughed. Fetchingly. Musically. Extravagantly. Her head back, a jeweled hand at her pretty throat. And she talked. Incessantly. About anything. Or nothing at all. Boys, shoes, cakes, dresses . . . It didn't matter. Talk a lot, laugh a lot, and you could drown out the noise made by the shattered, jangling pieces of your broken heart.

A small boy, brutalized. Innocent hounds, dead. When she thought of Tom and the dogs he'd loved, it felt as if each one of those jagged shards were trying to work its way out of her chest, piercing her flesh and drawing blood.

So she didn't think of him. She pushed him from her mind, set her glass down, and snapped her fingers at a serving boy to fill it, just as her stepmother would have done. It didn't matter that she wasn't having a good time; the important thing was that she appeared to be.

Rodrigo approached her and made fun of Haakon; she laughed and joined in. Hussein, the sultan of Asir's son, handed her a rose and asked her to dance. She refused it and teasingly told him to come back with two dozen. Alexander, a Hinterlands duke, offered her a sweet; she fed it to a spaniel.

The serving boy returned with her drink, but before she could take it, a voice behind her said, "Princess Charlotta-Sidonia Wilhelmina Sophia of the Greenlands, punch is for children."

Sophie turned. Haakon stood there, smiling. He was dressed in moss-green velvet, his blond hair long and loose around his shoulders. He was so beautiful, the mere sight of him made Sophie catch her breath.

"Try this," he said, thrusting a glass of champagne into her hands. "Thank you, my lord, but I cannot," Sophie said, trying to hand it back. "Champagne makes my head spin. It is the undoing of me."

But Haakon wouldn't take the glass back. "Well then, you cannot have me, either," he said. Quite loudly. "For I will make your heart spin." He tugged at the knot in the bottom of the silver laces that ran down the side of Sophie's bodice. "And *that* will be the undoing of you."

Gasps of surprise were heard. Sophie blinked, a bit taken aback herself. *This is very cheeky*, she thought. *Even for Haakon.* Well, she would play along. She had to. All eyes were on her. Her stepmother, the court . . . They expected a performance. They wanted a joust. And she would give them one. She knew that if she gave in to her shyness, if she ducked away blushing, she would be summoned, once again, to her stepmother's chambers.

"Shouldn't I *want* you, sir? Before I *have* you?" she boldly retorted. Scandalized oohs and aahs rose from the crowd.

Haakon feigned hurt. He banged his own glass down on a table. "Proud princess, do not scorn my declaration of love! Your words are a dagger to my heart!"

Sophie arched an eyebrow. "Ah! So you have one? I have heard the opposite."

"From whom? Show me the knave and . . . and"—Haakon looked around, snatched something from the table, and thrust it into the air—"I'll run him through!"

Sophie laughed. She couldn't help it. "With a *pickle*?"

He brandished it at her. "Tell me! Who said I have no heart?"

"Every girl at court, Your Highness. For you have wooed them *all*. Wooed, won, and declared yourself done."

"That is a killing blow, heartless lady!" Haakon staggered backward theatrically, then fell to the floor, limbs splayed, eyes closed.

Sophie rolled her eyes. She'd had enough. This was becoming a full-blown farce, and the effort of maintaining it was draining her. She leaned over him, careful not to spill the champagne she was still holding, and in a strained voice said, "Haakon, do get up. You're making a scene."

Haakon opened his eyes. "Dance with me. Or I'll make a bigger one."

"No."

Haakon let out a long, trailing howl. "A beautiful maiden's careless cruelty has mortally wounded me!" he cried.

"Stop it right now!" Sophie hissed.

He stretched out his hand and said, "And only her kindness can restore me."

Sophie softened a little at that. She drank the champagne all in one gulp, put the glass down, and then reached for him. *One dance*, she thought, *and then I'll find a dark, quiet corner.* Haakon tossed his pickle, grabbed her hand, and sprang to his feet. There was laughter and applause. Amid knowing glances, he escorted Sophie to the dance floor.

The volta had started. The drumbeats, loud and insistent, were calling out their challenge. The dancers turned swiftly clockwise, then counter, and then, with a crash of tambourines, the women leapt high, the men lifting them up, whirling them through the air. There were whoops and shouts of laughter.

Skirts flared. Hair came unpinned. The dance floor was a crush of movement.

Haakon pulled Sophie right into the middle of it.

The tempo picked up. The dancers whirled around each other again, faster and faster. Sophie felt a little giddy; the champagne *had* gone to her head. It was all she could do not to step on Haakon's toes. Or her own.

Then he pulled her close to him, so close it made her catch her breath. They turned in a circle; then Sophie leapt, and as she did, Haakon lifted her high into the air. She felt as if she were flying. The spinning, the pounding of feet, the quickening tempo—they took her breath away. Haakon's nearness, the smell of him, the warmth of his breath on her cheek, made her dizzy. His hands felt like a band of fire around her waist. And then the dance ended. The music stopped, and the dancers, flushed and laughing, clapped loudly and broke apart.

Haakon leaned forward, his hands on his knees to catch his breath.

Then he looked up at Sophie and said, "Run away with me."

Sophie reddened at his forwardness but tried to cover her blushes. "Don't be ridiculous," she said airily, as if handsome boys asked her to run off with them every day of the week.

"I've never been more serious. Either we run, right this second, or your next dance partner is Barse."

"Barse?" Sophie echoed, appalled. Barse was a sullen young man, an earl's son from the provinces. He picked his nose and taught filthy words to small children. "Barse doesn't dance."

"Apparently, he does. Don't look now, but—"

Sophie craned her neck and saw that the boy was indeed

making his way toward her. He wore a grimace on his face. It was as close as he ever got to a smile.

"Oh *no*," she whispered, horrified.

"I said *don't* look."

"What am I going to do?"

"We can still run for it."

"*How?*" Sophie asked. They were surrounded by a throng of people. The Great Hall had two doors. Barse, fording his way through the crowd, blocked the path to one. And the enormous banqueting table, arranged in the shape of a horseshoe, stood between them and the other.

Haakon dipped his head close to hers. "I'll save you, if you let me," he whispered in her ear. "I'm a prince. That's what we do."

Sophie risked a glance back again. "It's too late. The dragon's closing in."

"Trust me, Sophie. Do you?" Haakon asked, taking hold of her hand. Sophie's eyes found his.

"Not at all," she said.

Haakon tightened his grip.

And grinned.

And ran.

SEVEN

Sophie expected Haakon to pull her into a gavotte with his friends. Or lead her back to the huge silver punch bowl, where she could sip a cold drink and plead exhaustion when Barse approached her.

She never expected to find herself crawling under the banquet table. "Follow me!" Haakon had commanded, moving a chair aside. Then he'd ducked under the damask tablecloth. When Sophie hesitated, he pulled her in after him.

"Are you mad? What are you doing?" she'd spluttered.

"Spiriting the princess out of the dragon's lair. Hurry up!"

Then he'd commenced crawling across the floor. Sophie followed him. It was harder for her, as she was wearing a gown and petticoats, but she managed, bunching them up behind her.

Luckily, few guests were still sitting at the table. Most were up dancing. When Haakon reached the other side, he lifted the tablecloth. "There it is," he said, pointing at an arched stone doorway. "Our escape route."

He bolted from under the table, pulling Sophie with him. They startled a serving girl carrying a tray of cakes. Haakon swiped two, and then he and Sophie disappeared through the doorway and found themselves in a long hallway. Haakon pulled her close to the wall and held up one of the sweets he'd stolen. "Magic cake," he whispered. "Makes you invisible to dragons."

"You *are* mad," Sophie said, smiling.

Haakon popped the cake into his mouth. "So good!" He held up the second cake, and Sophie saw he meant to feed it to her. He teased her, holding the cake near her lips, then drawing it back and pretending he was going to eat it himself.

"Ah. I see how it goes, my brave rescuer," said Sophie tartly. "You eat the cake, and the dragon eats me."

"It's a tough choice," Haakon said. "You're very nice and all, Sophie, but this *cake* . . ."

"Haakon."

Finally, he fed her a bite. And then another. And Sophie found herself feeling a little warm, a little breathless. And then he clumsily dripped a bit of sweet, sticky icing onto her chin.

"Sorry," he said, thumbing it off. He licked his thumb, his beautiful sky-blue eyes on hers, and Sophie felt a warmth kindle in her chest. Its heat spread through her body. Her eyes darted to the cake, the wall, the floor, anywhere but to Haakon.

He grabbed her hand once more. "Come on," he said. "The dragon could still be lurking." They ran down one hall and then another and finally found themselves at a balcony. It overlooked the queen's gardens. Rose canes, laden with blowsy ivory blooms, climbed up one side of it.

Haakon leaned over, placed his hands on the railing, and said, "There. We've escaped. Barse won't follow us here. It's too far from the punch bowl."

Sophie joined him at the railing. "You are very brave, kind sir. Thank you for saving me."

Haakon smiled, but it wasn't his usual broad, cheeky grin. It was small and wistful. For a long moment, he didn't speak; he just gazed out over the garden. Then, all in a rush, he said, "I could, you know. I *would*. I want to."

"Want to what?" Sophie asked, puzzled.

"Save you. From Barse. From the queen. From what happened today." He paused. His eyes sought hers. "From yourself."

Sophie tilted her head. "What do you mean *from yourself*?"

Haakon looked away again. He straightened, then plucked a fragrant rose from a vine and twisted its stem into a loop. Its bloom was spent. The petals fell like confetti. Sighing, he tossed it over the railing and watched it fall.

Why is he suddenly being so strange? Sophie wondered.

And then she realized he wasn't being strange; he was nervous. Strutting, confident Haakon, who was always laughing and teasing, who turned every head in the room, was nervous.

"Haakon . . ." Sophie pressed. "What do you mean?"

Instead of answering, he reached for her hands, then turned them over. The thin red crescents she'd carved into her palms had stopped bleeding hours ago, but they were still there.

Haakon shook his head at the sight of them. "You could be onstage," he said. "You've been acting all night. All day, too." His eyes found hers again. "You try to hide your soft heart, but you can't. You're not a ruler, Sophie. It's not in your nature."

Sophie yanked her hands back. Anger flashed in her eyes. "What are you saying? The Greenlands are my home. I want to rule my realm. Of course I do!"

"Do you really? Can you do what's needed? Can you do what Adelaide does? Command armies? Catch spies? Condemn traitors?"

"Kill dogs? Whip children?" Sophie added bitterly. The champagne was still fizzing in her skull, making her bold.

Haakon hesitated. His eyes, always sparkling with amusement, were dark and still now, like the waters of a winter lake. "The little boy . . ." he started to say.

"Tom."

"I went to his family's cottage this evening. Before the ball. I brought medicines. A tincture for his pain. Salve for his wounds. Fresh linen to make bandages."

"You did?" Sophie asked, surprised. She would not have expected this from him.

"He's suffering tonight. Just taking a breath is agony for him. He's delirious. Doesn't even know his own mother."

Haakon's words hurt Sophie deeply. She couldn't bear to think of small, gentle Tom in so much pain. "Stop. *Please*, Haakon. No more," she begged.

"He will never do the wrong thing again. He will never shout at the queen or counter her wishes. He will simply follow her orders, quickly and without protest. As he must. And so will Adelaide's nobles, her generals, and her lord commander. As they must."

Sophie gave a sad laugh. "Tom will never do the *right* thing again. He'll never try to save an innocent life."

Haakon plucked another rose. He twisted its stem. "You would rule differently. With kindness, with mercy . . ."

"Yes, I would."

"Such a reign is a dream, Sophie. A pretty tale told to children. You might as well wish for a fairy queen to appear or seven little men to walk out of the woods."

Haakon stopped fumbling with the rose's stem. He had twisted it into a loop again. He took Sophie's left hand in his and pushed the loop onto her ring finger, nestling it against her unicorn ring.

"Marry me, Sophie," he said. "Let me be your king."

Sophie glared at him. This was a step too far. It was almost cruel. "There are some things you should never joke about, Haakon," she said briskly, moving to pull the ring off.

But Haakon stopped her. He caught her hand, raised it to his lips, and kissed it. "I've never been more serious," he said. "I'll do the hard, dirty work. I'll keep you safe. Keep our people safe. You can still do the kind things, the good things. Like giving alms to the poor. Visiting orphanages. Raising our beautiful children. Ruling is a brutal business, and you were not made for it."

Sophie's heart fluttered like the wings of a bird. She knew that politics drove royal marriages, not love. And yet, she loved Haakon. The way one loves stallions and storms, midnight and mountains and every other beautiful, willful, dangerous thing. And deep inside her soft, foolish heart, she hoped that he felt the same way.

Sophie lifted her eyes to his. "Do you . . . do you love me?" she asked. Haakon answered her with a kiss. He took her face in his hands and pressed his gorgeous mouth to hers. His lips tasted bittersweet, of chocolate and champagne. He smelled of costly things—leather and silk, ambergris and ambition.

Sophie's heart pounded against her ribs now. She forgot to breathe. To think. To be. There was only Haakon, his touch, his warmth. There was only this glorious, shining boy, and like ice in the sun, she melted into him.

After a long moment, he broke the kiss, then touched his forehead to hers.

Flustered and breathless, Sophie babbled. "My stepmother says love is nothing but a fable. She says I must box my heart away and put it on a high shelf. She says—"

Haakon kissed her again. Slowly. Deeply. "Silly girl," he said. "I've loved you from the moment I saw you. Put your heart in a box and give it to me. I'll keep it safe. Always. Say you'll marry me, Sophie."

Sophie's thoughts raced. *What do I do?* she wondered frantically. There was no reason to say no. Her stepmother would be delighted; she approved of Haakon wholeheartedly. More importantly, Haakon loved her. He'd said so. And she loved him. She must, because all she wanted to do was kiss that perfect mouth again. And he was right about her. Her stepmother was right. All the courtiers and nobles and ministers who'd ever mocked her, saying that she was too weak to be a good queen, that she followed her heart instead of her head—they were right, too. Better to let Haakon do the work of ruling for her. Better to give her heart to him—a man who was strong and capable. He'd promised to guard it carefully. He would make sure she never felt such terrible pain—for Tom, for the small hound, for the wolf—ever again.

"Sophie, this is agony," Haakon said. "Being so close to you yet not knowing if you're mine. Say no if you must, but—"

"Yes," Sophie said, cutting him off. "Yes, Haakon, I'll marry you."

Haakon smiled. His lips found hers once again. His kiss was as sweet as a pour of honey. "Tomorrow," he whispered. "We'll tell the queen tomorrow."

Sophie nodded, her head floating. From the champagne. From the kisses. From the warm, wondrous feeling of Haakon's arms enfolding her.

They stayed on the balcony for quite some time, until they heard the clock strike ten, and Haakon said they'd better rejoin the party before the queen sent her guards after them.

Sophie danced all night, her eyes sparkling, her steps light, her heart buoyant and joyous from the secret held inside it.

It was only much later, after the party was over, after her maids had undressed her, combed out her hair, slipped a linen nightgown over her head, that Sophie realized something.

Haakon had never asked, not once, if she loved him.

EIGHT

It was just after midnight, in the small hours—hours that weigh heavily on the soul.

The glittering ball was over. The palace was dark and quiet. All the revelers were abed.

Except for the queen.

She stood in front of her mirror, in her bedchamber, wrapped in a fur-lined robe, her golden hair trailing down her back, alone.

As she stared into the glass, the silver seemed to shiver and melt and then re-form, showing her not her own reflection but images of others.

She saw her ladies-in-waiting—Beatrice, Elizabetta, and Anna. They were leaving her chambers, hurrying down hallways. One carried a torn dress to the seamstress; another took a broken necklace to the goldsmith. A third went to the gardens with a basket on her arm to cut roses for the queen's chambers.

Adelaide knew that all three carried more than her possessions. She knew that there would be a folded note in the dress's pocket, another in the jewel box, one more in the willow basket. Every word of what had transpired during her meeting with the princess would be bartered to a foreign ambassador for a pretty ring or a length of fine lace. The crown would pass to Sophia tomorrow, but the cares of state would not. Adelaide would continue to bear them, for the princess was not even capable of putting a dog down, never mind a traitor.

"I went hunting this morning," she said to the glass. "And I caught a wolf. The kind who goes about on two legs . . ."

The glass shivered again. Now it showed her an elegant woman, beautifully dressed and riding a white mare.

"The Duchess of Niederheim, yes," the queen said. "She's as slippery as a weasel, and twice as rank. She changes alliances more often than she does her underclothes. See that new ruby brooch she's wearing? A stone that fine costs a fortune, and the duke gambled his money away years ago. So how did she pay for it?" Her gaze, fixed on the silvery glass, hardened. "By spying, of course . . . But for whom?"

The image changed again, this time to a heavily bejeweled man in flowing white robes. And then another, sitting on a throne of carved jade, and a third, walking along the ramparts of a fortress. The queen's eyes were bright, almost manic in their intensity now.

"They say they came to the ball to honor the princess. To honor me," she said. "But I know the truth. They came to *bury* me. The wily sultan of Asir, who pays pirates to plunder my ships. The emperor of Cathay, whose assassins move like shadows through Konigsburg. And the king of the Hinterlands, who puts poison in my rivers and rats in my storehouses."

The queen moved closer to the mirror. She pressed her palm against the glass. Her breath misted the silver as she whispered, "Mirror, mirror on the wall . . ."

Before she could finish her sentence, she heard it—the silken rustle of a bird's wings.

And then a man appeared in the mirror.

His eyes were as black as a crow's, his breath as cold as the grave.

He was standing right behind her.

NINE

The queen took a deep breath. Hands clenched, she forced herself to meet the man's gaze.

He came to her every night, whether she summoned him or not. Nothing could stop him. No matter how vast her armies were, no matter how many warships she commanded or fortresses she built, she could not keep him at bay.

He was tall and gaunt. His skin was so pale, fine blue veins showed at his temples. A crown of carved obsidian, studded with blood-red jewels, graced his head. A coat the color of shadows, buttoned high at the neck, hung from his narrow shoulders.

The man bowed his head. The queen returned the bow, for he was a king himself, descended from an ancient line.

"Your enemies mock you, Adelaide," the man said, his reflection speaking to the queen's. "Here, under your own roof, the sultan, the emperor, and the king say that you are a vain and shallow woman, in love with her own reflection, jealous of any other beautiful female."

The queen gave the glass a bitter smile. "I give them no actual cause to diminish me, so they must invent one.

46

Nothing scares a weak man more than a strong woman."

The man put a hand on the queen's shoulder. His thin white fingers were tipped with long black talons. Leaning in close, he whispered to her, "They say that you possess a magic mirror and that you ask it a question every night: *Mirror, mirror on the wall . . . who's the fairest of them all?*"

"The half-wits have it half right," said the queen. "Ah, well. Worse things have been said about me. Far worse. And yet this lie is a dangerous one. Slander a king, and the slanderer will lose his head. Slander a queen, and the queen will lose hers."

Anger hardened her voice, but under it, there was worry. The man heard it and smiled.

"They are plotting against the Greenlands, all of them. I know it," the queen said. "The king of the Hinterlands—"

"Is not your greatest threat," said the man, cutting her off. "Neither is the sultan or the emperor. There is one greater than all of them."

"Who?" asked the queen, her eyes widening in alarm.

The man tightened his grip. His talons pierced the soft fabric of the queen's robe and curled into her flesh. "Mirror, mirror on the wall . . ." he began, his dark eyes meeting hers in the mirror.

". . . who will bring about my fall?" the queen finished.

An image swirled in the silver. After a moment, it coalesced, then sharpened.

The queen's lips parted, but she could not speak. The color drained from her cheeks. "No," she finally said, her voice shaking. "No, it *can't* be."

The face looking back at her was drawn and downcast. Tearstained. Afraid.

The face in the mirror was Sophie's.

TEN

The queen turned away from the mirror, and the man. She crossed the room, then grasped the back of a chair to steady herself.

After a moment, she spoke. "You are *wrong*," she said forcefully. "In fact," she added with a dismissive smile, "you are *mad*. The princess is nothing but a softhearted and silly girl. She has no armies. No warships. She can't even find the courage to put down a useless dog, never mind threaten a powerful queen."

"I am not wrong or mad. I have seen it," said the man.

The queen's smile cracked and fell away. She approached the man. "What would you have me do?" she asked.

The man was holding an empty glass box. Its clasp and hinges were cast in gold. He set it down on a table. "Bring me her heart."

A maelstrom of emotion swept over the queen's face— disbelief, shock, horror. She took a faltering step back, her eyes on the glass box, and shook her head.

"For many years I've given you my counsel," said the man. "Ever since I found you cowering before this very mirror in your father's palace. I can still hear the soldiers' footsteps echoing in the halls. I can see the torchlight glinting off their swords. Have you forgotten?"

The queen lifted her gaze to the man's. Gazing into his eyes felt like staring into an abyss. Their dark depths rose to meet her, then swirled around her, pulling her ever closer to the edge.

"I cannot do what you ask," she whispered.

The man clucked his tongue. "You order thousands of men to their deaths in battle. You stand and watch, unmoved, as spies are broken on the rack. You smile as the ax comes down upon the necks of traitors. And now you cannot rid yourself of a mere girl?"

"She is an innocent."

"She is a *threat*," the man insisted. "She is foolish and weak. Did you not say so yourself? She can no more rule the Greenlands than a child could. You know it, and your enemies do, too. Did you not see them in the mirror? Already they circle, plotting your demise."

The queen closed her eyes. The man walked up to her. He came so close, she could smell him—midnight, iron, and ashes.

"Has the mirror ever failed you? Have I ever failed you?" he asked.

The queen did not answer.

"You have a choice to make," he said. And then he was gone.

The queen covered her face with her hands. "I cannot do it. I *cannot*," she said, anguish in her voice.

After a long moment, she lowered her hands again and caught sight of her reflection in the silver glass. Only it wasn't a grown woman she saw now; it was a young girl. She was on her knees. She was weeping. Her gown was covered in blood.

The pale man's words echoed in her head. *Has the mirror ever failed you?*

"Never," she whispered.

The man is far away now, but he hears the queen's answer; he knows her heart. He smiles. She believes she summons him. She believes she controls him. But this is a war, and she cannot defeat him. She does not know how.

Ah, how this pale man drives her, and has done all her life. From child to girl to woman. Even when he is gone, he is there. Whispering in her ear, running a talon down the back of her neck, sending a chill through her blood.

The sky begins to lighten. The stars fade.

The queen has decided.

She picks up the glass box.

And calls for her huntsman.

ELEVEN

The Darkwood

As dawn broke over the forest, seven brothers, each barely taller than a rain barrel, walked single file down a narrow path. They wore work clothes and caps and carried pickaxes over their shoulders.

A spider, nut brown with a cream-colored underside, and a foot taller than the men, brought up the rear. The handle of a willow basket was looped over one of his many arms.

As he walked, he shot a skein of silk into the air and snared a pretty white moth who'd been flying back to her home, tired and careless after a night spent chasing moonbeams. He reeled the silk in, then swallowed the creature whole. The moth's wings, still fluttering, tickled his throat on the way down.

"I'm hungry," said the youngest of the brothers, who was at the front of the line. "I wonder what Weber packed for lunch."

"We only just finished breakfast and already you're thinking about lunch?" asked the man behind him.

The youngest stopped. He looked over his shoulder fretfully.

"What if we only have sauerbraten and pumpernickel, and no bratwurst?"

"Schatzi, *walk*, would you?" said the man behind him, giving him a shove.

"Don't *push*, Julius!" Schatzi said, shoving him back.

"Stop it, you two!" another of the brothers scolded. "Weber packed bratwurst. I saw him. He also packed—"

A scream, thin and high, tore through the forest. It stopped them all dead.

The man who'd been scolding tightened his grip on the handle of his pickax. He eased the pointed metal head off his shoulder. "Did you hear that?" he asked.

"What a stupid question, Jakob."

"Of course we heard it."

"How could we *not* hear it?"

The replies were made in scoffing tones, but anyone listening could hear the uneasiness in them.

Jakob spoke again. "It's him," he said grimly. "He's taking another one."

"Mmm, no. I don't think so," Schatzi said, with a forced lightness. "I think it's just a bird. Or a squirrel."

"A *squirrel*? Squirrels don't scream, you fool," said Julius.

"Unless someone grabs their nuts."

"Do you think that's funny, Jeremias? Because it's not," Schatzi said testily. "How can you make stupid jokes after what happened to—"

"Ignore him, Schatz," interrupted Joosts, another brother. "It's a defense mechanism. Jeremias uses humor to mask difficult emotions."

53

"Oh, *please*," said Julius.

Joosts glowered at him. "Maybe he can't face his pain. Did you ever consider that?"

"Maybe he's a jerk."

"Will you be *quiet*?" Jakob hissed.

They all fell silent, tensely listening, waiting.

"See? It was nothing. Told you so!" said Schatzi, clapping his hands together as if clapping away his fear. "Can we get going now?"

Another scream pierced the morning. Jakob started running.

"Where are you going?" Schatzi shouted after him.

"We have to stop him!" Jakob shouted back.

"We can't . . . We've *tried*!"

"Then we'll try again!"

Schatzi closed his eyes. He clenched his hands. "I'm not doing this. Whoever it is, is already dead and it hurts too much to see them. Just like it did with Jasper. I can't go. I *won't*."

A rustling in the trees startled him. He opened his eyes. Everyone else had followed Jakob. He was alone, except for a crow sitting on a branch above him. It let out a harsh caw. A second bird joined it, then a third. They cocked their heads, pinning him like a juicy insect with their bright black eyes.

Schatzi shivered. They were gathering. Which meant their master wasn't far.

"Wait for me!" he shouted.

And ran to catch up with his brothers.

54

TWELVE

Jakob came crashing through the brush, his pickax raised, ready to swing it. He stumbled and dropped the ax, though, when he saw the poor creature. She was lying on her back in a pool of blood at the edge of a pond. Her chest was still; her eyes were open to the sky.

Two of his brothers, Josef and Johann, raced by him and dropped to their knees at her side. The others gathered around.

"It's too late," Schatzi said, distraught. "She's gone."

"She's not. She's warm," Johann said, pressing the back of his hand to the girl's cheek. "There's still a chance . . ."

"A *chance*?" Schatzi retorted. "In case you haven't noticed, she's missing a *heart*!"

"Where's Weber?"

The spider put his basket down and scuttled toward the girl.

"What can he do? It's gone, too," Schatzi said, wringing his hands. "It must be."

"It's *not* gone. It's right there. Can't you see it?"

The spider pushed his way through the men and crouched down by the girl's head. He tensed, all his eight eyes focused on the girl as something—something as soft as the dawn and as beautiful as the sun— rose from her lips. It lingered, shimmering like a pearl, then ascended into the air.

The spider started spinning, just as fast as he could.

"Hurry, Weber," Johann urged. "We're about to have company."

He pointed at the sky. It was darkening, not with clouds . . . but with crows. The birds, thousands of them, were gathering from all directions, swirling together in the air as one. It felt as if an unseen hand were pulling a curtain of night over the Darkwood.

"It's him. He's coming," said Schatzi, panic rising in his voice.

"Why?" asked Josef. "From the looks of things, he already has the girl's heart."

"Who knows? We've got to get out of here."

"There's no time. He'll see us."

"We'll have to hide, then. Come *on*, Weber; can't you go any faster?"

The spider had woven his sticky silk into a strong web. He stood now and, like a fisherman casting a net, tossed the web into the air and snared the glimmering object. Quickly, he pulled it back down. Then he gathered the edges of the web and cinched them, sealing the object inside.

"Well done!" Johann whispered. "Scatter, everyone! Quick!"

Julius grabbed Weber's basket and hid behind a rock. Jeremias joined him. The others climbed trees or crouched down behind brush.

The spider found a rotten log and hastily wedged himself under it. He lay there, his pale belly flattened against the loamy earth, his eyes blinking, his arms wrapped protectively around his webbed bundle.

He kept himself as still as death. He knew he must not be discovered. For he held something precious. Something radiant. Something that fluttered inside the silken skeins, just like the doomed and beautiful moth.

He held a girl's soul.

THIRTEEN

A woman, dressed in a tattered black gown, looked down at the dead girl and winced.

"Sometimes I destroy them, Brother," she said anxiously, tugging on a lock of her wild, matted hair.

"It wasn't you who killed the girl, Sister. It was a huntsman," said the man standing next to her. "He had a sharp knife."

The woman nodded but looked unconvinced. She tugged at the lock of hair again, harder this time. It came loose from her scalp with a sickening rip. She eyed the bloody roots, then tossed the lock away. "Sometimes I teach them. Sometimes I leave them gifts," she said.

"Sometimes," the man soothed.

The woman knelt. She touched the blood on the girl's jacket. It hardened under her fingers and turned into rubies. "Where has her heart gone?" she asked, peering at the girl's gaping wound.

"It's in a glass box. Waiting for me."

The woman tilted her face toward the man's. "How many hearts do you need, Brother?"

"All of them. Every last one."

"Then we mustn't dawdle. The palace is miles from the Darkwood."

The man offered her his arm. The woman stood and took it.

They were similar in looks, both tall and pale, with jet-black hair. Only their eyes were different. His were filled with darkness. Hers were red-rimmed, bloodshot, blazing with madness.

No sooner had they walked ten steps than the man stopped. He looked around, suddenly alert, like a wolf scenting the wind.

"What is it?"

"It's almost as if she were still here. Her spirit, I mean. Lingering. I feel her, don't you?"

He released the woman's arm and turned in a slow, uncertain circle. His gaze sharpened; it penetrated the gloom, taking in rocks and trees, and—at the edge of the pond—a rotten log. He started toward it.

The woman watched him. "Why, Brother," she said, a smile quirking her bloodless lips, "if I didn't know better, I'd say you were *afraid*."

The man stopped. He turned back to her and laughed as if she'd just told the funniest joke he'd ever heard. The woman joined him, her laughter not cold like his but manic and screeching. They moved off toward the palace, their voices carrying in the Darkwood. Above them, the crows launched themselves from the branches where they'd perched, cawing loudly.

A fox, standing nearby in some blackbriar, bared her teeth

at the harrowing noise, then nosed her kits into their den. A rabbit made for her burrow. A bullfrog shuddered and hid under a lily pad.

And nearby, seven small men and a large spider exhaled.

FOURTEEN

"Weber!" Johann hissed. "Psst . . . *Weber*! Are they gone?"

The voice came from high up in a tree.

The spider poked his head out from under the log. One leg followed it and then another. He pushed his upper body out, peered through the gloom, and nodded.

Johann jumped down. His brothers joined him, hurrying from their hiding places.

Josef stared down the path the man and woman had taken. "He *didn't* kill the girl," he said.

"He never does. He always gets someone else to do the dirty work for him, the bastard," Jeremias spat.

Schatzi, his face as white as salt, said, "Johann, can you save her?"

"I'm going to try," Johann replied, bending down to the girl.

"There isn't much time," Schatzi fretted, pointing at the webbed sack. The soul inside it was straining against the spider silk, trying to push its way out.

"I know, Schatz; I know. But as long as we've still got hold of it"—he nodded at the sack—"the girl's still got a chance."

Julius shook his head. "Why are we getting involved in this?" he asked.

"What should I do? Leave her here to die?" Johann snapped.

Julius winced. He looked away. "This will bring down trouble on our heads, mark my words," he muttered.

But Johann barely heard him. He lifted the body off the ground, and then he was gone, hurrying through the woods to the Hollow, the brothers' home.

Johann was strong and valiant, but his heart pounded under the weight of the human girl. His lungs labored as he ran. His legs trembled. Once or twice, he thought he might not make it, but on he ran, and as he did, a breeze moved through the branches above him. The leaves rustled and fluttered all around him.

Years later, recounting the story by a fire one winter's night, he would say that the trees themselves urged him on. That they whispered to him with the voice of a child, green and sturdy and full of hope.

The King of Crows has taken another heart, they said. *Hurry, Johann. Do not let him win. Do not let this girl die.*

FIFTEEN

Sophie dreamed that she was drowning in a sea of pain. Its fiery red waters swirled over her skin, burned in her blood, smoldered in her bones.

"Make it stop . . . *please*," she begged. "Let me go. Let me die."

A spider caught her in a cobweb net and gently pulled her to shore.

She fell limply to the sand. Her head rolled to the side. Through the red haze, she saw that she was lying on a wooden table. Tools were strewn all around—vises, pliers, tin snips, hammers. She saw gears, wheels, strikes, and springs. She heard the sound of a clock loudly ticking. Heard curses and hissed commands.

This is madness.

Do you have a better idea?

We're losing her!

A man, pale and gaunt, with a raptor's gaze, stared down at her. A woman joined him. She smiled, showing a mouthful of rotted teeth.

And then Sophie felt hands on her head; someone grasped her clenched jaw and forced it open. A bitter taste filled her mouth. Her vision faded; her eyes closed.

She slept. And dreamed again.

Of a sky black with crows.

SIXTEEN

As the princess struggled to hold on to the pale flicker of life still inside her, the queen sat on her throne, hands curled around the armrests, fingers digging in so hard that her nails had all broken.

She was waiting for me, her huntsman.

She had no doubt that I would carry out my task. She knew that, like her, I saw the world as it is, not as I would have it be.

I had seen the newborn fawn stand on shaky legs and the wolf rip out its throat before it had taken its first steps.

I had seen the fledgling fall from its nest and the fox snatch it up. I had seen the owl carry the shrieking young rabbit away.

I called myself a realist. I told myself this was the way things had always been, the way they would always be. And I believed it. But that belief did not help me. Nothing could help me, not then.

The entire court was assembled in the Great Hall for the princess's coronation. But the hour had come and gone, and the princess had not appeared. Her ladies were sent for. It was learned that she had gone out hunting very early and had not returned. And neither had I.

The lord commander ordered that a search party be sent to the Darkwood to find us, but as the words left his lips, a gasp rose from the assembly.

I stood in the soaring doorway of the Great Hall, my chest heaving, my eyes wild. I was clutching a glass box smeared with blood.

Did the queen know then what she'd done? Did she imagine that she was safe?

Step by shambling step, I made my way to the throne. Courtiers parted before me, some crying out in horror, for my clothing was soaked with blood. Guards, their hands on the hilts of their swords, advanced toward me, but the queen raised a trembling hand, stopping them.

When I was a few yards from the throne, I dropped to my knees. "The princess is dead!" I cried.

Screams were heard. Courtiers staggered ashen-faced to chairs. Some fainted. Young Prince Haakon stood perfectly still in shock.

The lord commander was on me in an instant. He drew his sword and pointed it at my chest. "You will answer for this, villain!" he thundered.

I did. I told my story. For the court's benefit. The queen knew it by heart, word for word, for she'd told it to me last night after summoning me to her chamber.

"We were attacked by a pack of wolves," I said. "I fought as hard as I could, but there were too many. One killed the princess, and then the pack . . . they savaged her body . . ."

My voice broke on the last word. My ravaged eyes found the queen's. I held out the glass box.

The queen stared at it, at the object inside it. Was she remembering how I'd wept when she'd handed the box to me? How I'd begged her not to ask this of me? She had no choice, she'd said. And neither did I.

"I killed some of the beasts, managed to drive a few more away," I lied. "I was able to retrieve the princess's heart."

Slowly, carefully, with the tip of the lord commander's sword still hovering by my chest, I placed the glass box on the floor. "I'm sorry," I whispered. To the princess. To the queen. To myself. And then, before anyone knew what was happening, I grabbed the sword with both hands and drove the blade into my own heart.

The lord commander shouted. He swore. He pulled the blade out, but it was too late. I toppled forward onto the marble floor. Blood pooled around me.

The queen's ladies rushed to her. She was as white as a skull. Lady Beatrice tried to lead her out of the Great Hall, but the queen pushed her away. She rose from her throne, walked down the steps of its platform, and crossed the floor to where I lay. Bending down, she picked up the glass box and made her way to her chambers.

She dismissed her ladies, her maids, and her guards and slammed the doors shut. The noise they made echoed through the palace.

Ominous. Final. Forever.

As if she were slamming the doors to a tomb.

SEVENTEEN

What dreams I've had, Sophie thought as she yawned in her bed. *Of large spiders and small men. Crows and ponds and . . . . . . faces.*

Two of them. Pale and strange, framed by black hair. A shiver ran through her at the memory. She pulled her sheet up around her neck. *Who are they?* she wondered. But the more she tried to recall the faces, the more maddeningly indistinct they became. So she gave up and stretched instead, but as she did a sharp pain sliced through her chest.

"Oh. *Ow,*" she cried, flinching. "I must've pulled something. Too much riding and dancing. Too much kissing."

Sophie smiled, warmed by the memories of Haakon's lips on hers, his touch. *Today's my birthday,* she thought, excitement bubbling up inside her like the champagne she'd drunk last night. There would be a quick breakfast in her room, then her coronation ceremony, and after that, feasting and music. When the revels were finally over, she and Haakon would go to the queen and tell her of their wish to marry. *For once, my stepmother will be pleased with me,* Sophie thought. She very much looked forward to that.

As she lay in bed, the pain in her chest persisted. Instead of ebbing away, it was worsening. Sophie decided a hot bath was required to soothe her strained muscles. She would summon her ladies to ready one for her. It was time to get up. She had to eat, then dress. There was much to do.

Slowly, sleepily, she opened her eyes halfway, expecting to see the high, painted ceiling of her bedchamber, with its flowers and cherubs. Instead, she saw pine boards. Her eyes shot open. This wasn't her bedchamber.

Panic gripped her. Quickly, she sat up. A lightning bolt of pain ripped through her torso, white and blinding. Her hands knotted in the sheets. She couldn't breathe or speak. She couldn't move.

Bit by bit, the pain released her. Air flooded back into her lungs. Her vision cleared. As she looked around, sweating and trembling, she saw that the room she was in was tiny, with lace curtains, a standing mirror, and a colorful rag rug. She tilted her head back and saw a tall wooden headboard behind her, carved with oak leaves and acorns.

Where am I? she wondered.

Images flashed in her mind again—the silver blade of a knife, birds taking wing, tears on the huntsman's cheeks.

She pressed the heels of her hands to her eyes. Dread as cold and heavy as a sea fog wrapped itself around her. She fought it down. Tried to think.

It was early in the morning . . . I was riding in the Darkwood. What happened? Did I fall?

"Yes, that's it," she said out loud, sounding surer than she felt.

I fell, hit my head, and lost consciousness. The huntsman brought me to the first cottage he could find. For help. To rest.

"But where is he?" she whispered.

More memories came, galloping through her brain like wild horses. Memories of unspeakable pain. Of the huntsman on his knees. Of something in his hands. Something red and small.

"M-my heart is gone. My h-heart is *gone*," Sophie stammered fearfully. "But h-how? *Why*? Why did this happen to me? How am I still alive?"

There was a reason . . . The huntsman had said something . . . But the red roar of pain had wiped his words away.

Sophie looked down at herself. She was wearing an old linen shirt. "Where did this . . . ?" she started to say, but her words trailed off. There was something under the fabric. Something dark. With trembling fingers, she unbuttoned the top of the shirt and looked at her chest. A long, livid incision, laddered with black stitches, was running down the center of it.

A dizzying sense of unreality gripped Sophie. She squeezed her eyes shut. "I'm still asleep," she whispered. "This is just a dream . . . a nightmare." But when she opened her eyes again, the bed, the room, the shirt, the stitches—they were all still there.

Gingerly, she touched the incision, and as she did, she felt something lurch under her rib cage. Then she heard clanking and grinding. It sounded like the noises the huge gold clock in her stepmother's chamber made before it struck the hour. She looked up, wondering if she'd somehow missed a clock sitting on a shelf or standing in a corner.

But no. The sounds, she realized, with horror, were coming from *her*. From inside her chest. Sophie's fear turned to terror. A cry tore itself from her throat.

An instant later, the bedroom door was wrenched open, and a ladybug, four feet tall and wearing a cap, an apron, and an expression of deep concern, entered the room.

Sophie's eyes widened. She took a deep breath. And screamed.

EIGHTEEN

The ladybug pressed a claw to her worried face, then turned and made a series of clicking noises over her shoulder.

Almost immediately, seven more faces appeared in the doorway. Sophie, her breath coming in short little bursts, shrank against the headboard. The clanking inside her chest grew louder.

"Do you *hear* that racket, Johann?" asked a short, bearded man. "This is a *disaster*. She won't last the night."

Johann, frowning thoughtfully, said, "It's just a sticky gear. It'll resolve." He paused, then added, "At least, I think it will."

"You *think* it will," said a third flatly.

Johann threw his hands up. "I had to work fast! There was no time for adjustments, for calibrations!"

Sophie's eyes darted frantically from the strangers to the window. It was only a few feet away, but even if she could get to it before they got to her, it was too high and too small to climb out of.

One of the men was carrying a tray. He made his way through the others, toward her. With a frightened cry, Sophie scrambled out of bed and pressed herself into the far corner, keeping the bed between herself and the strangers. A heavy brass candlestick stood on the night table. She grabbed it with shaking hands and held it before her like a sword. The clanking in her chest rose into a high, shrill screeching—the sound of metal scraping against metal.

"Look what you've done, Joosts. You've scared her. Put that blasted tray down."

"What's so scary about a bowl of chicken soup, Julius?"

The man who'd spoken of gears and calibrations took a few steps toward Sophie, his hands raised to show that he meant no harm. He opened his mouth to speak but never got the chance.

"I am Princess Charlotta-Sidonia Wilhelmina Sophia of the Greenlands!" Sophie shouted, brandishing the candlestick at him. "Touch one hair on my head and you'll answer for it!"

Julius closed his eyes. He pinched the bridge of his nose. "A princess. A *princess*! Didn't I say that this girl would bring trouble? The queen's cavalry will come riding through here any minute now, looking for her." Sophie blanched at the mention of her stepmother. Her chest made a deep grinding noise. All the strength in her body drained away. Her knees buckled. The candlestick hit the floor with a heavy thud.

She remembered now. The huntsman's words came flooding back to her. *Forgive me, dear princess . . . This foul deed was not my wish, but the queen's command.*

Sophie felt hands on her, lifting her up. It was Johann. She tried to shake him off but was too weak. He sat her down on the bed, eased her legs up, and then settled the covers over her. All she could do was sink back into her pillows and let him.

"Everyone out!" he ordered.

There were protests and grumbles. Joosts set the bowl of soup, along with a spoon and a napkin, on the night table; then he and the others left the room. When they were gone, Johann sat down on the end of the bed. It was much quieter in the room now, and the noises in Sophie's chest had stopped.

"Princess Charlotta-Sidonia—" he began.

"Sophie will do."

Johann nodded. "We scared you, Sophie. I'm sorry. We didn't mean to. My name's Johann." He nodded at the empty doorway. "The others are my brothers. We live here. Tupfen, the ladybug, is our housekeeper. She's been caring for you for the past few days."

"Days?" Sophie echoed, sitting forward. "How many . . . How long—"

"We found you in the woods twelve days ago."

It made no sense. It was *impossible*. Sophie shook her head. "How am I not dead?" she asked.

Johann hesitated, then gently he said, "Do you remember anything?" Sophie slumped back against her pillows like a broken doll. "A huntsman . . . someone I knew, someone I trusted . . . cut out my heart. Because my stepmother—the queen—ordered him to."

Johann's breath caught. "Why would she do such a thing?" he asked.

Shame clutched at Sophie. Her stepmother's words echoed in her head. *You are soft when you should be shrewd, forgiving when you should be fierce . . . How can you rule a country, Sophia, if you cannot rule yourself?*

"Sophie, *why?*" Johann pressed.

"Because I am so weak, so incompetent, so hopeless," Sophie

replied, her voice raw with despair, "that she would rather see me dead than sitting upon the throne of the Greenlands."

She turned to Johann then, expecting to see a look of contempt on his face, the same look she so often saw on her stepmother's. But he wasn't looking at her. He was looking out the window. His eyes were shiny. His jaw was working.

"How am I alive, Johann? *How?*" she asked. "I have no heart."

Johann brushed at his eyes. Then he turned to her and said, "Yes, Sophie, you do. I made you a new one."

NINETEEN

Sophie stared at Johann for a long moment, unable to take in what he was telling her; then she looked down at her chest. Slowly, fearfully, she pressed a palm flat against her rib cage, over the ugly black stitches, to the place where her small, perfect heart used to be.

The thing under her ribs felt big. Ungainly. Out of control. It seemed as if it were ticking rather than beating. It sped up, then slowed. It lurched and stuttered, wheezed, then thumped.

"It's a machine of sorts," Johann explained. "It pumps blood through your body, just as your old heart did."

Sophie knew what a machine was. Scientists and engineers from all parts of the world came to her stepmother's court to demonstrate their inventions. She had seen pumps and turbines—ugly, noisy monstrosities that belched smoke and spewed oil. Now one was inside her, under her flesh, her bones. For a few long seconds, she had to fight down the overwhelming urge to rip her stitches open and pull the thing out.

"What is it made from?" she asked, a tremor in her voice.

Johann took a deep breath, as if readying an answer, but

76

before he could speak, a reply came from the doorway.

"Tin. Gears and wheels. Wire."

Sophie looked up. One of the brothers—Julius—had returned. He was leaning against the doorjamb. His arms were crossed; his gaze was focused on Johann. She had no idea how long he'd been there.

"Johann is very crafty. Aren't you, Brother?" Julius asked. There was a bite to his voice.

Johann didn't reply; he just gave Julius a brittle smile.

Julius turned to Sophie. He was about to address her, when another of his brothers bustled back into the room, a plate in his hands.

"Weber sent up some fresh bread and butter," he said.

"Weber's our cook," Johann explained. "And this is Schatzi, our seventh brother."

"Seventh brother . . ." Sophie repeated. She'd been scared witless earlier, too frightened to think straight, to make the connection, but she did now. "Are you the seven men of the woods?" she asked wonderingly.

"We are," said Schatzi, setting the bread plate down on the night table.

"I remember the stories my nurse told me about you. I thought you only existed in fairy tales," she said, amazed. Her fear retreated a little. "You dig for gold and gems in secret mines," she added. "And each of you has a special talent. One is a carpenter . . ."

"Joosts," said Shatzi.

"Another's a hunter."

"Jeremias."

"There's a tailor . . ."

"That's me."

"An herbalist, a farmer, a blacksmith . . ."

"Julius. Josef. Jakob."

"And a clockmaker."

"Johann."

Schatzi pulled the single chair in the room close to Sophie's bed, picked up the bowl of soup, and settled it in Sophie's hands. "You're pale and thin," he said, giving her the soupspoon. "You have to eat. It's the only way you'll recover."

Sophie's fear returned. She looked at the bowl warily. Her own stepmother had tried to have her killed. Why should she trust seven perfect strangers?

Julius saw her suspicion. "Would we really go to all the trouble of keeping you alive just so we could poison you? You're a lot of work!"

"Julius, do you *always* have to be so rude?" Schatzi scolded.

"Why did you do it?" Sophie asked, wondering at their motives. "Why did you save my life?"

Julius's gaze slid to the window. He shrugged. "Why wouldn't we?"

Sophie persisted. "You built me a new heart. Nursed me through a long recovery. No one shows such kindness to a stranger."

"Maybe not where you come from," Julius said. "Here in the Hollow, we don't let h—" He stopped abruptly, as if he'd said too much. "We help people." He nodded at her bowl. "Eat your soup." And then he was gone. Sophie heard his feet pounding down a flight of stairs.

78

"Ignore him. He's grouchy today. His mugwort bush died," Johann said. "But you really should eat your soup."

Sophie looked down at the bowl full of egg noodles, carrots, chunks of chicken, and golden broth. Her stomach twisted painfully. She swallowed a spoonful and then another. Its nourishing warmth spread through her chest, her whole body. The thing inside her clicked and whirred. She tried not to hear it and kept eating. Before long, half the bowl was gone.

"Slow down," Schatzi cautioned. "You haven't had anything solid in well over a week."

Sophie didn't listen. She finished the soup, then wolfed the bread. "That was so delicious. Thank you," she said, wiping her mouth with the napkin Schatzi handed her. A bit of strength had trickled back into her. She felt more clearheaded, able to think straight. An idea had come to her, one that kindled a flicker of hope in the midst of her despair.

"Do you have a dress I can borrow? Are my boots around somewhere?" she asked, struggling to sit forward. "I need to go back."

Johann looked alarmed. "Back *where?*" he asked. "The palace? That's not a good idea."

"You're not strong enough to walk across the room, never mind travel!" Schatzi exclaimed.

"Back to where it happened," said Sophie. "The queen is hardly going to tell the court that she tried to have me killed. She'll make up a story. She'll tell them I got lost, or that I was injured and the huntsman went for help. Someone could be searching for me. Have you seen a search party?"

"No, we haven't, and thank goodness for that," said Schatzi.

"What do you mean *thank goodness?*" Sophie asked, perplexed.

"No sign of a search party means no one's looking for you. If the queen's huntsman brought her your heart—"

"He did?" Sophie cut in, confused. *How does Schatzi know that?* she wondered.

Johann gave Schatzi a deadly look, but Sophie didn't see it.

"I—uh . . . You . . . you *said* he did, didn't you?" Schatzi asked fumblingly.

"No, I didn't," said Sophie, wondering if he was hiding something from her.

"I—I guess I just *assumed* he did," Schatzi said. "Why else would he take it with him? And he must've. It's gone, isn't it?"

Sophie nodded. Schatzi's explanation made sense and yet she couldn't shake the feeling that there was something he didn't want her to know.

"And anyway," Schatzi continued, "the queen will never suspect—not for a second—that you survived, and as long as she believes you're dead, you're safe. Stay quiet, stay hidden, and you'll stay alive, Sophie. You mustn't leave the Hollow."

Sophie didn't want to stay in the Hollow. The brothers seemed very kind, but it was their home, not hers. Her heart made a low, grinding noise, echoing her feelings. She shuddered, horrified anew by the thing in her chest. When the noise finally stopped, she said, "What if there was someone whom I *wanted* to find me. Someone who could help me?"

"Who?" Johann asked.

"Lord Haakon, the prince of Skandinay. We mean to marry. He'll be looking for me; I know he will." The flicker of hope she'd felt earlier grew brighter. "Have you seen him?" she asked eagerly.

Johann shook his head.

"Tall, blond, blue eyes? Are you *certain*?" Sophie pressed, turning to Schatzi. But he, too, shook his head. "I—I don't understand," she said, deflated. Haakon had promised to keep her safe, to always protect her. "Maybe you missed him somehow," she ventured. "Or maybe he's looking in the wrong place."

"If the queen went to such lengths to arrange your death, I'd wager she also devised a story to tell the court," said Johann. "I'm sure the poor boy believes that you're dead."

Sophie nodded unhappily. She fretted the edge of her quilt, her hopes crushed. What Johann said made sense. The whole court, Haakon included, had likely been told that she'd been killed by robbers, carried off by a bear, or some other lie. Haakon wasn't looking for her. Nobody was. The realization made her feel frantic and desperate. As if someone had sealed her into a coffin, and all she could do was scream powerlessly as shovelfuls of earth hit the lid. Her future was gone. Her marriage to a prince. Her crown. Her stepmother hadn't managed to kill her, but she'd stolen her life nonetheless.

Schatzi saw her distress. "You're here, Sophie. You're alive. That's what counts," he said, patting her hand.

"Yes," she said. "I'm alive. Thank you for that." She closed her eyes again. The strength she'd gained from eating was now ebbing away.

"You're exhausted. You need to rest," said Schatzi. He stood, returned the chair to its place, and closed the curtains. "Get some sleep."

81

He picked up the dishes and left the room. Johann followed him. He was just about to close the door, when he stopped and turned back to Sophie.

"I almost forgot," he said, pulling a small cloth pouch from his jacket pocket. "We found these lying in the grass near you. Jeremias gathered them up."

Sophie forced her eyes open. She took the pouch from Johann and poured its contents into her hand. Six perfect rubies, the color of blood, glinted up at her.

"They're not mine," she said.

"They're not from a necklace? A bracelet? Perhaps broken in the struggle?"

Sophie shook her head. She tried to hand them back, but Johann wouldn't take them.

"Maybe you don't remember," he said. "They're certainly not ours. Keep them."

As he closed the door behind himself, Sophie put the rubies back in their pouch, then put the pouch on her night table. Sleep was pulling at her.

Stay quiet, stay hidden, and you'll stay alive, Sophie, Schatzi had said. But for how long? She couldn't remain in the Hollow forever.

Her thoughts drifted to Haakon. She pictured his beautiful face, his warm smile. Johann said that no one had come searching for her. But Haakon wasn't a no one. He was a prince. *Her* prince. Surely, he wouldn't accept the queen's lie. He would want proof. He would sense that she was still alive. He would feel it in his heart because he loved her, and he'd keep searching for her until he found her.

I'm a prince. That's what we do.

Sophie closed her eyes. The heart in her chest was quiet now. It made only soft rhythmic clicking noises, like clock weights slowly descending on their chains.

Sleep spread its dark cloak over her. The last hour and all its shocks and frights were receding now.

Fading.

Unwinding.

TWENTY

"Princess Charlotta-Sidonia Wilhelmina Sophia," Sophie said, regarding her reflection in the mirror. "You look like a circus clown."

Her shirt was an old striped nightshirt. Her skirt, which stopped well above her ankles, was stitched from a red-and-white-checked tablecloth. And her bodice had been fashioned from a grain sack. It was laced in front with a pair of red shoelaces.

Sophie looked absurd, she knew it, but she didn't want to complain. Schatzi had made the skirt and bodice. He'd left them on the foot of her bed moments ago.

"I hope you like them," he'd said shyly. "I've never made a skirt before. Tupfen helped me with the measurements."

Sophie had thanked him, and then he'd ducked out of the room, shutting the door behind him so that she could dress.

She adjusted her skirt now and tugged on her bodice. Her new clothes were her only clothes. Her riding outfit had been stained with blood, and Jeremias had burned it. *At least my boots survived*, she thought, looking down at them. Joosts had polished them for her until they gleamed. Haakon would already have covered much of the woods near the Hollow, she reasoned, and in a few days, maybe three or four at the most, he would arrive at the Hollow. She had to be ready when he did.

Today, two weeks after she'd woken up at the brothers' house, and not quite a month since she'd ridden out from the palace with the huntsman, was the first day Sophie felt strong enough to leave her bedroom. She'd put on a little weight, her stitches were out, and a bit of color had returned to her cheeks. But what would her strange, noisy new heart do when she started to move around? It had kept her alive so far, but then again, she'd barely taxed it. All she'd done was sleep, eat, and sleep some more. What would happen when she walked? Climbed up and down stairs?

Sophie wanted to go outside into the yard so that she could see Haakon when he came riding through the woods for her. He would come; she was certain of it. *I've loved you from the moment I saw you*, he'd told her. And not only would he find her, he would spirit her away to Skandinay, to the safety of his family's towering castle. From there, he and his realm's commanders would plot the best way to take her throne from her brutal stepmother.

Sophie took a steadying breath now and held it. She walked the length of her bedroom, expecting disaster with each step, but nothing happened. There was no pain, no noise from her new heart. She didn't feel light-headed or dizzy. She didn't collapse. She took a few more steps, then turned in a slow, cautious circle. Nothing hammered or banged. Everything was perfectly fine. She let her breath out in a long whoosh of relief. Then she opened her bedroom door and walked across the landing.

The brothers, and Tupfen, were waiting for her at the bottom of the stairs, anxious expressions on their faces.

"Sophie! You're up and walking!" Schatzi exclaimed when he saw her.

"You look well!" said Josef.

"Thank you. I feel well," Sophie said, carefully making her way down the steps. When she reached the bottom, she looked around. "What a sweet cottage!" she exclaimed brightly.

Built from pinewood, the Hollow was rustic and cozy. There were several separate bedrooms upstairs, but the downstairs was one open room. Sophie moved through it now, a broad smile on her face. The cottage was charming. It filled her with a sudden and deep delight.

"Look at these pretty curtains!" she said, running her fingers over the lace panels hanging in a window. "And this chair!" She sat down in an overstuffed easy chair, sighed happily, and then hopped up again.

As she did, her heart, which had been perfectly quiet, started to make a low, purring noise. Carried away by curiosity, Sophie didn't seem to notice it, but the brothers did. They traded anxious glances.

"Oh, just *look* at this painting!" she exclaimed, pointing to a pretty woodland scene hanging on the wall. "Look at the little deer! The little badgers! It's soooo *cute*!" She turned back to the brothers and Tupfen, put her hands on her hips, and said, "This cottage is A-DOR-A-BULLLLL!"

Josef held up a finger. "Um, Sophie, I think maybe—" he

started to say, but Sophie cut him off. She'd spotted something lying on a side table.

"What's this?" she asked, picking up a leather collar. A silver tag dangled from it. *Henrik*, it read.

"That's a dog collar," Joosts replied. "It belonged to a little schnauzer we had. He died a few months ago."

Sophie's eyes grew round. Her lower lip quivered. *"No,"* she said. "Oh, dear God, *no*." She clutched the collar to her chest. "Your . . . your little schnauzer . . . *died*? H-h-he *died*? Your little Henrik *died*?"

The last word rose in a wail. Sophie bent her head, still pressing the collar to her chest, and sobbed piteously. Her heart rumbled and clunked. "Poor Henrik! Oh, the tragedy of it! He was taken too soon. Too soon!"

"Um, Sophie? Henrik was twenty-two years old," said Jeremias. "It was his time."

"He had atrocious gas," Julius said.

"He snored all night long," Josef added. "Honestly? I don't miss him." Sophie held up a hand. Little by little, she got herself under control, then said, "We mustn't speak ill of the dead. Henrik will forever live on in your hearts and . . ." Her eyes fell on the kitchen table. "Oh, my goodness! What's all *that*?"

She was across the room in two strides, her heart pounding like a foundry. The table had been readied for lunch. Blue-and-white plates had been set out atop a pretty yellow cloth. But it was the platters in the center that had captured Sophie's interest.

One was piled high with sauerkraut and topped with

fat bratwursts. A flaky mushroom strudel graced another. There were golden slabs of schnitzel. Crispy potato pancakes dolloped with sour cream and applesauce. There was a loaf of pumpernickel bread, a dish of yellow butter, and a jug of fresh milk. And for dessert, apple dumplings with custard sauce.

Sophie picked up a potato pancake and downed it in three bites. "Mmm!" she purred, wiping grease off her lips with the back of her hand. She snatched a schnitzel and demolished that in six bites.

"Thith ib *tho* good!" she said through a mouthful of food. Next, she reached for a bratwurst.

"Would you like a plate? A fork?" asked Johann.

Sophie waved him away. Never had she tasted such delicious food. She couldn't get it down fast enough.

"The cook will be pleased," Julius observed. "This is quite a compliment on his work. A messy compliment, but still . . ."

Sophie heard them. And remembered her manners. Sort of.

"Where is the cook? I must thank him!" she said, holding a half-eaten bratwurst in her fist. She'd been at the Hollow for weeks and had eaten such delicious food, yet she'd never met the person who made it.

"Weber? He's right there," said Josef, gesturing to a figure standing at the far end of the kitchen, stirring a pot on the big iron stove.

Sophie looked at the cook, sucked in a lungful of air, and screamed. Even harder than when she'd first seen Tupfen. Her heart clanged like an alarm bell. She ran around to the far side of the table and screamed again. Then she threw the bratwurst she was holding. It bounced off Weber's head.

"Sophie, stop that!" Josef scolded. "Weber is gentle. He wouldn't hurt a fly!"

"Actually, he *would*," Julius said. "In fact, he hurt a few dozen of them at breakfast."

"Will you *hush*!" Josef hissed.

Weber rubbed the spot where the bratwurst had hit him. He blinked his eight eyes, then burst into tears.

Sophie pressed her hands to her cheeks, ashamed of herself. "What have I *done*?" she whispered. "I'm sorry. I'm so, so sorry. Spiders frighten me. But I can see that you're a perfectly lovely one. Will you ever forgive me?" She rushed to the creature and took hold of two of his many claws. "Please, please, please say that you will!"

Weber sniffled; he nodded hesitantly. Sophie clapped her hands happily, then threw her arms around him and wouldn't let go. Weber raised four of his arms in the air and gave the brothers a helpless look.

Julius pulled a chair over to Sophie, stood up on it, and then gently peeled her arms off their cook.

Sophie took a few steps back. She pressed a hand to her forehead, disoriented and confused. "I—I don't know what's gotten into me. I'm usually a bit more . . . controlled."

Johann approached them. He pulled a stethoscope out of his pocket. It was made from pieces of an old bugle and some bendy copper tubing.

"May I?" he asked.

Sophie nodded. She sat down, suddenly tired. Julius bent toward her. He pressed the stethoscope to her chest and listened. Then he scowled, nodded, and straightened again.

"Well?" said Julius, his voice sharp with concern.

"It's ticking . . . I mean, *beating* beautifully," Johann began. A look passed between him and Julius, a look of deepest worry. Sophie, her eyes closed, missed it.

"And?" said Julius.

"The rhythm is perfect at the moment," Johann said. "Everything's moving smoothly. I can't hear hissing, dripping, or any other sign of a leak. The regulators I put in to manage blood flow and timing seem to be working very well . . ."

"But?" Julius prompted.

Johann shrugged sheepishly. "But I, um . . . well, I think I forgot to put in a regulator for emotion."

TWENTY-ONE

Fear spiraled up Sophie's spine. An out-of-control heart was her worst nightmare. One of those had nearly gotten her killed.

"What's a regulator, Johann?" she asked anxiously. "What does it do?"

"It keeps things balanced and smooth. Like water flow in a mill, for example. Or in this case, feelings. Yours seem to be a little out of whack."

"What am I going to do?" Sophie asked as Johann's words sank in. "I'm behaving like a lunatic. Saying whatever comes to mind. Crying. Laughing. Throwing sausages. I can't go on like this. It's . . . it's *exhausting*."

But what she really meant was *dangerous*. Being led by her heart had raised her stepmother's ire. It had caused pain and suffering for an innocent child, for innocent animals. Even Haakon, who cared for her, thought her too kind, too soft, too emotional. He'd advised her to let him keep her heart for her. What would he think if he could see her now, completely unable to control herself? Would he still want her? Would he still love her?

Sophie reached for Johann's hand. "Tell me what to do," she begged. "Tell me how to regulate the heart myself."

Johann frowned thoughtfully. Then he said, "Maybe some fresh air would do you good. A bit of exercise. That might calm things down. You haven't been outside in a month."

"That sounds like an excellent idea," said Julius.

Sophie agreed, and Josef suggested they stroll to the garden to pick some strawberries. He got a bowl down from a shelf, and they left the cottage. As they did, the rest of the brothers sat down to their lunch.

Things didn't go any better outside, however. The instant she walked out the door, Sophie gushed loudly over the cottage's red shutters and pretty flower boxes. Only the sight of Josef's face, with its dismayed expression, simmered her down.

"Stop," she told herself, clutching her head with both hands. *"Stop."*

Josef led her to a stone path that wound from the cottage through the yard. At first, Sophie proceeded at a stately pace, but after only a few seconds, she was skipping down the path, her heart thumping joyfully. She buried her face in a fragrant rosebush and got her cheeks scratched. Plucked a daisy and tucked it behind one ear. Petted a slug. All before she'd even set foot in the garden.

Sophie was despondent when Josef caught up with her at the garden's gate. "It's no use," she said. "This heart does as it pleases."

"Try holding in your feelings, " Josef suggested. "As if you were holding your breath."

Sophie nodded. She straightened her spine, pushed the

gate open, and stepped into the garden. Her resolve lasted for exactly one second.

"Oh, Josef, *look*!" she exclaimed. "Have you ever *seen* such a *beautiful* cabbage?"

She trotted up and down the garden's tidy rows, astonished by the eggplants, the beans, the brussels sprouts. How had she never noticed the beauty of a peapod before? The elegance of dill fronds? Everything seemed like a miracle to her. She helped Josef pick berries for a few minutes, then waltzed off, unable to stay in one place, eager to explore.

Meanwhile, Johann, anxious to find out how Sophie was doing, ate a few quick bites of lunch, then joined Josef at the garden gate.

"How is she?" he asked his brother.

Josef shrugged. "We've had yelps of joy, manic laughter, but no screaming or tears. I guess that's an improvement . . . Wait a minute . . . What's she doing now?"

Sophie had finished admiring the swedes, when she saw something that wasn't so lovely—a big, lumpy brown heap at the very bottom of the garden. It was a jumbled dump of eggshells, spent tea leaves, sawdust, chicken poop, peels and pits, grass clippings, and dead leaves.

She walked over to the pile and wrinkled her nose. "Josef, what's this?" she called over her shoulder.

"That's our compost pile," Josef called back. "We put garden waste and kitchen scraps in it. They break down and become fertilizer for the plants. It's a bit smelly, Sophie, and full of bugs and worms. Come away."

Sophie was just about to heed Josef's warning, when a

movement in the compost pile caught her attention. But how could that be? It was nothing but garbage. She took a step closer. Had she imagined it?

But no! There it was again! The pile seemed to bulge out on one side. The bulge disappeared, then reappeared. It moved higher and higher until it reached the very peak of the pile, and then, like a volcano erupting, the top exploded open. A dirty pink nose poked out. Whiskers. Beady black eyes. They belonged to the biggest, filthiest rat Sophie had ever seen.

She gasped at the sight of him. Her heart shuddered and wheezed. She waited for the emotions she knew were about to take hold of her: fear, disgust, horror. But the emotion that gripped her was one she never expected: love.

Sophie plucked a peapod from a vine and held it out to the creature. "Sophie, don't! That's a very large rat!" Josef warned.

Sophie paid him no attention. "Rattie! Come *here*, sweet little thing!" she trilled, waving the peapod. "You are the most wondrous animal I've ever met. I shall make you my pet."

The rat sniffed at the peapod and ventured close. Sophie gave it to him to eat. Then she snatched him up and hugged him to her chest.

"Sophie!" Josef shouted as the rat squirmed and squealed. "Put that vile creature down!"

"But, Josef, I love him!" Sophie shouted back.

"Here we go again," said Johann with a sigh.

The rat jumped out of Sophie's arms and quickly tunneled down into the compost pile. Sophie pleaded with him to come out. When he would not, she burst into tears.

"It's just a sticky gear, you said. *It'll resolve*, you said. This

heart is a *disaster*, Johann! She loves bratwursts! She loves slugs! She loves a disgusting *rat*!" Josef whisper-shouted.

Johann, watching Sophie digging through the compost, frowned deeply. "The heart is flawed, yes," he said. "But it's working, Josef. It hasn't—"

"Hush. Don't even speak of it," said Josef. "I care for her. Already. As if she were my own child. I couldn't bear to lose her."

Johann turned to his brother; he patted his back. "I know. I feel the same way. But what can we do? I made her heart like the one I made for Jasper."

Josef looked stricken at the mention of the name. "But with improvements. You *said* so."

"Some. But we both know what's going to happen. It's just a matter of time."

Josef shifted his gaze back to Sophie. "What can we do?" he asked, echoing his brother's question. "We can hide the truth from her. As we have been."

"Is that fair?"

"We're keeping other things from her, aren't we? Like the name of the one who *really* has her heart. We have to. How else can we keep her safe?"

"How long do we hide the truth, Josef?"

Josef watched the girl in his garden as she smiled at a butterfly, picked up a grasshopper, and laughed with abandon at a chattering squirrel. As he did, sadness spread across his face like spilled ink across parchment.

"As long as we possibly can."

TWENTY-TWO

The woman leaned over the bleeding woodcutter.

He was lying on the ground, screaming. Seconds ago, he'd missed the log he'd been splitting and had buried his ax blade deep into his right foot.

It had cleaved through his leather boot, his heavy woolen sock, and his bones, too. He'd pulled the blade out, then collapsed. Blood was flowing out of the gash.

The woman's eyes traveled from the woodcutter's foot to his face. It was gray with shock. He was still screaming, though not quite as loudly. His eyes had rolled back in his head.

Clucking her tongue, the woman straightened, then continued on her walk through the Darkwood.

She'd been busy that morning. She'd visited a woman in labor, and together they'd invented some colorful curse words. Then she'd watched as a dentist's apprentice—a lad with thick fingers and poor eyesight— removed a wisdom tooth. After that, she'd attended a hanging. Good knot, thin neck—a quick affair.

The woman walked for miles through the forest, blending into the shadows in her dark garb. Plants withered under her feet. Tree trunks turned black where she touched them. Animals ran to escape her mad gaze.

After an hour or so, she passed a clear blue pond, then reached the edge of a sunny clearing. A tidy cottage stood in the middle of it, white with red shutters. Flowers bloomed in window boxes. A wisp of smoke rose from its chimney, carrying the scent of fresh bread.

The woman gazed at the cottage balefully. "The Hollow," she muttered. Her eyes followed the picket fence that enclosed it. Neither she nor her brother had ever been able to breach it.

"It's enchanted. It must be," she said, biting her thumbnail with her crumbling teeth.

The seven brothers were vigilant about keeping the siblings at bay. They had strong defenses, stronger than any charms. They had books and songs, flowers and plum cake. They had one another. When they sat together around the hearth at night, warming their toes by the fire, telling stories, and drinking schnapps, no one could break their circle.

The woman ripped her nail off with her teeth in a fit of pique, then watched the blood drip from her thumb. It soothed her a little, but the calmness didn't last. For a moment later, a girl walked out of the cottage and into the yard, a basket over her arm. As the woman watched, the girl clipped roses from a bush and carefully laid them one by one in her basket.

"It *can't* be." The woman's eyes narrowed. She moved closer to the fence, careful to stay in the shadows of the pines. But it was. The girl . . . the princess . . . she was *alive*. "*How?* My brother has her heart. I *saw* it in its box."

The woman took a few steps closer to the fence. She

squinted. Was that a scar on the girl's chest? Rising above her neckline? "What have those wretched little busybodies done?" she wondered aloud.

The girl turned suddenly to clip blooms from another bush, and the woman stepped back into the shadows, but her gaze lingered. She could teach this remarkable girl. Show her things about herself that no one else could. She could make her see that she was stronger and braver than she ever thought she could be.

Part of her very much wanted to.

"Because sometimes I help," she whispered.

As the words left her lips, a shiny green beetle landed on her skirt. The woman lowered her hand to the creature and coaxed it onto her palm, smiling crookedly. Then she raised her hand to her face and blew on the little insect. Instantly, it fell over onto its back, tiny legs scrabbling in agony.

"But not always."

She shook the beetle off. It landed on the ground and scuttled away. The woman raised her red-rimmed eyes to the girl again. She ripped off another nail; then she turned in a swirl of black skirts, droplets of blood pattering onto the forest floor, and disappeared into the gloom.

TWENTY-THREE

"Come on, Weber; try me," Sophie said gamely.

For the last five days, ever since she'd hugged the rat in Josef's garden, she'd been trying to train her heart to behave itself, and she was eager to test her newfound control.

She'd worked hard at keeping her feelings hidden, just as she used to, and she'd gotten a little better at it, but only a little. Most of the time, her new heart still revealed her emotions. Everyone knew how she felt about everything, all the time, and she hated it. Haakon was coming for her. How would she conduct herself at their court with her heart reeling around like a drunken bumpkin, embarrassing her ten times a day? How could she be the queen that Haakon wanted her to be?

The brothers had departed for their mines, pickaxes over their shoulders, hours ago. Jeremias and Joosts weren't with them. They'd left on a hunting trip yesterday and would be gone for a number of days. With two brothers gone, the remaining five were working longer hours. Tupfen had gone into the forest to hunt for mushrooms. Only Weber was at home. He was standing at the huge iron stove, preparing delicious things for supper. He turned around now, a claw on his hip.

"Go on," Sophie urged him. "Give me a test!"

Casting a skeptical look at her, Weber reached behind himself, took hold of something that Sophie couldn't see, and thrust it in front of her. It was a loaf of golden rye bread, freshly baked. Sophie leaned forward, inhaled the mouth-watering scent. There was no clanking or thumping.

"See?" she said. "I told you! Try something else. Anything!" She pressed her palm to her chest. "It won't make a sound."

Weber walked into the pantry, then reemerged a moment later carrying a large round plate. The instant Sophie saw what was on it, her heart clanged like church bells on a king's wedding day.

"A Black Forest cake?" Sophie said, stamping her foot. "Weber, that's not *fair*!"

The confection, a good ten inches high, was Sophie's favorite dessert. It involved layers of chocolate cake soaked with cherry syrup and sandwiched together with whipped cream. More cream, piped into swirls, graced the top of it, with dark, sweet cherries set into them.

Impulsively, Sophie snatched a cherry and bit into it. Juice dribbled down her chin. Her heart purred. Weber glared. He made loud, squeaky noises that sounded a lot like scolding, and Sophie realized how rude she'd been.

"Sorry," she said sheepishly. "I guess things aren't quite as under control as I thought. Are there any more cherries? I'll fix it. I—"

Her words were cut off by a loud, ratcheting clatter. There was a sudden pressure inside Sophie's chest. It grew, squeezing the air out of her. She tried to catch her breath but couldn't.

Seconds ticked by, and still she couldn't breathe. Frightened, she grabbed the edge of the table and willed her lungs to pull in air, but they would not. She was dimly aware of Weber's panicked squeaking. She stumbled, fell, and landed on the hard wooden floor on her hands and knees.

The shock jarred her, and as suddenly as it had started, the pressure eased, the noise stopped, and her lungs opened again. A moment later, she felt Weber helping her up. He sat her down at a bench by the table. Kneeling, he pushed a loose tendril of hair off her flushed, sweaty face and squeaked. She didn't understand all of his words, but she knew their meaning nonetheless.

"I—I don't know," she replied, her voice shaky. "One second I could breathe, the next I couldn't. It must be something to do with the heart. Something got stuck, I think."

Earlier, Weber had made a pot of tea. He poured a cup now, carried it to the table, and put it down in front of Sophie. He brushed another lock of hair off her cheek, concern clouding his many eyes. He was just about to say something to her, when a loud, angry hissing was heard.

His cream of leek soup was boiling over. It hit the hot iron burner, where it bubbled and burned, sending up a horrible smell.

"I'm so sorry, Weber!" Sophie said. "It's my fault. I distracted you."

She felt terrible. The spider had work to do, and she was keeping him from it. She stood and offered to help him clean up the mess, but he waved her away. She sat down again, sighed disconsolately. As she took another sip of her tea, she noticed that one of her sleeves was flapping open. Upon a closer look, she discovered that it was torn from elbow to shoulder. *Great. I must've snagged it on the bench when I fell*, she thought.

"Weber, I need to mend my sleeve," she said. "Where can I find another old shirt to wear while I fix this one?"

The spider, cleaning up the burned soup, shaking a pan of brussels sprouts, stirring a pot of simmering lentils, and salting a chicken—all at the same time—pointed up.

"In the attic?" she asked.

Weber nodded. Sophie finished her tea, then made her way to the house's second floor, her footsteps as heavy as her new, noisy heart. A doorway at the end of the hall opened to another flight of stairs. The attic was at the top of them. Sophie was familiar with it. She stole away, several times a day, every day, to look out its narrow window for Haakon. A month had gone by since the huntsman had taken her real heart, and still there was no sign of Haakon. Every day, she woke up and told herself, *Today is the day*. And every night she fell asleep bitterly disappointed. Sometimes a small voice inside her said, *He's not looking for you. If he were, he'd have found you by now*. Sophie did her best to smother the voice, but it lingered nonetheless.

She walked to the attic window now. It was hard to see much through the dense canopy of trees surrounding the cottage, but if she craned her neck one way, she could just glimpse a sunny clearing in the woods. And if she leaned in the opposite direction, she could see a stand of silver birches and the path that led to the Hollow.

"Where are you, Haakon?" she whispered.

He was out there, looking for her. He was. *He'll come. Just give him a few more days*, she told herself. She had to believe that, for without him she had no future, no hope.

"And when he does arrive, I don't want to greet him in torn clothing," she said aloud, reminding herself of the task at hand. Though Sophie visited the attic daily, she'd never actually had to search for anything in it, and she saw now that finding a shirt, or anything else, would be a daunting task. The brothers had arranged nothing neatly. Neatness was not their strong point. Tupfen was forever picking up after them, putting away stray clock parts, bowstrings, and tools.

Sophie smiled now, thinking of the brothers as she started her hunt. She was so grateful for their kindness and care, and she had already grown very fond of them. Schatzi, she'd learned, was a sensitive soul. He had red hair and a round face that was often flushed with emotion. Jakob, a decisive man of action, was the eldest. He had gray in his hair and beard, and lines in his face. Jeremias was salty-tongued and merry, though Sophie had the feeling his bluff good cheer was a defense, for she'd caught glimpses of a deep sadness in his eyes. Johann was quiet and deliberate, always lost in thought. Joosts was the peacemaker. Josef, who always had hay stuck to him, was happiest tending his chickens, cow, and pigs. Julius was gruff but smart and insightful, and kind, too, in his way. He was the one who'd read to Sophie at night as she'd convalesced, to keep her boredom at bay.

Moving carefully, Sophie navigated past crates stacked on tables, baskets balanced on boxes, and a jumble of broken furniture the brothers intended to fix one day. Sophie had to squeeze between chairs and a bedframe, fight with snowshoes

103

and fishing rods, and nudge aside a stuffed moose head, all to get to a basket of old clothing teetering atop a pile of books that had been stacked on a trunk. As she reached for the basket, she knocked into the books and sent them toppling to the floor. Sophie closed her eyes. She shook her head. Nothing was going right.

Swearing under her breath, she opened her eyes again, set the basket down, and started to pick up the books. And that's when she saw the name embossed on the trunk in neat block letters, a single word.

JASPER

TWENTY-FOUR

Sophie knelt down. She placed the books she was holding on the floor and brushed dust off the trunk's lid.

"Jasper?" she whispered, her brow furrowing. "Who are you?"

Was he one of the brothers? The fairy tales she'd heard only ever mentioned seven, and the brothers themselves had never spoken of an eighth.

Sophie's curiosity was piqued; she had to find out. She unbuckled the leather straps, opened the latch, and eased the lid back. Then she caught her breath as she saw what was inside—stacks of small paintings, dozens of them, each more beautiful than the next.

The scenes were so vivid, they leapt off the canvas. Sophie recognized the Hollow and its garden. The stream that ran through trees, out beyond the fence. A stand of silver birch trees. She lifted the paintings out, one by one, taking great care with them. She saw Jakob's face as he said grace. Josef drowsing by the hearth. Speckled blue eggs in a nest. Schatzi nose to nose with a fawn. Sophie took her time with the paintings, marveling at the detail and depth of emotion, in every single one. They were small, intimate things, and as Sophie viewed them, she felt as if she was looking directly into the painter's heart. Her own heart purred warmly.

"I wonder why the brothers don't frame these and hang them on the walls," she said; then she dug deeper. She saw Julius, holding up a sprig of rosemary, and frowning, as usual. A bear cub standing in a patch of woodland flowers. A fox peeking out from some blackbriar. A flock of crows in a tree . . .

. . . and a man standing under them.

Sophie's smile slid off her face like ice off a roof. She leaned in close to the picture, peering at it.

The man's face was as pale as bone. His long hair swirled around his shoulders. He wore a crown of obsidian, studded with dark jewels.

"I've seen him," Sophie whispered, her heart knocking loudly. A memory pressed in at her, shadowy and vague. The man was looking down at her, smiling cruelly. A woman was with him.

But where had this happened? And when? She'd never met this man. She would have remembered him if she had. How could anyone forget the bottomless depths of those black eyes? That awful smile?

Sophie tried to hold on to the memory, to make sense of it, but it was like trying to grab a handful of smoke. The brothers had never mentioned this man, and yet here he was in a painting. Had Jasper, whoever he was, known him? And then a chilling thought gripped her—could Jasper *be* him?

She set the painting down on the floor, then rummaged in the bottom of the trunk. Paintbrushes lay in a neat row next to an artist's palette and glass jars containing ground pigments. There was a green wool cap and a pair of spectacles.

106

A tweed vest. Several sketchbooks. A pocketknife. Everything, it seemed, but an answer.

"Sophie!" a voice bellowed from the floor below.

It was Josef. Sophie, still bent over the trunk, sat up straight. The brothers were home already? How could that be? It wasn't evening yet. She glanced at the attic window and saw that she was wrong. The shadows were lengthening. Dusk was settling over the Hollow. She'd completely lost track of the time.

Feet clattered up the stairs. "Sophie, are you up here? Supper's ready, and I—"

Josef's words died in his throat as he saw her sitting on the floor with the paintings spread out around her. He was across the attic in a few quick strides. Wordlessly, he gathered the paintings and placed them back in the trunk.

Sophie could see that they upset him. "I'm sorry. I—I guess I shouldn't have opened this," she said, helping him. "I was curious about Jasper. And then I saw this"—she held up the painting of the pale man—"and I wondered if he was Jasper."

Josef looked at the picture, and an expression of hatred spread across his face, so pure and so deep that Sophie was shaken.

"That's *not* Jasper," he growled. "Jasper was our brother. The youngest of us. He died. A long time ago."

"Josef, I'm so sorry," Sophie said, taken aback by the anger in his voice. "What did he die of?"

"Wasting sickness."

Sophie could see that he was lying. His face, always open and frank, was closed. He wouldn't meet her eyes.

"You never talk about him," she said. "Any of you."

"It's hard, Sophie. Very hard."

Sophie nodded, unwilling to press him any further. She asked another question, though. "Do you know who the pale man is? The one standing under the tree full of crows?"

Josef shook his head. "No idea."

It was another lie. He knew who the man was—she'd seen the recognition on his face only a moment ago—but he didn't want to tell her. *Why?* she wondered.

Josef closed the trunk and buckled it securely, careful to tuck the ends of the straps into their keepers. Then he placed the books that Sophie had knocked over back on top of it.

It's as if he's afraid the memories are going to get out, she thought. "Supper's ready," Josef said again. Then he started for the stairs.

Sophie followed him. As she reached the top of the stairs, she realized that she still needed a shirt to change into. She hurried back to the basket of old clothes, dug through it, and found one. As she pulled the garment out, she heard a scrabbling on the roof and a sudden burst of movement.

She jumped, pressing a hand to her chest, then laughed at her own foolishness as the cause of the noise flew past the window.

It was nothing but a large black crow.

TWENTY-FIVE

The coffin in the king's chapel was small and draped in black.

The child inside it, a boy, was dressed in his white christening gown. His eyes were closed, his tiny hands folded over his chest. He was only four months old.

The boy's father, the king of Saxony, was kneeling by the coffin, his head bent.

The boy's mother, broken by grief, was weeping in her bed.

Adelaide saw them. Her brother. Her father. Her mother. Long dead, all of them, but alive again in the depths of her mirror.

And then she saw herself, a little girl of five. Her hair was braided. Her eyes were solemn. She was clutching a bouquet of flowers in her small hands. She'd picked them herself. A few had wilted, for it had taken her some time to make her way from the queen's garden to the chapel.

She walked down the aisle to the altar. Her father was weeping. She could hear his sobs. It made her heart ache to see him so sad.

"Don't cry, Papa," she said as she came up behind him, but he didn't hear her.

Unsure what to do, she moved closer and patted his arm. The king startled at her touch. He raised his head. Adelaide barely recognized him. Grief had ravaged his once-handsome face.

"Papa, look," she said, offering her bouquet. "I brought you flowers."

The king stared at the blooms but didn't take them. Then he looked at her.

"Three sons dead in as many years. But you, Adelaide, you thrive. You grow tall and strong." He raised his eyes to the ceiling. "God in heaven, why? Why do you take my sons and leave me with a useless girl?"

Adelaide's hand fell slowly to her side. Tears smarted behind her eyes. She had not known that she was useless. Her tutor said she was smart. Her nurse said she was kind.

The king stood. He looked into the coffin. "My son, my little boy . . ." he said, pounding the heels of his hands against his head.

Adelaide wiped her eyes. The movement caught her father's attention. "Come here, child, come . . ." he said, beckoning her.

But Adelaide, afraid now, shook her head. She backed away. The king lunged for her. His hand closed on her shoulder. The flowers fell on the cold stone floor.

"Look at him, Adelaide," he said, pushing her up to the coffin. "Look at your poor dead brother lying there. Do you see him?"

Adelaide nodded, trying hard to be brave. She didn't like the baby anymore. His eyes were sunken under their paper-thin lids. His face was stiff and gray.

"Why, Adelaide?" the king cried. "Why wasn't it *you*?"

The image faded, but the pain of her father's words remained. Still.

After all these years.

"I remember that day," said a voice from behind her. "You and I were just getting to know each other then."

Adelaide slowly turned around.

"Only a few years after the boy's death, your parents died, too. But not you, Adelaide. You survived. You always survive." He tapped a black talon against his chin. "Why is that, I wonder?"

"Because of you," Adelaide whispered.

"Yes. Because of me. I help you vanquish all threats." He was smiling, but there was a coiled menace in his voice. "I cannot help you, however, if you do not do as I ask."

"What do you mean?"

"The girl still lives," the man said.

"No," Adelaide said vehemently. "That's *impossible*. The huntsman brought me her heart. I gave it to you."

"The seven men saved her. They gave her a new heart," said the man. "She's in the Darkwood. In a cottage called the Hollow."

Adelaide stiffened with anger. And fear. The girl was a threat to her. The mirror had told her so.

"As long as she lives, you are not safe," the man said.

"What can I do?" she asked the man. "My huntsman is dead."

The man reached inside his coat and drew out a pair of pretty laces, meant to fasten a bodice. They were made of lustrous black silk, threaded with gold. He put them into the queen's hands.

"You'll find a new horse in your stables, a gray stallion. He was born of a storm and is faster than the wind. Disguise yourself and ride to the Hollow. Give these to the girl. Make sure she laces her bodice tightly with them. That's all you need to do," the man said. And then he was gone and the queen was alone.

She turned back to her looking glass. "Mirror, mirror on the wall . . ." she began, entranced once again by the images she saw within it. "Who will bring about my fall?"

Had anyone else been in the room with her, they would have seen that there was nothing in the glass.

No king, no coffin, no heartbroken girl.

There was just a woman, thin as a whisper. Hollow-eyed. Haunted.

TWENTY-SIX

Sophie, one hand on the gate, the other clutching a small bundle, cast a last, guilty glance behind her.

No one was in the yard to see her. The brothers were in their mine. Weber was in the kitchen. Tupfen was washing windows.

Sophie knew she shouldn't be doing this. The brothers had sternly warned her never to leave the Hollow. But she had to. A little over a month had now passed since she'd ridden out from the palace with the huntsman, and there was still no sign of Haakon.

The Hollow was well-hidden, and Sophie was certain that when Haakon had ridden out searching for her, he'd missed it completely. Last night, as she'd helped clear the supper dishes, she'd come up with a plan—she would go back to the pond, to the place where the huntsman had taken her heart. Royal parties often galloped past it on hunts, and it was likely that Haakon would ride past it, too.

She would spend a few hours there, and with any luck, she would see him as his search party approached. She would run out to the path and wave them down. She would tell Haakon what the queen and her huntsman had done, and then they would ride, fast and hard, for the border. They'd have no choice. Haakon was the queen's esteemed guest, but he would not be able to return to her palace once he'd learned what she'd done to Sophie.

It pained Sophie to disregard the brothers' instructions and sneak off. And she knew that when she and Haakon were reunited, there would be no time to ride back to the Hollow to tell the brothers that she was leaving, so she'd put a note on her pillow, explaining where she'd gone and why, thanking them for all they'd done for her, and promising to come back one day.

Sophie took almost nothing with her, just an apple, a bit of bread, and the little pouch of rubies, tied up in a napkin. She had no idea if her plan would work, but she had to try. A month was a long time. What if Haakon was losing hope? What if he stopped searching for her and returned to his own realm? If that happened, she would lose her only chance of being saved. She would lose *him*.

Sophie unlatched the gate now and pushed it open. An instant later, she was running down the stone path. She had a rough idea in which direction the pond lay—she'd watched Johann head off toward it in the evening sometimes, a fishing rod over his shoulder, and half an hour later, she found it.

With difficulty, she made her way around the pond's marshy edge, startling some bullfrogs and stepping into soft, squelchy mud a few times. She was sweaty and winded by the time she reached the grassy bank where riders stopped to let their horses drink, and she leaned against a tree to catch her breath. As she did, her heart suddenly stuttered and whined, and then it slowed dramatically, with seconds elapsing between each beat.

Sophie felt so light-headed, she almost collapsed where she stood, but she managed, barely, to stumble to a log and sit down. Eyes closed, she took deep breaths, waiting for her heart to right itself.

A sticky gear. It'll sort itself out, Johann always said with a reassuring smile when this happened. But it never seemed to. Instead of diminishing as the days went by, these spells were happening more frequently.

After several minutes, the heart finally resumed its normal rhythm, and Sophie opened her eyes. She sat perfectly still, listening in eager anticipation for the sound of horse hooves. Maybe Haakon was on his way this very moment. She imagined the happiness on his face when he spotted her. She imagined him jumping down from his saddle and embracing her, telling her that he'd never believed she was dead, that he'd searched for her faithfully, every single day.

Sophie listened, but she heard nothing, just the breeze sighing through the pines. She resigned herself to a long wait, to the possibility of returning tomorrow. And the next day. She stood, thinking she'd walk down the riding path a ways. Instead, she stopped dead. A shiver ran through her.

This is the place, she thought, her gaze sweeping over the bank, the edge of the water, the tall reeds that lined it. *This is where the huntsman took my heart.*

The muddy smell of the pond, the whispering of the pines—they brought it all back. Ever since the day she'd woken up in the Hollow, Sophie had pushed the memories down, but they welled up now, flooding her mind with horrible images, sounds, and feelings. She felt the shock of surprise again as the huntsman pulled her to him; she felt the blade bite. And she saw the faces—two of them—leaning over her, pale and cruel. The man, the one wearing the obsidian crown, the one Jasper had painted . . . She *hadn't* imagined him. She'd seen him for real. Right here. He'd come to her as she'd lain dying. *Who was he?*

Sophie's heart stuttered and whined, and then it sped up. *This wasn't a good idea*, she thought. *I need to go back to the Hollow.* Jittery, anxious, driven by her emotion, she hurried away from the pond. Hugging the edge of the water once more, she retraced her steps. A few minutes later, she was fording her way back through the trees.

She walked for nearly an hour before she realized that nothing looked familiar. She'd passed a big gray boulder on her way from the Hollow to the pond. A huge blackbriar patch. A tree charred by lightning. Where were they?

A shrill, screeching noise made her jump. She looked up. A flock of crows had gathered in the branches above. Her eyes went to the sky. The sun had dropped low. The brothers would be home soon. They would be so worried if they discovered that she'd left. She hurried her pace so that she could get back before they did.

Panic chattered inside her head, telling her that she was hopelessly lost. That dusk was coming, and wolves would soon be on the prowl. "Which way do I go?" she murmured, trying to get her bearings.

Sophie had the vague notion that she'd walked east from the Hollow, so she decided to head west now, in the direction of the setting sun. Flustered, she looked every which way except

116

where she was going and never saw the thing on the forest floor until she caught her toe on it and nearly went sprawling. She righted herself, then turned around to see what had tripped her.

She expected a jutting rock or a gnarled tree root.

Not a skeleton.

Crying out in horror, Sophie staggered back from the bones. Her eyes roved over the remains. A small brown toad peeped out of a mossy eye socket. The jaw hung open in a silent wail. Scraps of fabric, rotted by the weather, draped the long bones. A hunting knife lay by a hip, half-buried in the ground. Vines snaked through the skeleton's rib cage. Some of the ribs were broken. Their blackened edges framed a jagged hole over the place where a heart had once beat.

As Sophie gazed at the hole, fear dragged a sharp fingernail down the back of her neck. She sidestepped the skeleton and hurried on. Her panic had swelled into full-blown fright, making her breath come in short little gasps. She had not gone more than twenty yards when she saw another skeleton on the ground, this one older and almost fully covered by moss.

She stumbled on, down through a gully, up a hill. And then she saw something worse. Not a skeleton, not yet. A body. It was propped against a tree. Decay had not yet taken the young woman's face, but birds had taken her eyes. Her heart was missing, too.

Sophie's heart slammed inside her chest. She didn't know whether to scream in terror or weep. Shaking badly, she turned around in a circle. This woman, the other people . . . they'd all died because someone had taken their hearts. Just as the huntsman had taken hers. Whoever that someone was, the Darkwood was his hunting ground. And she was out in it, all alone. No one was here to help her, not the brothers, not Haakon.

A sob of terror escaped her. And then another. She pressed her hands to her mouth to stop them, certain that if she started to cry, she wouldn't be able to stop, that she'd dissolve into a heap on the forest floor. Trudging forward on legs gone rubbery and weak, she crossed a stream and struggled through thick brush. And then, as she crested another hill, she saw a stand of silver birches. She remembered seeing birch trees from the cottage's attic window.

"Please let them be the same trees. *Please*," she prayed. If they were, the Hollow couldn't be far.

Sophie kept her eyes trained on the trees, took a deep breath, and ran.

TWENTY-SEVEN

Sophie heard the brothers before she saw them.

They were calling her name. Over and over again. At the top of their lungs. As she got closer to the Hollow, she saw lanterns bobbing in the dusk.

"I'm here!" she shouted, weak with relief. "Over here!"

A moment later, Josef was at her side. "Where have you been?" he asked, his voice sharp with worry. Then he held his lantern up and got a good look at her. "What happened to you?"

Sophie's boots were covered in mud. Blackbriar thorns had torn her skirt. Her hair, which she'd pinned up in a coil earlier, was down around her shoulders. Her face was flushed.

Jakob joined them, out of breath and panting. "We were so worried! We got home, and you weren't there!" He turned, cupped his mouth, and bellowed. "We found her!"

Together, the three made their way back to the cottage. By the time they reached the gate, the others were inside the yard, waiting for them. There were plenty of questions to answer.

"Why did you leave?"

"Where did you go?"

"Thank goodness you're all right!"

"Can we please go inside? Tupfen won't stop crying, and Weber's so upset, he burned the dumplings."

"I'm so sorry I gave you a scare," Sophie said as they headed toward the door. "I went to the pond."

"To the pond," Julius said, aghast. "Why?"

"To see if Haakon was there, looking for me," Sophie admitted.

"That was a foolish thing to do," Julius said. His voice was stern, but Sophie heard fear in it, too.

"I know," Sophie said. "I—I saw them. The bones. I saw a body, too."

Grave glances were exchanged between the brothers. Sophie caught them.

"What?" she said. "What is it? Why are those remains in the woods?"

"Come inside, Sophie," Julius said heavily. "Get out of your wet boots and change your clothes."

"I don't have any other clothes," said Sophie.

"You can borrow a pair of trousers and a shirt. Tupfen will get them for you. Then we'll have supper. Weber's been keeping it warm."

As they all trooped into the mudroom, Sophie fought down the urge to argue with him. She wanted answers, and the brothers had them. She could see they did, but she'd caused a lot of trouble, so she bit her tongue and decided to ask her questions later, when they were all seated at the table.

After kicking her boots off, Sophie walked into the kitchen.

Tupfen and Weber both rushed to her. Sophie kissed their cheeks and apologized to them, too, for causing so much worry. Some of the brothers set the table; others lit candles or stoked the fire.

Sophie was walking out of the kitchen toward the stairs, intending to go up to her room to change, when Johann, thinking she was already gone, bent his head to Josef's and said, "It's him."

He'd spoken in a low voice. His words had been meant for his brother's ears alone, but Sophie heard them. She turned around.

"Who?" she said, looking at Johann. "You said, *It's him*. Who are you talking about?"

Johann's eyes widened. He realized he'd been overheard. He stammered and stuttered, trying to backtrack, but Sophie wasn't fooled.

"Those bones in the woods . . . they were people once," she said. "Their hearts were taken. Just like mine was. There are things you're not telling me." Images came back to her—of black eyes boring into her, of a cruel smile. "It's the pale man, isn't it? That's who you're talking about. The one in Jasper's painting. Who is he?" She looked from one brother to the next, her eyes beseeching them for the truth.

And finally, she got it.

Julius placed his hands on the back of a chair and leaned on it, his head bent. "He's called Corvus, the King of Crows."

Anger flared inside Sophie. The brothers *had* kept things from her, and they had no right to.

"He's the one who took the hearts of all the poor people in the woods, isn't he?" she said. "When I was dying, I saw

121

him. He leaned over me. Does he have my heart, too? Did the huntsman lie to me? Did *you*?"

"No, Sophie, the huntsman didn't lie," Julius said heavily. "Corvus has your heart. The queen gave it to him."

"How do you know this?" Sophie asked, her anger growing.

"When we found you, you were almost gone," Julius continued. "Your soul was leaving you. Corvus was coming. With his sister, Crucia. Weber snared your soul in the nick of time, but catching it left us with no time to run. So we hid. That's when we heard Corvus tell Crucia that he was going to the palace to get your heart from the queen."

"But why? What does he want with my heart?"

"He collects them. He keeps them in a room in his castle in enchanted glass boxes, red and alive."

Sophie sat down at the table, more stunned than angry now. It felt as if someone had kicked her legs out from under her. "What does he do with the hearts?"

"We don't know."

Sophie's head was spinning. "Why didn't you tell me these things weeks ago?"

For the first time since he'd started speaking, Julius raised his head. Sophie saw that his eyes were filled with tears. Gruff, grouchy Julius was crying. That scared her more than anything he'd said.

"Julius, who *is* this King of Crows?" Sophie asked. "Where did he come from?"

"No one knows," Julius replied. "What is certain, though, is that he's a powerful, dangerous man, and you're a girl with a faulty heart. People get lost in the Darkwood, Sophie, and most of them never make it back. That's why we kept things from you. Why we tried to keep you here, in the Hollow, safe and protected . . ." Julius's voice cracked. He couldn't finish.

So Johann did it for him. "He took Jasper, Sophie," he said softly. "He took our little brother. We won't let him take you."

TWENTY-EIGHT

Candles had been placed on the table. Everyone was seated now. Weber poured the wine.

Johann was talking. His brothers were staring into the fire. Or their goblets. One had his eyes closed, a defense against the pain. They all knew the story he was telling. They'd lived it.

Sophie sat forward in her chair, elbows on the table, listening raptly. Johann had already told her that Jasper had been the baby of the family, gifted and sensitive.

"He was an artist," Johann said now. "He painted what he loved, a basket of apples or a duck on her nest. One day, he decided to take his paintings to Konigsburg to see if he could sell them."

Johann paused here to swallow a mouthful of wine. His eyes, always soft and faraway, took on a flinty hardness. "It didn't go well. The dealers laughed when they saw his work. *Nobody wants pictures of apples or ducks*, they said. *They want portraits of royalty. Or, better yet, portraits of themselves. In borrowed furs and fake diamonds. There's plenty of money to be made doing those, boy!*

"Jasper didn't sell a single painting. He changed after that day.

124

He became melancholy and quiet. He believed that his paintings were all wrong, that *he* was all wrong. He put his colors and brushes away and started going for long walks in the woods. That's where we found him. With a hole in his chest. His heart gone. A split second away from death."

"And you saved him," Sophie said.

Johann nodded. "I made him a heart. Like I did for you. It malfunctioned, too, but in a different way. Instead of feeling everything, poor Jasper felt nothing. He said he'd rather be dead than live like that." As Johann spoke, sadness seemed to collapse him. His shoulders drooped; his body sagged. Sophie could see that he blamed himself. "The heart's physical action worked well, though. For a while, at least."

"For a while . . ." Sophie repeated, a heavy foreboding settling on her own heart. "What happened, Johann?"

But Johann wouldn't answer. Julius, who'd been playing with a candle while Johann spoke, running his finger back and forth through the flame, answered for him. "It wound down."

Like winds swirling ahead of a storm, carrying dust and dead leaves on them, Sophie's memory blew ragged scraps of a dream through her mind. She remembered drowning in a red sea of pain, then seeing gears, wheels, strikes, and springs spread out around her. She remembered waking up and asking the brothers what her new heart was made of.

Gears and wheels. Wire.

The truth hit Sophie with brutal force. "You're a clockmaker, Johann. And this thing inside me . . . the thing that's keeping me alive . . . it's a clockwork."

"Yes," Johann said. "It is."

Clocks kept time, Sophie knew that. Some were slow, others fast. Some were simple, others diabolically intricate. Some were dependable, others unreliable. But they all had one thing in common: No matter how much you wound them, you had to re-wind them, or they stopped.

The light-headedness, the spells that took her breath away, these were all signs—signs that her heart was winding down. "H-how long did Jasper live?" she asked in a small voice.

"Not quite a month. He died on the way to Nimmermehr, the King of Crows' castle," Johann said.

Sophie felt the breath go out of her. *Only a month*, she thought. "Jasper couldn't bear living without his feelings," Julius explained. "He decided that he was going to find a way into the castle to steal his heart back. He'd heard there was magic, some sort of spell, that could put his heart back into his body. There are witches in these woods. Some of them are very powerful."

Hope sparked in Sophie. "Is there such a spell?"

"We never got to find out," said Josef. "We went with Jasper to Nimmermehr. We couldn't let him go alone. It was a hard journey. A week's walk from here. When we finally reached the castle, the trees were so tall, the branches so dense, light barely penetrated them. There were things in those woods . . ."

"What things?" asked Sophie.

Josef shook his head, as if at a loss. "Shadowy things. Nightmarish. With long claws. Some had red eyes. And some had no eyes at all. They lurked in the gloom. They kept their distance at first, but then they came closer. Some whispering.

Some wailing. We hurried along, trying to keep ahead of them, but it was too much for Jasper. His poor heart gave out only a mile from the castle. We brought him back to the Hollow and buried him."

A heavy silence settled over the room. The only sound to be heard was the crackling of the logs in the fireplace.

"How long do I have left?" Sophie finally asked.

"You've already lived longer than Jasper did. I've learned from the mistakes I made with his heart," Johann quickly said, avoiding her question. "I made improvements. I added weights and counterweights. More springs. Better strikes. I was able to lengthen the amount of time—"

"Johann, how long?"

Johann looked down at his plate. He brushed some imaginary dust off it.

"A month, I think. Give or take a few days."

Sophie lowered her head into her hands, feeling as if she were made of the thinnest glass, so brittle and fragile that the softest tap could shatter her. She had escaped death only to come face-to-face with it once more. "All that agony, all that fear . . . to gain so little time?" she said brokenly. "Why did you even bother, Johann? You should have let me die."

Johann didn't reply. No one did. Weber, upset, insisted on serving the supper. He placed a platter of sauerbraten on the table, the tender beef melting into its gingery gravy; a bowl of red cabbage studded with plump raisins; and another containing buttery, parsley-flecked spaetzle. No one felt like eating, but they didn't say so. They knew that feeding them was the spider's way of comforting them.

127

After a moment, Josef cleared his throat.

The others looked alarmed. "Josef, *don't*—" Julius started to say.

Josef cut him off. "I have to. No more lies. She needs to know," he said.

Sophie raised her head; she slumped back in her chair. "Is there *more* bad news?"

"Jeremias and Joosts didn't go on a hunting trip."

Sophie shrugged uncomprehendingly. "What does that have to do with my rapidly dwindling lifespan?"

"They went to Nimmermehr, Sophie. To steal your heart back."

For a long moment, Sophie said nothing, for the words wouldn't come. Jeremias and Joosts had undertaken a dangerous journey, they were planning to break into the castle of a murderous king—for her. She was deeply moved by their selflessness.

"Why?" she finally asked.

The brothers all looked at one another, puzzled expressions on their faces.

"What do you mean, *why*?" asked Schatzi.

"Why would they risk their lives for me? Why would you let them?"

Johann laughed, as if the answer couldn't have been more obvious.

"Because they love you, Sophie. We all do."

Sophie looked down at her plate. Inside her clockwork heart, a gear stuck and stuttered as warring emotions did battle—gratitude, doubt, wonder, unworthiness.

"It's a great kindness. Too great," she said quietly.

"You make it sound as if kindness is a bad thing," said Jakob.

Sophie raised her eyes to his. "Because it is. Kindness is weakness," she said, echoing her stepmother's words. "Kindness is dangerous."

Jakob clucked his tongue. "Kindness is many things," he said. "It is gentle. Tender. Tolerant. It is born of patience and faith. And sometimes, yes, it's dangerous. Helping a wounded animal that's likely to lash out, standing up for someone who's being taunted by bullies, breaking into the King of Crows' castle . . . these things are all dangerous. But to try to understand another creature, to put ourselves in their place, to help them—even when it costs us—that shows strength, Sophie, not weakness."

With everything inside her, Sophie longed to believe him. And yet her stepmother's voice rang out loudly in her head, and Haakon's, too. They told her that no ruler could afford to be kind, that brutality and fear were what kept one's commanders loyal and one's subjects obedient. She cringed to think of what they would say about her clockwork heart and how it revealed her emotions.

"Do you think they'll succeed? Jeremias and Joosts?" she asked. "Do you think they'll actually get my real heart back?"

Julius held up his hands, as if to push away too much hope. "We don't know. Which is why Josef should've kept his big mouth shut. We've been to Nimmermehr. We've seen what's lurking in the forest there. Jeremias and Joosts will have to be very wily, and very lucky, if they're to get inside the castle, snatch your heart, and get out again. Until they return to the Hollow with it, you're no better off than you were."

129

Sophie understood what he was saying—Jeremias and Joosts had only the slimmest chance of succeeding. "But I can hope," she ventured.

Julius scowled. "If you must," he grumbled.

Weber gestured at the food on the table. He squeaked irately.

"Yes, yes, you're right, Weber," Schatzi quickly said, picking up the platter of sauerbraten. "It *is* an insult to the cook to let his food grow cold." He served himself, then passed the platter. The others did the same, and soon everyone was eating. The candles were glowing. The fire was burning high. Everyone's spirits were bolstered by Weber's delicious cooking. Witches were not the only creatures in the Darkwood with magic; the spider had plenty of his own.

As they ate, Sophie asked when Jeremias and Joosts would return. "Two weeks, we hope," said Jakob. "Maybe three."

Sophie's stomach clutched with anxiety. Three weeks was a long time when you only had a month to live.

"You must not venture out again while we're waiting for them, nor must you let anyone in through the gate. The King of Crows might be near," Julius cautioned, giving Sophie a stern look. "I've always thought that Jasper might've lived longer if he'd stayed home. His heart might've been slower to wind down if he hadn't overtaxed it. If he hadn't forced himself over bad terrain and through rough weather to get to Nimmermehr. A month isn't long, but it might well be all you need. *If* you conserve your energy. *If* you sit still and wait for Jeremias and Joosts to return. *If* you're careful."

Sophie took his meaning. "If I don't leave the Hollow again," she said. "If I don't venture through the woods. If I don't try to find Haakon."

Julius nodded. He covered Sophie's hand with his own. "If you don't demand more from your heart than it can give."

TWENTY-NINE

There are many ways to take a heart.

And the King of Crows uses all methods; he shies from none. He's happy to have it cut out all at once as I, the huntsman, did.

He's happy to have it taken piece by piece, year by year, like a miser hoarding coins, with punishing silences, biting glances, and love served cold.

Poisonous words do the job, too. They are as sharp as knives and leave their victims hollow.

In the Darkwood, a princess stares out of her bedroom window at the stars. She was told that she is all wrong. And now she believes she's even more wrong, with a clanking, banging heart that's a greater liability than her old one was.

Miles away, in the palace, the queen stares into her silver glass. She is so many things: powerful, brave, intelligent, fierce. But the glass never lets her forget what she is not—not a boy, not a son, not a man, not a king.

Are you frightened by what you see when you look into the mirror? Too much? Not enough? All wrong? Never right?

Hear me, child. You should be far more frightened by what sees you.

THIRTY

Sophie lifted her face to the sun, taking a few moments' break from her chores.

There were dark smudges under her eyes. Two days had passed since she'd learned the truth about her new heart, and her old one, and she hadn't slept much. She ran to the attic window more frequently than she had before, looking not only for Haakon now but also for Jeremias and Joosts. She was worried for the two brothers. The King of Crows was a deadly foe—what if he were to capture them? She was worried for herself, too. Time was not on her side. Her heart was winding down with each passing minute. She wondered with a strange, cold detachment how it would feel to hear the last few seconds of her life ticking away. Would it hurt? Would she suffer? Or would everything simply stop? Like the hands of a wound-down clock?

A cuckoo called out from a high branch, scattering her morbid thoughts. Sophie opened her eyes and listened to his song, determined to put her worries away, if only for a little while, and enjoy the beautiful day. The sky was a clear, heartbreaking blue, and a gentle breeze wafted across the garden, carrying the scents of lavender and rosemary. The sun's warm rays were lengthening, though. The brothers would be home soon, and so would Weber and Tupfen, who'd gone to the woods to hunt for blueberries.

Sophie knew that she should finish her sewing so that she could help Weber get their supper ready. She was sitting on an old quilt in the cottage's yard, mending tears in her skirt. Blackbriar thorns had shredded the hem during her frantic run through the Darkwood, and she'd been wearing an old pair of Jeremias's trousers with the cuffs let down, one of his linen shirts, and her bodice ever since. Picking up her needle, she worked it in and out of the skirt's fabric. A few minutes later, as she knotted the thread, a voice called out from behind her, making her jump.

"Good afternoon, pretty miss! Can I interest you in my wares? I have many lovely trinkets—rings and brooches, thimbles and scissors—I'd be happy to show them to you!"

Sophie got to her feet, startled, but then relaxed a little when she saw it was only a peddler standing at the gate—an old woman, wearing a threadbare cloak, with a pack basket on her back. She had gray hair and kindly eyes. She seemed very nice, but when the brothers had left for their mines that morning, they'd warned Sophie, yet again, not to venture out past the fence.

"I don't need anything today, thank you," Sophie said.

The woman's face fell. Sophie felt sorry for her. She was thin and so weary looking.

"Might I trouble you for a drink of water? I've walked a long way, and I'm so thirsty," the woman said. She nodded at the well in the yard. "I'll help myself. I won't be any bother to you. If I could just come in and sit down for a moment . . ."

Sophie shook her head. "I'm not allowed to let strangers in."

"I understand, child. Thank you, anyway. May God keep you." The woman mustered a smile as she turned away, but her wrinkled face, framed by the cloak's hood, looked downcast.

The poor thing, Sophie thought, *walking for miles with that heavy pack. Surely there can't be any harm in handing her a cup of water.*

"Wait!" she called out. "Don't go! I'll get you a drink."

The old woman turned around, smiling with relief. She took her pack off and placed it on the ground. "Bless you, child," she said.

"Stay there," Sophie told her. "I'll be right back."

The woman nodded gratefully, and Sophie hurried off. A few minutes later, she returned, carrying a cup of cold water and a plate with a ham-and-cheese sandwich on it that she'd hurriedly slapped together. She handed them over the top of the gate, and the woman took them eagerly, gulping down the water right away.

"You are a kind girl," she said, sitting down on a stump. "What's your name?" she asked as she bit into her sandwich.

Sophie hesitated, then scolded herself for being silly. An old woman couldn't hurt her. "It's Sophie. And yours?"

The woman swallowed. "Ada," she said, wiping her mouth with the back of her hand. She put her plate on the ground, leaned over her basket, and dug down inside it. When she straightened again, she was holding a pair of pretty laces. They were made of black silk, with threads of gold woven through them. "For you. They're a gift. To thank you for your kindness."

Sophie tried to refuse them, but the old woman stood and walked to the gate. She held the laces out. "Go on, take them," she said. "They suit you."

Sophie bit her lip. The laces *were* awfully pretty, and they'd look so much nicer than the old red shoelaces that were currently holding her bodice closed.

"All right, then," she said delightedly, reaching over the gate. "Thank you."

"Put them in," the old woman urged as Sophie took the laces from her hand. "I'd love to see how they look on you." A small, secret smile curled the corners of her mouth. Her indigo eyes glinted darkly. But Sophie, eagerly undoing the knot that held the pretty new laces together, didn't notice.

As soon as she had them separated, Sophie draped the laces over the gate. Then she undid her old ones. As she pulled them free, the bodice loosened and sagged. Pinning it against her body with her elbows, Sophie tossed the old laces on the ground and began threading the new ones through the eyelets. When her nimble fingers had finished the task, she looked down at herself and smiled. They were a huge improvement. "How pretty they look, my dear!" the old woman exclaimed. "But they're too loose. Here, let me help you." She reached over the gate, undid the knot Sophie had made, and pulled the laces tight. "Oof!" Sophie said with a laugh. "I can barely breathe!"

And then the old woman knotted the laces, and Sophie couldn't breathe at all. It felt as if every last ounce of air had been squeezed out of her. "They're too tight!" she tried to say, but she couldn't get the words out. The woman stepped back from the gate, and as she did, her hood slid off her head. Her gray hair turned blond. Her wrinkled face became smooth. Her kind eyes turned cruel.

Sophie's heart slammed with fear. She tried to scream, but all that came out was a ragged groan.

"Will you never, ever learn how dangerous kindness is?" the queen said, her voice icy with derision.

Sophie stumbled. She fell against the gate. Struggling, she pulled herself up on it. "Please . . . *please*," she begged, reaching for her stepmother. But she was already gone.

Her chest hitching, Sophie turned and stumbled back toward the quilt where she'd been sitting. A pair of scissors lay on top of it. If she could just get to it, she could cut the laces. But she fell to her knees gasping before she'd made it halfway. She looked down at her bodice, ready to rip it off with her bare hands, and opened her mouth in a long, silent scream of horror.

Two black snakes, their scales tipped with gold, were twined around her chest. Tighter and tighter they squeezed, coiling themselves up her torso. They opened their mouths, hissing at her. *Weak, foolisssssh girl . . .*

. . . Not ssstrong enough, not ssssmart enough . . .

The venomous words seared Sophie's ears. The lack of air seared her lungs. She arched her back, trying to draw a breath. Above her, the sky started to spin.

The last thing she saw before she crumpled to the ground was a snake's head rising up above her, its tongue flicking in and out, its red eyes blazing, drops of poison hanging from its fangs.

THIRTY-ONE

Schatzi stopped in front of the gate, closed his eyes, and took a deep breath. The smell from the iron cookpot that Weber had set over the coals before he'd left to go berry picking was wafting on the evening breeze.

"Meatballs," Schatzi said dreamily. "Meaty, meaty meatballs in cream gravy! I hope we're having boiled potatoes, too." He opened his eyes. "That's my very favorite supper," he added, pushing the gate open. "With the possible exception of hasenpfeffer. And I hope there's a butter cake for dessert. With vanilla ice cream."

"Do you *ever* talk about anything other than food?" asked Jakob, pushing his way past him.

Schatzi looked at him as if he were crazy. "Why would I?" he asked, following his brother through the gate.

The others were right behind them, tired and dirty from a long day's work. They were all looking forward to a wash, then supper. Julius had just started toward the well when he saw her.

"Sophie! No!" he cried, dropping his pickax.

"What's wrong, Julius?" Jakob asked. "Why did you—" His words fell away. His face blanched with fear as he saw Sophie sprawled on the ground, her hands clutching at the grass. Her face was gray. Her lips were tinged blue. Two snakes, each as thick as a man's arm, were twined around her.

"Get a bow, some arrows . . . *Hurry!*" Julius shouted.

Johann was already running for the cottage. Jakob and Josef grasped their pickaxes and swung at the snakes, but the creatures were fast and dodged the blows. The ax heads sailed past them and lodged with thuds in the dirt. The snakes struck at the men. Jakob managed to jump clear. Josef's sleeve was ripped open by a pair of fangs.

Sophie was wheezing loudly, desperately struggling for air. Puncture wounds dotted her arms.

Johann returned with a bow; he aimed an arrow at one of the vipers, but both slithered close to Sophie, making it impossible for him to shoot them without hitting her.

"Keep distracting them. Don't let them bite her again!" Julius shouted, pulling a dagger from his belt. He started toward the snakes. "We need to get them off her! If we don't, she'll die!"

"Julius, what are you doing? Don't! You're too close!"

"I have to. They're going to kill her."

"They'll kill *you!*"

Sophie's eyes rolled back in her head. Her body went limp.

"No!" Julius shouted, lunging for her. One of the snakes reared up high, ready to strike at him, but as it did, there was a movement by the fence, distracting the creature. Something darted through the open gate and shot past the brothers in a blur. And then, before they knew what was happening, the snake's head, its fangs still bared, its eyes open in surprise, went flying through the air. It landed at Johann's feet with a wet, bloody thud.

The dead snake's body, coiled tightly around Sophie's torso, slackened, then fell to the ground. The second snake whirled around, eyes narrowing in fury as it saw its dead mate. It lunged, striking at the blur, but its rage made it clumsy, and it missed.

"What in the world—" Julius started to say. "It's a hound!" Schatzi exclaimed.

A small, wiry brown dog was growling and leaping around Sophie, antagonizing the snake. Dancing on her light, dainty feet, she taunted and teased, moving back from Sophie bit by bit, drawing the snake with her. One coil slipped off Sophie's body, then another.

The snake swayed from side to side, then struck. Again and again. The dog stayed just ahead of it, but then the snake suddenly reversed its direction, slithered to the side, and came up under the animal. The dog leapt sideways, but not quickly enough; she yelped in pain as the sharp fangs cut two grooves into her haunch. Bleeding, whimpering, she limped away, dragging her hind leg.

The snake reared again, gathering itself for the killing blow. Its black tongue flickered. With all the speed and fury of a whip cracking, it lunged. Its fangs buried themselves. They sank deep. But into the ground, not into the dog.

The wily hound had only pretended that her injury was bad. The wounds were bloody but not deep, and no poison had entered her flesh.

She'd jumped easily to the side as the snake struck. As the viper struggled to free itself now, the dog came around behind it and bit down into the soft flesh below its skull. There was a ripping sound, and then a second snake head went flying through the air.

As the brothers watched, too astonished to speak, the dog—panting, her hind legs shaking—walked back to Sophie. She licked the girl's face, nudged her with her nose. Then she let out a long, sorrowful howl and collapsed on the ground beside her.

THIRTY-TWO

"Wake up, wake up . . . *please* wake up!" Jakob said. He was on his knees by Sophie, gently slapping her cheeks.

"Is she dead again?" Schatzi asked tearfully.

"She's not dead. She's breathing . . . Look!" Johann said. Sophie's chest was rising and falling. Her breath was shallow, but she was alive. Happiness flooded through him, but then he saw the punctures on her arm. "The venom has to be drawn out," he said tersely.

Weber, who had come into the yard with a basket of berries, joined the brothers. When he saw Sophie and the dead snakes, he pushed everyone aside. He knew exactly what to do. Working quickly, he spun a length of silk, wadded it up, and pressed it against Sophie's wounds. As the brothers watched, the white silk slowly turned a murky, oily green.

Weber spun more silk. He changed the dressings again and again, drawing all the poison out. As the venom left her body, Sophie's eyelids fluttered open. She cried out, beating her hands wildly against the air.

"Stop, Sophie; it's all right," Johann soothed. "The snakes are dead."

Sophie pressed a shaky hand over her eyes. She took a few deep breaths, then lowered her hand.

"What happened?" Josef asked.

A shudder ran through Sophie. "It was *horrible*," she said, her voice ragged; then she told them what her stepmother had done.

"The queen found out that you're here, but how? Who told her?" Josef asked.

Johann looked up, searching the tree limbs for crows, but none were there. "*He* did. Corvus. Somehow, *he* found out that she's here."

As Johann finished speaking, Julius knelt down beside Sophie. He'd run into the kitchen a moment ago to fetch a small glass bottle. He picked up one of the saturated wads of spider silk and squeezed the venom into the bottle. Then he held the bottle up to the light, swirling it. He tipped out a drop onto his finger and tasted it.

"Grausamsprache," he declared. "It's a very potent poison. It travels quickly through the blood vessels and stops the heart."

"Then why am I still alive?" Sophie asked, confused.

"Because it only paralyzes flesh-and-blood hearts; it has no effect on clockworks. In fact . . ." He took Sophie's hand and placed two fingers on her wrist, feeling for her pulse. Then he smiled. "That heart of yours is ticking well. The rhythm is strong."

Sophie realized that this was the second time the metal heart had saved her from death. She was surprised to feel a grudging gratitude toward the faulty, noisy thing.

"I'm so glad you came home when you did," she said to the brothers. "Thank you for killing the snakes."

"We didn't," said Schatzi.

"But Johann said they were dead."

"*She* killed them," Schatzi said, pointing to the ground near Sophie. Sophie turned to see what he was pointing at. Her heart whirred as she saw the little hound lying in the grass, exhausted. Her sides were heaving; her eyes were closed.

"She's the bravest dog I've ever seen," Schatzi said. "The dirtiest, too. She's covered in mud. She's so dirty I thought she was a brown dog, but she's not. She's—"

"Cream-colored," Sophie said with tears in her eyes.

Schatzi looked at her. "How did you know that?"

"I saved her life once," Sophie said, laying a gentle hand on the skin-and-bones creature. As she did, the dog opened her eyes. "Now you've saved my life. Looks like we're even, girl." Then she leaned over and kissed the top of the dog's head.

Zara wagged her tail.

THIRTY-THREE

Carefully, cautiously, Sophie stepped out of her bedroom onto the landing, hoping against hope that the floorboards wouldn't squeak. She closed the door behind herself, then headed for the stairs, feeling her way down them in the dark.

She was leaving.

She'd made her decision right after the snakes had attacked her, before she'd even walked back into the house.

No good plans are made in the dark, Julius was fond of saying. But hers would be carried out in the dark. She would be gone before the brothers woke.

She was going north, to Skandinay. She had no choice.

The queen had found out that she was in the Hollow. Someone had told her. Johann thought it might have been the King of Crows. Had he seen her as she'd made her way through his hunting ground? Or was he even closer? Lurking just past the Hollow's fence. Watching. Waiting.

Sophie smiled bitterly, thinking of how, only weeks ago, she'd vowed to put her heart in a box. Now someone else had done it for her.

Sophie was scared but resolute as she made her way down

the stairs. The trip would be hard, and she would be alone. She'd never navigated through the woods before. She'd never walked for days, slept outside, or procured her own food, but she knew that she could bear every hardship the journey threw at her, as long as they brought her to Haakon.

As she lay in her bed earlier, upset—as she had been every night—that another day had passed and he had not come for her, she'd realized something—her stepmother, being a cruel woman, had most likely sent him home immediately after telling the court that Sophie was dead. He hadn't come for her because he hadn't even been allowed to look for her. If he couldn't get to her, then she would have to go to him.

Sophie knew that time was not standing still. After supper, she'd sneaked up to the attic to hastily consult a map that was stored there and had calculated that it would take her six or seven days to reach the border. She had just under a month now before her new heart wound down. Jeremias and Joosts might succeed in regaining her old one for her, but they might not. They'd already been gone a long time, which did not bode well. What if they'd been captured as they tried to sneak into Nimmermehr? What if they'd been imprisoned there? Sophie couldn't bear the thought of the two brothers languishing in a dark, dank cell. If they failed, her last hope—for them, and for herself—would be Haakon. He would have to assemble a fighting force and attack Nimmermehr before it was too late.

Her plan was perilous. It was crazy. If the brothers had known what she was doing, they would have been angry at her, they'd have tried to stop her. But they were the main reason she was leaving. She didn't know why the King of Crows wanted her heart or why her stepmother wanted her dead. But she did know that if the queen found out that she'd failed—a second time—to kill her, she would be back to try again.

Sophie wasn't the only one in peril now. By staying at the Hollow, she was endangering the brothers, Weber, and Tupfen, and she would rather die than bring any harm to them.

Sophie reached the bottom of the stairs now and made her way to the kitchen. She was carrying a rucksack she'd taken from the attic. Inside it was the map, an old brass compass, a bedroll, a battered tin canteen, a dagger, a woolen cap, and the little pouch of rubies that Johann had given her. She would fill the canteen with water from the well on her way out of the Hollow. She planned to sell the rubies in Drohendsburg, a village on her route, and use the money they brought to buy food and a horse to speed her journey.

Zara, who was sleeping by the hearth, heard Sophie walk into the kitchen. She opened one eye.

"I'm leaving. I have to," Sophie whispered, patting her on the head. "But you're staying here. The brothers will take good care of you. Stick close to Schatzi. He'll slip you bratwursts under the table."

Sophie rested her rucksack on the table and packed some food—a chunk of cold ham, a salami, a wedge of hard cheese, some plums, and a thick piece of apple strudel—enough to last her until Drohendsburg. She moved as quietly as possible, for Weber, who liked warmth, was asleep in the kitchen. She could just make out his shape in the darkness. He was up in the rafters, suspended in a hammock of spider silk, snoring. Her heart clicked softly at the sight; she would miss him.

When Sophie finished packing the food, she buckled the rucksack. As she did, she heard an inquisitive squeak from above her. *Weber*, she thought, her heart grinding. *I've woken him*.

She looked up to see eight black eyes blinking at her in sleepy confusion. As the spider's gaze moved to her rucksack, his expression changed from confusion to alarm. He shook his head and started to speak to her in his language. Sophie understood more of it now.

"No, don't wake them up. They'll try to stop me, but it won't do any good. I *have* to go," she said. "The King of Crows has my heart, Weber. My *heart*. I want it back."

Weber blinked his eyes. He heaved a sigh. Then he held up a claw, signaling that Sophie should wait for a minute. She could hear him rummaging in the rafters. A moment later, he let himself down on a skein of spider silk, carrying something under one of his arms. He walked over to Sophie, shook it out, and handed it to her.

"What is it?" she asked, taking it from him. "Is it a blanket?"

Weber nodded as Sophie marveled at the gift. It was a four-foot square, pure white, as soft and as light as a breath. Intricate patterns were woven into it, of flowers and flies, grasses and moths, all the things that spiders loved. Weber took it back and proceeded to fold it down to a small square. It was no bigger than a potholder by the time he'd finished. He tucked it inside her rucksack.

"Thank you," Sophie said, her voice suddenly husky. "Tell the others not to follow me. Tell them I'll come back if . . . if I can." Then she threw her arms around the spider and hugged him hard. He hugged her back with all his arms. When he finally let her go, she saw that he was crying. Big silver tears splashed onto the kitchen floor.

"Stop, Weber," she scolded fondly. "You have so many eyes, you'll flood the place."

The spider mustered a smile. Sophie kissed his cheek, asked him to take good care of Zara, and then shrugged into an old leather jacket, patched at the elbows, worn at the cuffs, hanging on a hook in the mudroom. Like the broom that stood beside it, the jacket belonged to no one and everyone, and she knew that as angry as the brothers would be with her when they discovered she'd left, they would want her to have taken it. They would want her to be warm.

Then she picked up her rucksack, stepped out of the cottage, and set off. There was no moon out tonight, only stars. The dawn was hours away.

It was the other things that would light Sophie's way through the forest, though she didn't know it. Not then.

It was the old, worn jacket that smelled of pine needles and woodsmoke, bacon and nutmeg. It was the soft blanket, so patiently woven, so generously given. It was the slice of strudel, slightly squashed, that she would eat with her fingers one night as she sheltered from the cold rain in a dark, dank cave.

Love is a soft thing. It smells like woodsmoke and sounds like rain. It tastes like sugared apples. It costs nothing to give yet is more precious than a sea of diamonds.

How I wish I'd learned that before it was too late. How I wish Adelaide had.

How I hope this scared, lost girl will.

THIRTY-FOUR

For once, Sophie's stomach was making more noise than her heart.

It growled and yarped, twisting with hunger.

She'd been walking through the Darkwood for two days and had run out of food last night. All she'd had for breakfast was a drink of water from a stream and a few handfuls of berries. Luckily, Drohendsburg had just come into sight.

Zara had caught a squirrel for her breakfast. Though Sophie had told her to stay home, the dog hadn't listened. Clever and quiet, she'd squeezed out of an open window and tailed Sophie for miles, only making her presence known when Sophie had walked too far to turn around and march her back to the Hollow.

The two were entering the village now, where Sophie planned to sell one or two of her rubies. She would use a little of the money to pay for a room at an inn. She needed a bath and a hot, filling meal, and she longed to sleep on a mattress for a night instead of the cold hard ground. A narrow main street ran through the center of the village. Stone houses lined both sides of it. Some had flower boxes in their windows, but the flowers had withered. Sophie was unsettled to see that the front doors of two or three houses were splintered or off their hinges, as if they'd been kicked in.

As she continued down the street, the houses gave way to shops. Signs for a butcher, two cheesemongers, a fishmonger, and a greengrocer hung over them. Crowds of people thronged the thoroughfare. Sophie had to work hard to make her way through them. *It must be a market day*, she thought.

Images of the delicious things she would buy for her breakfast—a wedge of buttery yellow cheese; slices of smoky, silky ham; fresh bread; figs—swam before her eyes. Her stomach growled painfully. She was so hungry, she felt faint.

But Sophie soon saw that the people were not on their way to a market. No one was carrying a basket or walking home with a fine fat hen under her arm. Instead, they were all clustered in a semicircle around a house, grim-faced, talking in low, hushed tones. A wagon stood in front of the house, too. Several soldiers idled near it.

Curious, Sophie drew closer. As she did, she saw a pot come sailing out of the doorway and land with a clang on the cobblestones. A soldier picked it up and put it in the wagon. Next came several feather pillows. Two soldiers carried a bed out. Another carried some earthenware bowls. One fell out of his hands and smashed in the street. Zara did not like the noise. She stayed close to Sophie.

A woman was standing at the edge of the crowd. She was thin. Her eyes were sunken. Her clothing hung off her frame like cobwebs. She watched the soldiers with a bitter expression.

"What's happening?" Sophie asked her.

"Same thing that happened to the Muellers and the Linds," the woman replied, nodding at a house with a battered front door. "Now the Beckers are being thrown out of their house because they can't pay their taxes. Their goods will be taken away and sold off."

"Why can't they pay their taxes?"

"Because they're too high," the woman said, looking at Sophie as if she were stupid. "They were doubled."

"Who raised them?"

"The queen, of course. Warships cost money. Someone must provide it."

Something else smashed on the street. There was the sound of a child crying. An old woman emerged from the doorway. She carried a bundle of clothing in her arms. Her back was stooped; her movements were slow. She wore a thin chain around her neck. A small silver angel dangled from it.

As Sophie and the townspeople watched, a soldier strode up to the old woman and ripped the chain off her neck. The woman cried out; she begged for it back, but the soldier ignored her and carried the necklace to his captain.

"Give it to the lord bailiff," the captain said.

Sophie's blood ran cold. The lord bailiff was Baron von Arnim. She'd known him ever since she was tiny. He was a member of her stepmother's inner circle, a trusted advisor. *Where is he?* she wondered frantically. He mustn't see her.

"That foul old pig," muttered the woman near Sophie, glaring at a high-sprung, costly carriage.

Sophie followed her gaze. The baron was visible through the carriage's open window. He was biting into a cake. He licked crumbs from his lips as the soldier approached, peered at the angel dangling on the chain, and then waved it away with a jeweled hand. A lackey, standing at attention outside the carriage, was holding a cloth bag. The soldier dropped the necklace into it.

The old woman, bereft at the loss of her necklace, shuffled toward the carriage, pleading for its return. Not aware of where she was walking, she stepped on a piece of the earthenware bowl that had shattered in the street. It skidded across the cobbles and sent her sprawling. She landed on the hard stones with a yelp of pain.

The soldiers burst into laughter. Not one of them moved to help her as she struggled to get up, her gnarled hands scrabbling at the cobbles. As they continued to laugh and make cruel jokes, a pregnant woman came out of the house, shepherding three small children before her. A man, hollow-faced, his head lowered, followed them. He lifted his head just in time to see a soldier plant his boot in the old woman's backside. She fell again, and this time she could not get up. She just lay on the cobblestones, groaning.

In a heartbeat, the man was on the soldier. He threw him down, then cocked his arm back to punch him, but a neighbor pulled him off.

"Are you insane?" he yelled. "They'll kill you!"

"You there!" It was the captain. "You just attacked a member of the queen's guard!" He motioned at two of his men. "Hold him!"

The soldiers grabbed the man. One twisted his arm behind his back. The man's wife ran to him but was caught and held fast by two more soldiers. His children, seeing their father being hurt, started to wail. Another soldier backhanded the eldest, bloodying his nose.

"The rest of you brats want some?" he yelled.

The captain, meanwhile, had drawn his dagger. He walked over to the man. "Kneel!" he barked at him. The soldiers holding the man kicked the backs of his legs. He dropped to the street.

The captain turned to the people assembled. "This man's house belongs to the queen!" he shouted. "His possessions belong to the queen. *He* belongs to the queen. I'm going to make sure that he never forgets it, that none of *you* ever forget it!"

And then he took his dagger and carved a Q in the man's cheek.

Sophie's heart twisted inside her, metal scraping on metal. The sound it made was like a shriek. But no one heard it, not over the man screaming, and his wife and children wailing, and the old woman weeping on the dirty cobblestones. Without thinking, forgetting all about Baron von Arnim, forgetting the wolf-faced soldiers, driven by her clockwork heart, Sophie pushed through the crowd and ran to the captain.

"Stop, please. I'll pay the taxes. I'll pay whatever they owe."

The captain shook his dagger. Drops of blood pattered across the cobbles. "Who the hell are you?" he said.

Sophie was suddenly aware that every villager was looking at her. All the soldiers. And their captain. She realized that she knew him. His name was Captain Krause. Did he recognize her? Did von Arnim? She stole a panicked glance at the baron's carriage. He was busy biting into another cake. To her relief,

Krause didn't seem to know her. Then again, she didn't look much like her old self; she was dirty and wearing trousers. Her hair was tucked up under a cap.

"I'm . . . I'm a relative," Sophie stammered, turning away from the carriage.

"You have five silver marks, relative?"

"No."

Krause shoved her away. "Then don't waste my time."

Sophie stumbled but managed to catch herself. "Captain, wait . . . *please*. I have something more valuable than silver coins."

The captain arched an eyebrow. He motioned her back to him. Sophie hurried to his side. She pulled the little sack of rubies out of her rucksack, opened the top, and tapped one of the gems into his hand.

The captain picked the ruby up between his thumb and forefinger. He held it to the light. Greed kindled in his eyes. "Is that all you have?" he asked. His gaze dropped to the ring she was wearing.

Sophie started to tap another stone into his palm, but before she could, he snatched the bag and dumped all the rubies out. Six large, perfect stones glittered in the sunshine. The captain smiled. He put them back in the sack.

"Take these to the lord bailiff," he told one of his men, motioning him over.

"What?" Sophie said, outraged. "*All* of them? One is enough to cover—" Her words were cut off by a sharp, loud crack. Her head snapped sideways. Lights burst behind her eyes. A rusty taste filled her mouth. *Blood*.

The captain had backhanded her so hard he'd split her lip.

"I'll have *that*, too," he said, roughly pulling her ring off her finger.

"No!" Sophie cried.

Zara growled, ready to lunge at the man, but Sophie stopped her. She had no doubt that Krause would kill the dog. She watched as the captain handed the ring to a soldier and the soldier started toward the carriage, her heart crashing in her chest. It was the Ruler's Ring. Baron von Arnim would recognize it instantly. He'd demand to know where it had come from.

"It's not fair!" Sophie protested, hoping to change the captain's mind. "The rubies covered the bill!"

"Would you like a memento of the day, too? To match his?" the captain asked, pointing at the man whose face he'd ruined. The man was still sitting on the ground, a hand pressed to his cheek, blood flowing through his fingers.

"N-no, sir," Sophie stammered.

"Stop sniveling. Your family's taxes are paid. They can stay. Consider yourselves lucky."

The captain turned to bark an order at his men. The man with the cut face got to his feet. And Sophie cast another frightened, furtive glance at the carriage. The soldier showed the ring to the baron, who made as if to wave it away into the bag with the other disappointments, but then the oval of diamonds that framed the unicorn glinted in the sun, catching his eye. He motioned for it.

Sophie's heart lurched. She had to get out of there. *Now.* But how? She couldn't backtrack; the street was too crowded. She couldn't walk forward, either. Doing so would take her right past the baron's carriage. As she frantically searched for a way out, she saw the open door of the Beckers' house. Grabbing a cookpot out of the wagon, she headed toward it, Zara at her heels.

"What are you doing? Where are you going with that?" a voice demanded. It was the wife.

"I'm carrying it into your house."

"But—"

"You can stay. I paid your debt," Sophie said.

The woman blinked at her, dumbfounded. "You did *what*?" she said. "Why? Who are you?"

Sophie glanced at the carriage. The baron had stopped eating cakes. He was beckoning for the captain. Her stomach plunged. "I'm nobody. Can I just carry this pot inside?"

"I know you . . ."

Sophie ducked her head. "You don't."

"I do! You're the princess! They told us you were dead! Thank you, Your Highness," the woman said, clutching Sophie's arm. "You saved us. All of us. We had nowhere to go. We—"

"Shh!" Sophie hissed. "Don't say anything else. *Please*."

The woman stopped talking. She nodded hesitantly, confusion in her eyes.

The baron was now motioning for the captain to open the carriage door. Sophie's breath caught in her throat. "Is there a back door in your house?" she whispered.

The woman nodded. "Are you in trouble?"

"Very much so."

The woman led Sophie into her house.

"The back door leads to a yard," she said. "Go over the

wall. You'll land in an apple orchard. Run to the far end of it. You'll come out at the edge of the woods." She gave Sophie's arm a squeeze. "Hurry!"

Sophie handed her the pot and ran for the back door, with Zara right behind her.

"Thank you, Your Grace," the woman whispered as she watched her go. "And Godspeed."

THIRTY-FIVE

A pale man on a jet-black stallion rode through the forest.

The sun was sinking in the sky. A blue-gray dusk brooded amid the trees. Night insects were singing; bats were on the wing.

The man came to a pond and dismounted. As his horse raked at the ground with a hoof, the man walked to the water's edge. A breeze curled through the trees, rippling the pond's surface.

Corvus, the King of Crows, barely noticed. He was gazing across the water at two creatures, a girl and a dog. The girl was leaning against the trunk of an ancient oak. She was tired from running; her shoulders were sagging. Drops of sweat had cut tracks through the grime on her cheeks.

She had stopped to pick blueberries, collecting them in her cap. She ate some now, sharing them with the dog. Then she unscrewed the top of her canteen and took a deep drink.

She is hungry and thin. Frightened and alone. Yet she endures, the man thought. *The huntsman did not kill her. Nor did the snakes. How can that be? My sister thinks the seven men might have fashioned her a new heart. Can she be right?*

Corvus's eyes glinted malevolently in the gloom. He rarely failed. Failure was unsettling. It made him uneasy. "And that takes some doing," he said.

The girl was stronger than he'd realized. Stronger than she herself realized. He had seen her today in Drohendsburg.

Oh, yes. He was there. Moving through the crowd. Whispering in the villagers' ears. Planting seeds in the rich red soil of their battered hearts. He saw the girl give all that she had to save a poor family. He saw her stand up to the captain and outfox the baron.

She is growing clever and tough, he thought, *and that will not do.*

He had convinced Adelaide that the girl was a threat to her. He had persuaded the queen to get rid of her.

But he had lied.

The girl was a threat, yes. But not to Adelaide. To him.

She was weak, soft, stupidly kind. She was a fool, a bumbler. And yet she might very well undo all his well-laid plans.

As Corvus continued to watch, hidden under the low branches of a pine, the girl bedded down for the night, stretching out on a borrowed bedroll, covering herself with a white blanket. The dog nosed its way under the blanket and curled up beside her.

"Spider silk," Corvus spat. It would keep the girl warm, protect her against wind and rain. Which was exactly why that wretched arachnid had given it to her.

Corvus would go to the palace to visit the queen. But first he would finish his ride through her realm.

He would bring her people flowers. Grown in his own garden.

Their petals are the color of blood and midnight. Their names are hatred, chaos, grief, despair.

Ah, Adelaide, beware.

The seeds of fear yield such dark blooms.

THIRTY-SIX

Sophie knelt down on the forest floor and stared at a clutch of mushrooms. Her mouth watered.

"What did Josef say?" she wondered aloud. "That the ones with brown caps and white spots are safe to eat? Or was it the ones with white caps and brown spots?"

She berated herself for not having paid more attention when Josef sorted through the baskets of mushrooms Tupfen gathered. She was starving. It felt as if her stomach had tightened itself to the size of a walnut, but she didn't dare eat mushrooms she couldn't identify.

She'd outrun Captain Krause and his men, but she couldn't outrun hunger or exhaustion. They circled her like vultures.

Dirty and sweaty, twigs and leaves in her hair, her split lip still throbbing—a full day later—from the captain's quick backhand, Sophie sat down, opened her canteen, and took a drink of water. She hoped it might lessen the pain gnawing her guts, but she knew it wouldn't do anything for the panic in her heart. She would soon become another skeleton in the Darkwood if she didn't find something to eat, but she had no idea how to do that. All she had of value—her rubies and her ring—were gone. And even if she still had the means to buy food, the next village—Grauseldorf—was miles away.

Her heart knocked against her ribs with anxiety. "Be quiet," she told it. "This is all your fault."

If she hadn't listened to it, if she hadn't helped the Beckers, she wouldn't be here right now, penniless and starving.

Sophie had run for her life after Captain Krause had stolen her things. Out of the Beckers' house and across their yard. After lifting Zara over the wall, Sophie had clambered over it herself. Then they'd raced through the orchard to the safety of the woods. Once there, Sophie had stopped briefly to catch her breath, but the sound of shouted commands, rising up over the houses, got her moving again.

Baron von Arnim and Captain Krause knew that it was the princess whose ring and rubies had paid the Beckers' debt, and Sophie was certain that by the time the sun had set last night, the queen had known it, too. Sophie could picture her stepmother's enraged reaction to the news that she was still alive, and she had no doubt that a fresh set of soldiers had already been dispatched to hunt for her. She felt like a fox who could hear the howls of the queen's hounds coming ever closer.

But it wasn't herself, or the danger she was in, that weighed heavily on Sophie's heart as she hurried through the woods. It was the Beckers. In her mind's eye, she saw the old woman, taunted and kicked. She heard the man's screams as the captain's blade cut into his cheek, and his children's cries. Sophie had never witnessed such suffering, and it had scarred her. Terror, pain, sorrow—these were the consequences of the queen's harsh rule, and the people of Drohendsburg did not deserve it.

Sophie wished desperately that she had more to give the villagers. She longed to help them. But what could she do? Nothing. She couldn't save them. She needed to continue to Skandinay. It would take her longer without the horse she'd planned to buy, but she would do it anyway; she had no choice. She needed Haakon's strength more than ever. Marrying him, making him king of the Greenlands—it wouldn't only save her, she saw now; it would save her people from a tyrant. Haakon would be a fair and just ruler. He would not throw villagers out of their homes. Sophie was sure of that.

A loud, deep growling in her belly scattered Sophie's tortured thoughts. She had to find something—*anything*—to eat.

She stood up now and looked around. As she did, a movement on the ground caught her eye. It was a rabbit. The creature was nibbling some greens. It locked eyes with Sophie, then shot off through a gap in a blackbriar bush. Sophie had seen quite a few rabbits as she'd made her way through the woods. Zara had loped off after one a few minutes ago.

Maybe I can catch one, too, she thought.

Jeremias was a hunter. Before he'd left for Nimmermehr, he'd let her shoot his bow, and he'd showed her how he trapped rabbits, carefully constructing snares out of thin strips of leather. Sophie didn't have any of those, but she did have a belt.

Excited by the thought of a filling dinner, she quickly unbuckled her belt and pulled it free of her waistband. Then she looped the end through the buckle to make a noose. She found a downed limb and propped it up in the blackbriar. After knotting the long end of the belt around the limb, she

164

arranged the noose so that it dangled just off the ground in front of the gap the rabbit had darted into.

"A rabbit, just one nice fat little rabbit . . . that's all I need," she said, stepping back.

A second later, the brass buckle slid over the leather, closing the noose. Sophie frowned. She pushed it back into place, praying it would stay, but as she did, the limb topped down. Groaning with frustration, she propped the limb up again. Blackbriar caught her hand; its sharp thorns tore red lines in her skin; Sophie swore; then she took a deep breath and tried again. Setting a snare took focus and precision, and she was so hungry, she could barely think straight. Her hands were shaking. Her entire body was trembling.

After a few minutes, the limb was rebalanced and the snare reset. Crossing her fingers, Sophie hurried away from it, flattened herself on the ground, and waited.

Please work, she prayed. *Please. Please. Please. I don't want to die in these woods.*

She picked her head up a little, the better to see the snare. But there was no sign of a rabbit. How long would it be before the creature ventured out? Minutes? Hours? Days? Her stomach squeezed again. The hunger was merciless. Tears of frustration stung behind her eyes; she blinked them back. And then a pink nose poked out of the blackbriar.

Sophie caught her breath. The rabbit's head appeared. "Come on . . . just a little farther . . ." she urged it.

The rabbit stretched toward the noose and sniffed at it. Sophie's heart thrummed. She realized that it was a very cute little rabbit, with a sweet face and large brown eyes.

"Maybe you have brothers and sisters," she whispered. "Maybe you have a whole big family." The thought made her feel sad. "I'm sorry," she said. "I wish I didn't have to trap you. It's just that I'm so, so hungry." The rabbit's ears stood up straight. Had it heard her? It backed away from the noose. Sophie's heart lurched. "No!" she pleaded. "Go forward!" The rabbit's nose twitched. It raised its head, eyes wide. And then, suddenly, inexplicably, it was lying on the ground, perfectly still, with an arrow through its skull.

Sophie gave a startled yelp, but then she realized what had happened— a hunter had shot her rabbit.

"*No!* That's *mine!*" she shouted, lurching toward the animal. She had to get to it before the hunter did. It was a kill for him, whoever he was, but it was life-or-death for her. She grabbed the rabbit, pulled the arrow out, and spun around, ready to defend her claim.

A boy was standing there. He was tall and thin, eighteen or nineteen years of age, with long brown hair and gray eyes. He held a bow in one hand.

"It's dripping blood all over you," he said, nodding at the rabbit. "Here . . . Why don't you give it to me? I'll clean it and—"

"It's *mine*," Sophie said fiercely, clutching the dead animal to her chest. The boy arched an eyebrow at her tone. "Actually, it's *mine*," he said. "Since I shot it."

"I made that snare. It was just about to step into it. It would've. If you'd just left it alone."

"No, it wouldn't have. It was spooked. It heard you talking. Every animal in the forest did." He smirked. "Why didn't you just ask it to jump into the stewpot while you were at it?"

166

Sophie clutched the rabbit tighter.

"You know how to clean and skin that? And cook it? Or are you planning to eat it raw?"

"I'm going to roast it. Over a fire."

The boy looked around. "Where's the fire?" he asked. He looked Sophie up and down. "Do you even know how to start one?"

Sophie's heart slipped a gear and made a harsh grinding noise. The boy's tone was mocking. His glance was dismissive. He made her feel small and diminished. Like she was back at court. Like she was all the things the people there said she was—foolish, weak, incompetent.

The boy cocked his head at the grinding noise. "What was—" Sophie cut him off. "I don't need you to save me!" she snapped.

The boy backed away. He held his hands up. "I never said you did. How about some help, though? Do you need that? Or are you good?"

"I'm good. In fact, I've never been better."

The boy snorted. "You don't look good. You look hungry. And tired. And whoever split your lip for you did a good job of it. The cut's wide open. It's still bleeding."

Sophie touched her fingers to her lip. They came away crimson. She stood up, eager to get her rucksack, call for Zara, and leave. But her vision swam, making her feel dizzy. She stubbed her toe on a tree root and stumbled but managed to catch herself.

The boy took a step toward her. "Why are you out here? Where are you headed?"

Sophie didn't answer him. For all she knew, he was another

monster in disguise, sent by her stepmother or the King of Crows.

"You could die out here, you know," the boy said. "Plenty do." Laughter, hysterical and convulsive, bubbled up from deep within Sophie's chest. It spilled out of her mouth. "Is that so? Do they really?" she said, still giggling. "I wouldn't know. I—"

Sophie never finished her sentence. Her eyes fluttered. Her legs gave way.

The archer rushed to her. He caught her just before she hit the ground.

THIRTY-SEVEN

Sophie woke to the smell of roasting meat.

Slowly, she opened her eyes. She was lying on the ground, on a carpet of pine needles. Her head was cushioned by her rucksack. She was drooling.

"The rabbit's almost done. I have pears, too. And cheese," said a voice. "Would you like some?"

Sophie's stomach growled like a tiger. "I'll take that as a yes."

Sophie sat up warily. She wiped the drool off her cheek with her sleeve. Looking around, she saw that she was sitting under a tall, sheltering tree. It was almost dark. The boy was turning a rabbit on a spit made of notched branches over a fire ringed by stones. Juices dripped from the meat and hissed in the flames. Zara was sitting near him, staring unblinkingly at the rabbit.

"Where am I? How—how did I get here?" Sophie asked.

"I carried you," the boy said, never taking his eyes off the meat. Sophie wasn't sure how to feel about that. Her wariness grew.

"This dog showed up and growled at me," the boy added. "I figured she was yours."

Sophie nodded. She looked closely at the boy. Who was

he? Had the King of Crows sent him? Did it even matter if he had? She couldn't fight or run away. She was too weak, too hollowed-out from hunger, to even stand up.

"Are you a monster?" she asked, her voice ragged with weariness.

"No."

"Are you going to kill me?"

"No."

"Because if you are, do it now, do it quick, and don't hurt my dog. She's been through enough."

The boy looked up at her. "Let's get one thing straight right from the start . . . I would never, *ever* hurt a dog."

Sophie's suspicion lessened a little. In her experience, people who didn't hurt dogs, didn't hurt people, either.

The boy turned his attention back to the rabbit. "My name's Will."

"Sophie."

Will slid the rabbit off the spit, laid it flat on one of the rocks surrounding the fire, and cut it down the middle with a hunting knife. He handed one half to Sophie. She took it in trembling hands. Then he tore the leg off his own half and tossed it to Zara.

"Be careful," Will cautioned. "It's very . . ."

But Sophie wasn't listening. She tore into the meat like a wolf, ripping off a chunk with her teeth.

". . . hot."

The meat was bland, for there was no seasoning. It was charred in some places, ropy and tough in others, but it was the best thing Sophie had ever eaten. Tears leaked from her eyes as she swallowed it. She brushed them away. Will pretended not

170

to notice. When she'd picked every bone clean, Will handed her a pear. And then a chunk of hard, salty cheese. Sophie devoured it all. The food warmed her. It gave her strength. Enough to run, if she had to.

"Thank you," she said when she finished it all, wiping her mouth with the heel of her hand.

Will nodded. The neckline of her shirt had come unbuttoned, revealing several inches of her scar. His eyes traveled down it.

Sophie saw him looking. She buttoned her shirt. His gaze drifted to her arms and the puncture wounds from the snakes' fangs—healing but still livid—that dotted them.

"Where are you headed?" he asked.

Sophie hesitated, still mistrustful, then decided if he was going to harm her, he wouldn't have fed her first.

"Skandinay."

Will let out a low whistle. "That's a long way from here. About five or six days on foot, and that's if you're fast."

Sophie's spirits sank at the reminder of how far away she still was from Haakon, and safety.

"I'm headed to Grauseldorf," the boy added. "It's in the same direction. I'll get you there, if you want, then show you the road north."

Sophie stiffened. "Why? Why would you help me? Why did you share your food with me?"

Will gave her a look. "Um . . . because that's what people do?"

"Do they?" Sophie asked. She didn't know many people who would help a stranger. Most of the people she knew wouldn't even help a friend.

"You might want to get some sleep," Will said, shaking his head. "I'm heading out at dawn."

Sophie wondered if sleeping only a few feet away from a stranger was wise. She felt a little stronger now; she could simply pick up her rucksack and leave.

And do what? she asked herself. *Walk through the Darkwood at night?*

She decided that she would stay but sleep with her dagger tucked inside her shirt. Just in case.

"All right," she finally agreed, still uneasy.

But Will barely heard her. He was busy pulling the branches that had formed the spit out of the ground and feeding them to the fire. As he did, Sophie dug in her pack for her canteen. She drank a bit of water, then used the rest to wash her face and hands. Together with Zara, she ducked into the woods. When she returned, Will was already bedded down by the fire. Sophie laid her bedroll out on the opposite side of the fire, then took Weber's blanket out of her rucksack.

"Thank you," she said again quietly as she settled down, Zara curling into the crook of her knees. She was amazed that Will had persisted in his kindness to her, even though she hadn't deserved it. She wasn't used to that. At the palace, bad behavior only inspired worse behavior, and any resulting wounds were rubbed with salt, not honey.

Without warning, the sticky gear in Sophie's heart caught again. The grinding noise was even louder than it had been earlier, right before she'd fainted.

Will looked up at her through (she now noticed) very long, dark lashes, a puzzled expression on his face.

"It's . . . um . . . it's a clock," Sophie said lightly.

"Where do you keep it?" he asked. "In your pocket?"

"Ha! Close," said Sophie.

Will raised an eyebrow but didn't pursue it. "Well, good night, Sophie. Sleep well."

"I will, Will. Hey, *will Will* . . . ha."

"Will Will. Yeah. Ha."

Sophie gave him a crooked smile. "You've probably heard that before."

"No. First time."

"Really?"

Will smiled.

"Oh. It isn't, is it," Sophie said, feeling a little foolish.

Will closed his eyes and pulled his blanket up around his shoulders.

Sophie watched him fall asleep. Until the fire burned down. Until the darkness enfolded them. Then she closed her own eyes.

Her heart whirred loudly.

It didn't matter. He couldn't hear it now.

Sophie felt something. Lying here in the forest. Only a few feet away from this boy.

She couldn't name the feeling right away, for she didn't recognize it. She hadn't known it in a very long time.

Not since her mother had sung her to sleep. Not since her father had held her in his strong arms, pointing out the stars, telling her their names.

But as sleep pulled her under, she remembered. For the first time in a long time, Sophie felt safe.

THIRTY-EIGHT

The sun was rising. Its pale golden rays slanted through the tree limbs and across the forest floor. Sophie and Will had broken camp an hour ago, after a quick breakfast of bread and cheese. They'd been walking ever since.

Will suddenly stopped dead. He often did that when he heard something, or saw something, remarkable. Sophie knew that now. The first few times, she'd crashed into him on the narrow forest path.

"Did you hear that?" he asked. "It's a kestrel. She's overhead." Will looked up. His eyes followed the bird as she darted through the air. "Probably looking for a tasty wren for her breakfast."

Sophie wasn't looking at the bird; she was looking at him. He loved the forest and its creatures, she'd discovered, and he made the long, boring walk interesting, pointing out animal tracks and woodland flowers. He was a puzzle, a very different creature to the boys at court, who constantly flirted and flattered and were absolutely allergic to silence. He was a quietly kind boy, one who spoke only when he had something to say. Sophie had learned this almost immediately.

"Where do you live?" she'd asked him shortly after they'd set off.

"In the woods."

"Do you have a family?"

"Yes."

"Why are you going to Grauseldorf?"

"Need some things."

After a while, she'd given up and had just trudged behind him silently. She had better things to do than chat, anyway. Like figure out how she was going to get all the way to Skandinay on foot with no money.

Five precious days had passed since she'd left the Hollow, which gave her a little over three weeks until the clockworks inside her stopped. Sophie felt as if she were standing inside a giant hourglass, desperately trying to keep the sand from pouring down on her. She needed help if she was going to complete her journey; that much was clear. She needed a supply of food, and she needed to take the quickest route to the border. Will was a good shot. He seemed to know every inch of the woods. As Sophie walked along, staring at his back, she wondered if he would take her to Haakon's palace. She had no doubt that Haakon would reward Will richly for returning his intended to him. But she wasn't sure that Will would agree to do it. She decided to wait a little, to get to know him a bit better, before she asked him.

They continued on after Will spotted the kestrel, walking through the dense woods, and up and down hills, for hours. They'd just made their way into a valley, and Will had suggested that they take a break to rest and eat, when out of nowhere, a voice said, "Stop right there. Hands up. Don't move."

Will did as he was told. Sophie, looking around wildly for the one who'd spoken, followed his lead.

A man stepped out of the trees. He was holding a knife. Sophie swallowed fearfully. She glanced around. More men emerged from the woods; they gathered around Sophie and Will.

Beyond them, hidden deep in the trees, stood half a dozen canvas tents, their sides covered with brush. A campfire burned in front of one. Neither she nor Will had smelled it because the wind was carrying the smoke away from them.

Sophie realized that she and Will had stumbled into an encampment. She squinted in the gloom and saw that a group of men, some young, some older, sat on logs that they'd drawn up to the fire. They all wore dark blue jackets that were faded but brushed and tidy, and they all appeared to be injured. One man's arm was in a sling. A boy, no more than fifteen or sixteen, had lost both eyes. A drum lay at his feet. Another man, thin as a wraith, shivered convulsively by the fire. Yet another sat slightly away from it on a chair with an elongated seat that someone had fashioned from tree limbs. The seat supported what was left of his legs.

Will, who walked with his bow over his arm, always at the ready, let one of his hands dip down toward his quiver to draw an arrow.

"I wouldn't, boy," the man with the knife cautioned. "Not unless you're sure that arrow can get to me before this knife gets to you."

Will let the arrow slide through his fingers and drop back

into the quiver. He raised his hands high again. "We're just passing through," he said. "We don't want any trouble."

"Don't give none, and you won't get none," said the man. He motioned to the path ahead with the tip of his dagger. "On your way."

Will nodded. He and Sophie lowered their hands. Will grabbed the sleeve of her jacket and tried to hurry her along. But Sophie's steps were slow and stumbling, because she couldn't take her eyes off the men.

Those jackets . . . the tents . . . the orderly campsite . . . she thought. *Why are they out here?*

She'd seen these things before, riding with her stepmother as she drilled her troops. Her gaze settled on the man, thin and ashen-faced, who was shivering by the fire. Impulsively, she broke free of Will's grasp.

"What are you doing, Sophie? He told us to *go*."

"But that man by the fire . . . He's ill. We should help him."

Will gave an ugly snort. "Do as you like. I'm leaving. I want nothing to do with these men."

Sophie looked at him, taken aback by the emotion in his voice. "Why would you say that?" she asked.

"They wear the queen's uniform. I despise the queen. The princess. Their so-called nobles. And all the thieves and murderers who make up the Greenlands' godforsaken army."

Sophie felt as if he'd slapped her. Will—kind, quiet Will—hated her, the real her, and she had no idea why.

Will didn't notice her reaction; he was still staring at the soldiers. "If you were smart, you'd leave, too," he said. "While you still have the chance."

As Will spoke, a fit of coughing gripped the man by the fire. Sophie's heart hurt at the sight of him hunched over, struggling for breath. She left Will and walked up to the man with the dagger.

"He's sick," she said, nodding to the one by the fire.

"That he is. Red fever."

"You're soldiers," Sophie said. "From the queen's army."

The man gave her a menacing look. "We ain't deserters, miss, if that's what you're about to say. We was good fighters, all of us. Still would be if we was allowed."

"Why are you out here?" Sophie asked.

"Too ashamed to be anywhere else," said the man in the makeshift chair. "Fighting was my life." He looked down at his ruined legs. "Who wants a soldier who can't march?"

The man sitting by the fire spoke. His head was down. He didn't bother to look up. "They tossed us away when we were wounded. Like rubbish. Didn't they, Hans?"

The man with the dagger—Hans—nodded.

"But there's a hospital for wounded veterans," said Sophie. "In Konigsburg."

"It's barracks now. We was told we cost the crown too much money. That we needed to make way for soldiers who were fit and could fight," Hans explained.

"The queen said this?" Sophie asked, appalled but not surprised.

"The lord commander did. Said it was on the queen's orders."

King Frederick, Sophie's father, had been a soldier. He'd died in battle, fighting against the king of the Hinterlands. The hospital for the war wounded bore his name. He'd believed veterans were heroes and that they deserved the highest honor their country could give them. Never would he have allowed these men to be treated so badly.

And neither will the king's daughter, Sophie said to herself.

Sophie's heart, quiet all morning long, banged like a foundry now.

The men all looked at her, alarmed by the noise, then at Will. "It's a clock," Will said.

Hans looked baffled by his explanation, but Sophie didn't notice. She wasn't aware of anything except the swell of compassion in her heart for the wounded men. All they wanted was to be soldiers, to fight for queen and country. Instead they'd been stripped of their dignity, robbed of their pride, and forced to hide themselves away in the Darkwood.

Sophie took off her jacket and draped it over the shivering man's shoulders. The man looked at the warm garment that had suddenly appeared with surprise. Then he looked up at Sophie. "I can't take this, miss."

"Yes, you can."

She pulled Weber's blanket out of her rucksack and spread it over the ravaged legs of the man in the chair. It eased his suffering some. Zara nudged her head under the man's hand, and he smiled. Next, Sophie pulled off her woolen cap and gently placed it on the head of the boy who'd lost his eyes. As she did, her long black hair tumbled free.

"Well, I'll be damned!" Hans exclaimed, his voice an awed hush. "It's *you*! I've seen you at drills and marches, ever since you was a tiny girl!"

Sophie glanced at him, then nervously looked away. She

shouldn't have removed her cap; she should've considered the consequences. It wasn't wise to reveal her identity—not in Drohendsburg, not to these strangers, and not to Will, but her heart had given her no choice, and it was too late to undo her actions now.

"I knew you wasn't dead! I never believed what the queen said. Not for a minute!" said Hans. "I knew it was a lie." He looked at Will and frowned. "Take that hat off, lad. Show some respect. Don't you know who this is?"

It was Will's turn to look baffled. "Um, yes. She's a girl . . . Sophie."

"*Princess Sophia* to the likes of you," the old soldier sniffed. He took Sophie's hand and kissed it.

Will's eyes widened. He took a step back. Not in awe, however, like the others. Not with deference.

"You're on the run, aren't you?" Hans asked.

Sophie didn't reply. She thought it best not to say what she was doing or where she was going. Her stepmother's spies were everywhere.

"Of course you are. Why else would you be dressed like that?" Hans continued. "Don't worry, Princess. Your secret's safe with us."

Sophie squeezed the soldier's hand. Then she straightened and addressed all the men in what she hoped was a magisterial tone. "I'll return for you. All of you. As soon as I can. You'll be taken back to Konigsburg and cared for. I promise."

The men dipped their heads to her. They smiled. The smiles were polite but skeptical. Sophie could see they didn't believe her. Why would they? They'd undoubtedly heard what had

180

been said about her at court. How could a weak young girl champion their cause against the decrees of a powerful queen? Sophie wished she could tell them about her plan, that she would be returning with the might of Skandinay's army behind her, but they would find out soon enough. She would not forget them.

Sophie took her leave. The soldiers wished her safe travels. She and Will started walking again. It was quiet between them for quite some time; then Will said, "You're going to be cold tonight."

"I'll get another coat," Sophie said crisply. Silence descended again.

"Why didn't you tell me who you were?" Will asked.

"How much farther to the village?" Sophie asked brusquely.

"So, it's none of my business? I'm walking a dead princess to Grauseldorf, but I don't need to know why?"

"No, you don't."

He looked at the side of her face. "Are you in trouble, Sophie?"

"Yes. Does that make you happy, Will?"

Will flinched. "No. Why would it?"

"Because you despise me. You said so."

"Yes, I did."

Sophie was surprised by his honest admission. It was not what she was used to. There were no denials, no excuses, no flowery words to perfume his earlier unpleasant ones. Sophie waited silently, to give him time to make his apology, but he didn't. Finally, her patience gave out.

"You're not sorry for what you said?" she asked huffily.

181

Will frowned thoughtfully. "Maybe. Maybe not. I don't know yet."

"You should be. Your words were cruel. You don't even know me."

"You're right. I don't." Then he said, "Why are you going to Skandinay?"

"I need to get to Prince Haakon," Sophie replied. "I need his help to fight some powerful adversaries."

She was about to ask him if he would help her, if he would take her to Haakon's palace—she didn't want to, not after what he'd said—but she was desperate. Before she could, though, he spoke. "Who are you fighting? The queen? Can't you do it yourself?"

Sophie shot him a scalding look. "Fight the queen of the Greenlands? *Myself*? No, Will. Funnily enough, I can't."

Will smirked. "Handsome princes certainly come in handy, don't they? Wish I had one."

There was the mocking tone again. It made Sophie bristle. "Haakon's my protector. We're betrothed, the prince and I."

"Hmm."

"*Hmm*? That's what you have to say? What does *Hmm* mean?"

"I heard that you were killed by wolves . . . that they dragged you off."

"You heard wrong."

". . . so I'm wondering . . ."

"What?" Sophie snapped.

"Why Prince Charming isn't searching for you."

The same question had pricked at Sophie like a thorn. She told Will what she'd been telling herself. "Because he believes I'm dead. Just like you did."

"Even so, you'd think he'd want to find your skeleton, at least. To give his lost love a proper burial. Maybe keep a finger bone for a little memento. Some teeth. A few toes."

Sophie stopped dead. Will did, too. "Do you have to be so horrible?" she asked angrily.

"He *didn't* search," Will said.

"He did."

"The why didn't he find you? Clever guy like him?"

"He ran out of time. The queen sent him back to his realm."

"So why doesn't he come back? He could search for you disguised as a woodcutter or a merchant."

Sophie walked ahead of him, irate. She couldn't believe she'd ever considered asking this troll of a boy for help. "Haakon has responsibilities! He has affairs of state to attend to! You just don't understand!" she called over her shoulder.

Will watched her as she stalked down the path.

And then, quietly, so that she couldn't hear him, he said, "Neither do you."

THIRTY-NINE

Sophie groaned. She huffed. She kicked at some dead leaves.

Will, a few yards up the road, paid her no attention.

They'd trudged through the woods for six hours yesterday after they'd left the soldiers and almost twelve hours today, walking, making camp, and breaking camp, mostly in silence. Neither of them had talked much since their fight.

Sophie was tired. Her feet ached. She thought constantly, longingly, of her soft bed back at the Hollow.

The road sloped down now; it curved around the base of a hill. As it did, an old church at the top of the hill, gray and decrepit, its bell tower crumbling, loomed into view.

"That's St. Sebastian's. The village is on the other side of it," Will called back to her. "We can save a bit of time if we cut through the graveyard. Come on." He shot up the hill.

Sophie followed him but at a walk.

"Are you coming? Hurry *up*!" Will shouted. He was already halfway to the church.

Sophie rolled her eyes.

She was still smarting from Will's harsh declaration. She still didn't know why he'd said that he despised her, and it wasn't likely that she would find out, for she refused to give him the satisfaction of asking.

Sophie had decided that she wasn't terribly keen on Will, either, though she was—grudgingly—grateful to him. For someone who couldn't stand her, he took pains to help her. He'd made it his mission to teach her what she could and couldn't forage from the forest. In less than two days, she'd learned which mushrooms were poisonous, how to set a proper snare, and what forest plants were safe to eat.

"Pay attention," he'd insisted as he showed her the difference between two types of swamp cabbage. "Green leaf fills you. Red leaf kills you. You need to know these things if you're going to make it to Skandinay." A shiver ran through Sophie now as she followed Will up the hill. She didn't like the look of the spooky old church, or the notion of taking a shortcut through a graveyard, but the day was lengthening and she knew that Will wanted to get to the village before the shops closed. He intended to make his purchases and start back for his home before dusk fell.

When she reached the top of the hill, she saw him walking through the grassy graveyard, past crypts and through rows of headstones. "How much farther?" she asked breathlessly as she caught up with him.

"Watch it, you blockhead! You stepped on me!"

Sophie stopped dead. That was the last straw. "*What* did you call me?" she asked.

"I didn't call you anything," said Will.

Sophie gave him a sharp look. "Oh, really? Then who did?"

Will stopped, too, and turned in a circle, his eyes on the grass.

"What are you looking at? I don't see anything but mushrooms," Sophie said, pointing at a patch of fungi sporting red caps with white polka dots.

"That's because mushrooms are what they want you to see."

"Who's *they*?"

"Ground pixies. Ever wonder why mushrooms seem to pop up from the ground overnight?" he asked. "It's the pixies moving around. They wear red hats that look just like mushroom caps as camouflage."

Sophie bent down and stretched her hand out toward one. "Be careful. They can be nasty," Will warned.

Just as she was about to touch a spotted cap, it shot out of reach. The cap tilted back. A tiny face, with a sharp nose and shrewd eyes, appeared underneath it. "Hands to yourself, strudel brain," the pixie said.

Sophie gasped. A little man was standing before her, wearing a white tunic and green clogs. He had pointy ears and sharp teeth.

"You shouldn't call people names," scolded Will.

"Sez who, cabbage head?"

"You are the *rudest* little thing!" Sophie sputtered, straightening. "I should cook you and eat you!"

The pixie made a rude gesture. "Eat *that*, fartsack!"

Will burst into laughter. Sophie did not. She stamped her foot at the pixie. But instead of running away, he and ten more of his kind charged at her, snapping their teeth. She gave a shrill cry and ran behind Will.

"You think kugel boy there is going to protect you?" the pixie scoffed. "Pul-*lease*!" He sucked his lower jaw in to give

186

himself buck teeth, stuck his neck way out, and imitated Will's loping walk.

"Hey!" said Will, scowling. "That's not funny!"

But Sophie thought it was hilarious; she couldn't stop giggling. Zara, meanwhile, had walked up to one of the pixies and had nudged it with her snout. This infuriated the creature; he kicked dirt in her face. "Don't breathe your smelly dog breath all over me, you spindly-legged, bugeyed, bony-ass fleabag!"

Zara took a step back. She barked uncertainly. Then she lunged at the pixie, grabbed it by its cap, and shook it violently. The strap that held its cap on its head snapped. The pixie went flying through the air, trailing a string of obscenities. Zara ripped the cap to shreds.

It was a mistake. A good fifty of the creatures ran out from the long grass, yelling at the top of their lungs.

"Um, Will? I think we made them mad," Sophie said, backing away.

"We sure did. Time to go," said Will.

They turned and started to walk away. Sophie looked over her shoulder. The pixies kept coming. They were gaining on them. Their teeth looked very sharp indeed. She tugged on Will's sleeve.

Will glanced behind himself. "We're in trouble," he said. "Where's a handsome prince when you need him?"

"Guess you'll have to make do with a handsome princess," Sophie said, impulsively catching hold of his hand.

Will's hand closed on hers, and Sophie pulled him along. They broke into a trot, laughing with each other this time. Zara, her ears flapping, loped along behind them.

Sophie didn't let go. Not until they were out of the graveyard, down the hill, and well on the road to Grauseldorf.

Neither did Will.

FORTY

Grauseldorf was as gray and dreary as the gravestones Sophie had passed in the churchyard, and she couldn't wait to leave it.

She had to be patient, though. Will was in the apothecary's shop. He'd buttonholed the owner as he was locking up and had persuaded him to open again for just a few more minutes. He couldn't wait until morning, he'd explained to the man. He had to get back on the road. Someone was waiting for him, someone who needed what he'd come to buy.

Sophie's ears had pricked up at this. He was so close-mouthed about his family, his whole life, that she was sure he hadn't meant for her to hear all that, but she had. *Who's the someone?* she wondered. *Does Will have a wife?* Her heart had sunk noisily at the idea of Will being married.

"Clock?" Will had said as the shopkeeper unlocked the door. "Clock," Sophie had replied, smiling brightly.

Will had followed the man inside, and Sophie had lingered in the street, waiting for the noise to stop, but to her mortification it continued, shifting down into an ugly, low hissing. She didn't understand why, and then, glancing in through the windows at Will, she did: Her heart was jealous.

The realization shocked her. It made no sense. What did she care if Will was married? She was soon going to be reunited with her beloved. That was the only thing that mattered. She wasn't jealous. How could she be? She didn't even like Will. And he certainly didn't like her. It was just her strange, unfathomable clockwork heart malfunctioning yet again.

A moment later, the noise stopped, and Sophie and Zara joined Will inside the shop. Sophie didn't want to be there. She was as impatient to get out of Grauseldorf as Will was. She felt exposed here. What if Krause was out looking for her and rode through the village? But Will made her wait. There was a public house on the edge of the village, he said, a rough one, and he didn't want her walking past it alone.

As Sophie wandered around in the shop, she looked at the jars lining the walls. Some contained wonderfully fragrant things like cinnamon, cloves, and nutmeg. Others contained substances that made her wrinkle her nose, like dried black beetle and pickled toad.

"Two ounces of eldertree bark, two of foxnettle, and an ounce of ground barberry . . ." she heard Will say. Sophie knew what these things were for. What she didn't know was why he was buying them.

The apothecary finished measuring out Will's order, folded the substances into squares of brown paper, and pushed them across the counter. Will paid the man, then carefully tucked his purchases into his rucksack. They made it to a few more shops before they closed. Will bought a few things at each one, then tucked four plums, some bread, and a hunk of cheese into Sophie's rucksack. She tried to thank him, but he wouldn't let her. Instead he lectured her, yet again, on the differences between stagleaf, which was delicious, and stagwort, which would turn her tongue blue.

Sophie listened dutifully as they walked past the shuttered shops, but when Will paused to take a breath, she said, "Why all the painkillers?"

She didn't get an answer, so she shot Will a sideways glance. His jaw was set hard.

"I guess it's none of my business," she said.

"I guess not."

They continued their walk in silence until the buildings fell away. Sophie could see a fork in the road up ahead, and to the left of it, just as Will said, an unsavory-looking pub. Sophie had to pick her steps carefully in places. A farmer had clearly recently been through with his cows; the animals had left plenty of cowpats in the road.

A few men idled at a handful of rickety wooden tables on the pub's porch. More came out to join them, pints in their hands. Gusts of raucous laughter burst through the open doors after them.

Will, his hands jammed into his trouser pockets, glanced at them. Sophie didn't. If she had, she would have noticed that they were wearing navy-blue uniforms. But she was staring hard at the road, trying to keep her unruly heart under control. She could feel it starting to thump. She hoped it wasn't going to embarrass her again.

A moment later, they reached the fork. Will inhaled deeply, then blew a heavy breath out. He shifted his weight from one foot to the other, then all in a rush he said, "I wish you weren't going alone. I'd go with you, Sophie. I want to . . . but I can't. There's someone at home . . . She needs me and . . . and I've got to get back."

Once again, Sophie's heart began making a low, ratchety clatter.

She started talking, a little louder than usual, to cover up the sound. "There's no need to apologize, Will. I wouldn't be here right now if it wasn't for you. I can never thank you enough for all the help you've given me. I'll be fine."

"Well, I guess this is it."

"I guess so."

Awkwardly, Sophie extended her hand, thinking Will would take it, shake it, kiss it . . . *something* . . . even though he didn't like her, if only for courtesy's sake. Instead, he hugged her. It was awkward and stiff. He patted her back too hard, as if she were a horse or a big dog. And he held her for a beat too long, which brought a catcall from the direction of the pub. A few whistles, too. And a rude comment.

Sophie broke the hug. She darted a glance at the man who'd made the rude comment. And sucked in her breath.

The rude man had just been lifting his pint of ale to his lips. He lowered it. His eyes locked on Sophie's.

He knew her. And she knew him.

He was the captain of the queen's guard.

FORTY-ONE

Sophie's heart clanged in her chest.

Will gave her an uncertain smile. "Hmm. That's not just any old clock in your pocket, is it? It's an alarm clock," he joked.

Sophie pushed him away. "Go back to the village," she hissed, and then she headed up the road as fast as she could.

Will caught up to her. "Sophie? Is something wrong?"

"Pretend you don't know me!" Sophie said, breaking into a trot.

"It's a little late for that. I just hugged you," Will said, hurrying to keep up with her.

Sophie cast a glance over her shoulder, back at the pub. "Go, Will! *Please.* Before they hurt you."

Will followed the direction of her gaze. They both saw the captain put his glass down. He motioned two of his men over.

"Is this the trouble you're in?" Will asked.

"Some of it."

"There's a farm up ahead. Just off this road," Will said tersely. "If we cut through its meadows, we can reach the hill to St. Sebastian's, where we came in. The Darkwood's on the other side. If we can get to it, we can lose them."

Sophie's eyes, still on the captain, were huge in her face.

193

"Sophie!" Will barked at her. "Look at me . . . *Me*, not him."
Sophie did so. His gray eyes looked as hard as steel.

"Hey! You there! Girl!" the captain shouted.

"You ready?" Will said. He took hold of her hand. Sophie
nodded.

Will tightened his grip. An instant later, they were running
like the wind.

FORTY-TWO

Horses, Sophie thought, her heart seizing with fear.

She and Will were pounding down the dirt road. They'd covered about a hundred yards when she heard the hoofbeats.

Why hadn't she thought of horses? Of course Krause and his men had them. Her stepmother made certain that her guard had the fastest, strongest mounts in all the realm. She and Will had no hope of outrunning them. Krause would capture her and take her back to her stepmother, or simply do away with her in the Darkwood. Her bones would join all the others there, moss-covered and forgotten.

It's over, she told herself, fear giving way to despair. *The queen, the King of Crows . . . They've won. I'll never make it to Skandinay. I'll never see Haakon again.*

Sophie's lungs were bursting; her muscles were screaming from the exertion of running flat out. She glanced back in terror. Krause, a few lengths ahead of his men, was riding at a full gallop. He would close the gap between them in mere seconds.

"It's useless, Will. I can't run anymore," Sophie shouted, starting to slow.

"Yes, you can!" Will shouted back. "Just a few more yards,

and we'll lose them! Come on!" His grip was like a vise; she had no choice but to keep up with him.

We can't lose them. He's crazy, Sophie thought.

And then they rounded a bend in the road and Sophie saw them—cows, at least fifty of them.

The farmer and his son were driving their herd home from a pasture to be milked. The animals were walking along at a leisurely pace, swishing their tails, the tin bells around their necks ringing. They'd spread out across the entire breadth of the dirt road.

Without slowing, Will pulled Sophie right into the herd. Zara was behind them. They moved through the cows like fish through reeds. Sophie remembered sidestepping all the cowpats, back by the pub. *Will knew they'd be here*, she thought. She ran faster, energized by new hope.

The cows took little notice of the two humans on foot, and a dog, but the riders were a different story. The thunder of the horses' hooves, their shrill whinnying, the shouts of the men—all the noise and commotion upset the peace-loving creatures. Some bolted ahead, which upset the farmer and made him yell. Some stopped dead and refused to budge, lowing loudly. Others turned and charged the horses. The soldiers could not get through the herd, nor could they go around it, for the road was walled in on both sides by tall hedgerows.

"Go back to the village!" Captain Krause shouted. "They're heading for the Darkwood! We'll cut them off on the far side of the church!"

Sophie and Will, meantime, had run through the farm's open gate, through a squawking flock of chickens, past barns and pens. They hopped a wooden fence, then made for the open meadow. By the time they'd reached the foot of the hill that rose to St. Sebastian's Church, Sophie felt as if her lungs were on fire. She wanted to stop, to catch her breath, but Will wouldn't let her.

"If we don't beat them to the woods, we're done for," he said.

A moment later, they crested the hill. Looking down the opposite side, they could see the Darkwood and the road that curved alongside it.

"They're not here yet," Sophie said, casting an anxious glance up the road toward the village.

"They will be," Will said.

He and Sophie wove in and out of the headstones. They were halfway down the hill, and Sophie had just started to believe that they would make it into the forest, when they heard hoofbeats again.

Will swore. He reversed direction. "Run for the church!" he shouted. Sophie's heart was battering against her ribs as she followed him back up the hill. They got to the church's door just as the riders rounded the bend. As Will opened it, they could hear the captain's voice.

"You four . . . search in the woods!" he bellowed. "The rest of you search the graveyard!"

Will pushed Sophie inside, then closed the door after her. The centuries-old church was enormous and empty. Sophie and Will ran down its center aisle, looking for a place to hide. There were wood pews, an altar. There were dark alcoves dedicated to saints and martyrs, with candles burning in them, but the soldiers would surely search all those places.

"Look!" Sophie said, pointing ahead of them. Inscribed over a stone archway to the right of the altar were the words: *To the crypts.*

Will nodded. They hurried through the archway, then down a spiraling flight of stone steps into the bowels of the old church. Oil lamps set into niches in the walls lit their way.

When they reached the bottom of the stairs, they found themselves in a long, low-ceilinged room that was musty and cold. Vaulted crypts, each enclosed by an iron gate, lined both sides of it. An avenging angel carved from marble stood guard at the left of the stairwell.

Sophie could see coffins through the iron bars. Some were made of wood; others were carved of stone. All were thickly covered in dust. "Will, there's no place to hide down here!" she said frantically.

Will tried the handle on the gate of the nearest crypt. It was locked. He tried the next one, and the next, making his way down one wall. Sophie started down the other side, but every gate she tried was also locked. Zara stuck close to her.

A deep booming crash was heard above them. Sophie and Will turned to look at each other.

"They're tearing the place up . . ." Will started to say, his eyes on the ceiling.

". . . looking for us," Sophie finished.

They redoubled their efforts. Sophie moved like lightning down her row, desperately trying one handle after another, fear churning in her belly, but she had no luck.

And then she did.

As she reached the last crypt, the handle turned, the catch released, and the gate swung open on creaky hinges.

"Will!" she whispered. "Over here!"

She stepped inside the ancient crypt. Zara ran in after her. Coffins lay in rows, some stacked two and three high. Mice, dampness, and time had destroyed many of them. Their tops were cracked; their sides had caved in. Sophie recoiled in horror as she saw bones spilling out of one. Another crash was heard from above them, followed by the sound of tinkling glass. The noise got Sophie moving again. She walked past the stacks of coffins, looking for a good hiding place.

As she did, she heard another noise, small and soft and close. Too late she realized that something was in the crypt with her.

Sophie stifled a scream as it loomed out of the shadows and grabbed her.

It was a man. He was holding a knife. He was pointing it at her throat.

FORTY-THREE

"Don't hurt her. *Please*."

Will was in the crypt now, too, his hands raised to show that he wasn't a threat.

Sophie's breath came in short gasps. The man's fingers curled cruelly into her arm, but she barely felt them. All her attention was focused on the tip of his knife.

"Who are you?" the man growled. His face was scarred. He was shaggy haired and dirty.

"She's the princess of the Greenlands," Will said. "The queen's guards are upstairs. They're after her."

There was another crash from above. It sent tremors down the walls. "The queen wants me dead," Sophie said. "If they get hold of me, I will be."

"And him?" He motioned at Will.

"He's my . . . my friend," Sophie said. "Can you hide us in here?"

The man sighed unhappily, but he lowered his knife. "May as well. Looks like I'm going to have to hide myself, too. Captain Krause and I are not the best of friends."

"You know him?" Sophie asked as Will closed the gate.

"He gave me this." The man pointed to his cheek.

The hair on the back of Sophie's neck prickled. The scar she'd glimpsed on the man's cheek had been branded into his skin. It was a T. For *Thief*. She quailed at the thought of being trapped in a crypt with a criminal.

"Captain! Down here!" a voice shouted from the top of the stairwell. Sophie froze.

"You going to stand there like a pair of turnips? Hide!" the man hissed. A large stone sarcophagus stood at the back of the crypt. Will and Sophie crouched down behind it and pulled Zara in close to them. As they did, the man took an iron skeleton key out of his pocket. He snaked his hand through the bars and locked the gate from the outside.

Just as the first soldier reached the bottom of the stairs, the man disappeared behind a stack of wooden coffins. Sophie leaned her head against the cold stone, willing her heart to be silent. She couldn't see the soldier from where she was, but she could see the light from a lantern playing over the walls.

More soldiers joined the first one. Sophie could hear them. They fanned out through the room, shaking the bars of the gates, holding up their own lanterns and peering into crypts.

Go, she silently urged them. *Leave.*

Light suddenly poured into the vault where she was hiding, washing over the floor and ceiling. Sophie did not move. She did not breathe. And finally, the darkness returned.

"They're not here, Captain!" a voice called out. "All the crypts are locked up tight."

"Where the devil did they go, then?" Captain Krause said, smacking the marble angel with his riding crop.

While the captain and his men talked, someone else walked down the length of the outer room. Sophie could hear his footsteps, slow and measured. Then he stopped.

"Sophie? Are you in here?"

Sophie's heart skipped a beat. It couldn't be . . . Could it?

"Don't be frightened, Sophie. I've been searching everywhere for you."

Sophie angled her body so that she could peer around the side of the sarcophagus. She didn't see Will shake his head. She didn't see the thief hold a finger to his lips.

All she saw was a tall, broad-shouldered man with a lion's mane of blond hair standing in the center of the room. He was holding a torch, shining its light into one of the crypts.

"My beloved girl, don't you know my voice? It's *me* . . ."

Sophie felt herself crumble, felt her whole body go limp with relief.

She breathed the man's name as he himself spoke it.

"Haakon."

FORTY-FOUR

With a cry, Sophie sprang from her hiding place and ran to the gate.

She wrapped her hands around the bars, tears welling in her eyes. She'd been wrong, so wrong. Captain Krause and his men hadn't been pursuing her to hurt her; they'd been trying to rescue her, on Haakon's orders. He must've been inside the public house when she and Will had passed it.

"Haakon," she said. "You came for me. You *did*."

Haakon smiled, his stunning blue eyes crinkling at the corners, and it felt to Sophie as if the sun had just come out. All her hardship was behind her. He was here with her. At last, she was safe. She would never have to run or hide or be afraid again. He was across the room in two quick strides, windblown and worn from riding but so impossibly handsome.

"My darling, darling girl," he said. "I thought I'd never find you. I knew you weren't dead. My heart knew."

Sophie reached through the bars for him. He caught her hand in his gloved one, lifted it to his lips, and kissed it. Sophie squeezed his hand tightly, as if she would never let go.

"Was this another of your cruel games?" he asked teasingly.

"Designed to taunt a poor lover, to lead him on a wild-goose chase?"

Sophie's heart whirred with happiness at his kiss, his words. Haakon heard it. He blinked in surprise. "What on earth is that noise?" he asked. Sophie's chest tightened with dread. She didn't want to answer that question, not here in front of so many strangers. She wanted to have time alone with Haakon to explain how she'd survived, and who had her real heart.

"I have so much to tell you, my love," she said. "And I will. But not here. Not now."

Haakon nodded. He held his torch high, shining its light into the crypt; then he said, "How did you manage to lock yourself in there?"

"I didn't. A man did. He hid us when we thought you meant us harm," Sophie said, gesturing for the man to come forward. "I don't know his name," she added with a laugh. "There was no time to find out. He has the key, though."

"I'm sure he *stole* the key," said Krause, contempt in his voice. "Right out of the vestry." He walked up to the gate, then banged on it with the side of his fist. "You in there, Schmitt?" he shouted, peering through the bars.

Sophie shrank back as Krause came close but then reminded herself that he was there to help her.

"Arno Schmitt! Show yourself!" Krause barked. The thief stepped out from behind the coffin. "Give me the key. *Now*," Krause ordered.

Swearing under his breath, the thief approached the gate. He reached inside his jacket, pulled out the key, and handed it through the bars. Krause took it, then snapped his fingers.

A soldier hurried to his side. Krause whispered something to him and the man disappeared up the staircase.

"Captain Krause, what are you doing?" Sophie asked, confused by his behavior and angry at having her command ignored. "Unlock the gate. Prince Haakon and I must ride to Skandinay. Immediately."

But instead of responding to Sophie, the captain inclined his head toward Haakon's. In a voice so low that Sophie could barely hear him, he said, "The road to the village is busy at this time of the evening, my lord. There may be a great many . . . *witnesses*."

Understanding broke over Sophie. She realized that it was still unsafe for her to be seen in the Greenlands. There might well be agents of the queen in the area. The captain was only protecting her.

"We'll have to resort to other methods, then," said Haakon.

He pulled his hand away, but Sophie did not want to let him go. Her fingers scrabbled at his glove. It came off and fell on the floor. As it did, something glinted brightly in the torchlight.

Sophie stared at the glimmering object, bewildered. "You're . . . you're wearing my ring," she said, raising her eyes to his. "Why?"

A sharp, bright stab of possessiveness pierced her heart. Her father had given her that ring. It was for her, the blood heiress, to wear. Only her.

"Baron von Arnim brought it back to the palace," Haakon said, picking up his glove.

"The queen . . ." Sophie said, fear pooling in her belly. "Did she see the ring? Does she know that I'm alive?"

Haakon didn't answer her question. Instead, he asked one of his own. "The boy that was with you . . . Is he here, too?"

"Yes, he is. Will, come out!" Sophie said, deathly worried by what her stepmother might or might not know, and thrown off balance by the abrupt change of subject.

Will was still crouched down behind the sarcophagus. Sophie didn't see him shake his head, then pound the heel of his hand against the stone tomb. He stood, then slowly walked to the gate.

"Haakon, this is Will. He saved my life. We must reward him. I'd like to give him a good horse to get home and some gold."

Will bowed to Haakon. Haakon looked the boy over. "Are there any others?" he asked.

"No," Sophie said, growing impatient with his questions. The sooner she and Haakon crossed the border, the better. "Open the gate and let us out. I want to leave this horrible place."

"I can't do that, I'm afraid," Haakon said with a smile of regret.

Fear skittered across the back of Sophie's neck like a spider. Something wasn't right. "Haakon, what are you doing? Let us *out*."

Footsteps were heard. The soldier who'd run up the stairwell had returned carrying two stoppered stone jugs.

"You can't do this," Will said, looking at the prince.

"Do what?" Sophie asked, her eyes darting from Haakon to Will and back again. "Can someone please tell me what's going on? Haakon, answer me."

Captain Krause was still holding the key. He handed it to Haakon. As the beautiful prince dropped it into his pocket, Sophie had her answer.

FORTY-FIVE

"Haakon, no," Sophie said, blindsided by his treachery. *"No."*

Haakon held out his hand and admired the Ruler's Ring. "After the wolves killed you—"

"Wolves *didn't* kill me," Sophie countered. "Is that what the queen told you? It's not true. She ordered—"

"The details don't really matter, do they?" Haakon asked impatiently. "After you died, I persuaded the queen to name me her heir."

"How?" Sophie asked, wooden with shock.

"She believes the king of the Hinterlands is going to attack her. Her fear of this is so great, she talks of nothing else. I promised to defend the Greenlands with the full might of Skandinay's army—*if* she promised that I would inherit her crown. But now I have a problem—you're *not* dead after all. How can I be heir to the Greenlands' throne if you're still alive?"

Sophie's fear blazed into full-blown terror. She wrapped her hands around the iron bars. "Open this gate, Haakon."

"It's time a man ruled the Greenlands again. I plan to make it part of Skandinay as soon as I take the throne."

Sophie knew she had to dissuade him from his plan. It was her only chance to free herself, Will, and Arno Schmitt. "But you *won't* take the throne, don't you see? Not for years. Decades, even. The queen is still young. She won't relinquish her crown."

Haakon smiled. "Adelaide is such a bold rider. It's amazing that something hasn't happened to her on her gallops through the woods, chasing wolves like a daredevil. She could fall. Break her neck. So easily."

Sophie stepped back from the gate, reeling. "Who *are* you?"

"I am a ruler, Sophie. One who's not afraid to seize the opportunities that present themselves."

"You asked me to *marry* you," Sophie said. "But it was all a lie."

"I *would* have married you. You were an easy means to acquire another realm." He shrugged. "But now I've found a way to acquire two. I plan to marry the princess of Cathay right after I take over the Greenlands. The emperor is old and ailing. He won't be around much longer."

"You told me that you loved me," said Sophie tearfully.

Haakon laughed. Pity filled his beautiful eyes. "Poor, foolish, softhearted Sophie. Still talking about love, even after all you've been through. Love doesn't matter. All that matters is that the girl can breed. I need sons to help me rule my realms."

"I believed you . . . I believed *in* you," Sophie said, her voice breaking. But Haakon was no longer listening. He was glancing at the stairs. Sophie saw she had little time left to convince him to free Will and Arno. "Haakon, spare these two men," she begged. "Let them out. They have nothing to do with this."

"Too much of a risk. They'd talk."

"You can't be this cruel. You can't just walk away and let us starve to death!"

"Sophie, *Sophie*," Haakon said, clucking his tongue. "I'm not going to let you starve. That *would* be cruel. I need to get the job done quickly. No witnesses. No bodies. Nothing to upset the peasants." With a rueful smile, he took a few more steps back from the gate.

"Where are you going? What are you doing?" Sophie asked.

"Captain Krause . . ." Haakon said.

Krause stepped forward. "Yes, Your Grace?"

Haakon handed Krause his torch. "Burn this place to the ground."

FORTY-SIX

With a bow of his head, Haakon turned and walked away, disappearing up the stairs.

"No!" Sophie screamed at his back. "Haakon, don't do this!"

Captain Krause and his men set to work. They unstoppered the two jugs that one of the soldiers had carried down and splashed their contents over the floor and through the bars of the crypts, including the one Sophie and her friends were in. Acrid fumes of lamp oil rose, searing Sophie's nose.

"Please let us out," she begged Krause, weeping. "You can't leave us to die!"

If Krause heard her, he gave no indication. His men followed their orders, and when the jugs had been emptied, they made their way to the stairwell.

Krause paused, waiting for them to leave. As soon as they were gone, he turned and touched his torch to the oil, and then raced up the stairs himself. There was a loud, sucking whoosh as the oil ignited. Will grabbed Sophie and pulled her back from the gate. Blue flames traveled along the floor. They darted into the gated crypts, fed on the wood of the old coffins there, and quickly grew.

And so did Sophie's terror. With their arched stone tops and fiery interiors, the crypts looked to her like giant ovens.

As Will tried to stamp out the flames creeping toward them through the bars, Sophie realized that she was going to die. Slowly and painfully. And Will and Arno Schmitt were going to die with her. She started screaming then and could not stop. Zara, whimpering, paced back and forth.

Will was throwing himself at the gate now, trying to break the bars, or bend them, but they were made of iron and did not give. He found a chunk of stone, one that had tumbled off an ancient tomb, and used it to batter them, but the stone shattered in his hands.

Arno did not scream or throw himself at the gate. Instead, he busied himself at the back of the crypt. Pulling his belongings together. Tucking things into a rucksack. Finishing off a bottle of wine.

"Stop, Sophie, *please*," Will said. "Stop screaming. I can't think . . . I need to think . . ."

"No, keep it up, Sophie. If you could, scream even louder," Arno said. He went back to his work, whistling.

Will looked at him in disbelief. "We're about to burn to death and you're whistling Oompah tunes?"

Arno gave Will a dismissive look. "Foolish is the man who builds a house with one door."

He grabbed hold of a wooden coffin lid and, with effort, pushed it to one side. Will saw a skull and just under it, the rotted lace collar of a once-fine dress.

"Pardon me, darlin'," Arno said to the occupant. He stuck his arm way down into the coffin and scrabbled around, frowning.

"Ah! There we are!" he exclaimed, pulling out a bulging leather sack. He dropped it on the ground. It made a clinking sound. "I'll miss this old place," he said, looking around wistfully. "Quiet neighbors. Nice memories." His eyes fell on Will again. "You might want to start shouting, too, son," he advised, shoving another coffin lid aside. "We need to be as noisy as possible. It'll look suspicious otherwise."

"You're insane," Will said.

The fire was burning hotter now. Its orange tongues darted through the bars. Thick gray smoke billowed into the crypt. As Will backed up to launch himself at the gate yet again, he felt a tap on his shoulder. "'Scuse me, lad. Do you think you could help me move the lid off this tomb?" Arno asked. "It's damned heavy. And my back isn't what it used to be."

"We're going to die!" Will shouted at him. "Don't you understand that?"

Arno smiled slyly. "Not if you help me. Grab the short side," he instructed. "On three, give it a good hard shove. Ready? One, two . . . *three*!"

Will and Arno both pushed the lid with all their might. It slid off the tomb, hit the floor, and smashed into pieces. Will looked inside. There were no bones there. Instead, there was a rickety wooden ladder leaning against one of its inner walls. It led down into a black hole.

The fire was pushing through the gate now and licking at a coffin just past it. The choking smoke swirled around Sophie, blinding her and making her cough.

"Time to go," Arno said. He nodded at Sophie. "Get her, will you?"

212

"Sophie, come on!" Will shouted, reaching for her.

She was coughing uncontrollably. Tears had washed smeary tracks through the soot on her cheeks.

"I'm sorry, Will!" she sobbed. "I'm so sorry!"

"It's all right! There's a way out!" Will said, pulling her to the tomb. Sophie didn't believe him, not until she looked down into the hole.

"Where does it go?" she shouted over the noise of the flames.

"Out!" Arno replied. "Help me with my bags!"

Half a dozen leather sacks, their necks tightly cinched, littered the floor around the tomb. Arno picked one up and dropped it into the hole. Will did the same. Sophie, frightened and dazed, grabbed one, but her hands were shaking so badly, she lost her grip on it. Its side split open as it hit the ground. Jewelry spilled out. Rings. Necklaces. And an earring—still attached to a shriveled black ear. She gave a sharp cry at the sight of it.

Arno smiled sheepishly. "It was dark. I was rushing. Couldn't get the damn thing out," he explained. He scooped the jewelry up and stuffed it, and the split sack, into his rucksack.

Sophie lifted her eyes from the jewels to Arno. The T in his cheek stood out in the orange light. "You're a grave robber," she said.

"We all have our flaws," Arno said. "Pick up those bags now, would you? It's getting a little warm in here."

The fire had devoured the coffin near the gate and had leapt to several others. Flames crackled only a foot away from where the three now stood.

As Sophie and Will hurriedly tossed the rest of the sacks into the hole, and then their own rucksacks, Arno made a torch out of a coffin slat and a piece of someone's shroud. He dropped his rucksack into the tomb, then threw a leg over its side. He found the ladder with his foot and quickly brought his other leg over.

"Follow me," he said.

He was at the bottom of the ladder in no time. Will lowered Zara to him, then told Sophie to climb down. By the time Will was on the ladder himself, the flames were licking at the tomb. He speedily joined the others and found himself in a low, narrow passage, hollowed out of the earth.

"What is this place?" Sophie asked.

"An escape tunnel. Probably made for priests during one religious war or another," Arno said, shrugging into his rucksack's straps. "It was in bad shape when I discovered it. I fixed it up."

"Is it safe?" Sophie asked, looking around uncertainly.

Arno snorted. "Safer than death? Yes." He picked up two sacks, then motioned for Sophie and Will to do the same. "Stay close. Let's go."

The three made their way through the tunnel, crouched low. It was dark. Cold water dripped from the ceiling. After walking for about five minutes, they came to another ladder. Arno climbed the rungs first, then Sophie, then Will handed up Arno's sacks, Zara, and their own things, before climbing up himself. They found themselves in a mausoleum—a large one, about fifty yards down the hill from the church. Shouts, cries, and the whoosh and crackle of a raging fire carried in through the barred door. They all walked over to it. Careful to stay in the shadows, they peered through its iron filigree at the conflagration above them.

The villagers of Grauseldorf surrounded their ancient church, some pressing hands to their cheeks, others crying. Krause and his men, feigning concern, kept the people back from the fire, shouting that it was too dangerous for them to go close.

"I'm staying put for the night," Arno said. "There are too many soldiers around for my liking."

He made himself a bed in a dark corner of the tomb and was soon sound asleep. Will did the same.

Sophie sat down next to them but couldn't sleep. She stayed up all through the night, watching as Haakon rode off with Krause and his soldiers. Watching old men weep as the bell tower crashed down. As the walls caved in. She was still up at dawn, staring at the ruins.

FORTY-SEVEN

The sound of rattling startled Sophie.

She jerked awake. Opened her eyes. Light was pouring into the mausoleum through its windows and door.

She closed her eyes again, trapping vivid swirls of orange and gold behind her eyelids. For a few horrible seconds, she was back inside the crypt as the soldiers set the place on fire. She could see the fire rising, smell the smoke, hear herself screaming.

St. Sebastian's was a smoldering heap of ash and debris now, and so were her hopes, her future. Shame burned inside her, as hot as the flames that had devoured the church, as she realized that her stepmother, the people at court—they were right. She *was* foolish and weak. She'd trusted Haakon, because he was beautiful and dazzling, because he'd spoken a few romantic words to her and made her believe that he loved her. Her heart had been her undoing. Yet again.

Something moved underneath Sophie, jostling her. She became aware that her head was resting on a warm, breathing creature; her arm was slung across it. *Zara*, she thought, hugging the dog for comfort.

But Zara didn't feel like herself. And she didn't smell like herself. She reeked of smoke, but under that there were the scents of pine, leather, lavender, sweat.

Sophie picked up her head. It wasn't Zara she was hugging; it was *Will*. Mortified, she pushed herself up on her arms. She remembered sitting next to him in the dark as he slept. *I must've fallen asleep, then toppled over like a sack of onions*, she thought.

The rattling came again. Sophie blearily looked around. It was Arno. He was moving around the mausoleum, pushing on coffin lids, looking for loose ones.

"Morning!" he called out when he saw her. "Is your sweetheart up?"

Sophie blinked at him. "My what? Who ... *Him?* He's not ... Will's not my ..."

Arno looked at her, still half slumped across Will. He cocked an eyebrow. "Don't worry," he said. "I'll never tell."

Sophie quickly got to her feet. She brushed some imaginary dust off her trousers. Zara, who'd been curled up nearby, immediately settled herself in the warm spot Sophie had left. Will mumbled in his sleep, rolled on his side, and put his arm around the dog.

"Strange arrangement you three have," said Arno. "But who am I to judge?"

He rattled another coffin. "The villagers are gone. The soldiers, too. We might want to get gone as well. Captain Crappy and the pisspot prince think we're dead. Which means they won't be looking for us. That gives us an advantage."

Sophie nodded. Her hair was loose. It stunk of smoke. She bent down to her rucksack and rooted in it for a ribbon so that she could braid it out of her face. As she did, something winked brightly from across the tomb. Arno had pulled the bag of jewelry that had split open out of his rucksack and had placed it on a coffin. Pale rays of morning sunshine bounced off the rings, brooches, and necklaces spilling out of it.

Sophie looked at the ill-gotten goods with disgust, remembering the shriveled ear. Arno saw her eyeing his cache. "Fancy yourself a ruby ring?" he asked.

"I do not," Sophie said distastefully. "You took those from a corpse. You're a grave robber. You steal from the dead. How can you do that?"

Arno snorted. He gave her a scalding once-over. "You're royalty," he said. "You steal from the living. How can you do *that*?"

"I've never stolen anything in my life!" Sophie said, offended.

"You look more like a farmhand than a princess right now," Arno said, walking up to her. "But I bet before the wolves ate you, or whatever the hell happened, you wore silk gowns, diamond rings, and a gold crown, too."

"Yes, I did. What of it?"

"Where'd they come from? You earn them?"

"Well, I . . . It's not as if . . . We don't—"

"How 'bout the castles and palaces and carriages? You earn those?" He bent down to her and drew a T on her cheek with a dirty finger. "Thief," he said, chuckling.

Sophie smacked his hand away, scowling. She rubbed the T off, then resumed her search for a ribbon. Arno resumed his for a hiding place.

Will woke as Sophie was finishing her braid. Their eyes met.

218

"Not a word about handsome princes," she warned him, too raw for any mocking. "Not one."

Will winced at that, as if her assumption pained him. There was a beat of silence, and then he said, "What are you going to do? You can't go to Skandinay now."

"No, I can't."

Her hope of Haakon getting her heart back for her was gone. There would be no army to march upon the King of Crows' castle. Her clockwork heart would wind down. Soon. Probably out in some lonely, godforsaken part of the Darkwood.

"Where will you go?"

"To the Duke of Niederheim's . . . to his castle," Sophie said lightly. "It's not far."

"Did you know that your nose crinkles when you lie?"

Sophie scowled.

"You don't have anywhere to go, do you?"

"No," Sophie admitted, ashamed of lying, ashamed of needing to. But the truth was, she had no one, and it was painful to her. Her whole life, she'd been surrounded by people. Everyone from nurses and chambermaids to powerful dukes and ministers. But she could not trust any of them. They served her stepmother or Haakon now. There was not one person from her old life whom she could turn to.

"You could come home with me. Rest a little. Eat some home cooking."

"I'll come home with you," Arno said. "I could use a little home cooking."

Sophie and Will ignored him. "I can't do that, Will. I almost got you killed last night."

"I'm not afraid of Haakon."

"You should be," Sophie said. "You should be afraid of anyone who wants power as badly as he does."

"Sophie—"

"Will, thank you. Really. But I have bigger problems than Haakon. And I . . . I don't have time to . . . I—"

"I this and I that," Arno cut in. "Maybe it's not about you, Princess Precious. Ever think of that? Are you going to just let that vicious bastard Haakon run this country? If he was happy to burn us alive, what's he going to do to others who get in his way?"

Sophie had had enough of this rude man. "What do you want me to do, Arno?" she asked, getting to her feet.

"Take your damn crown back."

Sophie looked at him as if he'd lost his mind. "Me," she said flatly. "Just me. Without an army. Or weapons. Or a fortress. Just me and my skinny dog. I don't even have two pennies to buy breakfast!"

"Just because you don't have two pennies—or an army—today doesn't mean you won't have them tomorrow."

But I don't have a tomorrow! Sophie wanted to yell at him. Instead, she said, "Arno, you don't know what you're talking about."

"Neither do you, you silly git."

Sophie shook her head in amazement at his effrontery. "You know, maybe I *will* take my crown back. Just so I can have you beheaded."

"You ever stayed in a hunter's house? You know how big it is? What they eat for supper? You might learn something.

220

About your own people. About their lives. Go to the kid's house, for Piet's sake. Can't you see he wants you to?" Arno winked. He held up a hand to the side of his mouth. "I think he's sweet on you!"

Sophie turned crimson. "Oh, my God. Arno, that is so inappropriate. Will's married!"

Will, drinking water from his canteen, spat it out. "*What?* No, I'm not!"

"But you . . . You said . . ."

"I said *what?*"

"You said you had someone at home. Who needed you."

"My *sister*."

"Oh." Sophie's blush deepened. She wanted to fall through the floor.

Arno clapped his hands. "See? I was right! You learned something already!" He shrugged his rucksack on, picked up a sword he'd hidden in the tomb, and took out his key ring. He'd cached his jewelry and was ready to go. A minute later, he had the mausoleum's door open. "Come on, girl. Let's get some venison loin. Dusted with black pepper and coriander. Served with a red currant sauce. Maybe some hasselback potatoes on the side, and braised cabbage."

"How about rabbit stew?" Will asked. "If I'm lucky enough to bag a few on the way?"

"I'll take that, too."

The three walked out of the crypt into the sunshine. Arno lifted his face to the sun. He smiled. Stretched his meaty arms wide. "Ahh!" he said. "It's good to be dead."

FORTY-EIGHT

Sophie knew she was in trouble about a mile from Will's cottage. The ticking in her chest was slow and heavy and had been for the nearly two days' walk. It stuttered, stopped, and then started up again. It wasn't loud—Sophie could only feel it, not hear it—but somehow that scared her even more. She was weak. Her limbs felt as if they were filled with sand. She stopped every now and again to throw sticks for Zara to fetch as she, Will, and Arno walked through the woods, but the playful breaks were a ruse—she needed them to catch her breath and gather strength. She made it to the cottage only through sheer force of will.

As they reached the small, tidy garden that surrounded the humble dwelling, Sophie saw an old woman sitting in the sunshine, carding a basket of wool. A little girl sat next to her. Her eyes were closed; her face was tilted to the fading sun. She was bundled up to her neck in blankets as if it were January, not August.

"Oma?" Will called out. "I've brought friends."

The old woman turned around. Her eyebrows shot up in surprise. Her sharp eyes, the same gray as her grandson's, roved over Sophie and Arno. They lingered on Sophie's scar, peeking out from the top of her shirt, and on the T on Arno's cheek.

The little girl scowled.

"This is my grandmother," Will said. "And Gretta, my sister. Oma, Gretta—this is Sophie, Arno, and Zara."

"How do you—" Sophie started to say.

But she never finished her sentence, because her vision blurred, and she stumbled and fell to the ground. Will and Arno helped her up.

"Heavens! What's wrong with her?" the old woman asked, getting to her feet. "She's as white as a sheet!"

"I don't know," Will replied.

"Quick, boy. Sit her down."

As Will and Arno eased Sophie into Oma's chair, Oma hurried into the cottage. She returned a few seconds later with a bottle of vinegar and waved it under Sophie's nose.

The sharp smell shocked Sophie's heart back into a steady rhythm. "Thank you," she said gratefully. She felt a bit of strength return to her body.

"What's wrong?" Will asked.

"Nothing. It was just . . . just a spell," Sophie lied. "I felt dizzy. I have ever since the fire. It's probably from the smoke." She did not want to tell them the truth—that her heart was winding down. She could barely face it herself.

"Fire?" Oma said. "Smoke?"

"It's a long story," Will said.

Oma gave him a look. "Stray cats. Stray dogs. Now a stray girl and a stray thief," Oma said. "Do you find them, Will? Or do they find you?"

Will chuckled. Sophie looked up and saw that he was holding his sister tenderly in his arms. The girl's limbs were as thin as matchsticks. Sophie had thought she was very young when she'd first seen her, perhaps five or six, but now she realized that the girl was ten or eleven. Her body was wasted. Sophie could see that she was not strong enough to walk on her own.

The girl, her eyes huge in her drawn face, regarded Sophie closely. "Hello," Sophie said, smiling at her.

"You stink," the girl said.

"Gretta!" Oma scolded.

"Well, she does."

Sophie knew she reeked of smoke. And probably worse. It had been a long time since she'd had a wash. "May I use your bathtub?" she asked.

Oma laughed. She hooked her thumb over her shoulder. "You don't have to ask my permission. Our *bathtub* is out there."

Sophie craned her neck. She saw a silvery flow of water burbling behind the cottage. "But that . . . that's a creek."

"Yes, it is. Get her soap and a towel, please, Will. And for yourself and Arno, too."

Arno looked as if he was going to decline the bath, but then he surreptitiously sniffed his armpits and grimaced. Will put Gretta down and disappeared into the cottage.

"But there's no privacy," Sophie protested, still staring at the creek.

"Walk downstream if you're bothered about it. No one to see you there except the deer. The men can bathe upstream. You should make sure to wash the cut on your lip while you're at it. It's swollen. Use plenty of soap on it. And wash your clothes while you're there. You can hang them on the line."

"But they're all I have. What do I wear while they're drying?"

"You can borrow something. I can't have you bringing fleas into the house."

"Fleas!" Sophie exclaimed, mortified. "I don't have—"

"I bet you do," said Gretta, her eyes narrowing. "You look like the type."

"Will!" Oma bellowed. "Bring some old clothes!"

Will came back out of the cottage a few minutes later with everything his grandmother had asked him to get. He handed some things to Sophie, some to Arno.

"Will, did you get a rabbit? Can we have st—" Gretta called out. A fit of coughing cut her question off.

Will knelt down by his sister and rubbed her back. The coughing got worse. Sophie was already heading to the creek. She stopped and turned around, concerned. Gretta wasn't able to catch her breath. Her face was starting to turn blue; her small hands were knotted in Will's shirt. Sophie started back to them, her heart knocking, but as she did, Gretta managed to clear whatever was in her throat. She took a huge gulp of air, then sagged in Will's arms. He carried her into the cottage.

Oma was right behind him, grim-faced. Sophie took a few uncertain steps toward them but then stopped, feeling that she wasn't needed. Or wanted. So she continued on to the creek. When she got there, she saw that someone had dammed it with rocks to create a deep swimming hole. After hanging her towel and the clean clothes on a tree limb to keep them dry, she quickly undressed and dropped her filthy clothing on the bank. Then she waded in, soap in hand. Zara followed her.

The water was so icy it made her catch her breath, but it felt good, too. Especially when she ducked her head under and the water flowed over her swollen lip, numbing it. Nothing could numb the pain she felt over Haakon's betrayal, though. She'd believed him. Trusted him. Loved him, even. At least, she thought she had. She imagined her stepmother's smug satisfaction when Haakon told her that she, Sophie, was truly dead. Adelaide would smile and say what a hopeless fool the girl was, so softhearted, so clueless, so easy to manipulate.

Shame's cold, reedy fingers clutched at Sophie as if they would wrap around her legs, hold her down, and drown her. For a brief, bleak moment, she wondered if she should simply let them. What good was she? To herself? To anyone?

But then she realized something: She had escaped, and neither Adelaide nor Haakon knew of it. Partly through luck, yes—she wouldn't have survived Haakon's treachery if not for Arno—but also through having sense enough to trust a good person—Will—and having the guts to run and hide and fight for her life.

Let Adelaide and Haakon say what they liked. She *wasn't* hopeless. She'd escaped. She was alive. And neither of them knew it.

Emboldened by this realization, Sophie kicked the reedy fingers away. With a noisy splash, she surfaced and sucked in a huge lungful of air. "Who's the fool now?" she whispered.

And then she started to scrub. Sophie's last bath had been taken back at the Hollow, and she hadn't realized how grimy she'd become. She attacked her body with the bar of soap, scrubbing every inch of it and then working a cloud of lather through her hair. When she was done, she pulled her dirty clothing into the water and scrubbed that, too. Then she washed Zara. The dog submitted to the bath but ran out of the water as soon as she could and shook herself off. Sophie followed her out, dried herself off, and got dressed. The bath, the clean clothing— they made her feel as if she'd been reborn.

She carried her wet things back to the cottage and pegged them onto the clothesline. The smell of cooking wafted out of the window. Onions frying in butter. Chopped thyme. Her stomach growled outrageously. No one was in the yard, and the door to the cottage was open, so she went inside. Zara stayed outside to dry herself in the sun.

Will was standing by a big black stove, his back to her, browning pieces of rabbit in a large iron pot. His hair was wet. He was wearing clean clothing, too.

"Gretta? Is she—"

"She's lying down," he said curtly.

"Is she—"

"She's fine."

"Your parents' cottage is very nice."

"It's not my parents'; it's my grandmother's."

"Oh. But are your parents here? Where are they?"

"Dead."

"I-I'm sorry. What happened to them?"

"Death."

"Yes. Well. You know what? That rabbit sure smells good," Sophie said with a sigh, giving up on trying to make conversation. After days spent trudging through the woods with him, she knew better than to try to get him to talk when he didn't want to.

Will reached for a jug of ale. It was silent in the kitchen, except for a loud, steamy hiss as he poured the liquid into the hot pan. Sophie, standing self-consciously with nothing to do, leaned against a cupboard and watched him.

Will's face was flushed from the heat of the stove. She noticed that a tendril of hair trailed down the side of his face, curling like a question mark against his skin. His movements were deliberate and contained. *Like all hunters,* Sophie thought. He was wearing his grandmother's apron over a worn linen tunic and patched trousers. She liked the way it looked on him, the way it had settled on his narrow hips, the way the loosely knotted ties trailed down his backside.

It's a rather lovely backside, she thought, tilting her head to get a better look. As she did, her heart gave a deep, warm purr.

She straightened up, mortified.

Will turned his head. He raised an eyebrow. "Clock?"

Sophie smiled brightly. "Clock."

"You could set the table."

"Yes!" Sophie said eagerly. "I could. I could do that."

What is wrong with me? she wondered anxiously. Her clockwork heart was becoming more and more unreliable, behaving in ways that were totally contrary to her feelings. She didn't care for Will or his backside. Was this, and the spell she'd suffered, signs that the heart was winding down faster than the brothers predicted?

The idea worried Sophie, but she didn't have long to dwell on it. Will pointed to a cupboard. She opened it, found a clean cloth, and spread it over the round wooden table. Next, she set out napkins and cutlery, then decided that some flowers were needed. Taking a pair of scissors from a drawer, she clipped a few blooms from Oma's garden and arranged them in a vase.

Oma, who'd been with Gretta, making her drink a tea she'd brewed from the contents of the packages Will had brought home from the apothecary, now bustled by Sophie with a loaf of bread and a dish of butter for the table. "Quite a night you had in Grauseldorf," she said curtly. "Will told me all about it. And more besides."

"Yes, it was quite a night," Sophie said, uncomfortable under the old woman's disapproving gaze. "We have Arno to thank for getting us out of the crypt."

"Mmm. And I guess we have *you* to thank for getting my grandson into it," Oma said. Then she frowned. "That lip's bleeding again."

Sophie touched her fingers to the cut. They came away crimson.

"It's not going to heal by itself," said Oma.

"It'll be fine, I'm sure."

"I'm not," Oma said, fetching a bottle off a shelf and a scrap of linen. "Sit there," she instructed Sophie, pointing at a stool under a window. "The light's better. I need to see what I'm doing."

Oma steered a reluctant Sophie to the stool and settled her on it. She uncorked the bottle and poured a bit of foul-smelling liquid onto the linen. "Close your eyes," she said to Sophie.

"Does it hurt?"

"Yes."

Oma's concoction burned like liquid fire. "Oh! *Owwwwww!*" Sophie howled.

"Hold still. Don't be such a baby," Oma scolded.

"I *ot* a yayee!" Sophie protested as best she could without using her upper lip.

Tears smarted behind her eyes. Just as she thought they would spill over, she felt a hand slip into hers, rough and warm and strong.

"Squeeze hard," Will said. "That stuff is the worst."

Sophie did and Will squeezed back. And finally, after what seemed like an eternity, Oma finished.

"There. I'm done. It'll heal fast and clean now," she said, pressing the linen to the wound to blot the fresh blood. "Take this. Keep the pressure on for a bit."

"Thank you, I think," Sophie said, opening her eyes and taking the cloth. Her lip was throbbing.

Oma put the bottle back. As she turned around, her eyes went to Sophie's hand. And her grandson's. They were still clasped.

"I'm *done*," she said again.

Will went back to his stew. Sophie pressed the cloth to her lip with both hands.

And Oma walked outside to see where Arno was. As she did, she looked back over her shoulder at her grandson, humming now as he tended the stew. He never hummed. Then she looked at the girl, tilting her head, the better to cast glances in the boy's direction.

Her brow furrowed, she muttered to herself, "Encounters in the Darkwood, thieves, girls in trousers . . . Nothing good can come of this."

FORTY-NINE

Sophie had never smelled anything as delicious as Will's rabbit stew.

He'd brought it to the table in the pot in which he'd cooked it. They were all sitting down, napkins in their laps. Zara had crawled under the table, just in case anyone dropped anything.

After putting the pot down, Will sat, too. Arno was about to reach for a slice of bread, when he saw Oma bow her head. Will and Gretta did the same. Sophie followed suit, and Oma gave thanks for their meal.

As soon as she was done, Will took the lid off the pot, and steam wafted out. Sophie's heart clanked. Oma raised an eyebrow. Gretta, who'd boosted herself up out of her seat and was leaning on the table with her hands, and Arno, who'd done the same thing, were too busy gazing into the stewpot to notice.

"It's a clock," Will said to Oma.

"A small one," Sophie said. "That I keep in my pocket."

Will handed Sophie the ladle, and Sophie, carried away by the mouthwatering aroma, greedily scooped out vegetables, sauce, and a chunk of meat. And then another. And one more. It all smelled so *good*.

Oma looked at Sophie's plate, and Sophie realized she'd taken more than her share of the stew. "I'm so sorry," she said, blushing. She hurriedly shoveled most of it back.

"Food must be very plentiful where you're from," Oma said archly.

"It is," Sophie replied sheepishly.

She was used to food just appearing. Usually on silver trays. Until recently she'd never for an instant considered where it had come from, or what it was like not to have enough of it.

Oma served Arno, then herself and her grandchildren, and then everyone was eagerly eating. Sophie was ravenous. It was all she could do not to shovel the stew into her mouth.

"Will told me and Oma that you're the princess. But I heard the princess died. So are you a ghost, then?" Gretta asked.

Oma snorted. "With an appetite like that? Hardly!"

Gretta's face fell. "So you're *not* a ghost?"

"Not quite. Sorry," said Sophie, with a rueful smile.

Gretta was about to say something else, but before she could, she started coughing again. And just like before, she coughed so hard she couldn't catch her breath.

"What's wrong?" Sophie asked. But Will's and Oma's attention was on Gretta, and they didn't answer.

Luckily, the fit didn't last as long as the one before had.

"It's wasting sickness," Gretta said when she could speak again.

"Hush, Gretta!" Oma scolded, pained by the girl's words. "It is not. It's a bad cold that won't clear. You're under the weather, that's all. A bit run-down. You—"

Gretta cut her grandmother off. "This cottage isn't very big, Oma. I hear you and Will talking at night, you know."

Will said nothing, but he clenched his jaw so hard that a muscle jumped in his cheek.

Sophie's heart twisted painfully. She knew that wasting sickness was a cruel disease that sapped its victims' strength and vitality but took a long time to kill them. "How did you get it?" she asked.

"My mother. She had it. She was getting better, but then the queen took our farm, and she got worse."

"Why did the queen take your farm?"

"She wanted the crops to feed her soldiers. We had acres and acres and grew all sorts of things. My mother was sick before the soldiers came. She didn't last long afterward. And then my father got sick, too. Though Oma says *he* died of a broken heart."

Sophie's own heart felt as if it were breaking apart. It made a slow, thumping noise, like the sound of a drum beating out a dirge. Now she knew why Will had said he despised her, the queen, the palace, and everyone in it—because her stepmother had destroyed his family. Sophie ached for him, for Gretta and Oma, but her sadness was mixed with anger, too. Didn't Adelaide see what she was doing? Didn't she understand that her brutal actions carried terrible consequences for her people? She was so vigilant, so worried about threats from her enemies. She raised armies, built warships—all to keep her people safe. But in doing so, she herself had become their enemy. And what would happen if Haakon had his way and took over the Greenlands? Sophie knew—things would get even worse.

"I am so sorry, Gretta," she said.

"I hate the queen," said Gretta, clenching her fists. "I hate the palace and everyone in it. They take everything, while we barely have enough to eat. I hate you, too, Sophie!"

"Gretta, stop. That's rude," Will said.

Oma's eyes flickered to Sophie. "And dangerous."

"Sophie's not like the queen," Arno said, gnawing on a bone. "She's going to take her crown back. Change things."

"Are you?" Gretta asked, a mixture of hope and disbelief in her voice. Sophie dropped her gaze to her plate. She couldn't answer Gretta. Doing so meant extinguishing the hope in the sick girl's eyes. An uncomfortable silence descended, and as it did, a new kind of hunger gripped Sophie—this one was not in her belly; it was deep down in her faulty heart.

For the first time, Sophie hungered for her throne, and that hunger was so great, it was a physical pain. She hungered to sit straight-backed and regal upon the golden chair and to feel the sweet, somber weight of the Greenlands' crown upon her head. Not so she could frighten ambassadors in a jewel-studded surcoat. Not so she could build the world's greatest armada. But so she could make sure that a pregnant woman was never thrown out of her home. That a teenage boy who'd lost his sight fighting for his country was not discarded like a broken toy. That a young girl had something better to do than cough herself to death.

But Sophie knew it was a hunger that could never be satisfied, and that hurt more than anything that had happened to her. Her heart was not only flawed but failing; every second brought it closer to its final ticktock. And as she grew weaker, her

234

enemies grew stronger. The thought of her people enduring Adelaide's cruelty, and soon Haakon's, filled her with a deep, aching hopelessness.

Oma, staring at Sophie, was silent, the way a simmering pot of milk is silent right before it boils over. She looked at Will and said, "What have you dragged to our door?" Nodding at Arno, she said, "You're a thief, but that doesn't worry me because we have nothing to steal." Then she turned her gaze to Sophie. "But you're a dead princess who's not dead, and that worries me greatly. I heard about you days ago. Word travels fast in the Darkwood. You made quite an impression in Drohendsburg, saving that family from eviction. And those veterans? They'd march to the end of the earth for you." She buttered a slice of bread, then pointed the knife at Sophie. "You gave those people hope, girl, and that's a dangerous thing. There's no greater weapon in the whole world than hope. It's dangerous because it's powerful. And don't think for a second that this prince—Haakon—doesn't know it. If he catches wind that you escaped, he'll be kicking down doors trying to find you. You're going to bring a world of trouble our way."

"Oma," Will said sharply. "Sophie is here because I want her to be. The things that have happened . . . they aren't her fault."

Sophie looked up. "No, Will. Your grandmother's right to be worried. I shouldn't have come here. It's just . . . I was afraid. I wanted a safe place. Only for a few days. A quiet place. A place . . ." Her words trailed off.

"A place to what?" Will asked.

Sophie looked up at him. His gaze, clear and honest, gave her the strength to say it.

"A place to die."

FIFTY

"What do you mean, *a place to die?*" Will asked.

Oma flapped a hand at Sophie. "Never mind, boy. You're not going to get a straight story from this one."

But Will's eyes, as darkly gray as a storm now, were fixed on Sophie. "What do you mean?" he asked her again.

Sophie didn't want to do this. She didn't want to reveal herself, to reveal her heart. Not to Will. He hated her and what she stood for. His whole family did. And yet, that's what his gray eyes were asking her to do. They were challenging her. To be truthful. To trust him. And she knew that if she lied to him, those eyes would be shuttered against her, and for some reason, one known only to her faulty heart, she couldn't bear that.

Taking a deep, steadying breath, she unlaced the neck of her borrowed tunic and pulled it wide open so that he, Oma, Gretta, and Arno could see the angry red scar that cleaved her skin.

Will's gaze traveled from Sophie's collarbone to the top of her breast.

He winced but did not look away. Arno let out a low whistle.

"Ugly, isn't it?" Sophie said. "The story behind it's even uglier. Are you sure you want to hear it?"

"Yes," said Will.

Sophie glanced at Gretta, worried that what she was going to tell them was too harsh for the girl's young ears.

Gretta held up her spoon, brandishing it at Sophie like a sword. "Don't even think about not telling me," she warned. Turning to her brother, she said, "If you put me in my room, I'll listen at the wall."

Will sighed, resigned. "Go ahead," he said to Sophie.

And Sophie did. She told them what had happened to her, starting with her morning ride with her stepmother's huntsman and ending with her escape from Haakon.

"I believed in Haakon. Until he tried to kill me. I believed he would help me get my heart back. Now I'll never get it back, and the one inside me will soon wind down."

It was quiet when Sophie finished speaking. No one said a word for quite some time. No one rose to clear the dirty dishes or the empty pot. Dusk lapped at the windows.

Arno spoke first. "Even if Haakon was on your side, Sophie, I'm not sure he could breach Nimmermehr or best the King of Crows."

"Why not?" Sophie asked. "He would have an army with him."

"Doesn't matter. Many have tried. Kings. Emperors. Warlords. They don't even make it to the moat. The things in the woods . . ." Arno shook his head, at a loss to describe them. "Monsters, ghouls, terrifying things . . . They'll kill you if they get hold of you, but just a glimpse of them sends even the hardest soldiers running for their lives."

Sophie remembered the brothers telling her about the terrifying creatures that prowled the grounds of Nimmermehr and how they were too much for Jasper. His heart had given out at the mere sight of them. She feared greatly for Jeremias and Joosts. A part of her hoped that they'd given up and returned to the Hollow. If kings and warlords couldn't best the King of Crows, how could they?

"How do you know all these things?" she asked Arno.

"I've been there," Arno said. "Not *inside* the castle, but close to it. Rumor has it there's a tunnel—a hidden escape route in case Nimmermehr ever falls under siege. Many castles have them. I wanted to find it."

"Why?" Gretta asked.

Arno shrugged. "Corvus is a king, right? Kings have nice stuff."

"And you're a thief," said Gretta.

"Exactly, my clever girl," said Arno, patting her on the head.

"Arno, who is he . . . the King of Crows?" Sophie asked. "What does he do with the hearts he takes?"

"I don't know. I hear talk, though. People say that the King of Crows is from a foreign land. That he's a monster himself. A ghost. A vampire. People say there are magical spells to repel his creatures and to keep him away, but as far as I can tell, it's all nonsense. I've been to almost every village, town, and city in the Greenlands, and I've never met one person, not one, who has made it into Nimmermehr and lived to tell the tale."

Sophie's fear for Jeremias and Joosts deepened. Her fear for her own life grew, too. It took her a moment to work up her nerve and ask the question she was most afraid to ask: "Do you know if there are spells that can put a heart back?"

Arno hesitated slightly, then said, "I've never heard of one." He quickly added, "But that doesn't mean they don't exist."

Another silence descended. Sophie realized that she'd been fooling herself all along. Even with the might of Haakon's army, she wouldn't have been able to regain her heart. It was hopeless, and it always had been. The knowledge was as inescapable, and as crushing, as an avalanche.

This time, Gretta broke the silence. "I'm sorry I said that I hate you, Sophie."

"Don't worry about it, Gretta. I'd feel that way, too, if I were you," Sophie said.

"Why, Sophie? Why did all this happen to you?" Gretta asked. "Why did the King of Crows take your heart?"

Sophie looked down at her hands. "Oh, Gretta," she said, her voice heavy. "I wish I knew."

"It doesn't seem fair," said Gretta. Sophie smiled ruefully. "No, it doesn't."

"How long do you have before . . . before your heart . . . ?" Will didn't finish his question.

Sophie took a deep breath, then said, "Less than three weeks now, I think. Give or take a few days."

A pall fell over the room. The sadness was palpable. Zara, sensing Sophie's distress, put her head in Sophie's lap. As Sophie scratched behind the dog's ears, a volley of coughing burst from Gretta. Will was immediately at her side.

"I'm not going to bed!" she protested as soon as she caught her breath. "If you try to pick me up, I'll go limp as a noodle, I swear!"

"Calm *down*. No one's trying to put you to bed. Your hands are blue. You need to sit by the fire," Will said.

Gretta let him carry her to a chair by the hearth. Oma said

that she would brew some mint tea to warm everyone. As Will settled his sister and tucked a blanket around her, Sophie and Arno cleared the dishes and washed them, then joined Will and Gretta.

Will stoked the coals, then put a fresh log on top of them. Sophie stared into the flames.

"You're very unhappy, Sophie," Gretta said.

Arno snorted. "That's an understatement."

"I wish you weren't."

Sophie forced a smile. She was about to lie to Gretta, to say that she was fine, when Oma bustled over with the tea. She set the cups down, settled herself in her rocker, and said, "Don't wish Sophie's unhappiness away, child. She needs it. Right now, it's the most valuable thing she's got."

"She does?" Gretta said.

"It is?" Sophie said.

Oma gave a brisk nod. "Absolutely. It's the unhappy people who get things done. Have you ever noticed that? They build things. And discover things. And invent things. Like calculus. Only a very unhappy person could have come up with *that*. The happy ones just sit around eating strudel. They seldom amount to much."

Sophie gave her a sidelong look.

"You don't believe me," Oma said, "but I know what I'm talking about. Have you ever heard the tale of 'The Two Brothers and the Ogre'?"

Gretta clapped her hands. "I love stories!" she crowed.

Oma reached into a basket, picked up her knitting, and started to tell it.

241

FIFTY-ONE

"Once upon a time," Oma began, "there was a wealthy merchant who lived in a prosperous town. He had a beautiful daughter, and two brothers were in love with her. But an ogre loved her, too, and he said he would marry her on Midsummer's Day. If she refused him, he would kill her and everyone else in the town.

"The merchant was heartsick. He told the brothers that whichever of them could kill the ogre could marry his daughter. Both brothers asked Tanaquill, the fairy queen, for help. The elder, who was handsome and charming and always laughing, asked for a bag of gold and a jacket of yellow silk. He didn't need the jacket, it had nothing to do with his plans to kill the ogre; he just thought yellow looked good on him. Tanaquill granted his request. The younger brother was plain. He was also well-read and clever but so shy and quiet that no one knew it. He asked for a bag of gold, too, but not a yellow jacket. He thought that was pushing it. But all the fairy queen gave him was a ball of twine.

"How the townspeople laughed at him, standing in the square with a ball of twine in his hands. His own brother laughed at him.

242

"The younger brother felt hurt and humiliated. All his life, his older brother had been preferred over him. All his life, the world had underrated him. Why should now be any different? His dazzling brother would win the merchant's daughter; of course he would."

"This is the worst, most depressing fairy tale I've ever heard," Will said.

"I haven't finished yet," Oma retorted. "As the younger brother stared at the ball of twine, it seemed to mock him," she continued. "It seemed to be everything he was—plain and rough, with no charm and nothing funny to say. Angry and heartsore, he walked to the river and threw it into the water. But just as he turned to walk away, the ball of twine hopped out of the water and rolled to a stop at his feet.

"The younger brother was very unsettled by this, so he ran away, but the ball of twine rolled after him, growing bigger as it did. It rolled in front of him, blocking him no matter which way he tried to go.

"Scared now, the younger brother kicked the ball of twine away, over and over, but it rolled back every time. Growing bigger. Rougher. Uglier. Until it had become a monster. The boy punched it again and again, fighting with it, struggling against it, trying to escape from it, but he only managed to get himself hopelessly tangled up in it.

"Exhausted with no hope of getting free, the young man wept, ready to give up. On winning the merchant's daughter. On making something of himself. On everything. His heart ached so badly.

"That's when the ball of twine started to speak to him. This is what it said:

Run from me and you will see, I never go; I only grow.
Turn your back and I'll attack.
I'll knock you down, drag you around. But stand and face me,
let me speak, And I'll reveal what you must seek.
Your path, your way, the fork, a ford,
No more *from*, only *toward*.
The task is hard, but you are smart. Bold and brave and
strong of heart. And never forget when all is done:
Monsters can't chase unless you run.

"As the twine spoke, each tangled skein that held the boy down
slowly loosened until he was free. And then it shrank down,
becoming only a small ball again, still and silent in his hand.

"Now, while the younger brother had been fighting with
the twine, the elder brother had used his gold to buy cannons.
He'd arranged them around the ramparts of the town's wall
so that he could fire on the ogre the instant the horrible
creature was sighted. But several days passed, and no ogre
came. The elder brother, who was spoiled and not used to
things not going exactly the way he wanted them to exactly
when he wanted them to, grew bored, so he bought ten
barrels of wine with his leftover gold. He threw a party, got
drunk, and strutted all around the ramparts in his yellow
jacket.

"The younger brother, meanwhile, had grown hungry but
had no money to buy food. There was a forest outside the
town, though, so he used his ball of twine to fashion a snare,
caught a hare, and roasted it. The meat filled his belly and
gave him strength. When he finished, he reset the snare so

that he might eat again the next day, and as he did, he got an idea.

"That very evening, the ogre came. The elder brother was so drunk he never even saw him approach. But the ogre saw the elder brother. How could he miss him? The fool stuck out like a lemon in his yellow jacket. The ogre snatched him up and bit his head off. Then he squeezed his body like a wineskin and drank all his blood. But as the ogre was draining the very last drop, a rock hit him in the back of his head. Furious, he threw the elder brother's body down and turned around.

"The younger brother had thrown the rock, and as the ogre stomped toward him, he threw another one. It hit the ogre smack in the middle of his face and broke his nose. Roaring with fury, he chased the boy. Which was just what the younger brother wanted. He led the ogre—who was shouting and cursing and holding his gushing nose—through the woods to a ravine. When he got to the very edge, he turned around and pretended to be afraid. The ogre grinned. Step-by-step he drew closer to the boy, all the while telling him how he was going to rip off his right arm and eat it, and then rip off his left arm and eat it, and then—*TWANG!*

"The ogre, blinded by his rage, had stepped into a snare the younger brother had set for him. A loop tightened around his ankle, and the next thing he knew, he was dangling upside down. The boy grabbed him by his greasy hair, cut his head off, and brought it to the merchant. The merchant promptly presented the boy with his daughter and called for a minister to come and marry them on the spot, but the boy politely declined. He said he would only court the merchant's daughter

245

if she wished him to, for he knew very well what it was like to have to take what you were given whether you wanted it or not. The girl agreed. They courted, fell in love, and were married within the year. Weeks after the boy killed the ogre, he went back to the spot where he'd set the snare to search for the ball of twine. But it was gone. He never saw it again. He never needed to."

Oma smiled; she rested her knitting needles in her lap. "The end," she said. Then she looked at her sleepy-eyed granddaughter. "And now, miss, it's time for bed."

Gretta protested but only half-heartedly.

"Wait, Oma . . ." Will said. "Is there a point, any point at all, to this weird and gruesome story?"

"Yes, boy, there is." Her eyes found Sophie. "We must not run from our unhappiness. We must listen to it. It has much to tell us."

Will rolled his eyes. He got to his feet, picked Gretta up, and carried her to bed. Oma told Arno he could sleep on the floor in Will's room and gave him some bedding. She gave Sophie a pillow and a quilt, too, and told her she was welcome to sleep up in the loft, which was opposite the hearth.

Sophie thanked her. She turned toward the ladder that led to the loft, but Oma placed a hand on her arm, stopping her.

"So you thought a handsome prince was going to save you?"

Sophie gave her a bitter smile. "I guess I did."

"What does a queen need with a prince?"

"You mean my stepmother? Making Haakon her heir? I don't know why she—"

"No. I mean you."

Sophie tilted her head, puzzled by Oma's words. "But I'm not a queen."

"But you could be," Oma said, pinning Sophie with her steely gaze. "Adelaide's not your biggest enemy. Or Haakon. *You* are. They can tell you everything you're not, but they can't make you believe it—only you can do that." She released Sophie. "You want your heart back, girl? Go get it." And then she left the room to tend to her granddaughter.

Sophie watched her go, thinking about what she'd said. Then she climbed the narrow ladder and found herself among ropes of garlic, bunches of herbs, several salamis, and a large ham. After clearing a space on the floor, she made herself a comfortable place to sleep from her bedding. She cast a last glance down at the room below her to make sure Zara was all right but saw that she needn't have worried; the dog had curled into a ball on a soft rug in front of the hearth.

Sophie was exhausted but couldn't sleep. Her head was full of images. Of rampaging ogres. Of talking, tangled balls of twine. Of a sad boy who didn't have money, or an army, or weapons to defeat a fearsome adversary. Who had only himself.

Lying still, staring out of the loft's small window at the night sky, Sophie listened. Not to the whispers and the mocking laughter of the court. Not to her stepmother's lectures, her dire predictions, her threats. Not to Haakon's murderous goodbye. But to a voice inside that was small and tired. Tired of hiding. Of pretending. Of always being

247

wrong. It was hard to listen to the voice. It was painful. Silent tears rolled down her cheeks. But Oma was right; that voice had so much to tell her.

Sometime before midnight, Sophie made up her mind. Then she closed her eyes, and finally, she slept.

FIFTY-TWO

The fire had burned low, but its dim light illuminated Oma. She was wearing a white nightdress; her gray hair trailed over her shoulder in a long, loose braid. She was rocking Gretta by the fire. The child had woken in great pain. Oma had carried her from her bedroom to the hearth, where it was warm.

The little girl was suffering. Her body was rigid. Her eyes were squeezed shut. Oma reached for a cup on a nearby table that contained medicine and, with some difficulty, got Gretta to drink from it. It helped. After a few minutes, Gretta's body relaxed a little and she was able to lie down in a trundle bed that Oma had made up near the fire. She kept hold of her grandmother's hand, though, listening as Oma sang her a lullaby.

Finally, the child fell asleep. Oma gently withdrew her hand from Gretta's and pulled the child's blanket up around her shoulders. The old woman sat down again in her rocker, leaned her head back, and closed her eyes. Worry deepened the lines in her forehead and the hollows in her cheeks.

From the shadows, a figure emerged—a woman dressed in black, with wild hair and wilder eyes. She peered at the little girl's face with an expression of tenderness and sorrow, and then she touched the child's cheek. As she did, the silvery tears still clinging to the girl's skin turned to pearls and fell to the pillow.

Gretta groaned. She shifted in her sleep. Zara heard her. The dog was still curled up on a rug by the hearth. In an instant, she was on her feet, growling low in her throat.

Oma sat up and looked at Zara; she followed the dog's gaze, and then she and the visitor locked eyes. The woman in black retreated, melting back into the shadows.

"Hiding, are you?" Oma asked her. "I would, too, if I were you, given the damage you've done in this house."

The woman bit a thumbnail, her expression turned baleful.

"You're following the princess, aren't you? Why? What interest does she hold for you? Perhaps you simply enjoy tormenting her, but I think there's more to it. Why does your brother want the girl? Is she a threat to him? Is it possible that he, the King of Crows, fears her?"

Oma rose, picked up a poker, and prodded the logs in the fireplace.

Flames curled their thin fingers around it.

"Ah, who can understand you or your ways. I doubt even you do." She nodded at Gretta. "A chest full of pearls couldn't make up for what you've done to this child. People say what doesn't kill you makes you stronger. And sometimes that's true," she allowed. "But sometimes what doesn't kill you makes you wish to God it had."

She sat down again. "The princess will have to face him, and she may well end up a pile of bones like all the other poor souls who get lost in these woods. And the world will grow a bit darker when she does. Perhaps that's what you want, you and your brother both."

Zara whined. She walked over to Oma and put her head in the elderly woman's lap. Oma scratched the dog's ears, her eyes still on the visitor.

"I suppose you can't help who you are. None of us can. That girl sleeping in the loft cannot help who she is, either. Scared. Lost. So full of doubt. Maybe she is what her stepmother says she is . . . too soft, too kind. Led by her heart."

Oma looked down at Zara. Her lips curved into a small, defiant smile. "And if she is, what of it?" She chucked the dog under the chin. "Too small to kill a wolf, eh? But only a small dog moves fast enough to kill a snake. Sometimes the thing that makes us all wrong is the thing that makes us perfect."

When she looked up again, the woman was gone.

FIFTY-THREE

The queen sat on the floor, staring into her mirror.

Her hair cascaded down her shoulders. Her eyes were sunken and dull. She seemed to grow thinner with each passing day, as if she were being devoured from the inside.

There was no reason for it. She had gotten rid of the princess. She had made a strong, bold man her heir. Together they would invade the Hinterlands before the king of that realm attacked the Greenlands. All was as it should be, and yet Adelaide was more afraid than she'd ever been. It seemed as if the more she tried to diminish her fears, the bigger they grew.

She looked nothing like the young girl she was watching in the mirror. That girl was straight-backed and strong, with a general's bearing. The only thing they shared was a sadness in their intelligent blue eyes. The girl was sumptuously dressed and richly bejeweled. She was standing at an altar with a man who was twice her age.

Her brother, the king, beamed from his seat in the royal chapel. He was happy about the marriage and the alliance it afforded him. He was even happier to be getting rid of Adelaide. She had saved his life, saved his kingdom, and as soon as he'd turned eighteen, he'd thanked her by marrying her off to a man who did not love her, a man with a dead wife and a young daughter.

"Mirror, mirror on the wall . . ." Adelaide whispered.

". . . who's the fairest of them all?" a voice whispered back. A voice that sounded like footsteps in the dark, rats in the wall.

The King of Crows appeared. He knelt down beside her.

"Your own brother put that story about, didn't he? He said that you were vain. That you constantly asked the mirror *Who's the fairest of them all?* instead of *Who will bring about my fall?* He did it to diminish you. Because he was jealous. You were ten times the ruler he could ever hope to be. The king of the Hinterlands is fond of telling it. The emperor of Cathay, too." He peered into the glass. "Words spoken. Words written. In them, you find the story. But in the shadows they cast, you find the storyteller."

With effort, Adelaide tore herself from the images in the glass and faced him. Her weary eyes met his bright, busy ones.

"But you didn't summon me to talk about the past, did you?" he asked. "You wish to talk about the present."

Adelaide nodded. "I am uneasy. Unsettled. I can neither eat nor sleep."

"There is a reason for it, and you sense it. I know you do. The princess still lives. The snakes did not kill her. She's in the Darkwood, making her way to Nimmermehr. She must be stopped."

The King of Crows's words sparked anger in the queen. Dark flames burned behind her eyes. "Tell me how," she said, rising from the floor.

The king rose with her. "Take this," he said, drawing something from his pocket. "Find the girl and give it to her."

It was a large haircomb, exquisitely carved from jet, in the shape of a scorpion. The creature's eyes were faceted rubies. Its pincers and the sharp stinger at the end of its curved tail were black diamonds. The gems gleamed in the firelight.

"Hurry," the King of Crows said, putting the comb into the queen's hands. "The girl must not make it to Nimmermehr. She must not find her heart."

There is the sound of beating wings, and then he's gone. The queen trembles. Why, she does not know. For a moment, she feels breathless and weak, as if the king took from her all that is strong and sure. She stands tall, reminds herself that she holds the power. She summons this pale king, and he does her bidding.

But who is the real master here? Who grows powerful, and who grows weak?

Adelaide slips the comb into her pocket. She calls for her cloak. She calls for her horse.

As her ladies scurry to and fro, she presses a hand to her chest. Over her heart.

As if reassuring herself that it's still there.

FIFTY-FOUR

Will saw the note as he walked into the kitchen.

Sophie had left it on a chair, on top of the clothing she'd borrowed and the bedding she'd used, all neatly folded.

Dear Oma,

I'm going to get my heart back. And then I'm going to get my crown back. I have no idea how I'm going to do either of those things.

Yours, Sophie

PS—thank you for supper and for a nice, warm bed. Please tell Gretta goodbye, and tell Will thank you. I'm sorry to leave without saying goodbye in person, but I fear I'll lose my nerve if I see your kind faces. I'll miss you all. Even Arno. Please take care of Zara for me.

Oma came into the kitchen, carrying a pail of milk from their cow, as Will finished reading the note.

"What did you tell her?" he demanded.

"That if she wants her heart back, she should go get it."

"I can't *believe* you, Oma! You told her to go to Nimmermehr by *herself*? She won't make it within a mile of the place. She'll die!"

Oma shrugged. "She'll die if she doesn't go, too. Better to try than to just give up, don't you think?"

Will shook his head, muttering to himself. He put the note down, then returned to his room.

"Uh-oh, Oma," said Gretta from her chair by the fire. "Now you've done it."

Oma waved a hand at her. "He's just sulking. He'll get over it."

Gretta shook her head. "He's not, and he won't."

She was right. Ten minutes later, Will was back, his rucksack in one hand. Arno was right behind him. Zara danced a circle around the two men, yipping.

Oma looked up from the pan of bacon she was frying. "No," she said. "You're not going after her."

"Yes," said Will. "I am."

Oma glared. "Why don't you look for your own heart while you're at it? Seems to me someone took *that*, too."

"I have to go. She's all by herself. Someone's got to keep her from getting lost."

Oma laughed. It was not a happy sound. "You're the one who's lost, boy. She's a princess. You're a pauper."

"Really, Oma? I had no idea. Thanks for pointing that out."

"Say by some miracle you do get her heart back, then what? I'll tell you—"

"Thought you would."

"—she marries some king, and you're right back here."

"Right back here's not so bad."

Oma heaved a sigh of resignation. "Be careful, boy. We need you, too."

Will put an arm around his grandmother and kissed the top of her head. "I'll be back before you know it."

Oma dipped a hand into her pocket. "Here, take these. You can sell them for a few coins along the way. You may need some money."

She took his hand and put three pearls on his palm.

"Where did you get them?" Will asked, surprised.

"An old friend gave them to me," Oma replied.

"You ready?" Arno asked. "There's a nice graveyard just past the Black Hills. A fancy one. With roomy mausoleums. I can get us into the Schneiders' vault if no one's changed the lock. We should get going, though, if we want to make it there by nightfall."

"You're going, too?" Oma asked him.

"Think I will. It's been a while since I was over Nimmermehr way. Got someone I want to say hello to there."

Oma made bacon sandwiches for Will and Arno, then wrapped up one for them to take to Sophie. She also packed a loaf of bread, salami, cheese, and fruit for them. Then the two men left, and Oma and Gretta stood in the yard, watching as they walked down the path from the cottage into the woods.

"Sophie's wrong, Oma," Gretta said.

"About what, child?"

"About the queen. She didn't try to kill Sophie because she thinks she's weak. Or foolish."

"No? Then why did she do it?"

Gretta thought of the dirty, skinny girl she'd met. The girl with a scar running down her chest, bite marks on her arms, and smoke in her hair.

Then she said, "Because she's afraid of her."

FIFTY-FIVE

Sophie swung her rucksack off her shoulders, put it on the ground, and knelt down by a clumpy green plant.

"Stag*leaf* is safe to eat ... stag*wort* turns your tongue blue ..." she murmured, reaching for a broad green leaf. But then, instead of breaking one off, she drew her hand back, frowning. "Or was that the other way around?"

She bit her lip, wishing she'd paid more attention to Will's woodland lectures. She did remember that he'd said it was very important to forage all the time to build up your supply of food and to not wait until you were hungry. So far, she'd gathered two handfuls of hazelnuts and some angel wing mushrooms. All she'd taken from Oma's kitchen was a thick slice of buttered bread and two apples, and she'd already eaten the bread.

Deciding that a blue tongue was better than starving, Sophie picked the leaves. She had experienced terrible hunger after she'd fled Drohendsburg, and she knew that if she wasn't careful, it would kill her before the King of Crows ever got a chance to.

Sophie had left Oma's cottage only an hour ago, just before sunrise, and already she was missing its snug four walls. The tidy kitchen. The cozy hearth. The loft, with its collection of provisions for the coming winter. It had been hard to leave it, just like the Hollow. Everything about the little house spoke of thoughtfulness, care, and love.

The forest Sophie was walking through was magnificent, with its ancient trees, its rich scents of evergreen and earth, and its soft, mossy hush, but it was boundless and unknowable and made her feel small and vulnerable. Every animal—from the fiercest wolf to the tiniest mouse—had a den or bolt-hole, and she? She had nothing. Nowhere to shelter, nowhere to hide. No fellow wolves or mice who cared if she was hungry or cold.

As Sophie broke off a few more leaves—never take the whole plant, Will had told her—she wondered if she would ever know the feeling of home again. What she'd felt at Oma's cottage—it was more than the comfort of a good meal and a warm bed. Around the old woman's table, with Will, Gretta, and Arno, Sophie had felt as if she was being seen, truly seen, for who she was, for who she could be. Maybe for the first time in her life.

Snatches of her conversation with Oma returned to her now.

But I'm not a queen . . .

But you could be . . .

It didn't matter what her stepmother believed about her. Or Haakon.

Or, for that matter, what Arno and Oma believed.

It matters what I believe, she thought. *I'll never get my heart back, and my crown, unless I believe I can.*

259

Sophie sat back on her heels, clutching a handful of stagleaf, and looked up at the vast blue sky. "But do I?" she asked aloud. The sky had no answer for her.

With a sigh, she unbuckled the top of her rucksack and tucked the leaves inside it. She was just about to fasten it again when she heard it—the sound of a branch snapping. She froze.

A voice carried through the woods, low and quiet. And then another.

Men's voices.

Sophie crouched low, trying to make herself small, to stay unseen. The voices could belong to Krause and his soldiers. To Haakon. To robbers. She looked around wildly. There was a stand of shrubby evergreens about ten yards away. If she could get to it in time, she would be safe. Once she was inside the dense branches, no one would be able to see her. Slowly, quietly, she started to rise, determined to not make a sound. Eyes straight ahead, she never saw her assailant coming.

The force of the impact knocked her to the ground. It happened so quickly that there was no time to cry out. She landed on her back with a thud, smacking her head. Stars exploded behind her eyes. She tried to sit up, but there was a weight on her chest. Hot breath, steamy and rank, gusted in her face. Drool dripped onto her cheek. Sophie's vision cleared. She saw a furry snout. Big teeth. A lolling tongue. Her attacker whined, then barked in her face.

"Zara!" Sophie exclaimed. "I told you to stay with Oma! How did you get out?"

Zara barked again. Sophie pushed the dog off herself and sat up.

"You found her!"

"Good girl!"

Sophie knew those voices. "Will! Arno!" she called out as the two of them appeared. "What are you doing here?"

"Thought I might call for tea at the King of Crows's castle," Arno said grandly. "See how the other half lives." He hooked a thumb at Will. "And him? He's sweet on—"

Will quickly cut him off. "That's right. I'm sweet," he said, his cheeks coloring a little. "And sweet people do sweet things. Which is why I'm here. To do a sweet thing."

Arno shot him an exasperated look but said nothing.

Sophie shot him a puzzled one. *Sweet* was not a word she would have used to describe Will. She was touched and happy to see them both, but she was worried, too. "You weren't supposed to come," she said. "Oma needs you, Will. Arno, Captain Krause thinks you're dead. What if someone sees you and tells him that you're not? I can make it to Nimmermehr by myself."

Arno snorted. His eyes had dropped to the leaves sticking out of Sophie's rucksack. They moved to the half-picked plant. "Is that so?"

"Yes, that's so," Sophie replied indignantly, irritated by his tone.

Will peered at the plant, too, his face tight with concern. "Did you eat any of those leaves you picked?" he asked.

"No."

Will's expression softened. "Whew."

"Why?" Sophie asked, her brow crinkling. "Stagleaf's good for you. You said it was."

"That's not stagleaf. It's purgebush."

"Purgebush?" Sophie repeated. She'd never heard of it.

"Um. It fixes . . . *things*," Will explained, flustered and blushing again.

"What the boy's trying to say is, it's good for constipation. You eat all those leaves you picked, and you'll have the trots for a week!"

It was Sophie's turn to blush. She quickly dug the leaves out of her rucksack and left them on the forest floor. By the time she'd buckled the bag closed again, Arno was already back on the path, disappearing between two trees. "Hurry up!" he yelled. "Or we'll miss the finger sandwiches! I hope the King of Crows made us some scones, too!"

Will fell in behind him. Sophie threaded her arms through the straps of her rucksack and followed them.

"Will . . ." she called as she started down the path. Will turned; he raised an inquisitive eyebrow.

"Thank you. I—I know you don't care for . . . for royalty . . . for *me* . . . but I'm grateful for your help."

It seemed as if her words hurt him, for pain sliced across his face. Sophie had no idea why. He took a few steps toward her as if he were going to say something. For a moment, she thought he was going to tell her that she was wrong, that he *did* care, and her heart whirred softly, but then he abruptly stopped. Ran a hand through his hair. Looked away.

Finally, he did say something. "I care about my sister, and you're her last best hope." And then he hurried to catch up with Arno.

Sophie stood there, stung. A little embarrassed. And angry—at herself. *What did you expect?* a voice inside scolded.

She wanted some impossible things—her heart, her life, her palace, her crown.

But as Sophie watched Will disappear into the woods, she knew that any hope she had of this strange, silent boy caring for her the way she'd begun to care for him was the most impossible thing of all.

FIFTY-SIX

It was noon when Sophie, Will, and Arno crossed the road.

They'd been together for the last five hours, ever since the two men had caught up to her.

As they'd walked, Arno had told them that he thought it would take them four or five days to get to Nimmermehr, and that the King of Crows's castle was hard to find. The path that led to it was hard to follow and disappeared completely in places. He also warned them about the monsters again.

"There are all kinds of trolls there. You've got your mud trolls, of course," he said knowledgeably. "Your fungus trolls. Rock trolls. Ask me, though . . . worst of them all is your well troll. They live deep down in abandoned wells. And I swear, the smell alone will kill you dead."

"What else?" asked Will.

"Might see some makabers as we get close. They hunt for unburied dead. They like to take things from the bodies. Fingers and toes. Noses, too. They're more disgusting than dangerous, but they'll rush at you if you come close to a corpse they've claimed. They don't want you to steal it."

"As if," Will muttered.

"We might run into some wunschfetzens, too."

"What are those?" Sophie asked.

"Wunschfetzens? They're gray, drippy, mopey little creatures, with big sad eyes. They like damp places. They cling to ceilings in caves and basements with their long fingers, then drop down on your shoulder and stick those long fingers into your ears. They pull memories out of your head and make them seem real. You see someone you loved. A parent, long dead. A girl who married someone else. A brother you haven't spoken to for years. You're so happy to see them, you don't even question why they're there. You just follow them blindly as they lead you into a swamp or off a cliff. You're a goner if you encounter a wunschfetzen by yourself, but if there's someone with you, he might be able to draw the thing off with sweets. The little bastards love them."

Sophie shivered at Arno's descriptions. She thought of Jeremias and Joosts. What if one of these horrible creatures had gotten hold of them? They'd be lost in the Darkwood forever.

After another hour's walk, the three had come to a narrow road carving through the forest. They were surprised to see a caravan of people—at least two hundred of them—making their way down it. At first, Sophie thought they were simply villagers returning from a market day or a fair, but as they drew closer, she saw that they looked more like refugees than townspeople.

Some walked. Others rode in carts piled high with household goods and pulled by tired horses. They were thin and dirty. Some were coughing. Children straggled along at the edges of the group. A man was pushing an elderly woman, who was too frail to walk, in a wheelbarrow.

Sophie stopped him. She asked him his name and to tell her what had happened.

The weary man barely picked up his head as he spoke. "Name's Max. One of our townspeople discovered gold in our river. The prince—Haakon—he heard about it and turned us all out. His soldiers took over the village. Now all our gold goes to the queen's coffers, and we walk the roads, begging. Do you have anything you can spare? A bit of food?"

His defeated expression told Sophie that he'd been turned down many times and expected no help from her. But as Sophie put some hazelnuts into his hand, amazement replaced the hopelessness in his eyes.

"It's you! It's the princess!" he exclaimed.

He grabbed the woman next to him. "Look! It's her! It's the Princess Sophia."

Awed gasps and murmurs rose.

"It's her! She *is* alive!" a woman said.

"The stories are true!" a man shouted.

One by one, the people dropped to their knees. They bowed their heads.

"Hail to the princess!"

"Hail!"

"Long live the princess!"

Sophie felt seared by shame. She didn't deserve the honor they were showing her. There was nothing she could do for them, no help she could give them. Her clockwork heart stuttered painfully in her chest.

Arno moved close to her. She felt him put something into her hand. "Give it to them," he said. "Go."

Sophie looked down at what she was holding. It was a leather sack. She knew what it contained—stolen goods. Part of her wanted to hand it back, but she knew the jewels inside it would pay for the use of a farmer's barn to shelter these people. It would buy food, medicine, and clothing.

She took Max's hand and bade him rise. Then she gave him the sack of graveyard jewels. "For you and your people," she said. "Feed them. Find them shelter."

The man looked at her questioningly, then opened the sack. His eyes grew wide when he saw what was in the bag. A cry escaped him.

"Thank you, Your Grace. Thank you!" He handed the bag to the man next to him, took Sophie's hand, and kissed it.

A few others had gathered around. They saw the jewels. Word quickly moved through the crowd.

"God save you, Your Grace!"

"God save the princess!"

A woman with four children burst into tears. A man smiled at his elderly father. A boy with six young siblings clustered around him closed his eyes and exhaled.

And Will looked nervously down the road. "We've been standing here awhile, Sophie," he said quietly. "Krause and his gang of killers could be anywhere. It's time to go."

"We'll never forget this, Your Grace," Max said, releasing Sophie's hand. "One day, we'll help you."

Sophie smiled, moved by his words. He meant them, she knew he did, but what help could these poor people offer her? Some of them could barely stand. Others would not last the week.

"Take good care of them, Max," she whispered as she watched the people resume their trek.

Then she, Will, and Arno disappeared back into the Darkwood.

FIFTY-SEVEN

"Could we stop and rest for a few minutes?" Sophie asked, trudging behind Will. She was thirsty and drenched with sweat. Her feet ached. Her heartbeat was erratic. She'd started to feel weak and dizzy again. Two days had passed since she, Will, and Arno had met Max and his fellow refugees, and they'd been walking ever since, only stopping to sleep when it was too dark to see the path. "Will? Could we stop . . . *please*."

Head down, her attention fixed on her feet, she didn't see that Will had come to a halt and that he was looking at something just off the path. And so she crashed into him. Headfirst and hard.

"Oh! *Ow!*" she shouted, staggering backward. "Why did you do that?" she asked crossly, rubbing her forehead.

"Do what? Stop? Maybe because you asked me to?" Will replied. "Look . . ."

"At what?"

He pointed at a patch of dark purple blooms growing near a rotting log. "Foxflowers."

Sophie scowled at them. "You almost fractured my skull for *those*?"

269

"They're very beautiful. And useful. If you press the petals to a bug-bite, they take away the itch." He gave her a quizzical look. "Don't you know these things? What do they teach you in princess school?"

"Nothing useful," Sophie muttered.

At that moment, something inside her heart—a gear or wheel—caught on something else and made a high scraping noise. Sophie's chest tightened; she struggled to draw a breath. Her body became rigid.

"What is it? What's wrong?" Will asked, reaching out to steady her.

A few seconds later, whatever had caught shuddered free, and Sophie slumped against him, gulping air.

"Same thing that's always wrong," she said when she could speak again. "I have a faulty clock for a heart, and it's winding down."

Worry clouded Will's face. He shaded his eyes and squinted at the sun. Its rays, slanting through the leafy branches, threw shadows across the ground.

"The day's growing long. We're going to have to pick up the pace if we want to make the next graveyard by nightfall," Arno said as he caught up to them. "Otherwise we're sleeping under the stars again."

"Sophie needs a break," said Will. "Let her rest for a few minutes. I'll hunt for our supper. It'll save us time when we reach the graveyard. I've been seeing lots of rabbits."

"Rabbit *again*?" Arno echoed, making a face.

"What's the matter, Arno? Are you tired of rabbit? All right, then. I'll just shoot us a standing rib roast instead. Medium rare. How does that sound?"

"If only," Arno said longingly. "I'll go with you. Maybe I can find some juniper berries to flavor the meat. Mushrooms. Some wild thyme. A fine Burgundy."

Will shot him a look, then turned back to Sophie. "Will you be all right by yourself?" he asked, releasing her.

Sophie said she would, then sat down at the base of a birch tree, unscrewed the top of her canteen, and took a long drink of water.

Will dropped his rucksack on the ground, then took off into the woods with Zara at his heels. Sophie lowered her canteen and tried to slow her breathing, which was still too fast and too shallow. The frightening spell she'd just had reminded her of something she'd rather forget: that she had a little over two weeks to steal her old heart back, return to the Hollow, and hopefully find someone with magic strong enough to put the heart back where it belonged.

Thinking about how fast her time was running out didn't help Sophie's breathing, so she shook the dark thoughts from her head. Will and Zara had not yet disappeared from sight. She liked Will's easy, loping walk. He moved through the trees as effortlessly as the wind. She knew that he would only hunt for rabbits. They'd seen all manner of woodland birds as they'd walked—pheasant, grouse, quail, partridge—but Will wouldn't shoot them. He loved birds, he'd told her, and couldn't bear to kill them.

Sophie thought, yet again, how very grateful she was to Arno and Will for going with her to Nimmermehr. Arno hadn't exaggerated when he said that the trail was hard to follow. She would've gotten hopelessly lost on her own. As her breathing finally began to ease and Will walked out of view, Sophie looked around. They'd covered a lot of ground since they'd left Oma's cottage, and with every step they took, the Darkwood seemed to grow darker.

The pines were shaggier and impossibly tall. Thick moss, so darkly green it was almost black, carpeted rocks and stumps. During the day, crows screeched in the treetops, fern fronds beckoned in the breeze, and large, warty-backed toads blinked from under rotten logs. At night, moths with feathery antennae swooped down to the campfire, beating their jewel-tone wings, clouds of bats emerged from hidden caves, and animal eyes glowed eerily green in the darkness. Sophie and her friends had slept outside last night and had had to take turns keeping watch, for Will had seen wolf tracks. It would be good to find shelter tonight, even if that shelter was a tomb.

Sophie leaned her head back against the birch tree. She closed her eyes. The break from walking was doing her good. After a few minutes, she heard a branch snap, and then another. Footsteps crunched through the layers of dead leaves on the forest floor. *Will and Arno must've gotten lucky*, she thought. *They're back already.*

"What took you so long?" she teased. "Did you get lost?"

"Yes, I'm afraid so."

That wasn't Will's voice. Or Arno's. Sophie's eyes snapped open.

A strange man was standing a few yards away.

FIFTY-EIGHT

Sophie was on her feet instantly.

She grabbed her rucksack, ready to run with it.

The man took a step back.

"I-I'm sorry," he stammered, holding his hands up. "I didn't mean to frighten you. I heard voices. I've lost sight of the path and was hoping that you could tell me how to find it again."

Sophie relaxed slightly. "Where are you trying to go?

"Grauseldorf. I'm hoping to get there by tomorrow night."

"It's not exactly close," Sophie said. "It's going to take you a few days." The man looked so dispirited at her words that Sophie felt she had to say something to cheer him up. "You're on the right path. It's just hard to see it from here." She pointed back the way she'd just come, at a group of poplars. "It becomes easier to follow on the other side of those trees."

The man nodded. "Thank you," he said as he adjusted the heavy rucksack on his back. Sophie saw that he was thin. He looked as tired as she felt.

"Are you hungry?" she asked.

The man shook his head at Sophie's question, but his refusal faltered as she produced a bag of plums. Sitting back down, she gestured for him to join her. "I'm Sophie," she said, handing him a plum.

"Rafe," the man returned, with a smile.

"Have you come far?" she asked, setting the fruit on the ground.

"A fair distance," he said. He hooked his thumb behind himself. "I live back that way. Deep in the woods. With my wife."

"Why are you going to Grauseldorf?"

"To sell my wares. I'm a woodcutter by trade, but I carve, too, to make a little extra money. I have figurines to sell. Candle holders. Snuff boxes. Trinkets for ladies. I'll show you." He dug in his rucksack, frowning, squinting, moving things aside. "Ah, here we are. This one's very striking," he said, pulling out something small and wrapped in muslin.

He unfolded the cloth and placed what was inside it into Sophie's hands. She caught her breath. It was a haircomb, carved from jet, in the shape of a scorpion. Never had she seen a piece so finely made. The comb's teeth were long and impossibly thin, designed to sit atop a coiled braid or a twist. The scorpion was perched above the teeth, so lustrous and lifelike, Sophie half expected it to move. Its powerful pincers were raised, its tail arched high above its head.

"It's incredible," she marveled. "You're very talented."

Rafe smiled, pleased by her praise. "I'm hoping it will fetch a pretty penny, even though I hate to sell it. I wish I could keep it. My wife loves it."

"I can understand why," Sophie said wistfully, remembering all the exquisite combs she'd owned when she lived at the palace. It seemed like a lifetime ago.

Rafe had placed the muslin cloth on the ground between them. Sophie carefully laid the comb back down on it. As she did, he bit into the plum she'd given him. "Delicious," he said. "Thank you." He asked her where she was going.

"Schadenburg," Sophie said evasively, referring to the village nearest to the King of Crows's castle. She did not wish to share her real destination with a stranger.

Rafe made a face. "Why? It's a dreadful place."

"I have business there," Sophie said.

"I'd advise you to get it done as fast as you can."

There was a sudden, skittering noise behind them, like mice moving through dead leaves. Sophie startled a little. She looked over her shoulder but didn't see anything.

"Squirrels, I imagine," Rafe said. "Collecting nuts for the winter. Summer's on the wane."

A breeze moved through the trees. It tickled Sophie's neck. A shudder ran down her back.

She reached for a plum. As she did, her gaze fell on the muslin cloth. The carved scorpion was gone. She was certain she had laid the beautiful carving down on it. She hoped nothing had happened to it.

"Where did your comb go?" she asked, anxiously looking around for it.

Rafe unsheathed a slow, sharp smile. "Right where it belongs," he said.

As the words left his mouth, Sophie felt something scuttle up her neck. She gave a cry and tried to pull whatever was crawling on her off, but large, jeweled pincers parried her hands. One sliced into her finger.

Sophie screamed.

The carved scorpion had come to life. It was crawling up the back of her head, its tail arched, a glistening green drop of poison hanging from the tip. It raised its tail high, then struck.

Instantly, the venom spread though Sophie's body, burning like acid. She screamed and writhed, trying to pull the scorpion off, but the creature had grown. It was the size of a weasel now and had tangled its legs in her hair. *Foolish girl . . . too soft, too weak . . .* it hissed.

The scorpion's poisonous words pierced Sophie's heart. As she struggled, the creature stung her again and again. Its venom began to take effect, slowing her movements. She rolled onto her back, her breathing labored, her heartbeat heavy and slow. She could see Rafe. He was standing over her, looking down. She could see something she hadn't before—that his eyes were an indigo blue. That his hair was long and flowing. That he wasn't a man at all, but a woman.

The scorpion crawled down the side of her face, across her collarbone, and perched on her chest, pausing in its attack as if listening, waiting.

Sophie watched it, unable to move. Her lips worked, but no sound came out.

The queen looked down at her. Her eyes glittered as she spoke. "Aim for the heart. Make sure the girl dies for good this time," she instructed the creature. "She must not get to Nimmermehr."

The scorpion raised its tail. And struck deep.

FIFTY-NINE

"Sophie, we're back! I got two rabbits. Sophie?" Will shouted.

His voice sounded as if it were coming from deep underwater. Sophie forced her eyes open. Her vision was blurred, but she could make out Will's form.

She heard swearing, shouting. Will threw the rabbits down. In a heartbeat, he had an arrow nocked and aimed. But it was hopeless; he couldn't hit the scorpion without hitting her.

He drew his dagger from its sheath and swiped at the creature, but it was faster than he was, and it stung his hand. Will swore. He sucked the venom from the wound and spat it out.

"Sophie!" Arno yelled, thrusting his knife at the scorpion. "Fight the poison! Stay awake!"

"Can't . . ." Sophie murmured. "Too hard . . ." Her eyes were closing again. Her limbs felt so heavy.

Zara tried to kill the scorpion, too. The fleet-footed hound charged. She feinted to the left and attacked on the right, but she was no match for the fierce creature. It was twice as fast as she was, and more than once its stinger grazed the dog, raking bloody lines in its side.

"Draw it toward you, girl!" Will shouted at her. "Distract it!"

Zara tried, lunging and snapping at the creature, forcing it to face her and turn its back on Will. As it did, Will grabbed the end of Sophie's long braid and swiped his dagger through it, close to her head. As he pulled the severed braid free, the scorpion came with it.

Arno tried to stamp on it, but it darted out of the way and scuttled back toward Sophie.

"No!" Will cried, valiantly trying to block it.

The scorpion sunk its stinger into his calf. Will shouted in pain. His leg buckled. As he fell to the ground, he saw the thing crawl up Sophie's shoulder.

"Quick, Zara, try again," he said to the dog. "It's going to kill—"

The rest of his words were cut off as a streak of gold shot by him, snarling and snapping.

The attack came so fast, the scorpion had no time to defend itself. The large, brawny wolf lunged at the creature, bit down on one of its legs, and tore it off. The scorpion squealed in pain. It turned to strike, but the wolf had already jumped back. Shaking its head, it sent the leg flying. Then it advanced again.

The scorpion thrust its pincers at its enemy. As it did, a second wolf, this one black, grabbed another of the creature's legs and tore it away. The scorpion was yanked sideways. It lost its balance and almost fell off Sophie. Then a third wolf, this one with a tawny coat, joined the fray.

Tottering on its remaining legs, shrieking, striking out blindly, the scorpion didn't see the fourth wolf circling, the fifth, or the sixth. Piece by piece, they tore it apart until only its tail, twitching impotently on the ground, remained.

Will staggered to Sophie, sat her up, and leaned her against the trunk of a tree. "Wake up, Sophie," he said, gently slapping her cheeks. "Come on . . . Wake up!"

But Sophie, heavy as a sack of grain, toppled forward into his arms. Then a seventh wolf, with a gray coat, silver eyes, and a ragged ear, walked out of the woods. She held a branch in her mouth. Slowly, warily, she walked over to Will, but he was still frantically trying to rouse Sophie and didn't see her. The wolf pawed at the ground, but still Will didn't look up. Then she dropped the branch and barked at him.

That got his attention. He turned from Sophie to see the animal standing only a few feet away. She lowered her head and nudged the branch toward him.

"Waspbane," Will said, looking at it. His raised his eyes to the wolf's. "Will it work on scorpion stings?"

The wolf tilted her head.

"Of course it will," he hastily added. "Why else would you bring it to me?" He gently lowered Sophie to the ground. "Think, Will, *think* . . ." he said to himself. "Crush the leaves . . . No, wait! Make a mud paste first."

He ran to his rucksack and pulled a tin plate out of it. Then he raked dirt off the forest floor and heaped it onto the plate. He poured a little water over the dirt and stirred it with his finger. Under the wolves' watchful eyes, he stripped the waspbane leaves off the branch, crushed them in his fingers, and added them to the mud. The broken leaves oozed white liquid that smelled like rotten eggs. Together he and Arno rubbed blobs of the slimy mixture on every welt they could see. In no time, Sophie's face, head, and neck were covered with it. Will rubbed a bit on the sting on his own leg, too, and on Zara's side.

The waspbane worked like magic. The paste changed from brown to green as it drew the poison out. Slowly, Sophie's eyes opened, but they were unfocused. She sucked in a deep lungful of air. "Get it off me! Get it off!" she screamed, her hands scrabbling at her head.

"It's all right. The scorpion's dead," Will soothed. "Sophie, it's all right."

Sophie blinked at him. Her eyes focused. "Will?" she whispered, clutching at him.

"I'm here."

Sophie sat up and looked around, her heart heaving. She saw the wolves, all seven of them, sitting in a semicircle. Their leader sat at the center. "What are they doing here?" she asked.

"They killed the scorpion. And saved your life."

"But how . . . ? Why . . . ?" Sophie started to say. Then the leader stepped forward and Sophie saw the silver eyes, the ragged ear, the patch of white at her throat. "It's *you*," she whispered, remembering the hunt, remembering how the poor creature had been cornered.

The wolf raised her head. She let out a series of long, high yips. The others joined in, and then they all turned tail and disappeared into the Darkwood.

"I saved her life once," Sophie said.

"She just returned the favor," said Arno.

Sophie lowered her face into her hands. "It was so awful," she said.

"What happened?" Will asked.

Slowly, Sophie released him. Then she recounted how Adelaide had appeared, disguised as a woodcutter. As Will and Arno listened, their expressions, already grim, darkened.

Arno sat back on his haunches. "She knows you're going to Nimmermehr," he said. "I bet he knows, too—the King of Crows. I bet he had a hand in *that*." He pointed at the scorpion's remains. "He's going to be waiting for us. With all his monsters." Frowning, he looked up at the sky. Dusk was starting to edge the day away. "We need to get going, folks," he said. "I don't want us sleeping in the woods tonight. By the time it's dark, we need to be inside a safe, cozy crypt."

Will and Arno stood. They got Sophie to her feet, too.

Arno frowned at her. "If you want to make it to Nimmermehr, you need to do something . . ."

"What?" Sophie asked.

"Stop being stupid."

Sophie blinked at him, offended. "I beg your pardon?"

"People come out of the woods and pretend to be your friends. They offer you something—laces, a comb—and you take them. Stop it. Stop taking poison from fake friends. It'll kill you."

Sophie felt a lump rise in her throat. She tried to swallow it down. "Fake friends are the only kind I've ever had. I've never had a real friend. Not one."

Will, rubbing another blob of waspbane on Sophie's chin said, "Well, you've got some now. Even though you have tons of ugly red spots all over you."

"*Tons* of spots? Seriously, Will?"

He nodded.

Arno chimed in. "And even though you have no hair."

"What?" Sophie said. Her hands flew to her head. They told her that what Arno had said was true. "M-my hair," she stammered, horrified. "What happened—"

"I cut it off. I had to," Will said. "The scorpion was tangled in it, and I was trying to get it away from you. But even though you have no hair . . . Even though you're covered in slimy mud . . ."

"I have no hair," Sophie echoed in shock.

"And even though you really, really stink . . ."

"Wait . . . That smell is *me*?"

"Even though all those things, Sophie . . . I'm here," said Will. "And so is Arno."

Will finished smearing mud on her chin. Then he caught her gaze and held it.

"I guess that means we're your friends."

SIXTY

Sophie glanced over her shoulder. The von Stauffenzee mausoleum loomed in the distance, its white marble glowing so brightly in the moonlight that it would be easy to find her way back to it. Arno was right; the woods were no place for them tonight, and she didn't want to get lost in them.

Zara at her side, Sophie walked well into the trees to relieve herself. Her gait was slow. Everything hurt. The bites from the scorpion throbbed. Her muscles ached from all the walking she'd done. But it was her heart that hurt most of all. The encounter with her stepmother had left her despondent and scared.

The clockwork inside her was winding down, her stepmother and the King of Crows wanted her dead, and her only hope of survival—a castle called Nimmermehr—was surrounded by murderous creatures who would never let her pass. She was her people's only hope, and she had no idea if her unsound heart would even let her live through the night.

It seemed to Sophie that the deeper she traveled into the Darkwood, the more afraid she became—afraid that her quest was an impossible one, afraid that she would die in the woods, just as Jasper had.

And then what? Her mind answered the question for her, torturing her with images of Captain Krause brutalizing the villagers of Drohendsburg. Of the wounded soldiers succumbing to hunger and cold over the coming winter. Of Will and Oma standing by Gretta's grave.

The images were still swirling in her head as she stepped out of the trees, and she was so preoccupied by them that she almost didn't see the woman, dressed in black, standing at the edge of the graveyard.

With a jolt of recognition, Sophie stopped short. She'd seen her before; she was certain of it. Where had they met? Why couldn't she recall her name? Arno's warning echoed in her head. *Stop being stupid*. The woman could have been sent by the King of Crows. She could be her stepmother, disguised again.

"Do I know you?" Sophie asked, taking a wary step back.

"Everyone knows me," the woman said. She cocked her head, her red-rimmed eyes taking in the welts on Sophie's face and neck. "Do they still hurt?"

Sophie nodded, bewildered by this strange woman. *Where* had she seen her?

"The stings will heal. In a day or two, the pain will be gone. But the ache in your heart? That pain will never go away."

Sophie felt her whole body go cold. "How do you know—"

The woman didn't let her finish. "The pain will follow you as long as there is one hungry child in the realm. One family without a home. One sick man shivering by a fire. That pain is a queen's burden, one she must bear until the day she dies. Are you certain you want this burden, child?"

"Why are you asking me this?" Sophie demanded, spooked by the woman's ability to see inside her.

"Because sometimes I help," the woman replied. "You have a powerful weapon in your possession. But it takes courage to wield this weapon. A great deal of it. Do you have such courage?"

Sophie's heart raced. "What weapon?" she asked, looking around. "Where is it?"

The woman laughed mirthlessly. "Do you still not know?"

"No, I don't. What is it? Tell me, please." Sophie's excitement grew at the thought of having something, *anything*, to use against the King of Crows.

The woman stepped back, shaking her head. "You must find it for yourself."

"No, wait! Tell me! You said you help!" Sophie cried, crestfallen.

The woman smiled sadly. Sophie saw that her teeth were black. "Sometimes, but not always."

Then the woman turned and started to walk into the Darkwood. She'd only taken a few steps, and already she was fading into the gloom. "No!" Sophie shouted, desperate to keep her here, to find out about the weapon. She ran after her, reached for her. As her hand closed on the woman's arm, she felt a shock of pain move through her entire body. She staggered back, eyes closed, gasping.

When she opened her eyes, the woman was gone, and she was alone. Zara came running out of the woods and stood next to her, wagging her tail.

Sophie pressed her palm to her forehead. "There's no one

here," she said, a tremble in her voice. She wondered if her faulty heart was making her hallucinate now.

"Sophie!" a hushed voice called out. "Sophie, where are you?"

It was Will. He was walking toward the woods, trying to be as quiet as he could, to not alert anyone who happened to be passing by the graveyard to their presence.

"I'm coming!" Sophie called back. She got to her feet and looked around once more. "Did I imagine her?" she whispered. "I must have."

But as she hurried to meet Will, she felt something wet on her right hand, the one she'd used to reach for the woman. She turned it over and bit her lip.

Her palm was smeared with blood.

SIXTY-ONE

It was dark and quite late. Owls were on the wing, hooting softly as they flew over the mausoleum. Mice were scurrying in its dark corners.

The building was more like a mansion than a tomb. It had high, soaring ceilings, stone benches, and even a fireplace for winter funerals.

Arno had started a small fire, and the flames had chased the chill away. Sophie was warm and safe; her stomach was full. Will had made a delicious dinner of rabbit with wild sorrel. She should've been asleep long ago, but she was not. She was sitting on her bedroll, her arms wrapped around her legs, her chin on her knees, staring into the fire, brooding.

She'd wiped the blood off her hand before Will noticed it and attended to the long, thin cut on her palm once she'd gotten back inside the mausoleum, but the image of the woman, and the things she'd said, were haunting her.

Arno was whittling a figure of a fox with his knife. Will, stretched out on his bedroll, was looking up at the marble ceiling carved with figures of angels and saints.

"Should make Nimmermehr in two more days, if we set

287

a good pace," Arno said, taking a slug of brandy from a flask.

Neither Sophie nor Will replied.

"What's wrong? Somebody die? Heh-heh," said Arno, glancing around at all the von Stauffenzees, whose busts stood on pedestals and whose names were carved into the walls.

No one responded to that, either, but Will turned his head toward Sophie.

"Why aren't you sleeping? Is it because you're in pain from the scorpion?" he asked.

Sophie, still gazing into the fire, said, "No. It's because *they're* in pain. Because they're hurting. And hungry. And cold. Because they have nowhere to go."

"Who?"

"The soldiers. Max. The Beckers."

"You should get some sleep. You can't do anything for them tonight," Will said.

She looked at him. "Can I do anything for them ever?" she asked, doubt in her voice. "What if I don't make it? Chances are I won't. And I've dragged both of you into this fool's quest, too. What if something happens to you, Will? Where does that leave Oma and Gretta?"

"What if something happens to *me*?" Arno interjected.

"I'm scared," Sophie continued. "Not for myself. For them. I'm all they've got. *Me*." She gave a bitter laugh. "And I'm not up to the task."

Silence descended. Most people would have filled it with platitudes and empty promises of success, but Will and Arno weren't most people.

"If you can't fail, then don't fail," said Will.

Sophie squeezed her eyes shut. "Not helpful, Will," she said.

"Hey, want to hear a story?" Arno asked, trying to lighten the mood. "Good!" he said, when no replied. "This one's called 'The Maiden in the Tower.'" He took a deep breath. "Once upon a time, there was a girl who listened," he began. "She listened to all the people around her—parents, relatives, friends—as they told her about all the dangers in this world and the many harms that could befall her.

"Why, by just venturing into town she could be trampled by a runaway carriage, carried off by an invading army, or fall into the river and drown. On the other hand, if she stayed in the house, lightning could strike it and set it on fire. A tree could fall and cave the roof in. The girl grew very scared, afraid to venture out, afraid to stay in, afraid to do anything.

"'Not to worry,' the people said. 'We will keep you safe.'

"They were all carrying heavy bricks. They told her to build four strong walls around herself. Then they stood in line and handed her their bricks, one after the other.

"'Dolls,' said the first one as he gave her his brick.

"'Leeches,' said a second.

"Those bricks were followed by others—blue cheese, dentures, pirates, olive loaf, the Black Death. One by one, the girl took the bricks and laid them around herself in a neat square. She added another row and then another. The heavy bricks locked themselves together. Higher and higher she built the walls, standing on her tiptoes, until finally she could reach no farther.

"The girl smiled when she was done. Nothing could get in. Not through those sturdy brick walls. But neither could the girl get out. She'd built the walls so fast she forgot to make a door. She was safe from all the scary things in the world, yes. But she was safe from other things, too. Roses. Music. Sunsets. Peaches. Books. Pancakes. And kisses.

"She cried out to the people who had handed her the bricks, but they were gone. She was alone. No one could hear her. Frantic to free herself, the girl tried to climb the walls but only succeeded in bloodying her hands."

"What happened to her?" Sophie asked.

"She starved to death, slowly and painfully, staring up at the sky through the open top of her self-made prison."

Will drowsily said, "That is the second worst fairy tale I've ever heard."

"What a terrible ending," said Sophie, flopping back on her bedroll.

"Isn't it?" Arno said cheerfully. "I love fairy tales. They give it to you straight. Nothing the maiden was afraid of killed her; fear itself did. There's a lesson in that story."

"Yeah, there is: Fear is a lousy architect," Will mumbled.

"No," said Arno. "That's *not* it. Don't you see? People carry the heavy bricks around with them their entire lives. They burden themselves. They hand the bricks off and burden others. When all they need to do is put the bricks down."

"So what do we do? Build nothing? Live in a tree?" Will asked.

"How do we protect ourselves?" Sophie asked.

"Protect yourself? From what? Pain? Suffering? Misery? Loss?" Arno asked.

"Yes," said Sophie. "All those things."

"Plus rain, snow, and squirrels," Will added. Then he pulled his cap down over his ears and turned onto his side.

Sophie turned onto her side, too, with her back to Will. There was a good half foot of space between them. "Good night, Arno," she said. "Thank you for a truly awful story."

"My pleasure," Arno said, taking another slug of brandy.

Soon Will's breathing evened out and deepened. Sophie's did, too. Arno stoked the dying fire, then continued whittling. As the little fox took shape in his hands, Sophie twitched in her sleep. She dreamed. Of the girl who'd bricked herself up. In her dream, she was the one standing inside the tower. But the cries she heard weren't her own. They belonged to her people. Desperate to help them, she searched her small prison for a weapon—a knife, a sword, a bow and arrow, *anything*. She had a weapon. The strange, pale woman had said she did. So where was it? Frenzied, she dug in the dirt and clawed at the bricks until her hands were ripped and bloody, and as she did, she thrashed in her sleep, whimpering and moaning.

Arno leaned toward her to wake her. But he didn't need to. For Will, mumbling in his sleep, had rolled onto his back. Sophie whimpered again. "Shh," Will said. He turned toward her and threw an arm across her. "Shh," he said again, never waking.

Sophie stopped thrashing. Her body relaxed into his, her back against his chest. Zara rose from her place by the fire and walked over to Sophie. She turned in a circle several times, then nosed at Sophie's arms, which were folded in front of her. When the nudging failed to make Sophie move them, Zara pawed at them. As Sophie lifted one arm to push her away, Zara wormed under it and settled herself against Sophie's chest. Sophie mumbled something incomprehensible, then wrapped her arms around the dog. A moment later, all three creatures were sleeping deeply.

Arno chuckled. "How do we protect ourselves?" he whispered in the light of the glowing embers. "Ah, Sophie. The answer is right in front of you."

SIXTY-TWO

Sophie opened her eyes.

Will's face was only inches from her own. His arms were around her. Hers were pressed to his chest. She could feel it rising and falling, could feel his heart beating.

How did this happen? she wondered, but she didn't move away. The ground beneath her was cold, and he was so warm. The sound of his breathing soothed her. And the weight of his arm across her body felt sweet.

The silvery dawn light washed over him, highlighting the landscape of his face—his high cheekbones, the line of his jaw, his nose with the slight bump in the bridge. His closed eyes were in shadow, but she could see his dark lashes, sooty against his skin. The stubble on his chin. His lips.

Her heart purred softly. *He is lovely*, she thought. *So lovely.*

Sophie knew she needed to wake up. And sit up. She needed to remember who she was and where she was and what she had to do. But not yet. Not yet.

Just one more minute, she thought, nestling in closer to him. She allowed herself to imagine always being this way with him. What it would be like to hold him the way he was

293

holding her. To run her fingers through his hair, cup his face in her hands, kiss his lips.

It would never happen. The crown had taken his farm, killed his parents, made his sister sick. How could he ever forgive that? Forgive her. He hated everything she stood for, and she was falling in love with him.

Sophie sighed. Her eyes fluttered closed. And then Will licked her.

From her chin, across her mouth, then over her nose to her forehead, leaving a trail of slobber on her skin.

Sophie gasped. She sat bolt upright. "*Will!* That's disgusting. How—how *could* you?"

"What?" Will mumbled, opening his eyes.

"You *licked* me!"

Will blinked. "Have you lost your mind?"

And then it happened again. A long pink tongue trailed over Sophie's face, from her cheek to her ear. The lick was followed by a whine. And then a bark. Zara had to go out.

"Call me when there's coffee," Will said, yawning. "Drink some yourself. Then maybe you can tell the difference between me and a dog." He rolled over and closed his eyes.

Sophie blushed, embarrassed. Her heart made a noise that sounded like a wheel coming off a cart. Will pulled his blanket over his head. Zara whined again. She paced to the door and back.

"Hold on, girl. I'm coming," Sophie said, getting to her feet. She planned to follow Zara into the woods.

The fire was burning high, stoked with windfall gathered from the forest. Arno was nowhere to be seen. Sophie walked to the iron door and saw that it was ajar. Cautiously, she pushed it open. It squeaked loudly.

"You can come out," Arno said. "There's no one else here. This is a lonely graveyard."

He stood a few yards away, his back to her, watching a group of swallows fly. Sophie bade him good morning, and then she and Zara ran into the trees. When they returned, Arno was talking to the swallows. Several of them had lighted on nearby gravestones. They tilted their heads this way and that, regarding him with their quick, curious eyes.

"You speak to them so kindly, so warmly," Sophie said, joining him. "As if they were children."

"They *are* children. Swallows carry the souls of dead children. Don't you know that?" he asked her. "Haven't you ever watched them fly? So different from other birds, swooping and soaring out of sheer happiness. Just like children do. Haven't you ever wondered at that?"

Sophie didn't answer. Because just then the birds all took off from their gravestone perches at once, chirping and calling, flying low, like children running together over a field. Her heart pounded and clanked so hard she thought it would shake itself apart. She'd never seen anything so beautiful.

One swallow lighted again. On top of a very small gravestone. Sophie read the name carved on it. *Mattias Schmitt.*

She turned to Arno, stricken. "Your son," she said.

Arno nodded. "I came to say hello to him. He was three when he died. Fever. I was a carpenter but had no work. All the trees for miles around had been taken by the crown to build barracks. So I robbed a rich merchant to pay for a doctor, but it

295

was too late." He touched the horrible mark on his cheek, then said, "Matti died. I was caught. The queen's justice was served."

Sophie's heart slipped a gear, stuttered, and then found its rhythm again.

"Getting caught, getting branded . . . None of it stopped me," Arno continued. "It just made me smarter. An old woman was buried the same day Matti was. A wealthy widow. Went into the ground with a pound of gold on her. She never helped anyone when she was alive." He smiled. "She did when she was dead, though. She helped a child who took sick after Matti died. So did many others who lie here. The living can be so cold, so callous. But the dead? Ah, the dead are happy to help."

Sophie remembered how Arno had slipped the bag of jewelry into her hand to give it to the refugees. "You give it away, don't you?" she said. "You use it to help people."

Arno fell silent for a moment. He and Sophie watched the birds wheeling high above them. She remembered her harsh words in the crypts of St. Sebastian's when she'd seen what was in Arno's sacks and realized how he'd gotten them. She knew what it felt like to be judged.

"I'm sorry, Arno," she said.

Arno turned to her. "You want to find your heart, girl?" he asked softly. "Watch a child die for the lack of a few coins. Do that, and you might start to understand a few things, like the difference between a theft and a crime."

He walked away then, through the graves and back inside the tomb. The swallow flew up from the gravestone and landed on Sophie's shoulder. He chirped at her, then took off again.

As she watched the bird go, Sophie thought about many things. About seven brothers, once strangers to her, who had saved her life. About little Mattias, lying dead beneath her feet, and sickly Gretta, who might soon join him. About a grave robber with a bag of dusty jewels and a heart of pure gold. About a pretty boy who'd told her pretty things and made her believe them. About another boy, who was silent and strange but here. With her. When he had every reason not to be.

Love is a fearsome thing.

It is braver than generals, stronger than fortresses. It opens graves and pulls rings off corpses. It sits up through the long, lonely night with a failing child. It fashions hearts out of scraps and bits and rusty things and makes them beat on, no matter how many times they break.

"Coffee's ready!" Arno bellowed from the tomb's doorway. "Come eat some breakfast, Sophie. We need to get a move on. It's still a ways to Nimmermehr."

The three ate, then packed up their gear. Arno locked the crypt, and they set off. Zara ran ahead of them, veering off through the grass to chase squirrels.

As Sophie walked along, bringing up the rear, she watched Will. *A powerful king has taken my heart*, she thought. *But a penniless boy has stolen it.*

Will didn't know. He didn't know that he'd slept with his arm around her. That they'd breathed each other's breath all night. That she'd wished a thousand impossible things about him.

He didn't know.

And he never would.

For love is fearsome, and Sophie is frightened.

As the three left the graveyard and entered the Darkwood once more, a crow lighted on a high branch.

He tilted his head from side to side, watching Sophie. He saw sadness in the set of her shoulders. Uncertainty in the knots she'd made of her hands. He saw longing in her eyes.

He nodded. As if he knew her thoughts. As if he knew her fears.

And then, quietly, he flew away. Heading west in the gray light of dawn.

Toward Nimmermehr.

SIXTY-THREE

The King of Crows was angry.

His coat swirled behind him like smoke as he paced the queen's chamber. "The princess is becoming a heroine to her people," he said.

"*My* people," Adelaide said.

"Not for much longer. In every market square, in every public house and town hall, people talk about a rebel princess, an avenging angel come back from the dead to help them. And you?" He pointed a taloned finger at her. "You do *nothing*!"

"That's not true! I have the prince looking for her, and the captain of my guards. I've tried myself to kill her—twice!"

"And failed twice," Corvus said. He reached into his coat, drew something from its folds, and placed it on a table.

Adelaide arched an eyebrow. "An apple?" she said.

"A poisoned apple," said the king. "She is nearing Schadenburg. Go there. Put it within her reach."

"How? She'll be wary of strangers now. I won't be able to convince her to take anything from me again."

"You won't need to. She'll take it herself."

Adelaide hesitated, gripped by doubt. "She grows strong, Corvus," she said at length. "Perhaps stronger than either of us."

A lethal red rage flared in the depths of the king's black eyes. He waved his hand in front of the mirror. An image swirled and shimmered in the glass. It sharpened.

"Look, Adelaide," he commanded. "*You* are strong. Have you forgotten?"

Adelaide faced the glass. In it, she saw a girl of twelve. She was running down a long hallway. Her hair was loose. Her eyes were filled with fear. Blood stained her cheek. It dripped down the front of her dress.

With a cry, Adelaide turned away from the mirror, unable to bear the image and the memories it brought.

"You survived that day," Corvus said. "I helped you. I never abandoned you. Not once in all these years. And now I'm warning you . . . This is your last chance."

Adelaide bristled at his words. "*I* summon *you*. You serve *me*," she countered hotly. "You would do well to remember that."

The King of Crows smiled coldly. "Are you certain?" he taunted. And then he was gone.

Adelaide walked to her mirror. She touched its gilded edge. It was ancient. It had stood in her father's palace for centuries. As she gazed into its depths, the girl appeared again. She was just a child. Alone. Afraid. Turning in a frantic circle. Adelaide watched as the girl caught sight of herself in the silver glass. She heard the hitch in her throat, the racking sobs. *I don't know what to do . . . Help me . . . Somebody please, please help me . . .*

The King of Crows had heard her pleas. And he'd answered. He was the only one who ever had.

The girl pressed her palm to the glass. Adelaide did the same. Then she turned and picked up the apple.

SIXTY-FOUR

The scarecrow hung like a corpse on its wooden pole.

Its head sagged forward. One arm dangled limply at its side. The other, still attached to its cross pole, pointed east—the way Sophie, Will, and Arno had come.

As if it's telling us to go back, Sophie thought uneasily.

They walked past the scarecrow, past a tumbledown church and a cluster of rickety houses. Dingy curtains twitched in windows; pinched faces loomed behind them. Skinny dogs barked at gates. Children, thin and solemn-faced, with lank hair and shadows under their eyes, stood in doorways. They looked as if they'd been drained of color, like clothing washed too often.

Sophie and her friends were on the outskirts of Schadenburg, an old, walled town, the last one on the road to Nimmermehr. They would have to camp in the woods for one more night, and Arno wanted to buy the makings of a good supper.

"I can't eat one more damned rabbit," he'd said. And then he'd counted off all the things they would buy—a bottle of fine wine, three steaks, a loaf of fresh bread, butter, potatoes to bake in the coals, cheese, and fruit.

"You make it sound like the Last Supper," Will grumbled. It was the first thing he'd said in hours. He'd been quieter than usual since they'd left the von Stauffenzees' tomb.

"It might well be," Arno said philosophically. "So let's get a chocolate cake as well. I know of a pawnshop in the village. I'll sell the owner a ring or two."

Will offered to pawn the pearls Oma had given him, but Arno wouldn't hear of it. They continued walking, and a few minutes later, they were approaching the town's east gate. Five or so yards before it, though, Will stopped.

"I need to tell you something . . ." he said to Sophie.

Sophie looked at him questioningly. Will opened his mouth, then closed it again, grimacing. Sophie knew he wasn't much of a talker. She could see he was struggling to get his words out.

"I shouldn't have said what I said. Back at the soldiers' encampment," he finally blurted.

Arno regarded them both, his curiosity piqued. "What did you say?" he asked, using the break to take a drink from his canteen.

"He said he hates me," Sophie replied, flinching a little at the memory.

Arno spat his water. "You *said* that?"

Will shook his head, clearly pained. "No, no! *Despise.* I said I despised her."

"Oh, well, that's all right, then," said Arno with a snort.

"I'm sorry, Sophie. I lumped you in with every other person at the palace. You're nothing like the queen," Will said earnestly.

"Just what every girl wants to hear—that she's nothing like a deranged tyrant," said Arno.

Will gave Sophie a searching look. She could tell that he hoped his words would make things better. But they hadn't. In fact, they'd hurt her more.

Will saw her unhappy expression and blanched. "Did I say the wrong thing?" he asked anxiously.

Sophie gave him a rueful smile. "You're trying to make yourself feel better, Will—not me. You think I'm going to die soon. That's why you're telling me this. Because you might not get another chance and you want to clear your conscience while you can."

Will looked wounded. "No, that's *not* the reason," he quickly said. "It isn't at all. You see, it's like Oma said . . . *You*, you're a princess . . ."

Arno circled his finger in the air, trying to speed him up.

"And me? Me, I . . . Well, I'm *not* . . ."

"Not what? Not a *princess*?" said Arno.

"Yes," Will said, looking from Arno to Sophie, helplessly. "Not a princess . . ." His words trailed off. He looked away, crimson-cheeked, defeated.

Sophie almost felt sorry for him.

Arno didn't. "Sophie, let's continue into the town," he suggested, taking her arm. "Will, let's shut up."

The three walked through the arched gateway in an awkward silence and soon found themselves on its winding main street. It was market day, and farmers had come in from the countryside to sell their wares.

Sophie had never seen such a bleak place. The buildings that lined the main street were made of gray stone. They were tall and crooked and seemed to lean toward one another across the narrow main street as if they were weary. The people wore clothing woven of gray cloth and shawls knitted of gray wool. Even their faces were gray. It appeared as if the village, and everyone in it, were made of ash. Sophie half expected a strong wind to come along and blow them all away.

Unsmiling farmers, brusque and surly, exchanged cabbages and potatoes; tired hens; and small, spotty apples for dirty silver coins. Rangy men, arms crossed over their chests, stood sullenly in the doorways of shops and pubs, watching people walk by, sometimes nodding, sometimes spitting.

Crows, roosting between chimney pots, cawed harshly from rooftops. A few stood on the peaks or cornices and watched the people in the street. Their eyes lingered on Sophie.

"I hate this place," Arno said, pulling his jacket collar up around his neck, even though it was not cold.

He found the pawnshop and got a good price for an emerald ring. After parceling out the coins—and items on his shopping list—between himself, Sophie, and Will, he said, "Let's split up, buy our supplies, and then meet by the west gate in half an hour. We'll get out of here faster that way."

Will and Sophie agreed, and the three went on their separate ways, with Zara trotting along behind Sophie. A few minutes later, Sophie found a baker's stall and bought a loaf of bread. Next, she found a pastry shop and purchased a small chocolate cake. The last thing on her list was fruit.

As she walked down the winding street, it seemed to grow even narrower. Shopfronts and shoppers, wagons and carts, all crowded in at her. She eyed the hills of fruits and vegetables. They provided the only color in the dreary town, but even they looked washed out. She wanted to buy some apples, but everything she saw was crabbed and sour-looking.

A few minutes later, Sophie found herself at the end of the street, at the west gate, and still she'd found nothing worth buying. As she turned in a slow circle, looking to see if Will or Arno had made it to the gate yet, she suddenly spotted a bright daub of red against the backdrop of unrelieved gray. A lone farmwife, red-cheeked and smiling, her hair tucked under a straw hat, had set up her stall on a narrow side street. It was piled high with the most perfect red, ripe apples. Sophie decided that she would buy from the woman. She still had time. Neither Will nor Arno was anywhere to be seen.

"Come on, girl," she said to Zara. The two of them made their way through the stream of people to the stall.

"Three apples, please," Sophie said, pulling a coin out of her pocket.

"Only three?" the farmwife asked jovially as she took Sophie's money. "Clearly you've never had *my* apples. If you had, you'd buy a dozen. They're that good." She nodded at the pile. "Try one. On me. Then tell me if you still only want three."

Sophie smiled. "If you insist," she said. The apples looked so tasty and she *was* a little hungry. The farmwife had arranged the fruit in a pyramid. Sophie took the topmost one, rubbed it on her shirt, and then bit into it. It was crisp and tart. Juice ran down her chin. She wiped it off with the back of her hand.

"What do you think?" the farmwife asked her.

"It's delicious," Sophie said, taking another bite. But it wasn't. Not anymore. It was suddenly sickly sweet.

"What do you think?" the farmwife asked again.

Sophie coughed. She didn't want to hurt the woman's feelings. "I—I told you . . . It's delicious . . . It—" She wheezed, then coughed again, trying to clear her throat.

"No, you pathetic fool. What do you think you're doing? Traveling to Nimmermehr, to the King of Crows's castle? Did you really imagine you could win against an adversary like him?"

Sophie's head snapped up. She opened her eyes. The farmwife had raised her head. Sophie could see her blue eyes, her cruel smile. *Adelaide.* A movement caught Sophie's eye. The apple in her hand was crawling with maggots. With a cry of disgust, she threw it down.

Voices started chattering at her. Scores of them. *Weak . . . foolish . . . not strong enough . . . not smart enough . . .*

It was the apples. They were all whispering and hissing, shriveling and collapsing. Rot darkened their once-red skins.

Sophie gasped for air, but she couldn't get any. The piece of apple was lodged in her throat. Panic gripped her. She was dimly aware of Zara whimpering.

Please, Sophie mouthed, panic blooming into terror. She whirled around, hoping to motion to a passing shopper for help. But there were none nearby. They were all on the main street. No one was even bothering to cast a glance in her direction.

Sophie clutched at her throat. Her vision was dimming. Zara was barking madly.

"It shouldn't take much longer. Just another minute or two, and it will all be over," Adelaide said.

Sophie sank to the hard, cobbled street.

Another face looked down at her now, a man's face—pale, with cold black eyes and a cruel mouth. "Do you know me,

307

Princess?" he asked. "No? Well, no matter. I know you, and I've ended you. For good this time. I have your heart. Soon I'll have all hearts."

In the instant before darkness descended on her, sweeping across her eyes like a black wing, Sophie realized she did know him. He was Corvus, the King of Crows.

He is the villain of this story. And so many more.

SIXTY-FIVE

By a pushcart in a gray and heartless town, a small, thin dog barks frantically.

People gather around. They try to quiet her. To draw her away from the girl's body, but the dog stands her ground.

A man and a boy come running. They know the sound of this dog's bark.

The boy shouts. He falls to his knees. He calls to the girl. Slaps her cheeks. Pleads with her.

He knows what has happened. He remembers the scorpion. But this time the girl is not breathing. This time there is nothing to fight. He does not see the half-eaten apple, for it's been kicked under the cart by a careless foot.

The man turns around and around in a wild, furious circle, dagger drawn, looking for the murderer. But there is no sign of an assailant. There is only a shabby pushcart, weather-beaten and rusted, with a pile of apples on it, soft with rot.

The boy gathers the girl's limp, lifeless body into his arms and weeps into her neck.

And the small, thin dog raises her head and howls. It's not the poisoned objects that kill us.

It's not the poisoners who are the murderers. It is us. We, ourselves.

We listen to the snakes. We let the scorpions get close.

We believe the hisses, the whispers, the words that tell us all we are not and will never be.

We take the shiny red apple that the evil queen offers, and we bite right into it.

Venom can be drawn from flesh, but poisoned words lodge deep in our hearts, where no antidote can reach.

Above the sad gray town, a flock of crows rises high into the sky, shrieking in triumph.

Their master has won.

The princess is dead.

SIXTY-SIX

A light rain was falling as Will and Arno arrived at the Hollow.

Josef, who was repairing a broken slat in the fence, saw them coming. He didn't know the two men, but he raised his hand in greeting. They gave him their names, and he introduced himself, too. He was about to ask if they were thirsty, if he could get them some water, when his eyes moved to the horse they were leading, and the bundle, wrapped carefully in a blanket, that lay across its saddle.

Josef's hammer hit the ground with a dull thud. "No," he said, as if he could refuse what he knew was coming. *"No."*

"I'm sorry," Will said. "I'm so sorry. It happened in Schadenburg. On our way to the King of Crows's castle. We thought she would want to come back here to the Hollow. She told us about you. She loved this place. She loved you."

The other brothers joined Josef. They were wide-eyed, worried. Julius was holding his gardening shears. Johann was clutching an ax that he'd been sharpening. Schatzi was carrying a basket of carrots. Jakob was holding a hoe he'd just fixed. Weber and Tupfen followed. They wondered why Josef hadn't fetched the strangers a drink. They didn't understand why he was just standing there, his hands covering his eyes.

But as they drew close, they saw that Will had turned away, his head bowed, his hands knotted. They saw Arno gently lifting the bundle down off their horse. He carried it through the gate and into the yard. As he did, the blanket slipped open, and they saw that he was carrying the body of a girl. Their girl.

Julius's legs gave way. He sat down hard on an old stump. Johann sent his ax hurdling into the trunk of a tree with an anguished cry. Josef and Jakob wept. Schatzi dropped his basket, then took the body from Arno and laid it down on the ground under the sheltering branches of an oak tree. He kissed Sophie's cold hands, stroked her alabaster cheek.

"Why did you leave us, Sophie? You were safe here. Jeremias and Joosts are on their way back with your heart. They'll be here any day now. I *know* they will. If only you'd waited for them."

"Did you see our two brothers?" Johann asked hopefully. "Traveling back from Nimmermehr?"

Arno shook his head. And Will told them all what had happened, his voice ragged with grief. More tears came as he spoke. The brothers' hearts were breaking.

"But she doesn't look dead," Schatzi said when Will had finished. "There's still a bloom on her pale cheek, see? Her lips are still red."

"There's no breath," Arno said gently. "No life."

"Her heart is quiet," said Will. "I listened to it. For a long time. Until the sky grew dark. Until her body grew cold. Hoping the heart would suddenly knock, bang, clank . . . *anything*. Hoping the light in her eyes would come back . . . hoping I could hear her voice again, see her smile . . ." His voice broke; he couldn't go on.

Weber, silver tears falling from his many eyes, asked a question in his language.

"No, Weber, it's too late this time," Josef replied. "Souls don't stay for long after the heart stops. You have to be there quick to catch them." He shook his head, then said. "She should have a funeral, a proper burial—"

"No! She can't go in the ground!" Schatzi cried. "It's cold and dark and lonely there and she . . . she loved flowers and sunlight. She loved the lark's song and the crickets' call. She's *not* being buried. I won't have it!"

"All right, Schatz, all right," Julius soothed, patting his brother's back.

"She's *not*," Schatzi tearfully insisted.

"What are we going to do, then?" Johann asked.

They all fell silent for a moment; then Julius said, "We'll make her a coffin of quartz. Cut from the mines and polished until it's as clear as glass. With handles of gold. We'll set it under the silver birches that she loved. The spring rains will wash over her. The summer sun will shine on her. The autumn leaves will kiss her. The snow will swirl her in its embrace."

Schatzi nodded his assent. Arno said he would help them. And Will looked up at the sky, fists clenched.

Johann noticed. He walked over to him. "You loved her," he said.

"Still do."

"And she loved you?"

"She was a princess. I'm an archer."

"That doesn't answer my question."

"I have to go," Will said brusquely.

"Go where? Stay with us. For the night, at least. You must be very tired."

Will shook his head. Softly, he said, "I have birds to hunt." He stood gazing at the dead princess, the fringes of her badly cut hair resting on her cheek, her graceful hands resting on her chest, her beautiful lips so full and red. Still.

Then he dipped his head to the brothers, and to Arno, and was gone, melting into the forest's shadows as swiftly and quietly as the creatures who lived there.

A breeze moved through the pine branches, making them sigh.

And the rain came down harder, as if the Darkwood itself was weeping.

SIXTY-SEVEN

The brothers worked two nights and two days without pause to fashion Sophie's coffin.

They cut huge slabs of quartz from deep within their mines, polished them until they were as clear as water, trimmed them with gold, and lined the coffin with the softest spider silk. Then they set it among the silver birches on a carved wooden bier.

Only moments ago they'd laid Sophie to rest in it.

Tupfen had dressed her in a pair of soft deerskin trousers and a tunic of white linen, both of which Schatzi had made. Everyone had taken turns embroidering the tunic with images of the things Sophie loved—roses, Zara, plums, and Black Forest cake. Sophie's hair was neatly combed. A fringe of black swept across her forehead. There was still a kiss of pink in her cheeks.

"How can she be dead?" Schatzi wondered now, looking at her.

"Schatzi, she *is*. You have to accept it."

"But *look* at her. What dead person looks like that? Dead people are gooey. And crumbly."

"You make them sound like coffee cake," said Julius.

"It's some dark magic from the King of Crows, I think. He didn't want her to be buried. He wanted her to be seen, to serve as a warning," said Arno, who had stayed with the brothers and helped them build the coffin.

"Why did she do it? Why did she go after her heart?" asked Josef, his voice cracking.

Jakob shook his head. "People need to follow their hearts, or they die long before the thing stops beating."

The brothers, all standing around the coffin in a semicircle, their hearts heavy with grief, their eyes welling with tears, did not see the boy coming up behind them. They weren't aware of him at all until he spoke.

"Please, sirs . . . could you spare a bit of food?"

They all turned toward him. He was a small boy, no more than ten or so.

"Who are you, child?" Jacob asked. "Where did you come from?" He turned to Weber and Tupfen. "Get him a plate of food, please. And a glass of milk."

As the two servants hurried off, the boy said, "My name is Tom. I live in the woods."

"The Darkwood is no place for a child. Where is your home?"

"I ran away from my home. It's a cruel place. The woods are safer. I heard that kind people lived here and was hoping you could spare some bread. I don't need much, and I'm not looking for a handout. I'll work for my dinner."

Tom spoke manfully, pulling himself up to his full height. All four feet of it. Josef winced as he looked at the child. He was little more than skin over bones. His face and hands were clean—he'd obviously washed them in a stream or pond—but his clothing was filthy. His hair was matted.

"Work for your dinner?" Josef said, shaking his head. "Child, you're lucky you didn't become dinner! There are bears in the woods. And wolves."

"None worse than where I come from, sir." Tom looked past Josef to the quartz coffin. The sun, high overhead in the sky, glinted off the quartz, making it impossible to see the body inside it.

"You've lost someone," he said. "I'm sorry, sir. I lost someone, too. A few months ago. Grown-ups always say time heals all wounds. Maybe the outside ones. The inside ones only get bigger."

Tom's gaze drifted over the coffin to the bier and the ground around it, strewn with rose petals. He took a few awkward, halting steps forward, squinting at the coffin. He still couldn't make out who was lying in it, nestled deep in the spider silk, but he saw what was lying under it.

The little hound had refused to leave Sophie's body. She was lying under the bier, her head on her front paws, her eyes closed, grieving.

"Zara?" Tom said, astonished. "Is that *you*, girl?"

At the sound of the boy's voice, the dog opened her eyes and raised her head.

"It *is* you! You're alive," Tom exclaimed. "Do you remember me?"

Zara thumped her tail on the ground.

"You *do* remember." As he spoke, the sun went behind a cloud, and he saw who was in the coffin.

"That . . . that's my *friend*. That's the *princess*!" Tom said. "That's her for sure, but how is she here? She was carried off by wolves. That's what the huntsman said." He pressed his palm to his head, confused. Then tears welled in his eyes. "She looks alive. Like she never left me." He wiped his eyes on his filthy sleeve. "I wish she hadn't. She was my only friend. *Be careful, Tom. Slow down*, she would tell me. And she always made me feel better when other people made fun of me . . ."

The child took a few more steps toward Sophie's coffin. He was weary and hungry, in pain from the terrible scars on his back, and he stumbled, as he often did. His foot got caught in a clump of grass. He lost his balance and went tumbling headfirst.

Into the quartz coffin.

SIXTY-EIGHT

Everything happened at once. The heavy coffin shuddered, rocking slightly. Zara ran out from under it, her tail tucked. The wooden bier groaned. Jakob grabbed Tom and yanked him out of harm's way just as a crack opened up in the wood. An instant later, the entire bier collapsed, and the coffin hit the ground and shattered.

Sophie's body lay facedown in the rubble.

All the color drained from Tom's cheeks. "I'm sorry," he cried, cowering. "I'm so sorry. I'm clumsy. Everyone says so. But I didn't mean to. I didn't—"

Josef saw that the poor child was terrified. He put a gentle hand on his soldier. "Hush, Tom; it's all right. Don't fret. We'll fix it. Please don't—"

"Josef. Great God, Josef, *look*!"

It was Schatzi who'd spoken. He was standing as still as a tree, pointing at the shattered coffin.

The corpse that had been lying motionless inside it only seconds ago was now coughing and gasping. It rolled over onto its side and spat out what looked like a chunk of apple.

Then it sat up, dazedly looked around, and said, "Why is everyone crying?"

SIXTY-NINE

Sophie stood up on unsteady legs.

Schatzi's hands came up to his mouth. "Sophie, my darling girl . . . You're *alive*."

"How did I get here?" Sophie asked weakly. "How—"

A wave of dizziness, oily and sickening, washed over her. She swayed on her feet, squeezed her eyes closed. Arno took her arm and led her to a wooden bench the brothers had placed near the coffin. After a moment, the dizzy spell passed. Sophie opened her eyes again.

That was the brothers' cue. They all rushed to her, kissing her cheek or the top of her head, taking her hands in theirs. Tupfen and Weber joined them.

"Your friends brought you here, Arno and Will," Julius told her. "Do you remember anything at all?"

Sophie told them about the farmwife and the apple. And a man with cold black eyes.

"It was him, the King of Crows," she said, chilled by the memory. "He said that he had ended me." She stopped speaking for a moment, trying to recall her last moments at the market.

"But he didn't. The apple must've gotten stuck in my throat. I didn't swallow it."

"I think that's what saved you," said Arno. "You only got enough poison in your system to slow your heart and put you into a deathlike sleep, not enough to kill you."

"How much time has passed since I was in Schadenburg?" she asked.

"A week . . . I think," Johann said.

"No, eight days," Arno countered.

"What?" Sophie said, alarmed. She shot to her feet. "Where are my things?" she asked. "My rucksack . . . my canteen . . ."

"In the house," said Johann. "Sophie, sit down. You're still very pale."

Sophie shook her head. "I need them," she said. "And bit of food, too, if you can spare it."

"Why? What are you doing?" Jakob asked.

"I'm going to the King of Crows' castle."

"After what just happened? Are you mad?" Jakob spluttered.

"I have to. I'm running out of time," Sophie said, with steel in her voice. "I only have a week left, maybe not even, before my heart winds down. And it takes that long just to get to Nimmermehr."

"You can do it in six days if you hurry," Arno said. "Will and I did."

"But, Sophie, you don't need to go," said Schatzi. "Jeremias and Joosts will return with your heart any day now."

"It's been weeks, Schatzi," Sophie said, as gently as she could. "*Weeks*. Something has happened to them. Something must have, otherwise they'd be back by now. If I can find them on my way and help them, I will."

Schatzi lowered his head. He swallowed hard.

"Where's Will?" Sophie asked, looking around for him.

"He left," Arno said. "Guess he figured there was no point in sticking around, what with you being dead and all."

Sophie's heart sank with a soft, sad sound that was almost like a sigh. "Where did he go?" she asked. "Home to Oma and Gretta?"

"I'm not sure," Arno replied. "He said something about hunting birds."

Sophie didn't understand. "That makes no sense, Arno. He never hunts birds. He loves birds."

Arno shrugged.

I'll go back to Oma's cottage one day, Sophie told herself. *Once I have my heart again, and my crown. To say thank you. And goodbye.* It wouldn't change a thing between them. She knew that. It wouldn't make him care for her the way she cared for him. But she owed him her thanks, and she owed herself one last glimpse of him.

"Sophie," Johann said. "If Jeremias and Joosts are . . . are truly lost to us . . . if they couldn't best the King of Crows . . . what makes you think you can?"

"A sick girl. A blind boy. An old woman in a wheelbarrow. Orphaned children. A man with a Q carved into his cheek. *They* make me think I can," Sophie replied, looking from Johann to his brothers to Arno. "I know what the King of Crows means to do now—to take the hearts of my people, all of them. He told me so himself. Right before the poison took effect. But I won't let him. I swear I won't."

There was urgency in Sophie's voice, and a new determination.

They had not been there before. The brothers all heard it. Arno did, too.

Weber, who had disappeared, now returned with two schnitzel sandwiches, a jug of water, and two glasses. Sophie drank her fill, then reached for a sandwich. As she bit into it, she saw the spider carry the other sandwich away. He handed it to a small boy who was standing back from the group.

"Tom, is that *you*?" she said, breaking into an astonished grin. She put her sandwich down, hurried to him, and threw her arms around him. It felt like embracing a bundle of sticks. "What are you doing here?" she asked as she released him.

"I ran away. Weeks ago. After . . . after the queen had me whipped."

"I'm so sorry. It was my fault."

"You saved a life, Princess Sophie. There's no fault in that."

"You've been out here alone ever since?"

Tom nodded. Sophie, realizing that the thin, hungry boy was holding his sandwich out of politeness, instead of tearing into it, led him to the bench and told him to eat. They devoured their sandwiches together.

When they'd finished, Sophie went into the cottage and quickly gathered her things. Arno gathered his, too. There was no way he was letting her go alone, he said. He still had some jewels and would use them to buy horses from the first farm they came to. If they rode, they'd cut days off the journey. Weber packed food for them and then Sophie kissed the brothers goodbye. They wanted to go, too, but she wouldn't hear of it.

"You're my family now," she said. "I need you to be here when I come back."

Then she turned to Tom. "I'm leaving Zara here. Will you take good care of her for me?"

"I will. I promise," Tom said.

And then Sophie and Arno were hurrying down the path. The brothers watched her go, worry on their faces.

"Goodbye, Princess!" Tom called after her.

"I knew she wasn't dead," Schatzi said, dabbing at his eyes. "I knew she didn't die."

"I think she did," Johann said.

"Did what? *Die?*" Julius asked.

Johann nodded.

"What are you talking about?" Josef said. "She just stood up, ate a schnitzel sandwich, and took off into the forest!"

Johann did not reply for a moment. He stood at the gate, watching as Sophie grew smaller and smaller and then disappeared from view, into the Darkwood. She seemed taller to him. Bolder. Fearsome.

"The *princess* died in Schadenburg," he said with a small, proud smile. "And a queen was born."

SEVENTY

Sophie spurred her horse on. He was a stallion, young and strong. The best horse graveyard gold could buy.

Arno was right on her heels on a wild-eyed mare. The horses were fast, and they'd made it to Nimmermehr in four days. Hooves pounding, they galloped between the dense trees now, throwing up clods of dirt. Dusk was already descending. Sophie knew she and Arno needed to get to the castle, then find the entrance to the tunnel, and fast. They'd never locate it in the dark and they couldn't afford to wait until morning. If Johann's calculation—made back when he'd first told Sophie that her heart was a clockwork—was correct, she had two days before it stopped. Only two days to recover her heart, and then somehow find someone with magic strong enough to put it back into her body.

Give or take a few days, Johann had added to his estimate. Sophie prayed hard that the heart inside her would give her those days, not take them.

The forest path wound down through a valley, flattened, and then climbed again, narrowing to little more than a deer trail. Sophie and Arno had to slow to a walk as the terrain grew steeper and more treacherous. Finally, they crested the hill. Sophie halted her horse at the top. Her heart knocked loudly as she saw what lay beyond it.

In the distance to the north, a castle stood in a clearing, surrounded by a deep moat. The stones of its soaring walls had been hewn from black granite. Torches burned along its ramparts. Above them, towers rose so sharp and thrusting, it seemed as if they would pierce the sky and make it bleed.

Arno's gaze swept across the castle, to its grounds, and then to the river that flowed to the west of it. "The entrance to the tunnel is supposed to be near the river and under cover of the Darkwood, which is a good thing. We can ride down this hill, swing west, and stay within the woods. We don't want to set foot in the clearing." He nodded at the castle. "Who knows what's watching."

Sophie clucked her tongue at her horse, urging him on. Arno followed. They'd barely gone ten strides when they heard it—a violent, splintering crash, like the sound a tree makes when it topples over in a storm. And then a pounding, deep and booming, that made the ground shake.

Sophie turned around. Her stomach knotted in fear. A creature was coming up the path behind them—a living nightmare. Although it was large and ungainly, it ran fast, using its feet and hands. The knot tightened as Sophie saw that it was made entirely of branches, with broken twigs for teeth and dark, empty pits for eyes. It stopped halfway up the path, scented the air, and roared. A chorus of roars answered back.

"Arno, what *is* that?" Sophie whispered, her hands tightening on her reins. Her horse had heard the roars, too, and was dancing nervously underneath her.

"A waldwicht," Arno said tersely. "And he's bringing his friends. They can't leave the woods. Ride for the clearing, Sophie."

"But the castle guards . . . They'll see us."

"We don't have a choice. *Go!*"

Sophie touched her heels to her horse's sides, and the animal took off, galloping down the other side of the hill, his ears back.

Arno, his sword drawn, was so close behind her that Sophie could hear his horse breathing. "Faster!" he shouted.

Sophie kicked her horse on. The creature was flying now, but it still wasn't fast enough. Sophie heard another splintering crash. The waldwicht was gaining on them. And then, without any warning, it was there, right behind Arno, swiping its lethal claws at his horse's haunches, trying to bring the animal down. Arno yanked his horse's reins, pulling her up short. The horse reared, spinning around on her hind legs just as the waldwicht struck.

The move saved the animal. And Arno, too. The waldwicht's sharp, twiggy claws missed the horse and raked harmlessly through the air. Arno raised his sword and brought the blade down on the waldwicht's neck, slicing its horrible head off. Then he turned his horse and kicked the animal into a gallop, for more monsters were right behind the dead one.

Still brandishing his sword, Arno charged down the path after Sophie. Seconds later, they broke through the tree line and streaked into the clearing. Angry roars echoed after them. Sophie glanced back and saw a dozen of the things raging at the edge of the woods, snapping branches off trees, stamping their feet, and hammering the ground with their fists.

"That was close," Arno said as they slowed their horses to a canter.

"Thank you," Sophie said, getting the words out between gasps for breath. "You saved us both." She shuddered to think how close the creatures had come and what those terrible claws would have done to them.

"For now. Come on; we're making targets of ourselves out in the open. Let's cut over to the edge of the woods. I think we've lost the waldwichts."

Sophie cast a final look back. As she did, she thought of Jeremias and Joosts. Had they encountered the monsters? Had they been able to escape them? Or were those awful, empty eyes the last things they'd seen?

Arno turned his horse to the right. Sophie followed, and they ducked under the canopy of branches. As soon as they were hidden from view, they slowed the horses to a walk. The animals' coats were lathered. Foam flecked their lips.

"We've got to get them to the river and let them drink," said Arno.

"Is it far?" Sophie asked. She'd lost her bearings during their terrifying ride.

"Shouldn't be, if my memory's any good."

Sophie allowed herself a small sigh of relief. "Good. Maybe the worst is over."

"*Over?*" Arno echoed with a hollow laugh. "Girl, it's only just beginning."

SEVENTY-ONE

Sophie trudged through the dense brush, shoving aside branches with one hand and leading her horse with the other.

Arno's dire prediction had unnerved her. With every step she took, she expected to hear a bloodcurdling roar or see some ghastly creature bearing down on her, but she would not turn back, no matter how afraid she felt. She'd come this far, and she was resolved to do whatever it took to regain her heart.

Arno was certain that both the tunnel and the river were nearby, but he hadn't been able to find either one, so they'd decided to split up and search. If one of them found something, he or she would call like a raven to the other. If no one did, they would meet back by a gray boulder in half an hour. The dusk was deepening; soon they would lose the daylight completely.

Frustrated by clinging vines and branches that scratched and slapped, Sophie stopped bushwhacking for a moment and stood still, trying to reorient herself. Was she heading west or north now? Where was the setting sun? And what was the sound? Was it burbling, like water running over rocks, which meant she was nearing the river? Or was it something else?

As she looked around, the sound grew louder. It wasn't burbling; it was rustling, like something slithering through dry leaves. She stopped. And so did the rustling. Then it started again, closer this time.

Sophie remembered the snakes that had sunk their fangs into her and the scorpion that had mercilessly stung her, and she pulled out her dagger.

Holding it out in front of her, she kicked at the leaves, ready to strike at whatever was hiding in them before it struck at her. She laughed, a little embarrassed, when she saw there was nothing there, only a vine, with long, curved thorns and a curling tip.

Blackbriar, she thought. And that sound she'd heard? *Probably just a mouse*. But she still felt uneasy. "Arno? Arno, are you there?" she called out quietly, looking all around.

There was no reply.

Sophie took a deep, slow breath, trying to quiet her nerves. "Come on, boy," she said, turning to lead her horse on once more, determined to find the river. But as she tried to walk, she found that her left foot was stuck fast.

Looking down, she saw that the black vine had curled around her ankle. She tried to pull free of it, but as she did, it tightened. Its sharp thorns pierced the leather of her boot and dug painfully into her skin.

Wincing, she swiftly looped her horse's reins over her free arm, then bent down and sliced through the vine with her dagger. The piece around her ankle fell to the ground, wriggling like a tentacle. A shiver ran up her spine. As she straightened, she heard the rustling again. She tugged on her horse's reins, trying to hurry him away from the vines, but it was impossible. They were moving toward them from every direction, snaking along the ground or slithering up tree trunks and out along branches. Their thorns glinted like obsidian. Dusky roses bloomed along their lengths. As the flowers opened, they gave off spicy scents of myrrh and cassia. Sophie was scared, and her heart was hammering, but the rich, heavy smell had a strange, calming effect on her. Instead of trying to escape, she stood perfectly still.

The dark blooms were spellbindingly beautiful, but it was their voices that held Sophie transfixed. The roses were whispering. Their tones were low and silky and strange, but their words were so familiar.

You're just a girl . . . You can't best the King of Crows . . . Why try? You'll only fail . . .

There are bones all around you . . . They belonged to warriors and kings . . . What chance do you have?

Sophie shook her head, struggling against the sedative smell, the enervating words.

Move. Now, she told herself. *Go.*

But she couldn't. The words sapped her will; they slowed the noisy thrust and thump of her heart. She was like a mouse entranced by a cobra. Let the vines wrap around her. Let them cover her, strangle her. There was no use in fighting, no point in denying the truth.

Her horse's shrill, frightened whinny nudged Sophie from her trance, and then a bruising kick to her backside sent her sprawling. The animal was stamping and dancing, trying to break free of the vines that were encircling his legs.

Sophie got to her feet and shook off the vines that were curling around her wrist. She cut loose several twining around her calves and ripped away the one snaking up her back. The scent that had beguiled her only moments ago now sickened her. With an angry cry, she stamped the blooms into the ground, then turned to her horse. The stallion was wild-eyed, whinnying, bucking, and kicking out. Sophie knew that a hoof slamming into her skull could kill her.

"Shh, boy . . . Easy . . . Easy . . ." she whispered to him.

Keeping her distance, she hacked at the vine twisting around one of the horse's front legs. She grabbed another that was licking at a back leg and tossed it away. As soon as he was free, the horse spun in a wide circle, looking for a way out of the brush. He dragged Sophie with him. She stumbled and fell, then was scraped along the ground. It was all she could do to keep hold of the reins.

A vine slithered after her, its roses whispering.

Arno's dead . . . His eyes were pecked out by crows . . . It's all your fault, useless girl . . .

Finally, Sophie was able to find her feet, pull the horse's head around to her, and lead him forward.

That's when she saw the two men.

The blackbriar had lashed them tightly to the trunk of a tree, immobilizing them. More black, blowsy roses were blooming on the vines. *Give up. Let go . . . You failed . . .* they whispered.

Sophie could just make out the shapes of their vine-tangled

bodies in the dusk. She saw a flash of blue linen, a red cap. The thorns had torn the men's clothing and pierced their skin. Their eyes were closed. Their faces were drawn and gray.

But she knew them all the same.

"Jeremias!" she cried. "Joosts!"

SEVENTY-TWO

Sophie dropped her reins and attacked.

Like a girl possessed, she hacked, stabbed, and slashed at the blackbriar. She ripped the flowers off the vines and stamped them underfoot, heedless of their ugly squeals.

"Joosts! Jeremias! Are you all right?" she called out as she fought her way through to them. But the brothers didn't answer. "Please don't be dead," she begged. "Please, please, *please* . . ."

Sophie kept battling, tearing thick lengths of severed, writhing vine from around the brothers with her bare hands.

She heard Jeremias suck in a lungful of air as she unwound the blackbriar from his chest. His eyes fluttered open; his gaze was unfocused. For a moment, he didn't know her.

"Jeremias, it's *me* . . . It's Sophie!"

His eyes found hers. *"Sophie?"* he said, his voice like a rusted hinge.

"Yes, yes!" Sophie said with a noise somewhere between a laugh and a sob. "I'm getting you out of here."

"Water . . ." Jeremias rasped.

Sophie looked around frantically for her horse—her canteen was in a saddlebag—but the animal had bolted.

"There's a river close by," she said. "I-I'm not sure where it is, though."

"I know . . ."

"Can you walk there?" she asked him.

He nodded. "Joosts . . ."

"He's right here," said Sophie.

Jeremias found his feet. He took a few unsteady steps away from the tree. Joosts was in worse shape. His eyes fluttered but did not open. His body dropped to the ground as Sophie ripped away the last of the blackbriar. Together, she and Jeremias got him up, then set off, half carrying, half dragging him through the woods.

"What happened?" Sophie said at the exact same time as Jeremias said, "What are you doing here?"

Before either could answer, another voice was heard. "Sophie?" it hissed. "Sophie, are you there?"

"Arno?" Sophie called back as loudly as she dared. "Where are you?" She was so relieved to hear his voice. She'd been scared that the whispering roses had gotten him, too.

"Here! Over here!"

Sophie explained to Jeremias that Arno was her friend. They followed the sound of his voice. As they got closer to it, they heard rushing water. With a final push through the brush, they came out at the edge of a narrow river. Arno was standing a few yards away by a tree. He was tying Sophie's horse to a low-hanging branch, trying to soothe the animal.

"I found him standing in the water, drinking his fill," Arno said as he finished tying the horse. Then he turned and saw the two men with Sophie. Joosts was still not fully conscious.

His head was lolling. Sophie and Jeremias helped him to the edge of the river. They sat him down, and then Jeremias scooped water up in his cupped hands and trickled it into his brother's mouth.

Joosts eyes opened. He swallowed, coughed, and then heaved himself forward. Bracing himself with one hand, he used the other to scoop more water into his mouth.

"Go slow," Jeremias cautioned him, cupping water for himself now.

"What happened?" Arno asked as he joined them.

As Sophie started to explain, Joosts submerged his whole head in the river, then pulled it out again and shook the water off. He opened his eyes wide and asked for food.

Sophie and Arno quickly dug in their saddlebags and gave the brothers everything they had. As they wolfed the food down, Sophie told Arno about barely escaping the blackbriar and then finding Jeremias and Joosts. She washed her hands in the river as she spoke, rinsing away the blood the thorns had drawn.

"Those weren't blackbriar vines," Arno said. "They were Herzmord roses. They tried to get me, too."

"But you don't have any cuts," Sophie said, eyeing his arms.

"I whistled polka music. It's like poison to them. Next time they come after you, do the same. Herzmords *hate* polka music."

"I wish we'd known that," Jeremias said. "They were on us before we knew what was happening. We tried to get them off, but there were just too many of them."

"How long had you been like that?" Sophie asked, standing

"I've lost track. Days? A week? Longer?"

Sophie's heart clanked noisily, aching at the thought of the two brothers cruelly bound and suffering for such a long period of time. "How are you still alive?" she asked.

"Luckily, it rained a few times and we were able to get some water by opening our mouths. Otherwise, we wouldn't have survived." He swallowed another bite of food, then asked some questions of his own. "What are you doing here, Sophie? Why aren't you home, at the Hollow?" He nodded at Arno. "Who's that?"

"Arno's my friend. We're trying to find the tunnel into Nimmermehr. So I can get my heart back."

Jeremias shook his head. "You can't. It's too dangerous. We'll go," he said dismissively. He started to stand, but his legs shook so badly, he had to sit down again.

"I can do this. And I will," Sophie said. "Things have changed since you both set off from the Hollow. *I've* changed."

Jeremias's eyes roved over her, taking in her tunic and trousers, her cropped hair, the scars from the snakes and scorpion. Walking for days had made her limbs lean and hard. Sunlight had bronzed her skin. But the biggest changes were the determined set of her jaw and the confident light in her eyes.

"Yes," he said at length. "I can see that."

"We found the tunnel." That was Joosts. The food and water had brought a bit of life back to him. "We were just about to head into it, when the vines came after us. It's not far. About twenty paces south of the tree where you found us. Go. Hurry. It's almost nightfall."

Sophie and Arno set off. Sophie led the way back to where she'd found the brothers. Once they'd located the tree, Arno oriented himself toward the south, counted off twenty paces, and found himself staring at the entrance to the tunnel.

It was nothing more than an opening between two boulders, maybe eighteen inches wide, veiled by cobwebs. A sinkhole of dread opened in Sophie's chest as she regarded it. Who knew what waited for them in that darkness?

Arno quickly fashioned two torches from green branches he snapped off a tree, dry twigs, and pine cones sticky with pitch. He ignited the torches using a flint, a steel, and a bit of char cloth, all of which he kept in a small tin in his jacket pocket.

Sophie pulled the cobwebs down and ventured inside. Dampness hung in the stale air. Thin fingers of moss dangled from the ceiling. Water trickled down the walls and pooled on the tunnel's floor. Black millipedes, shiny and fat; glossy green beetles, and lanky white spiders scuttled away from the torches' light. Before Sophie and Arno had ventured fifty yards in, they had to step over the bones of a skeleton that was slumped against the wall. Sophie gripped her torch tightly. As her eyes adjusted to the darkness, she saw that smaller tunnels branched off from the main one. The floor dipped down as they walked. Cold, murky water rose up over her ankles.

"It's quiet in here," she said as the tunnel rose again and the water drained away.

"So far," Arno said. "I'll be amazed if we make it through without coming across a makaber or two. Maybe a troll as well."

The tunnel snaked sharply to the left, and as they rounded the curve, they saw that part of one wall had caved in. Stones and dirt were heaped on the ground. Luckily, the rubble didn't entirely block their way; there was an opening, about two feet wide, at the top of it.

Arno stopped and looked at it, one hand on his hip. "We can squeeze through that," he said.

Sophie went first. She climbed up carefully, mindful of her torch, expecting the stones to slide out from under her feet at any second, but they stayed in place. Just as she was about to crawl through the opening, she heard Arno gasp.

"What's wrong?" she asked, turning around.

Arno was staring down the tunnel, back the way they'd come. He didn't look scared, though. In fact, he was smiling.

"Arno? What is it?"

Arno's smile broadened. He took a few steps away from her.

"Matti?" he said in voice soft with wonder. "Matti, is that *you*?"

The hair on the back of Sophie's neck stood up. Matti was the name of Arno's dead son.

"My child . . . My darling boy," Arno said. "I've missed you so much."

"Arno?" Sophie said uncertainly, climbing back down the rubble. She looked past him into the darkness, hoping to see what he saw. But there was nothing.

Arno knelt down. He stretched his arms out before him. "Come, Matti," he said, his voice breaking. "Come give your papa a hug . . ."

"Stop this, Arno!" Sophie demanded. "You're scaring me."

"Matti? Matti, no! Don't run away! You'll get lost down here!" Arno cried. The happiness drained out of his voice. Fear took its place.

340

Sophie reached for him, to shake him and snap him out of the strange trance he'd fallen into. As she did, she felt something land on her shoulder, something damp and cold. With a cry, she batted it off. It hit the ground with a wet splat. *Where did it come from?* she wondered. Raising her torch high, she looked up.

Clinging to the ceiling like a colony of bats were hundreds of small, quivering creatures, no more than eight inches high. Their thin, jellylike bodies were translucent; Sophie could see black veins through their gray skin, and pulsing yellow hearts. Their eyes were large and pale, their mouths puckered. Sucker-like cups on their long fingers and toes kept them attached to their perches.

Sophie's stomach tightened. She knew what the creatures were. "Wunschfetzens," she whispered.

Arno had told her about them. They stuck their long fingers into your ears, pried out your memories, and made you think you were seeing someone who wasn't there, someone you loved and longed for. Several of the creatures tensed their bodies, ready to jump, but Sophie thrust her torch at them, and they scattered across the ceiling, screeching.

"Arno, it's an illusion!" she shouted, reaching for him again. "Matti's not there!"

But her hand closed on air.

Arno wasn't there anymore, either.

SEVENTY-THREE

Sophie ran.

"Arno! Arno, *wait*!" she shouted, following him back the way they'd come.

But Arno, desperate to catch up with his son, was running fast, and Sophie couldn't keep up. He turned down a twisting side tunnel and then two more.

"Left, left, right . . ." she said aloud—like a chant, a prayer—as she pursued him, adding a directional every time she turned so that she could remember the way back.

There was more standing water in the narrow tunnels. Scuttling things clutched at her ankles as she moved through it. Sophie kicked them away without a glance. She kept her eyes on the light of Arno's torch, but he was moving so fast that it was growing dimmer by the second.

Arno took a sharp turn and then another. Sophie caught her toe on something as she tried to keep up, and tripped. Frantic to keep her torch from falling onto the damp ground and snuffing out, she came down hard on one knee, stopping her fall. Pain shot through her leg, slowing her.

"Arno, *stop* . . . Please . . ." she cried, scrambling to her feet.

Arno's footsteps faded into the darkness. The light from his torch winked out.

He was gone, and Sophie was alone. Her chest was heaving. She could hear her own breath, rapid and shallow, echoing off the tunnel walls. Her heart urged her to keep going, to save her friend. Sophie looked at her torch. The flames were not as high as they had been. They would burn out soon. She knew she couldn't be down here when they did, or she would become another skeleton slumped against the wall. Who would fight for her people then?

"I'm sorry, Arno. Please, please forgive me," she whispered to the darkness.

And then she turned away, tears slipping down her cheeks.

SEVENTY-FOUR

"Left, right, right . . ." Sophie said, reciting her directionals in reverse, trying to make her way back to the main tunnel.

As she rounded each turn, she stopped to scratch an arrow in the dirt, pointing the way out, just in case Arno came to his senses and tried to retrace his steps.

She wanted to stop, to sit down on the ground and weep for her lost friend, but she forced herself to keep going. She would mourn Arno later; grief was a luxury she could not afford now.

"Left, left, *right* . . ." Sophie said, praying that she was remembering the turns in the correct order. As she neared another fork, her memory suddenly failed her. She could not recall which way to go. Trying not to panic, she stopped and held her torch out to her left. Its weakening glow illuminated yet another endless tunnel snaking away into the darkness. Then she moved the torch to her right.

What happened next made her scream.

A face, pale and eyeless, framed by a shock of white hair, loomed out of the darkness, snarling loudly. It raked its dirty claws through the air, aiming at Sophie but missing, then it scuttled back into the tunnel and crouched down over something.

Sophie saw that the something was a corpse and that the creature was stealing its toes and putting them in its pocket.

"A makaber," she whispered.

Arno had told her that makabers were possessive of the bodies they found and would fight anyone who tried to take them. The creature was gruesome to look at, with its ragged clothing, and tattered flesh, but it seemed to be too obsessed with its prize to want to pursue her. "Ugh," Sophie said, revolted. But at least she now knew which tunnel to take. She hadn't passed the makaber, or the body it was robbing, as she'd chased Arno, which meant she'd come down the tunnel to her left. Quickly, she made her way up it and after only two more turns found herself in the main passageway. A few minutes later, she was back to the place where the wall had caved in. She crawled through the opening to the other side, careful of her torch.

As Sophie started walking again, she noticed that the tunnel was sloping upward. She very much hoped that meant she was nearing the end of it, for her torch had begun to sputter. A few minutes later, her hopes were rewarded as the passage gave way to a flight of moss-covered steps, hewn out of rock. Sophie carefully picked her way up them and found that they brought her to a wooden door. It was old, pocked with wormholes, and as mossy as the steps were. Its large iron handle and hinges were covered in rust.

"This opens into the castle; it must," Sophie reasoned. "Please don't be locked. *Please*," she added, trying the handle. But it was.

"No," she whispered, distraught. She leaned her head against the door. Had she come this far only to have to turn back?

"No," she said again, louder this time, banging her head against the soft, spongy wood. She thought of the pale, powerful king, untouchable in his castle. She thought of her stepmother sentencing Tom to ten lashes. Of Captain Krause and his men setting St. Sebastian's on fire. And as she did, her despair hardened into something dark and lethal. "No," she growled angrily. "No, no, no, NO!"

Shaking with rage, Sophie kicked the door. Again and again and again, harder each time. Yelling. Shouting. Screaming. At the King of Crows. At her stepmother. At Haakon and Krause. And then, abruptly, she stopped. Because her foot had gone through the rotten wood.

Sophie's eyes widened. She kicked at the door again, and the bottom half crumbled away. She dropped to her hands and knees, crawled through the hole she'd made, still protecting her torch, and stood up in a cavernous vaulted cellar.

Huge oak barrels of wine lay stacked in rows in the center of the room. Casks of brandy lined the walls. Sophie's fizzling torch cast enough light to illuminate another flight of stairs at the far end of the room. She was up them in no time. Just before she reached the top, the flames finally died. She threw the torch down and let her hands guide her the rest of the way. Her fingers found the door; they closed on the handle. Would it be locked, too? She turned it and the door opened on squeaking hinges.

Sophie's heart was beating a staccato rhythm. She gathered her courage and stepped into Nimmermehr.

SEVENTY-FIVE

Lifeless swans hung from the ceiling on silver hooks. A basket of shiny black eels stood on the floor. A dead stag lay on a wooden table.

Sophie had walked out of the cellar and into a larder. Warily, she crossed the room, then leaned her head out of the doorway, glancing around for cooks or servants, but she didn't see any. She had no idea where the King of Crows kept the hearts he'd taken, but she doubted they were in the larder. Moving slowly, she left the room on silent cat feet. The stag's dead eyes followed her.

A dimly lit hall led her to an enormous kitchen. Careful to stay in the shadows, Sophie peered around the edge of the doorway, but the kitchen, too, was strangely empty.

Cautiously, she ventured into it, ready to bolt out again if anyone appeared. Pots simmered on a large iron stove. A boar's body roasted over glowing coals on a revolving spit. Its fierce, tusked head sat atop a platter on a wooden worktable that stretched half the length of the room.

It appeared that someone was in the midst of preparing supper. Cheeses stood on boards; some had ink-black rinds, others were furry with green mold. Baskets held mushrooms that were dark purple, bright green, or speckled yellow. A beautiful charlotte russe towered on a cake stand. It took Sophie a moment to realize that the ladyfingers edging it were real ones, with crimson nails, still wearing their rings.

With a shiver, Sophie made her way to another doorway on the opposite side of the kitchen. As she disappeared through it, the boar's head let out a loud, gusty snort. And from behind the coal bins, under the worktable, and beneath the huge stone sinks, a dozen frightful creatures emerged.

They were all about six feet tall, pot-bellied and round-shouldered, with gangling arms and legs, and skin as warty and mottled as a toad's. They wore black tunics that reached down to their knees.

Had he been there, Arno would have recognized them. They were kobolds, a particularly vicious strain of goblin. They smiled as Sophie left the room, showing mouthfuls of needlelike teeth, their dark eyes glittering.

Sophie saw a spiral staircase as she emerged from the kitchen and quickly climbed it. She was in a dangerous man's domain and didn't know where the stairs would take her. She had no idea where to even begin looking for her heart. All she knew was that she had an impossible task ahead of her and that the only way to finish such a task was to start it. The stairway stopped at one end of a long hallway, paneled in ebony.

She walked down the passage, trying to be as quiet as a mouse, and came to the castle's trophy room. Its tall wooden doors were open. Slowly, cautiously, she entered it and looked around. The room's walls were studded with the heads of glassy-eyed deer and elk. Predators, their preserved bodies frozen in a crouch or a pounce, stared down from tree limbs or stood atop logs.

Sophie threw open cabinet doors and searched shelves. She lifted the top of a desk and rifled through it. Just as she was lowering it again, the top slipped out of her hands and slammed down. A dead fox stood on it, snarling.

Gasping, Sophie stumbled back. A deep growl rumbled from behind her. She whirled around and saw a black wolf walking toward her, its head low, its teeth bared. A shriek sounded from across the room. A panther had leapt onto the mantel and was tensed to spring.

Terror propelled Sophie like an arrow from a bow. She shot across the room toward the doors. A split second later, the panther landed exactly where she'd been standing. Scrabbling on the smooth wood floor, the big cat tried to gain purchase but slipped and crashed into the desk. The wolf ran past it, gaining on Sophie. She burst through the doorway, grabbed both doors, and pulled them shut behind her.

Panting with fear, she took a step back and then another. A heavy thud against the doors made her jump. Something scratched against them furiously. She heard more snarling.

Will the doors hold? she wondered frantically, then decided not to wait to find out. Running down the dark hallway, she came to another doorway. She skidded to a stop in front of it and looked inside.

The room was an armory. Banners hung from the ceiling. Pikes and halberds were crossed on the walls. Suits of armor stood in rows in the middle of the room like silent sentries.

Sophie dashed inside, slammed the doors closed, and leaned against them, eyes shut, struggling to catch her breath.

She had made a great deal of noise. Someone—the King of Crows, his servants—must have heard her. She stood perfectly still, listening, her nerves taut, for several long moments. But all she heard was the thumping of her own heart—no voices, no footsteps.

"Get moving," she told herself.

At the back of the room were dozens of wooden chests. Sophie decided to search them. The first one held leather gloves. The next one contained chain mail hoods. Quivers filled a third. Nothing held a heart in a glass box.

"Where *is* it?" she said aloud, her desperation growing.

As the words left her lips, she heard a high, metallic scraping. One by one, the helmets atop the suits of armor turned sharply toward her. The darkness behind the sightless visors seemed to sense her. Metal-covered fingers clenched into fists. Metal-covered legs wrenched themselves off the floor and crashed down again.

The suits of armor were slowly coming to life. With a strangled scream, Sophie forded her way back through them. A chain-mailed hand swiped through the air and connected with her back, sending her sprawling. She hit the floor, then rolled away as an armored foot stamped down inches from her head. Crawling on her hands and knees, Sophie dodged more blows and managed to get to the doors. She scrabbled to her feet just as a halberd's blade came down. It kissed her back, neatly slicing into her tunic, barely missing her skin. She raced across the threshold, grabbed the doors, and heaved them shut.

There was clanking and crashing from behind the doors. Sophie flattened herself against the wall opposite them. She imagined a set of armor toppling over, and another and another until they were all piled up. At least, she hoped that's what was happening; it would keep them from getting out.

Shaking, she set off down the hallway again. Her search carried her into a small theater, where marionettes with painted-on eyes swiveled their heads and jerkily pursued her, trailing their strings and crossbars. She stumbled into a wallpapered drawing room with dark furniture and velvet draperies, a music room, and a library with thousands of leather-backed tomes. Nothing chased her in those rooms, but nor did she find what she was looking for.

Exhausted, she sat down on a tufted leather bench in the library and lowered her head into her hands. "Where is it? Where is my heart?" she whispered. Images came to her of the bodies she'd seen in the Darkwood the first time she'd left the Hollow. "Where are *all* the hearts?" she asked.

From deep inside, a voice answered. *They're here. You* must *keep searching. He wants you to quit. Don't do it.*

Sophie listened to the voice. She stood up and kept going. Up stairways. Down hallways. In and out of a ballroom, a billiards room. Until, hours after she'd entered the King of Crows' castle, she finally came to a pair of soaring black doors, with painted panels of snakes, scorpions, and apples.

Sophie felt, she *knew*, as soon as she touched those doors, that this was the room she was seeking. She grasped the handles, her hands trembling, and turned them.

The doors swept open on silent hinges.

SEVENTY-SIX

The chamber was magnificent.

Its coffered ceiling was two stories high. Moonlight pouring in through arched windows fell across an ebony dining table and glinted off crystal goblets and gilt-edged plates. Tapers burned in silver candelabra at either end of the table; high-backed chairs surrounded it. Heavy carvings of gargoyles adorned its thick legs. Across the room, flames leapt in a black-marble fireplace.

But Sophie saw none of that. Her eyes were glued to the shelves that soared from the floor to the ceiling. Each contained glass boxes. So many glass boxes. More than anyone could count in a lifetime. And inside every one of them was a human heart, as red and alive as the day it had been taken.

Some were large, and some were so, so small. Looking at them all, Sophie felt her clockwork heart stutter and wheeze as it filled with grief. "All stolen," she murmured. "Men's hearts . . . women's . . . *children's*." She walked up to a shelf and ran her fingers along the boxes. Each had a paper label affixed to its front with a name written on it. Some of the labels were bright and new; others were so old that their ink was faded and their edges curled.

"Mine is here, too. *Somewhere*," she said, overwhelmed. "But how will I ever find it?"

"That shouldn't be too difficult," said a voice from behind her, a voice as cold as the winter wind. "I have it right here."

SEVENTY-SEVEN

Sophie slowly turned around and faced him.

The King of Crows had been standing by the fireplace, in the shadows, but he walked out into the moonlight now. He was carrying a glass box.

His face was as pale as a gravestone, his eyes as dark as a murderer's heart. His long black hair flowed down his back. A fitted jacket, embroidered with crows, hung from his narrow shoulders.

Some part of Sophie knew that this meeting was no accident. He'd been here all along, waiting, knowing she would come to him. As she watched, he set the glass box on the table.

"My heart," she whispered, mesmerized.

"Indeed."

Sophie walked closer to it.

"It's smaller than you thought, no?"

She nodded.

"That's what every human says. The ones who make it this far, that is. The small, pretty, perfect hearts are the easiest to take. The bigger ones, full of breaks and cracks, hatched with scars, those are more challenging."

"Why did you take my heart?" Sophie demanded. "What are you going to do with it?"

Corvus's gaze drifted down to the table, to the porcelain plates, the linen and silver. Frowning, he nudged a knife into place, his talons clicking softly against the silver. Then his eyes met Sophie's again. With a smile, he said, "I'm going to devour it."

SEVENTY-EIGHT

The room and everything in it seemed to spin together like a child's pinwheel, then break apart in a jangle of fractured shapes and colors.

Sophie felt wildly dizzy. She couldn't keep her balance. Inside her chest, the clockwork heart slowed noisily.

"It sounds like you haven't got much longer," Corvus said. "Why those meddling brothers bothered to save you, I'll never understand."

Sophie pulled a chair away from the table and eased herself into it. She fought down the dizziness, the weakness. She could not give in to it. *Don't you quit on me. Not now. Don't you dare*, she warned her knocking, banging heart. Little by little, the ticking in her chest quickened, and the spinning inside her head cleared.

"You . . . you devour hearts . . ." she said to Corvus when she could find her voice again.

"Yes, there's nothing more delicious to feed upon than a human heart," he responded, walking out from behind the table. "And I've been saving yours for a special treat. It looks as if it will be exceptionally sweet and tender."

She forced herself to meet his gaze. His eyes frightened her. They pulled at her, like a bottomless chasm pulls at a person standing on its edge. "I'll die if I don't get my heart back," she said.

Corvus tilted his head, crow-like. "But I thought you wanted it this way? You wanted to put your heart in a box."

Sophie remembered standing in her stepmother's chamber, listening to Adelaide tell her that kindness was dangerous, that a soft heart would only bring her trouble. She remembered thinking that it would be better to feel nothing than to feel so much pain. In her mind's eye, she saw Haakon standing with her on the balcony, urging her to let him keep her heart.

"I did once, yes," Sophie admitted. "I don't anymore."

Gathering her strength, she broke his gaze and rose, determined to get her heart. *My people need me*, she reminded herself. *They have no one else.*

But as Sophie reached for it, ugly little faces with sharp teeth and bulging eyes appeared from under the table and heaved themselves on top of it. What Sophie had thought were merely carved gargoyles were real. The creatures gibbered and hissed and swiped at her with their sharp claws, blocking her from the glass box.

The King of Crows wagged a long finger at her. "My pets know you wish to rob me of my prize," he said.

Sophie tried again to get to the box, but one of the creatures flapped its leathery wings and flew at her, screeching. Its sharp claws raked her head, driving her back.

"I wouldn't touch that box if I were you," Corvus cautioned, calling the creatures off. "The heart is still alive, untouched by time or decay. But if you open the box, you'll break the spell, and the heart will wither and rot."

Sophie's forehead was wet where the gargoyle had scratched her. She wiped the blood away, then said, "There's magic. To restore the heart to me. I know there is. The brothers said so."

Corvus laughed. His eyes pulled at her again. "And people say *I'm* cruel. Nothing is crueler than hope. There's no magic to restore a heart once I've taken hold of it."

"That's a *lie*," Sophie insisted, but dread gripped her. What if he *was* telling the truth? How could she know, when she didn't even know him? Summoning all her courage, Sophie walked up to him. "Corvus . . . the King of Crows . . . These are just names," she said. "Who are you? Who are you really?"

And then she looked deeply into those terrible eyes and knew.

He was the creak on the stairs. A cold breath on your neck. Footsteps in the dark.

He was the figure who stood in the corner of your room at night, whispering to you all the things you were not and never would be.

He was the eater of hearts.

He was Fear itself.

SEVENTY-NINE

Fear placed a sharp talon on the soft underside of Sophie's chin and raised it.

"You've finally figured it out," he said. "And now you also know that your quest to retrieve your heart is futile. No mere human can defeat me. Look at what happens when you try." His eyes moved up and down Sophie, lingering on her shabby trousers; her dirty, ripped shirt; the scar under her collarbone; her spiky hair. He removed his hand, laughing. "Look at you, reduced to a ragamuffin from the princess you used to be. Look at your friend, wandering to his death in my tunnels, calling for a child who isn't there. And the other one . . . He's even *more* pathetic . . ."

"What other one?" Sophie asked. And then the blood in her veins turned to ice. *Will*, she thought.

After Tom had knocked the coffin over and she'd woken, she'd asked Arno about him. His words drifted back to her . . . *He said something about hunting birds* . . .

With a jolt of terror, Sophie realized Will had meant *crows*. He had come here, to Nimmermehr, to search for her heart. He'd probably hoped that if he could get it, he could bring her back to life.

"My kobold servants taught the foolish boy to think twice about trespassing," said Fear. "My gargoyles were just finishing him off when you arrived."

"Where is he? *Where?*" Sophie shouted. Fear pointed to the fireplace.

Sophie skirted around him. A cry escaped her as the fireplace came into full view. Crumpled on the floor in front of it was the body of a boy.

It was motionless.

It was bruised and bloodied.

It was Will.

EIGHTY

"No!" Sophie cried. "Will! *Will!*"

She fell to her knees beside him and cradled his head in her lap. "Please don't be dead," she whispered. "Please, Will . . . Wake up. Wake *up* . . ."

His eyelashes fluttered. A small groan escaped him.

"You're alive!" she said, squeezing his hand.

"Is he?" Fear asked with a frown of disappointment. "Well, not for much longer."

A woman entered the room in a swirl of black. Blood welled at the corner of her mouth. She had a tooth, its roots crimson, pinched between her thumb and forefinger.

Sophie looked up. She recognized the woman. She'd talked with her in a graveyard. She'd seen her in a fever dream.

"My sister, Crucia. Pain to her friends," Fear said to Sophie. "I believe you've met."

Sophie didn't answer him. Terrified for Will, she patted his cheeks, shook him, and tugged on his wrists, trying anything and everything to get him to wake up.

Pain dropped her tooth into a skirt pocket; then she looked at Sophie, her face streaked with tears; at Will, half-dead.

Wincing, she turned to Fear. "All of this started with a mirror," she said with a sigh. "A piece of silvered glass."

"Do wipe your chin."

Sophie heard them. She looked up again. "What mirror? What does it have to do with me? With my heart?"

Pain palmed away the blood dribbling from the corner of her mouth. "Queen Adelaide has a magic mirror. She speaks to it. Or so my brother says. You can't trust him, though. He's a liar."

Sophie looked at Fear. "Is it true? My stepmother really has a magic mirror? She speaks to it?"

A smug smile curled Fear's lips. "It's *not* magic. Not at all. But Adelaide does speak to it. She asks it who will bring about her fall. But the mirror only shows her what she already knows," he explained. "She is smart, bold, wily. Life taught her to be. She herself set up her network of spies. She places informants in the courts, halls, and bedchambers of her fellow rulers. She knows of every plot against her as it's being hatched, and she ends them—and those involved in them—long before they ever take wing. She was, for a time, one of the best rulers the world had ever seen."

"But you helped her, brother," Pain said accusingly. "Whispering to her. Advising her."

"Oh, yes. I helped her," Fear allowed. "I helped her when no one else would." His expression darkened. "And then once, just once, I asked her to help me. But she failed."

"It was you, wasn't it? You told my stepmother to kill me," said Sophie. "That was the help you asked of her."

Fear nodded.

362

"Why did you need the queen's help?" Sophie asked. "Why couldn't you kill me yourself?"

"It's damned hard to kill a princess," Fear replied, with an airy wave of his hand. "Royals have an annoying habit of surrounding themselves with guards."

His answer was too careless, too flippant, and Sophie saw right through it. "No, that's not it. You *can't* kill, can you? You need someone else to do it for you." This knowledge strengthened her; it made her brave. More questions came to her lips, the same ones she'd been asking herself since the huntsman had cut out her heart. "Why do you want me dead? Why am I your enemy?"

Fear arched an eyebrow. "You surprise me. You came here to face me. Most humans never do."

"Answer my questions," Sophie demanded.

But Fear was silent. Pain tapped the glass box that contained Sophie's heart with a filthy fingernail. "Do you know how your father died?"

"The king died in battle," Sophie replied. She turned back to Fear. "Answer my questions."

But Fear, adjusting the silverware again, still would not speak.

So his sister did. "Your father didn't simply die in battle. He sacrificed himself," she said. "Two of his generals had been cut off from their battalions. They, and a handful of their men, were under attack and greatly outnumbered. Your father was watching from a place of safety, high up on a hill. Without hesitation, he rode out onto the field, knowing that the enemy soldiers would leave the generals and pursue him, for he was the king, the greatest prize. His action allowed his generals to break free and return to their troops. Because of your father, the Greenlands' armies won the day. He gave his life for his people."

Sophie's anger grew. She didn't need Pain to tell her these things; she knew them. "Why won't you answer me?" she shouted at Fear.

As Corvus maintained his silence, another voice was heard. It was deep and rumbling; it sounded like the stone door of a tomb rolling open.

"Your father was one of the bravest men who ever lived. He had the heart of a lion. But bravery isn't fearlessness. Only a fool feels no fear. Bravery is being afraid but doing what you must anyway. And there is only one thing that allows mortals to do that. Your father possessed great reserves of it, and you do, too. That's why you are my son's greatest enemy. That's why he wants you dead."

EIGHTY-ONE

Sophie turned toward the voice.

It belonged to a man. He was standing in front of the high windows at the farthest end of the study, his back to her.

Like Fear and Pain, he was tall and dressed in black. His shoulders were broad, his arms and legs powerfully built. He wore leather britches tucked into high boots, and a tunic of chain mail. A rippling mane of steel-gray hair flowed down his back. A sword hung at his hip.

"Fear rightly sensed that you were just like your father and that you would rule your realm wisely and well, with mercy and justice. He knew that you had something powerful inside you, something that could best him, and that once you were on the throne, you would drive him from the land. He could not have that. I cannot have that. If a mere girl conquers Fear, the strongest of my children, what message will that send to the world?"

The man turned around then, and Sophie drew a sharp breath. His face was a skull. His hands were bleached white bones.

"May I introduce my father?" Fear said. "His name is Death."

EIGHTY-TWO

The gears of Sophie's heart spun wildly. They slipped, faltered, and then caught again.

Death started toward her, his footsteps echoing in the room. Sophie was paralyzed by the sight of his ghastly face.

"My son has tried to kill you—and failed—several times," said Death. "It's my turn now, and I never fail."

Closer and closer he came, and as he did, he drew his sword. The blade glinted in the candlelight. Sophie saw a word etched down the length of it: *Aeternitas*. Everything inside her, flesh and bone and blood, told her to get up and run, but her faulty heart told her to stay, to protect Will.

Death's words echoed in her head. *He knew that you had something powerful inside you, something that could best him . . .*

What is it? she desperately asked herself. *What thing can best Fear?* She needed the answer *now*.

"Dispatch the boy first, Papa," Pain said with a sigh. "Put him out of his misery. And mine."

"You always were a softhearted girl," said Death, stopping in front of Sophie and Will.

Pain smiled, showing her rotten teeth. Fear adjusted a crystal goblet. And Death loomed tall, gripping the hilt of his terrible sword tightly. "No," Sophie cried, crossing her arms over Will's chest. *"Please."*

Time seemed to slow down, yet everything that happened next happened in the space of a heartbeat. Death raised his sword, then thrust the blade straight at Will's heart.

Sophie screamed.

And threw herself in front of it.

EIGHTY-THREE

The blade of Death's sword, a blade so sharp it could cut stars from the sky, pierced Sophie's skin and the muscle beneath it. It slid between two of her ribs, severing cartilage.

Had it hit the soft red creature that used to lie under Sophie's ribs but now lay in a glass box on Fear's table, it would have killed her.

But it didn't.

It hit a heart built from metal scraps and crooked gears and old springs, a heart that was faulty and flawed, noisy and troublesome.

Death's sword hit Sophie's clockwork heart.

And shattered into a million pieces.

EIGHTY-FOUR

Death stared in disbelief at his sword, in pieces on the floor.

Pain ripped a hank of hair out of her scalp.

Fear snarled.

And Sophie looked down at her chest. Blood seeped from the wound over her heart and soaked into her tunic. But it wasn't much. It wouldn't kill her. She'd suffered far worse.

Grabbing an iron poker from a stand near the fireplace, Sophie stood up, placing herself between Will and Death. She would not give the gray-haired killer a second chance.

Holding the poker out before her like a sword, she said, "You can't have him."

Sophie looked straight at Death as she spoke. She gazed into his hollow eye sockets, into the eternal darkness inside them, and though she was more afraid than she had ever been in her life, she thought of Will and held her ground.

Death looked at Sophie, at this thin, dirty, tear-stained girl. Her hand was shaking so hard she could barely hold the poker.

He laughed and took a step toward her, his chain mail clanking. "I am *Death*, you foolish girl," he said. "I have the abyss and all its terrors at my command."

Sophie took a step toward him, her heart clanking. "Yes, you are. But I am Queen Charlotta-Sidonia Wilhelmina Sophia of the Greenlands, and I have this poker. Don't make me use it."

Sophie looked absurd trying to fend off Death with what was little more than a stick, but there was something in her stance, something in her gaze, that said if Death wanted Will, he would have to take her down first. And she wouldn't go easy.

Death regarded Sophie.

He looked down, again, at the glinting shards of steel on the floor.

And then Death bowed his fearsome head.

EIGHTY-FIVE

Some think that courage comes from the belly.

I don't have the stomach for it, people say. Or, *He hasn't got the guts*.

The truth is, courage comes from the heart.

The word *courage* was born of *cor*, the Latin word for *heart*. Courage requires love, and love demands great courage— the courage a frail boy shows in speaking up for a small dog, the courage a king shows when he willingly rides to his death, the courage a scared girl shows as she throws herself in front of Death's sword.

Though Sophie is wounded, trapped in the castle of Fear, she stands tall and strong now. Because she finally understands. Fear has kept her heart in a box, but no more, never again. She knows what the thing is—the thing that will defeat Fear. And Pain. And even Death himself.

That thing is called love.

EIGHTY-SIX

Death stepped back.

Fear and Pain followed.

And for a moment, it felt to Sophie as if the world had stopped spinning. The floor shook beneath her feet. And then a sound like cannon fire tore through the air. She flinched, crouching protectively over Will. A long, juddering crack was traveling the length of the wall. Plaster tumbled down. The shelves all began to shake; the glass boxes slid across them, knocking into one another, clinking, fracturing. Some fell, shattering on the floor.

Nimmermehr was crumbling. Sophie knew she had to get her heart, get Will, and get out of the castle. She dropped her poker. Another crack tore across a wall. Windows exploded. Shards of glass rained down. The floor pitched violently. She lost her balance, fell, and whacked her head against a chair. Shaking off the pain, she picked herself up and lurched toward the table.

She was only a few feet away from it, reaching for the glass box, when a heavy chunk of plaster plummeted from the ceiling. Sophie saw it but could not stop it.

It hit the glass box that contained her heart and smashed it to pieces.

EIGHTY-SEVEN

"No!" Sophie screamed.

She grabbed the chunk of plaster and threw it to the floor. Her hands scrabbled for her heart. But it was too late. She picked it up but could only stand there watching in despair as it shriveled and cracked, then turned to a glittering ruby-red dust and slipped through her fingers.

Sophie sagged against the table. A wail tore itself from deep within her. It had all been for nothing. Her suffering at the hands of the huntsman. The clockwork heart the brothers had made for her. Her journey into the Darkwood. She would never take back her crown. Her people would be ruled by tyrants. Arno had died here. Now she and Will would, too.

Pain, circling the table, approached her. Sophie did not back away. What more could the woman do to her? She pointed at Sophie's chest. "That patched-together heart took a direct hit from my father's sword. The sword is shattered, but you're still here. Perhaps you should not wish such a heart away."

"But the clockwork will stop. Any moment now. Johann told me so. He said I had only a month to live."

Regarding Sophie with a rueful smile, Pain said, "Perhaps

Johann is a better clockmaker than he thinks he is. Every human heart is faulty, full of cracks and scars. And every heart winds down one day. Yours will, too. But today is not that day. And today is all that humans are given."

She touched the blood soaking Sophie's tunic. A shower of crimson rose petals fluttered to the floor. "Goodbye, Sophia. For now."

Pain turned away in a swirl of black, and then she was gone, and a crow, its feathers blue-black and glossy, rose in the air. Two more joined it, cawing and flapping, and then all three flew through a ruined window, out into the moonlit night.

EIGHTY-EIGHT

The castle shuddered.

Windows were breaking in every room. Mirrors were falling and smashing. Paintings crashed to the floor. Armor toppled over. Outside, the castle's towers and ramparts were tumbling down.

Sophie needed to get out of Nimmermehr *now*. She needed to get Will out, but she couldn't; he was slipping away. Kneeling over him, her hands on his chest, she could feel no breath, no heartbeat. Frantic, she yelled at him. Shoved him. Grabbed his shoulders and shook him.

"Don't die, Will. Please don't die," she said, her voice breaking. "I love you."

She leaned over him, then kissed his lips, lingering there. Making the kiss long enough to last forever. Closing her eyes, she touched her forehead to his. "I love you," she said again. "I should have told you long ago. But now it's too late. I'll never get the chance again."

"Would you take it if you did?"

Sophie gasped. She raised her head. Will was awake. His beautiful, bruised eyes were open.

"Will!" she whispered.

"Would you?"

"Yes," Sophie said. *"Yes."* She kissed him again and again, and she might've kept on kissing him if another piece of the ceiling hadn't crashed down only feet away from them.

"What's happening, Sophie? Where's Corvus?"

"Gone. Nimmermehr is falling. We have to get out, too, before we're crushed."

She helped Will to his feet. He was hurting and limping, but he could walk with Sophie's help. She put his arm around her neck, and together they made their way out of the room.

"Arno . . . Did he come with you?" Will asked. "Is he here?"

"A wunschfetzen got him. But there's a chance he's still alive, I think."

"How?"

"Corvus talked about him. He didn't say he was dead. He said he was wandering in the tunnels. We can't leave him here, Will."

"No, we can't, but we've got to hurry. When this place comes down, it'll crush the tunnels and anyone in them."

Sophie led Will back the way she'd come, past the ballroom and the music room, the armory, the trophy room. They ducked falling books and chandeliers. Doorframes cracked above their heads; floorboards separated under their feet. The goblin servants were running for their lives, too, and paid no attention to the two fleeing humans in their midst.

When Sophie and Will finally reached the kitchen, thick black smoke was billowing from the ovens, making it hard to see. The floor was slippery from water flowing out of burst pipes. Sophie skidded in it and fell, nearly bringing Will down with her, but she caught herself, kept going, and found the way to the larders.

Will swiped a handful of small cakes off a table. "If we do find Arno, we can use these to draw the wunschfetzen off," he said, stuffing them into a pocket. Sophie grabbed a blazing lantern that someone had left on a shelf.

They were able to move quickly from the larder down through the cellars, but their progress from cellars to the tunnel—over the slippery stone steps—was painfully slow, and all the while, the ancient castle above them shuddered and groaned.

As they climbed down, Will told Sophie how he'd tried to find the tunnel, too, but had failed. So he'd tried to sneak across the bridge instead, under the cover of darkness, but a goblin guard had grabbed him before he'd even made it halfway across the moat. Beatings followed, and several long days in a dungeon cell. He'd never expected to make it out of the castle alive.

When Sophie finally got Will down the steps and into the tunnel, they were able to move faster. Their only obstacle was the caved-in wall. More rubble had been loosened by the shaking going on above them, but the opening was still there. Sophie went first while Will waited on the other side. When she'd crawled through, she turned around so that he could give her the lantern. Handling it carefully, for it was the only light they had, she placed it on the ground, then reached back through the opening for his hand.

But before she could take it, a meaty arm hooked around

her neck and jerked her backward. Sophie had no time to scream.

Her attacker tightened his arm, squeezing her throat. Fireworks exploded inside her head. She fought, clawing at him, feet kicking wildly, but she could not free herself.

"Where is he?" a voice shouted. "Where's Matti? Where's my boy?"

It was Arno, and he was throttling her.

Sophie tried to call his name, to beg him to stop, but no sound would come. Her lungs were hitching. The fireworks were fading. She felt her body go limp, felt the fight draining out of her.

And then Arno threw her to the ground like a sack of garbage. Clutching her throat, Sophie looked up at him. He was a shambling wreck. His face was wet with tears; his eyes were unfocused. Half a dozen wunschfetzens were clustered on his shoulders. Two had their fingers in his ears. The others were pushing and shoving, trying to knock them away so that they could have a turn tormenting him.

"Hey! Look! Look over here, you jackasses!" Will yelled.

He'd somehow managed to crawl through the rubble. One hand was braced against the wall; the other was thrust out in front of him.

"Come on, come here . . . See what I've got for you?"

In his hand were the cakes he'd taken. They were squashed; the icing was cracked, but it didn't matter; the wunschfetzens shrieked with greed at the sight of them. They stretched their skinny arms toward Will; their long, sticky fingers clutched for the sweets.

"Come closer," Will coaxed. "That's it . . ."

The wunschfetzens jumped from Arno's shoulders to the tunnel floor. As they did, his eyes cleared. His back straightened. He looked as if he'd stepped out of a fog.

The creatures hopped and danced around Will's legs, clamoring for the cakes. Will lowered his hand but still held the sweets just out of reach. The wunschfetzens drooled; their huge eyes grew even bigger.

"Here you go, you little creeps," Will said, and then he chucked the cakes through the opening in the rubble.

The wunschfetzens screeched with rage. They clambered up the debris, pulling on one another's legs and arms, each trying to prevent the others from getting to the cakes.

"That'll keep them busy for a bit," said Will.

"Will, is that *you*? How did you get here?" Arno asked, dazed. "Sophie, why are we standing around? We have to go . . . We have to get into the castle . . ."

"I went without you, Arno. I had to," Sophie started to explain, but one of the wunschfetzens shrieked, cutting her off. Arno looked down at the noisy creatures, still brawling in the rubble.

"I'm guessing that they were involved," he said.

"I'll tell you everything once we're out of here," Sophie promised. "Help Will. We've got to keep moving. Nimmermehr is crumbling."

As the words left her lips, a thundering boom was heard from above them. The tunnel shook. Dirt and stones rained down from the ceiling.

Sophie snatched the lantern. Arno grabbed Will's arm and

looped it around his neck. The three dodged more falling rubble and climbed over another cave-in, but half an hour later, they'd made it out of the tunnel.

Arno sagged against a rock, weak with relief. Will joined him. But Sophie wouldn't let them rest. "We need to find Jeremias and Joosts. And the horses," she said. "If nothing else has," she added grimly.

They pushed past trees and through brush, led by the sound of rushing water. The two brothers, drawn and worried looking, were standing on the riverbank, staring at the castle in the distance. Flames were devouring it now, burning so hot and high that they cast an orange glow over the entire landscape.

"Jeremias! Joosts!" Sophie called, running to them.

"Sophie!" the two brothers shouted. They embraced her, and the three stood together, arms around one another, for a long, teary minute.

"We thought you were in *there*," Joosts said, nodding at the inferno.

"We thought we'd lost you," said Jeremias, with a tremor in his voice. "Did you—"

His words were cut off by the roar of a tower toppling. Will and Arno had joined the others. They all watched in silence as another tower collapsed. A moment later, the ramparts crumbled, and then with a shudder, the castle itself fell, imploding with the force of an earthquake. Stone blocks rained down, raising geysers of water from the moat, punching holes in the ground, smashing the drawbridge. The noise continued for what seemed like an eternity, and then all was eerily still.

The King of Crows' castle was gone. There was only a cloud of dust rising from the crater where it used to stand.

As the five friends stood, watching and listening, the shouts and cries of goblins rose on the night. They were answered by the roars of trolls, the screams of waldwichts, and more sounds—sounds that Sophie couldn't put an image to and didn't want to.

Arno winced as a particularly bloodcurdling howl rose. "Fear has left, but his creatures are still lurking," he said. "We need to get going. We're not safe here, not by a long shot."

He and Joosts untied the horses. Will bent down to the water, cupped his hands, and drank.

And Jeremias laid a hand on Sophie's arm. "I tried to ask you something, but the castle collapsed before I could . . . Did you find your heart, Sophie?"

Sophie wasn't sure what to say. She'd found it in Nimmermehr, only to lose it again. Forever. But then she thought of Jeremias and Joosts, and the other brothers back at the Hollow. Of Weber and Tupfen. Tom. The Beckers. Max. The soldiers. Oma and Gretta. Will.

Sophie smiled. "Yes, Jeremias," she finally said. "I did."

EIGHTY-NINE

The night was dark and deep, but the silver moon, high and shining, provided enough light for Sophie and her friends to see as they made their way through the Darkwood.

Will and Joosts had trouble walking, so they were on horseback. Sophie and Jeremias were leading the horses, and Arno was leading them, for he knew the woods best.

They were all trying to be as quiet as possible so as not to alert unfriendly things to their presence. They were also trying to figure out their next step.

"We'll take Will home first," Arno said, his voice low. "He needs care. Then we'll go to the Hollow—"

Sophie cut him off. "Do what you need to do. I'm going back to Konigsburg, to the palace," she said. She had bested Fear, bested Death. Her heart was strong, stronger than either she or the brothers had realized. Now it was time to face the queen.

"How?" asked Will. "Adelaide . . . Haakon . . . They'll have you killed."

"You can't go there, Sophie. It's madness," Arno said.

His dismissive tone angered Sophie. She lengthened her

horse's reins and caught up to him. "You're the one who told me to take my crown back, didn't you?"

Arno didn't answer her.

So she raised her voice. "You're the one who said, *Just because you don't have two pennies—or an army—today doesn't mean you won't have them tomorrow*."

Arno jutted his chin. "Didn't know you then. Didn't care for you. Lost my family once. My little boy. You're my family now, Sophie. I can't lose you."

"Sophie, it's suicide," Jeremias argued. "You need help. Allies. You need soldiers and weapons. You'll have to ask the emperor of Cathay for help. Or—"

"Shhh!" Will suddenly hissed, holding up a hand.

Everyone stopped. They fell silent. A rustling sound was heard. It came from behind them. And in front of them. Whatever was making it was all around them.

"Someone's out there," Sophie said quietly.

"A lot of someones," Will added. He held up the lantern he was still carrying. Its light reflected in scores of eyes. They glinted green in the darkness.

"Who are they? What do they want?" Joosts asked.

"Fear sent his army to finish the job," Arno said.

No sooner had he finished speaking than the attack was launched.

There was a series of heavy, thumping booms, and then a tree, merely steps away from where Sophie was standing, exploded into shards. The horses reared, whinnying shrilly. Will and Joosts only barely managed to keep their seats.

A stone troll, eight feet tall and made of rocks and rubble, pounded into the clearing, his massive hands clenched into fists. Dozens of goblins followed him, their dark eyes—and sharp teeth—glinting in the torchlight. They were armed with clubs and pikes.

Hands went to weapons, but Sophie and her friends were greatly outnumbered, and they knew it. A goblin stepped forward. Sophie tensed, clutching her dagger, ready to fight for her life. But then, to her astonishment, instead of attacking her, the goblin swept her a bow.

"Forgive us. We did not mean to frighten you," he said, tossing the troll a stern look. "Some of us do not know our own strength."

The troll shuffled from foot to foot, shamefaced. He banged his fist on his head.

The goblin rose. His eyes met Sophie's. "Fear enslaved us," he said. "He made us vicious. You freed us. We are here to thank you for that and to pledge our allegiance to you. Our code of honor demands no less. You will be our ruler now. We are yours to command, your loyal servants."

As Sophie watched in astonishment, a thousand torches flamed to life within the woods. She saw hundreds of goblins. Stone trolls, moss trolls, river trolls, mud trolls. There were waldwichts and makabers. Pixies with mushroom caps and acorn hats—some of them rode squirrels or rats, others sat in wooden wagons drawn by weasels.

Their eyes—hopeful, expectant, determined—were all on her. And she didn't know what to do. They wanted her to be their leader, but she'd never led anyone before, never mind such ferocious creatures.

Another goblin stepped forward. He was carrying a crown. It was made from Herzmord vines twined together. The blooms that decorated it no longer whispered poisonous words but shimmered like dark jewels in the moonlight.

The goblin leader's words sounded in her head. *He made us vicious . . . You freed us . . .*

Sophie knew it was love that had freed them. Love had given her the courage to face down Fear. Love had made her strong. She thought of another creature driven by Fear—Adelaide. Perhaps she could be freed, too. Perhaps this whole ravaged realm could.

Sophie took a deep breath. She knelt down. The goblin stepped forward and placed the crown on her head. As Sophie rose, he—and all the other creatures—raised their fists, their weapons, their voices.

"Hail to the queen! Hail to the queen! Hail to the queen!"

The sound whirled through the woods like a hurricane's roar.

The stone troll, the one who'd crashed into the clearing, approached Sophie. He bent down and set his huge hand on the ground, palm upturned, and tapped his shoulder with his other hand.

Sophie understood. She stepped onto his palm, then climbed up his arm and sat down on his shoulder. He tilted his fierce face to hers. In his eyes was a question.

Sophie whispered the answer. The troll nodded. He stood straight, turned to the east, and started to walk, the ground shaking with his every step.

Will called after Sophie, his voice tight with fear. "Sophie, what are you doing? Where are you going?"

Sophie turned to him, smiling, and said, "To my palace. With my army."

NINETY

They came.

In twos and threes. Or one by one.

From Schadenburg. Grauseldorf. Drohendsburg. And a thousand other places.

In wagons. On foot. Carrying rucksacks and bundles. Laden with food and provisions, or with nothing but the clothes on their backs.

Word had spread far and wide about the young queen on her march to the palace to take her throne.

In the towns and villages, people threw open their shutters. They ran into the streets. In the countryside, they stopped tilling their fields or milking their cows and hurried to the road to catch a glimpse of her.

Max caught sight of the procession from the topmost window of the barn he'd bought with Arno's graveyard jewels to house his fellow refugees. He and a hundred others hurriedly packed their bags and were waiting at the side of the road when she arrived.

The wounded veterans, every last one of them, met her by the burned-out ruins of St. Sebastian's. A stone troll carried the soldier with no legs. A goblin took the blind drummer's hand, and together they walked along.

The Beckers joined—the husband with his scarred face, the pregnant wife, the grandmother, the children—and so did most of their village.

The elderly and the young came. The strong and the weak. The rich and poor. Young mothers with small children in their arms. Old mothers in their grown children's arms. They all joined Sophie. Promised to fight for her. To die for her.

The trolls hoisted the infirm onto their shoulders. The waldwichts made baskets of their arms and carried the babies. At night, in the camps, children braided the river trolls' long, reedy hair out of their faces and brought soupbones to the makabers. Little ones curled up in the soft arms of the moss trolls. Old ones told stories.

Their numbers swelled from hundreds to thousands to tens of thousands. For days they walked through the Darkwood, in sunshine and rain, up hills and through valleys, until they finally arrived at the outskirts of Konigsburg one evening at dusk, and made camp for the last time.

The young queen sat up through the night, her eyes on the palace, with its thick stone walls, its drawbridge. Its cannons and swordsmen and archers.

By morning, she knew what she had to do.

NINETY-ONE

A sentry, bleary-eyed and tired after a long night, stopped dead atop the ramparts.

"I'm dreaming. I must be," he said, unable to believe what his eyes were telling him.

He rubbed his weary face, but he was not asleep. As he continued to gaze west, he saw something that would stay with him the rest of his days.

A girl, her black hair cropped short, was making her way from the Darkwood, across a clearing, to the palace.

She was bruised and battered, dirty and scarred. She was alone.

A huge crowd of people ringed the clearing but did not approach the palace. The girl seemed to have asked them to stay back, to stay safe.

For a moment, the sentry thought she looked like the princess come back from the dead. But he dismissed the thought as a trick of his bleary eyes. This thin, ragged girl could not be the princess. No proud warhorse carried her. No robes of satin and silk fluttered around her. She wore ripped trousers and a tattered shirt. A simple crown of black roses adorned her head.

On she walked until she was only yards away from the palace wall.

"Sentry!" she bellowed. "Lower the drawbridge! Let me in!"

"Who are you? By what right do you demand entry to the palace?" the sentry shouted back.

"I am Queen Charlotta-Sidonia Wilhelmina Sophia, rightful ruler of the Greenlands! I've come to take my crown from a cruel queen and her murderous heir!"

The sentry did not know what to do. He'd been told that the princess was dead. Yet here was a girl who looked like her, demanding entry to the palace. As he stood in place, deliberating, several other soldiers joined him. One shouted for their sergeant.

"Soldiers!" the girl bellowed. "I will have my crown! Lower the drawbridge!"

Shouts went up from the soldiers. The girl's words were treason. They demanded the crown; they threatened the queen. An alarm was sounded. Soldiers ran shouting from their barracks. Archers took their positions. The lord commander appeared, his long cape billowing behind him. He was followed by Prince Haakon.

"What's going on here? Where is the queen?" Haakon demanded.

"Queen Adelaide is safe in her quarters, my lord. Surrounded by guards," the lord commander replied.

"This girl," the sentry said, pointing at Sophie, "says *she* is the queen."

Haakon turned and looked out over the ramparts to the clearing. His face flushed crimson with anger. "How is she not dead?" He said the words under his breath, but the lord commander heard him, and his shrewd eyes sharpened.

Haakon took a breath, ready to shout orders, but before he could, Sophie spoke.

"Lord commander! Soldiers!" she cried. "Look! Look at these people with me! Your people! Your friends and neighbors! Your families! Do you know what's happening to them? They're being turned out of their houses. Their crops and possessions are being taken to build fortresses and buy warships so that a heartless queen and a false prince can attack realms that have not attacked us. The same will happen to you. When you're wounded, you'll be tossed aside. When your father's farm proves valuable to the queen, she will take it. When the prince needs your horses for his generals, your livestock to feed his soldiers, he will snatch them."

"She is a traitor! Shoot her!" Haakon bellowed.

"But, my lord," one of the soldiers said. "She says she is the princess. We cannot shoot the princess!"

Fury twisted Haakon's handsome features. "She is *not* the princess! The princess is dead! She's an imposter, a troublemaker! Shoot her, I said! Did you not hear me?" he yelled. "Nock!"

The archers, all one hundred of them, notched the ends of their arrows into their bowstrings and readied themselves to aim. One hundred arrows would obliterate Sophie, strong heart or not.

But Sophie did not cower. She did not run. Instead, she strode forward and ripped open the neck of her shirt, exposing the scarred skin under her collarbone.

"Here is your target, archers!" she shouted. "Shoot if you will! You have deadly weapons. I have only my heart."

"Draw!" Haakon yelled.

The archers raised their bows, drew the strings back, and aimed, waiting for him to shout the final command: *"Loose!"*

But before he could, a young mother, her baby in her arms, broke from the line of people ringing the clearing and ran to Sophie. She was panting for breath by the time she reached her.

"No!" Sophie shouted, terrified for the woman and her child. She motioned at her to go back.

But the woman would not. She stood next to Sophie, facing the palace and all its soldiers. She held her child tightly to her chest and lifted her head. "If you shoot our queen, you'll have to shoot us, too!" she yelled.

Sophie's heart clenched. Never had she seen such bravery. "Don't do this. Go back. *Please*," she said.

"To what? Wandering the roads? Begging? Those are slow deaths. I'd rather a quick one for me and my baby. My husband's dead. My house is gone. We have nothing. You gave us something. You gave us courage. Hope. Love."

Tears threatened, but Sophie swallowed them down. She felt for the woman's hand. It was shaking. Sophie squeezed it hard.

The two women turned and once again faced the archers. Sophie prayed that if the end was coming, it would be quick. But the gods had other ideas, for one by one the archers lowered their bows.

"Draw, damn you!" Haakon thundered. "Or I'll have you all hanged!"

But the men would not shoot a child.

Sophie and the young mother did not stand by themselves for

long. The blind drummer was the next one to walk across the clearing, helped by his new goblin friend. Then came heavily pregnant Mrs. Becker and her family. Max. A woman in a wheelbarrow, pushed along by two boys. Old people. Children. Trolls and pixies. They all joined hands, making a circle around Sophie. Bigger and bigger it grew, spiraling outward, until it filled the clearing.

The lord commander looked out over the sea of people. His people. Tired, hungry, thin. Injured, some of them. Homeless. Hurting. Discarded.

But brave, so brave. So full of hope.

"Do you *dare* to disobey your prince?" Haakon screamed. *"Draw!"*

"He is not your prince!" Sophie shouted. "He cares nothing for you and will use you for cannon fodder to satisfy his own ambition. You will die for him, because that is the kind of ruler *he* is. I will die for you, because that is the kind of ruler *I* am. Arrest him, Lord Commander!"

Enraged now, Haakon tore a bow and arrow out of an archer's hands.

In one quick, fluid motion, he fired.

But the lord commander was quicker. He grabbed hold of the bow and pulled it down. The shot went low; the arrow splashed harmlessly into the moat.

"Arrest this man," he commanded.

"Arrest *me*?" Haakon said, incredulous. "On whose orders?"

The lord commander turned to Sophie. He bowed.

"On the queen's," he said as he rose.

NINETY-TWO

Sophie rode over the drawbridge on the shoulder of a stone troll.

Soldiers dropped to one knee as she entered the Queen's Court. The troll knelt, too, and stretched out his palm. Sophie stepped onto it, and he lowered her to the ground. The troll let out a menacing growl as a reminder of what would happen if anyone harmed her.

The lord commander was waiting there for her.

Sophie looked around, amazed to find herself in the court. There were days when she thought she would never see the palace again.

Now she was here, and the responsibilities that lay ahead of her would soon descend, but she had another task to attend to first. Haakon had been arrested, but Sophie's greatest enemy was still at large, and she would not be safe, nor would her people, until Adelaide was in a prison cell.

"Welcome home, Your Majesty," the lord commander said.

Sophie gave him a curt nod. "My stepmother . . . where is she?" she asked.

"In her chambers," he replied.

"I'll need you to accompany me, together with two dozen loyal soldiers," Sophie said as she prepared for the confrontation. "The men guarding her may not wish to stand down."

The lord commander ordered his soldiers to Sophie's side and said he would go with them as well. Just as they were about to enter the palace, Haakon—frog-marched down from the ramparts—appeared in the Queen's Court on his way to the dungeons.

His wrists were manacled. He had a cut above one eye, a bruise on his cheek. He'd obviously resisted his captors.

He and Sophie locked eyes. "Stop," she ordered as he and his guards approached her.

"Sophie, I—" he started to say, but Sophie cut him off.

"My ring, please," she said, nodding at the gold unicorn ring on Haakon's left hand, the Ruler's Ring.

One of the soldiers removed it and handed it to Sophie. She pushed it onto her left ring finger, where it belonged.

"I'm sorry, Sophie . . . so sorry. For everything. What have I done? It should've been me putting a ring on your finger," Haakon said, his voice heavy with remorse.

"It almost was," said Sophie, her eyes lingering on him, on his tumble of golden hair, his handsome face, his sky-blue eyes. She remembered the flower ring he'd given her, here in the palace, not so long ago. The promises. The kisses.

Haakon caught her gaze and held it. "You won't believe me . . . but it's you I'm worried about now," he said.

Sophie gave a mirthless laugh. "You're right, Haakon. I don't believe you."

"Put me in prison. Keep me in a cell, but let me help you," Haakon said earnestly. "Let me spend the rest of my life making amends. Or at least trying to."

"Why would I do that?"

"Because you can't do this, Sophie," he said, his voice urgent and low. "You can't rule. You *know* you can't. You're too softhearted. Your enemies will eat you alive. How will you deal with them? Love them to death?"

Sophie cocked her head, her gaze unwavering. "How would you have me deal with my enemies?"

Haakon straightened, emboldened by her question. "The king of the Hinterlands will invade as soon as he hears that you've taken the throne. The emperor of Cathay is sure to follow his lead. Let them cross the borders, burn a few towns, kill a few villagers—"

"You are so smart, Haakon. So certain," Sophie said, cutting him off. "You always see what needs to be done."

Haakon nodded in perfect agreement with her. Women always succumbed to his charm, his intelligence, his confidence. How could they not? "I can help you, Sophie. Truly. If you'll let me."

Sophie arched an eyebrow. "Like you helped me in St. Sebastian's?"

"That was a misunderstanding."

"Ah. Is that what it was?"

Haakon risked a smile. The sort that could melt the iciest of hearts. "All's fair in love and war, my darling girl. But we're on the same side now. At least, we *could* be . . ."

"Go on."

"You must deal with your enemies quickly and decisively," he instructed. "Capture their captains and generals. Capture their king, if you can. Then send a message. Show no mercy. Take the prisoners straight to the executioner's block—before their commanders send reinforcements—and cut off their heads."

"Cutting off my enemies' heads . . . What an excellent idea, Haakon," Sophie said.

She turned to the two soldiers holding the handsome prince and said, "Start with his."

NINETY-THREE

Without a glance back, Sophie headed into the palace and made her way to the main staircase. She took the steps two at a time. The lord commander and his soldiers followed her.

The hall leading to Adelaide's chambers was blocked at both ends by members of the queen's guard. The lord commander explained to their captain what had happened and ordered them to stand down.

Krause's eyes flickered over Sophie. A sneer curled his lip. He hesitated, just for an instant, then obeyed his commander. Sophie remembered him setting fire to St. Sebastian's and throwing the Beckers out of their home.

Adelaide had once told her that cowardice could infect a population. Looking at Krause, Sophie knew that viciousness could, too. She would find a new captain of the guards. Immediately.

Sophie tried the doors to her stepmother's chambers, but they were locked. She called to her, asking her to open them. When she got no response, she motioned to her soldiers to batter them down—a task they quickly accomplished.

Sophie moved through her stepmother's rooms—her

antechamber, her study, her dressing room—warily, fully mindful that the woman had tried to kill her several times. As she did, she saw the familiar furnishings, the jewels and gowns, the gilt mirror. How many times had she been summoned here to endure the queen's searing words, her excoriating looks? How many times had she been forced to hear her shortcomings, her failings? To be told all that she was not?

Many would have forgiven Sophie for feeling exultant as she walked through the rooms, but all she felt was a deep, aching sadness for the hours, the days, the life wasted here.

Sophie found Adelaide in the last room—her bedroom. She was standing by a pair of French doors that led to her balcony, gazing out at a courtyard.

"It's really you," Adelaide said as she turned to regard Sophie. "You died from the poisoned apple. I saw you. And yet here you stand. You are impossible to kill." She circled Sophie. "Look at you. So different. Scarred and dirty, skinny as a broom yet marching on palaces and toppling enemies," she marveled. "I did that. I made you tough. Made you shrewd. I made you who you are."

Sophie slowly shook her head. "No, Adelaide. *I* made me who I am. With the help of my friends, and my people."

"You must come with us now, madam," the lord commander said to Adelaide as two of his soldiers advanced toward her.

But the queen was quicker than they were. She opened the French doors and darted through them. Her intention was clear.

Sophie held up a hand, stopping the men. "Come in from the balcony, Adelaide," she said.

But her stepmother would not. She was facing Sophie but kept walking backward, taking one slow step after another until she reached the railing.

"Stop, Adelaide."

"Why not? Isn't this what you came for? Revenge? I shall make it easy for you."

"Revenge is not why I came."

"What do you want, then?"

"I've met the King of Crows. He told me that he helped you when no one else would. Tell me, Adelaide. Tell me what happened. I want to understand."

"Why should I? It will do me no good."

"It will do us both good," Sophie countered. She waved the men back. They retreated into the adjoining room.

Adelaide regarded Sophie for a long moment, deliberating; then she walked back into the room. She stopped in front of her mirror and gazed into it. Her eyes were not focused on herself; they were far away. She was seeing a time, and a place, that Sophie could not.

"When I was twelve years old, Edward, the treacherous duke of Saxony, attacked my father's palace. He wanted the crown. There was no warning, no time for my father to muster his army. The king's guard fought valiantly, but they were quickly overpowered. Edward's men spared no one in the palace, not even the smallest kitchen girl. They killed my parents in front of me. My mother tried to protect me. She pressed a dagger into my hands. As my father died, he begged me to save his son. *Promise me, Adelaide*, he said. *Promise you'll save him, no matter what. Even if it costs you your own life . . .*"

401

Sophie listened raptly to her stepmother. She had heard the story of the murder of Adelaide's parents but never from Adelaide. "I was small and quick. I managed to escape the soldiers and find my way to the nursery using a secret passage. My brother was there, alive. His nurse was with him. She'd bolted the door, but Edward's soldiers were pounding on it. The baby was shrieking with fear . . ."

Adelaide's words trailed away as emotion engulfed her. She took a moment to gather herself. Sophie waited, watching her in the glass. After a long moment, Adelaide spoke again.

"There was a mirror in the nursery. This very one," she continued, touching her looking glass. "I caught sight of myself in it. I was drenched in blood. My legs buckled, and I fell to my knees in front of the glass. The nurse pleaded with me to get up. To save my brother. But I barely heard her. I was so terrified, I couldn't move. All I could do was stare into the glass. And that's when I saw him . . . behind me in the mirror . . . the King of Crows. He promised to help me. He told me to get up and get my brother. *The soldiers are almost through that door*, he said. *Hurry.* Just then the door burst open. Edward's men came into the room, but as they did, they were attacked by some survivors from my father's guard. One of the enemy soldiers broke free and killed the nurse. He started for my brother . . ."

"What did you do?" Sophie asked.

Adelaide shook her head.

"Adelaide, what did you do?"

"I killed him, at Corvus's urging. I used my mother's dagger."

Sophie took a sharp breath. Adelaide kept talking. Her words tumbled out in a gush, as if they'd been pent up behind a dam for too long and the dam had finally burst.

"I was lucky. The first cut went deep. He dropped his weapon. I stabbed him again and again, even though he begged for his life. That soldier visits me often. In my nightmares. It did not cost me my life to save my father's son, no. It cost me much more."

Sophie moved closer. She could see the anguish in her stepmother's eyes and knew that in her mind, Adelaide was a girl again, back in that room, with the dying man and the wailing child. She ached for that girl.

"I was able to snatch my brother and escape. Two of my father's guards got us to the earl of Coburg's castle. As my father's eldest child, I had suddenly become queen regent, the ruler of my realm. With the earl's help, I assembled an army that very night. We rode on the palace the next morning and routed Edward's soldiers. I ruled for seventeen years. Until my brother came of age and married me off to your father, like a horse put out to pasture."

Adelaide fell silent, still standing in front of her looking glass. Her eyes were red with unshed tears, her face was ravaged by remorse. As Sophie watched, her stepmother whirled around and snatched a heavy crystal inkwell from her writing desk. With a wrenching cry, she heaved it at the mirror. The silver glass shattered and a million glittering shards rained down on the floor.

The lord commander, watching from the doorway, hurried into the room, his hand on his sword, but Sophie stayed him.

Adelaide stared down at the shards. "I let Corvus into my

heart the day Edward's soldiers came, and he's been there ever since. Devouring it bit by bit. Every decision I made was led by Corvus. Every cruelty I inflicted. Every life I took. He convinced me that mercy was weakness. That kindness would be repaid with treachery. And I believed him. And now? Now there is nothing left of my heart." Tears slipped down her cheeks. She started for her balcony once again.

"No, don't," Sophie said, moving toward her.

Adelaide picked up a large shard of silver glass from the floor. She held the shard out like a dagger, warning her off.

"I do not relish what lies before me," she said. "I've sent many to the palace dungeons. And the executioner's block. I will not spend whatever time I have left in a rat-infested cell, awaiting your vengeance."

"I seek justice, Adelaide, not vengeance. For crimes committed against my people."

Adelaide opened her hand. She watched the shard fall. "He will find me in the dungeons," she said softly, more to herself than to Sophie. "He will wait for me at the scaffold." She lifted her eyes to Sophie's once more, and in them Sophie saw a deep, aching weariness.

"I was a great queen but not a good one," Adelaide said. "You must be both, Sophia."

She bowed her head, and then before Sophie could stop her, she darted the rest of the way across the room to the balcony.

Sophie screamed. She rushed to the railing and leaned over it, clutching futilely for her stepmother's arm, her skirts, anything. But it was too late. The queen's body lay broken on the stones below. Blood pooled around her head, a final crimson crown.

NINETY-FOUR

Sophie, dressed in a gown of white, a golden crown on her head, stepped out onto the palace balcony and waved.

A roar like a tidal wave rose from the thronging crowd below her. It was her coronation day. She'd been crowned queen of the Greenlands at dawn. The cathedral bells were still ringing, and millions of rose petals fluttered in the air.

Sophie waved to her people, her heart clanking with joy.

Then she invited her fellow monarchs, who were all inside the Great Hall, waiting to be seated for the celebratory dinner, to join her on the balcony.

They stood together, shoulder to shoulder, all the rulers of all the world's realms, and then Sophie spoke, her voice ringing out strong and clear. She told her people about her experience with Fear and how he had taken her heart, how he wished to take every human heart. And then she had called upon them never to give in to Fear, and to guard one another's hearts as carefully as they guarded their own.

"As long as we treat one another with kindness, we will keep our hearts whole. Let us all live, from this day forward, with peace in our hearts, and with love."

The rulers applauded, and then one by one they all turned and walked back into the hall, giving Sophie her moment.

Basking in the love of her people, Sophie smiled. Will was in the Great Hall, too, to celebrate with her. Oma and Gretta as well. The little girl was getting stronger. Sophie had brought her to the palace, where she was receiving the best of care. The brothers were here. Weber and Tupfen, too. Arno. Tom. And Zara.

Sophie lifted her face to the sky. A crow was flying above her, making circles against the blue.

The queen's guard knew about the King of Crows and how he had tried, many times, to have Sophie killed. They were constantly on the lookout for him.

Two members of the guard had been posted on either end of the balcony, archers both. They spotted the bird and aimed at it. But before they could fire, Sophie stopped them.

"The crows will always be here. With me. With all of us," she said. "Arrows may kill one or two, but they won't keep Fear at bay."

Sophie raised her forearm. The crow slowly spiraled down and landed on it. It cocked its head, eyeing her. Then it clicked its beak. Sophie pressed her hand to her heart.

"Only they can keep your master at bay," she said, nodding at the joyous people thronging the streets, at the trolls and goblins and pixies rejoicing with them. "I have them, you see. I have my friends. I have a warm jacket. And strudel. I have Will. They fill my heart. They *are* my heart."

The crow bowed to Sophie and gave a single, shrill caw. Then it flapped its wings and flew away.

Morning had broken over the palace that day as it had months ago, when a girl had ridden out past the walls to the forest, following where I, the huntsman, led her.

That girl had been afraid.

That girl had sought to protect her heart by boxing it away.

That girl had died in the Darkwood.

And another girl had been born. A girl with a heart that refused to be hidden. One that was willful and noisy and out of control. A heart of cracks and patches, one that leaked emotion like a broken bucket leaks water.

A girl who understood that a queen's heart was made to break. Over and over again. And Sophie knew that hers would, too. When crops failed and people starved. When plague descended. When war swept its red cloak over the land.

Like blood that turned to rubies, and tears that turned to pearls, the ache that would rack her heart was just another of Pain's strange gifts. From sadness came empathy. From grief came compassion. From anger came resolve. From loss came love.

These are the things that make us get up when we fall. Try again when we fail. These are the most valuable jewels.

Once upon long ago, always and evermore, a girl road into the forest.

Started off for her grandmother's house.

Met a witch in the woods.

And then that girl came back. Led no more, but leading.

With the smell of burned witch in her clothing.

With the wolf's head in her basket.

With an army at her back.

She requires no mirror to tell her what she always knew.

That she is everything she needs, that she has everything she needs, to make a path through the Darkwood.

And find her way home.

EPILOGUE

"I thought we'd have a picnic," said Fear, smiling brightly.

"A *picnic*?" said Death, incredulous. "That's why you invited us here?"

"Yes. And I thought we could take a nice ride first. Work up an appetite."

War turned to Pestilence. "Our baby brother has lost his mind," he said.

"Indulge me, won't you?" Fear said. "There's something I want to show you."

"It *is* a lovely evening. And it's not often I get to see so many of my children all in the same place," Death said wistfully. "Everyone's so busy these days."

"Good! Hop in," said Fear, opening the door of his shiny black carriage. It was standing at the bottom of a steep mountain. A narrow road zigzagged to the top.

Death climbed in first. He was followed by his daughter Pestilence. She wore a sweat-stained linen shift. Her hair was cut short and bristly; her lips were cracked. She was covered with oozing sores, pustules, and blisters.

Sunken-eyed Famine, his hair falling out in patches, his

clothes hanging from his bones, shuffled in behind his sister, whining the whole time. "Oh, come *on*, Pesti. Don't drip on the seat. Other people have to sit there, too, you know."

Pain, with her red-rimmed eyes, climbed in next, and then War, bronzed and muscular. The springs creaked and groaned as he sat down. Scars, livid and shiny, laddered his face and his bald head. He left bloody handprints on the door, the seats, everything he touched.

Once they were all inside, Fear joined them, closed the door, and then rapped on it. The driver, a cadaverous-looking man wearing a bowler hat, cracked the whip. Four glossy black stallions started off.

"The girl . . . Sophia . . . I hear she won. I hear she beat you," War said to Fear.

Fear arched an eyebrow. "I suppose *you've* never lost a battle?"

War grinned widely, stretching the scars on his face. Stitches ripped. Blood trickled down his cheek. "I *am* the battle, Little Brother," he said.

The siblings and their father spent the ride catching up. They were all happy to hear of War's successes in the Lowlands, and Pestilence smiled shyly when they congratulated her on the latest outbreak of plague.

After an hour or so, the carriage stopped, and the family climbed out. They had arrived at the top of the mountain. Most of it soared up into a high, rocky point, but part of it was flat. As the driver spread a picnic blanket on a smooth patch of rock, Fear led his family to the mountaintop's edge. They all looked down at the sheer rock face sweeping away below them.

Fear took a deep breath, then thumped his chest. "I like it

here," he said. "The air's good. I like the neighbors, too. Look over there . . ." He pointed to a wisp of smoke curling up through the treetops. "An old woman lives in those woods. In the sweetest—literally—gingerbread house you've ever seen."

Next he pointed to a village, the spires of its churches and town hall just visible. "In that charming burg, there's a widow with a daughter. The little girl has the prettiest hooded cloak. It's a deep bloodred. And she *loves* to visit her grandmother." He turned in a semicircle toward the sea and nodded at a tower, tall and gray, protruding up from the craggy coastline. "Only one person lives there. She has the whole place to herself. I see her sometimes at night, looking out the window and combing her long hair. You know . . . I can really picture myself here. Setting down roots."

"And why are you telling us this?" Famine asked.

"I'm thinking of building."

Death smiled proudly. He clapped Fear on the back. "That's the way. Get right back on the horse, my boy!"

"Building . . ." Pestilence started to say, but then a coughing fit gripped her. She spat a bloody gob onto the ground. "Building what?"

Fear put his hands on his hips. He nodded.

Then he smiled and said, "A big, beautiful brand-new castle."

Acknowledgements

Those Grimm brothers, they don't pull any punches.

In their version of Snow White, the queen orders her huntsman to cut out Snow White's heart and bring it to her—not just so she has proof that the young princess is, in fact, dead—but so she can eat it. Yes, you read that right: eat it.

When I first read the story, as a kid of nine or so, I thought the whole heart thing was gross. Now, as a slightly older kid, I think it's brilliant. What an incredible metaphor for what fear does to us—it devours our hearts. Hollows us out. Leaves us empty.

As I wrote Sophie's story, I saw that all too often, we believe what others tell us we are. We listen to the golden-eyed snakes and the glittering scorpions and let their words define us and direct us. We take the poison apple the evil queen hands us and we bite right into it.

Sophie showed me that it's possible to crush the snakes and scorpions, spit out the apple, and look fear right in the eye. All we have to do is listen to our hearts—no matter how battered and broken they may be.

Once again, I would like to thank my incredible editor,

Mallory Kass, for having my back as Sophie and I made our way through the Darkwood, and for always being at the ready with advice and encouragement. Thank you to Maya Marlette for helping me brainstorm my way through dark tunnels and past whispering roses, trolls, and makabers. Thank you to Dick Robinson, Ellie Berger, David Levithan, Lori Benton, Erin Berger, Rachel Feld, Shannon Pender, Lizette Serrano, Emily Heddleson, Lauren Donovan, Alan Smagler and his team, Melissa Schirmer, Jody Corbett, Maeve Norton, Elizabeth Parisi, and the rest of my Scholastic family for your enthusiasm for Poisoned. You are true believers in the power stories have to inspire and uplift children, and I feel so very fortunate that I get to work with you all.

As always, a huge thank-you to my agents, Steve Malk and Cecilia de la Campa, and my family—Doug, Daisy, and Omi. I'd be lost without you guys.

And last but never least, thank you to you, dear reader. You are the reason I do what I do.

Read on for an excerpt
from *Stepsister* . . .
A stunning and shocking retelling of the Cinderella
fairytale
Available now!

Prologue

Once upon always and never again, in an ancient city by the sea, three sisters worked by candlelight.

The first was a maiden. Her hair, long and loose, was the color of the morning sun. She wore a gown of white and a necklace of pearls. In her slender hands, she held a pair of golden scissors, which she used to cut lengths of the finest parchment.

The second, a mother, ample and strong, wore a gown of crimson. Rubies circled her neck. Her red hair, as fiery as a summer sunset, was gathered into a braid. She held a silver compass.

The third was a crone, crookbacked and shrewd. Her gown was black, her only adornment was a ring of obsidian, incised with a skull. She wore her snow-white hair in a coil. Her gnarled, ink-stained fingers held a quill.

The crone's eyes, like those of her sisters, were a forbidding gray, as cold and pitiless as the sea.

At a sudden clap of thunder, she raised her gaze from the long wooden worktable at which she sat to the open doors of her balcony. A storm howled down upon the city. Rain scoured the rooftops of its grand palazzos. Lightning split the night. From every church tower, bells tolled a warning.

"The water is rising," she said. "The city will flood."

"We are high above the water. It cannot touch us. It cannot stop us," said the mother.

"Nothing can stop us," said the maiden.

The crone's eyes narrowed. "*He* can."

"The doors are locked," said the mother. "He cannot get in."

"Perhaps he already has," said the crone.

At this, the mother and the maiden looked up. Their wary eyes darted around the cavernous room, but they saw no intruder, only their cloaked and hooded servants going about their tasks. Relieved, they returned to their work, but the crone remained watchful.

Mapmaking was the sisters' trade, but no one ever came to buy their maps, for they could not be had at any price.

Each was exquisitely drawn, using feathers from a black swan.

Each was sumptuously colored with inks mixed from indigo, gold, ground pearl, and other things—things far more difficult to procure.

Each used time as its unit of measure, not distance, for each map charted the course of a human life.

"Roses, rum, and ruin," the crone muttered, sniffing the air. "Can you not smell them? Smell *him*?"

"It's only the wind," soothed the mother. "It carries the scents of the city."

Still muttering, the crone dipped her quill into an inkpot. Candle tapers flickered in silver candelabra as she drew the landscape of a life. A raven, coal-black and bright-eyed, roosted on the mantel. A tall clock in an ebony case stood against one wall. Its pendulum, a human skull, swung slowly back and forth, ticking away seconds, hours, years, lives.

The room was shaped like a spider. The sisters' workspace, in the centre, was the creature's body. Long rows of towering shelves led off the centre like a spider's many legs. Glass doors that led out to the balcony were at one end of the room; a pair of carved wooden doors loomed at the other.

The crone finished her map. She held a stick of red sealing wax in a candle flame, dripped it onto the bottom of the document, then pressed her ring into it. When the seal had hardened, she rolled the map, tied it with a black ribbon, and handed it to a servant. He disappeared down one of the rows to shelve the map, carrying a candle to light his way.

That's when it happened.

Another servant, his head down, walked between the crone and the open doors behind her. As he did, a gust of wind blew over him, filling the room with the rich scent of smoke and spices. The crone's nostrils flared. She whirled around.

"You there!" she cried, lunging at him. Her clawlike hand caught hold of his hood. It fell from his head, revealing a young man with amber eyes, dark skin, and long black braids. "Seize him!" she hissed.

A dozen servants rushed at the man, but as they closed in, another gust blew out the candles. By the time they had slammed the doors shut and relit them, all that remained of the man was his cloak, cast off and puddled on the floor.

The crone paced back and forth, shouting at the servants.

They poured down the dusky rows, their cloaks flying behind them, trying to flush the intruder out. A moment later, he burst out from behind one of the shelves, skidding to a stop a few feet from the crone. He darted to the wooden doors and frantically tried the handle, but it was locked. Swearing under his breath, he turned to the three sisters, flashed a quicksilver smile, and swept them a bow.

He was dressed in a sky-blue frock coat, leather breeches, and tall boots. A gold ring dangled from one ear; a cutlass hung from his hip. His face was as beautiful as daybreak, his smile as bewitching as midnight. His eyes promised the world, and everything in it.

But the sisters were unmoved by his beauty. One by one, they spoke.

"Luck," hissed the maiden.

"Risk," the mother spat.

"Hazard," snarled the crone.

"I prefer Chance. It has a nicer ring," the man said, with a wink.

"It's been a long time since you paid us a visit," said the crone.

"I should drop by more often," said Chance. "It's always a pleasure to visit the Fates. You're so spontaneous, so wild and unpredictable. It's always a party, this place. A regular bacchanal. It's so. Much. *Fun*."

A handful of servants spilled out from a row between the shelves, red-faced and winded. Chance pulled his cutlass from its scabbard. The blade glinted in the candlelight. The servants stepped back.

"Whose map have you stolen this time?" the crone asked.

"What empress or general has begged your favor?"

Still holding his cutlass in one hand, Chance drew a map from his coat with the other. He tugged the ribbon off with his teeth, then gave the parchment a shake. It unrolled, and he held it up. As the three women stared at it, their expressions changed from anger to confusion.

"I see a house, the Maison Douleur, in the village of Saint-Michel," the crone said.

"It's the home of—" said the matron.

"A girl. Isabelle de la Paumé," the crone finished.

"Who?" asked the maiden.

"All this trouble for a mere girl?" asked the crone, regarding Chance closely. "She's nothing, a nobody. She possesses neither beauty nor wit. She's selfish. Mean. Why her?"

"Because I can't resist a challenge," Chance replied. He rerolled the map with one hand, steadying it against his chest, then tucked it back inside his coat. "And what girl wouldn't choose what I offer?" He gestured at himself, as if even he couldn't believe how irresistible he was. "I'll give her the chance to change the path she is on. The chance to make her *own* path."

"Fool," said the crone. "You understand nothing of mortals. We Fates map out their lives because they wish it. Mortals do not like uncertainty. They do not like change. Change is frightening. Change is painful."

"Change is a kiss in the dark. A rose in the snow. A wild road on a windy night," Chance countered.

"Monsters live in the dark. Roses die in the snow. Girls get lost on wild roads," the crone shot back.

But Chance would not be discouraged. He sheathed his cutlass and held out his hand. As if by magic, a gold coin appeared in his fingers. "I'll make you a bet," he said.

"You push me too far," the crone growled, fury gathering like a storm in her eyes.

Chance flipped the coin at the crone. She snatched it from the air and slammed it down on the table. The storm broke. "Do you think a *coin* can pay for what you've set loose?" she raged. "A warlord rampages across France. Death reaps a harvest of bones. A kingdom totters. All because of *you*!"

Chance's smile slipped. For a few seconds, his fiery bravado dimmed. "I'll fix it. I swear it."

"With *that* girl's map?"

"She was brave once. She was good."

"Your head is even emptier than your promises," the crone said. "Open the map again. Read it this time. See what becomes of her."

Chance did so. His eyes followed the girl's path across the parchment. The breath went out of him as he saw its end . . . the blotches and hatches, the violent lines. His eyes sought the crone's. "This ending . . . It's not . . . It *can't* be—"

"Do you still think you can fix this?" the crone mocked.

Chance took a step towards her, his chin raised. "I offer you high stakes. If I lose this wager, I will never come to the palazzo again."

"And if *I* lose?"

"You allow me to keep this map. Allow the girl to direct her own steps forevermore."

"I do not like those stakes," the crone said. She waved her

hand, and her servants, who had been slowly edging closer to Chance, charged at him. Some were bearing cutlasses of their own now. Chance was trapped. Or so it seemed.

"There's no hope of escape. Give me back the map," said the crone, holding out her hand.

"There's always hope," Chance said, tucking the map back into his coat. He took a few running steps, launched himself into a somersault, and flew over the heads of the servants. He landed on the worktable with the grace of a panther and ran down its length. When he reached the end, he jumped to the floor, then sped to the balcony.

"You are caught now, rogue!" the crone shouted after him. "We are three storeys high! What can you do? Leap across the canal? Even *you* are not that lucky!"

Chance wrenched open the balcony's doors and leapt up onto its railing. The rain had stopped, but the marble was still wet and slippery. His body pitched back and forth. His arms windmilled. Just as it looked as if he would surely fall, he managed to steady himself, balancing gingerly on his toes.

"The map. *Now*," the crone demanded. She had walked out onto the balcony and was only a few feet away from him. Her sisters joined her.

Chance glanced back at the Fates; then he somersaulted into the air. The crone gasped. She rushed to the railing, her sisters right behind her, expecting to see him drowning in the swirling waters below.

But he was not. He was lying on his back, cradled in the canopy of a gondola. The boat was rocking violently from side to side, but Chance was fine.

"Row, my fine fellow!" he called to the gondolier. The man obliged. The boat moved off.

Chance sat up, eyeing the Fates with a diamond-bright intensity. "You *must* accept my stakes now! You have no choice!" he shouted.

The gondola grew smaller and smaller as it made its way down the canal. A moment later, it rounded a bend and disappeared.

"This is a bad state of affairs," the crone said darkly. "We cannot have mortals making their own choices. When they do, disaster follows."

The maiden and the mother stepped back into the room. The crone trailed them. "Pack a trunk," she barked at a servant. "I'll need quills and inks . . ." Her hand hovered over the bottles upon the table. She selected a deep ebony. "*Fear*, yes. *Jealousy* will be useful, too," she said, reaching for a poisonous green.

"Where are you going?" the maiden asked.

"To the village of Saint-Michel," the crone replied.

"You will stop Chance from taking hold of the girl?" asked the mother.

The crone smiled grimly. "No, I cannot. But I will do what we Fates have always done. I will stop the girl from taking hold of a chance."

Jennifer Donnelly

Jennifer Donnelly is the author of thirteen novels and a picture book for children. She grew up in New York State and studied English Literature and European History at the University of Rochester.

Jennifer's first novel, *The Tea Rose*, is an epic historical novel set in London and New York in the late 19th century. Her second novel, *A Gathering Light*, set against the backdrop of an infamous murder in the Adirondacks of 1906, won the Carnegie Medal, the Los Angeles Times Book Prize, the Borders Original Voices Award, and was named a Printz Honor book. In 2014, Jennifer teamed up with Disney to launch the bestselling Waterfire saga, an epic series about six mermaids on a quest to rid the world of an ancient evil. In *Stepsister* Jennifer turned her feminist eye to the Cinderella story.

Jennifer lives in New York's Hudson Valley with her husband, daughter and two rescue dogs. Follow Jennifer at www.jenniferdonnelly.com or on Twitter: @JenWritesBooks

HOT KEY BOOKS

Thank you for choosing a Hot Key book.

If you want to know more about our authors
and what we publish, you can find us online.

You can start at our website

www.hotkeybooks.com

And you can also find us on:

We hope to see you soon!